Unexpected Princess

THE ROYALS
BOOK TWO

C. R. RILEY

 Created with Vellum

Hermosa Islas

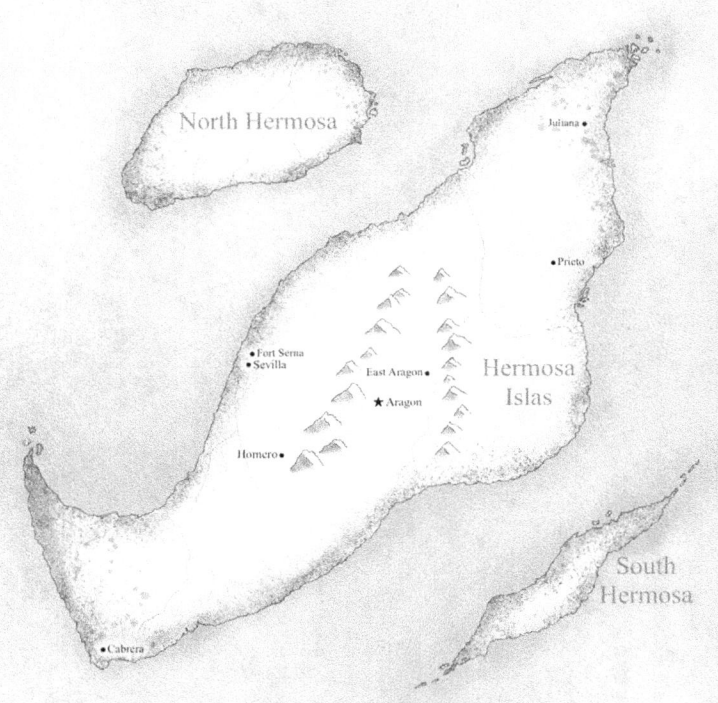

*This book is dedicated to all the moms out there
raising strong independent girls.
Keep encouraging them go after their dreams.*

Dreams are what makes the world go around.

CHAPTER 1
Winifred

The Royals

Standing in front of the mirror, I stare at the image I present. I can't believe I permitted my mother to dress me for such an important event. I realize I don't have the most flattering figure out there. Or perhaps I should disclose I'm not supermodel-skinny like my three sisters. To be clear, my dress isn't flat out ghastly. It's similar to every other dress I have ever worn.

I was hoping since tonight was my night, I'd be wearing a dress that flattered me more than this one. Instead, it appears I'm doomed to wear another with quarter length-sleeves and a high neckline. It drapes loosely off of my frame, with a straight unflattering skirt that touches the floor, concealing any curves I possess. The color is even plain, ensuring I don't stand out in the crowd. Making it difficult for anyone to notice me once in the ballroom. Even though everyone attending is here so they can take note of the woman I have become.

It is an observed tradition in Hermosa Islas when a young lady reaches the age of adulthood—eighteen—she be thrown a debut soirée social. It is more customary for those who have grown up in high society, as opposed to those who have not. Mainly because it is when negotiations often begin.

A negotiation for what exactly is what you are asking, isn't it? Well, believe it or not, most raised in the lifestyle I have been brought up in don't get to decide who they will one day marry. That decision is usually left to both sets of parents, but not always.

My oldest sister, Dalia, sealed my fate when she wasn't able to lock down the man my father had selected for her. He'd allowed her to do her best to obtain her young man's attention without interference. She had almost done it, even, came very close. However, when this man overheard her gloating to my mother and my two other sisters about how she was confident to soon be getting everything she ever wanted, the affair ended abruptly.

Now my father is not about to allow any of his other daughters to make the same error. And because I am the youngest, and the least attractive—my family's words, not necessarily mine—he has made it clear I will get no say in the matter. A fate I have accepted only because I see no other way around it.

"I guess this gown will have to do." My mother steps in behind me so she can study my reflection. "I just don't understand how you manage to maintain all this extra weight. No matter what I feed you, it doesn't seem to make a difference. Are you sneaking food again, Winifred?"

A common lecture I have listened to most of my life. Apparently, I'm blind, because I seriously don't get what she is talking about. This last year I've dropped a considerable amount of weight. I'll admit I went through a chubby stage between ages twelve to sixteen, possibly enough that one could have gotten away with calling me fat. Although that is no longer the case, I'm not skinny by any means, never will be, but I'm not carrying *extra* weight.

My sister Karina starts, "She was in the kitchen again after we—"

"I was only there to grab an apple," I cut her off.

I fail to mention anything about the half sandwich I ate to go with my apple. Seriously, who can live on a small salad—sans the dressing—and water? No wonder they all look as if the wind blew just right, they'd fall over. Sue me. I like food. Real food, not rabbit food.

Paschal steps up next to me, wearing a sour frown and dares to inspect my reflection. "I'd die if I had to wear something like that to cover my fat arse."

I don't have a fat arse. I mean, not really. I just happen to have one. Along with breasts and a little shape in my hips. Like I stated earlier, I'm not supermodel skinny, but I'm not fat. Unlike my sisters, God has blessed me with a few female curves.

I glance around the room at my sisters who are all dressed in gowns full of color, hugging their bodies. Dalia's is burgundy with a sleeveless bodice and a sexy mesh panel between her average-size breasts. Karina's is dark blue with a deep V-neck and spaghetti straps that crisscross in the back. Paschal's is strapless and purple, with a slit up to her thigh, which enables her to move freely since it is that tight. There is no way anyone will miss those three tonight in their colorful gowns. My gray dull gown will simply blend in, keeping most of the male guests—especially their eyes—off of me, like always.

My mother shakes her head as she waves my sisters away, pointing them toward the door behind us. At first, after they disappeared, I thought she was about to report they were wrong. However, I once again underestimated her.

"I don't know what you expect me to do, Winifred, when you provide them with every reason to voice all those truths. I just hope the men your father invited tonight for you will be able to look past this." She gestures up and down my reflection. "It wasn't as if we had a large pool to choose from. Not many men can see the potential in a woman like you. Make sure you smile, appropriately respond to any questions they might ask, and only talk when instructed to do so. Don't go off-topic or discuss anything that—"

"I know, mother." I force a smile. I am always forcing a smile around her. "I promise to not disappoint you or Papa."

"I highly doubt that, dear. And please remember to not eat the hors d'oeuvre, no man wants to observe you stuffing your face." She shakes her head, disgusted again, before offering a sigh. "It will be a miracle if your father gets any offers at all."

Wow.

Thanks for the encouraging words, Mother.

"Also, remember, tonight is not all about you. We have taken the liberty of inviting a few influential men for your sisters. King Antonio, along with his brothers, will be attending. I do believe Prince Esteban would make a wonderful companion for Paschal." My mother's eyes get a little glazed over. "If we are lucky, the king will realize how much he needs Dalia now that he has been doing life in his station alone for almost a year. Perhaps he will finally be able to appreciate how a woman like her could benefit him in so many ways."

"One can only hope." I smile the best I can, even though I don't agree.

She scans over me one more time before leaving me alone to wait for my father. That gives me time to reflect on all that was disclosed.

I should have known this night would end up being more about my three sisters than me. That is the way these events always seem to go for me, where I stand in line with the family dynamics. I'm merely the background noise that is an inconvenience, as far as they are concerned. The fourth child who was not planned, a thorn in all of their sides, my father's last disappointment. I have never fit in. So many times, I was the one they blamed whenever things went south.

When Dalia's engagement fell apart, it was my fault because I hadn't noticed Prince Antonio standing just outside the private dining hall. Just like it was my fault when Karina got drunk at her debut soirée, then threw up all over one of her more prominent suitors. My fault, when Paschal was found making out with *two* young gentlemen down a dark, hidden hallway at her soirée. No matter what went wrong, it somehow always ended up being my fault. Before this night is over, I'm certain to be blamed for at least one issue, if not more.

My father enters my room and grunts. That sound indicates it's time to pretend we are one big happy family. I'm not at all surprised to have to endure a lecture on our journey to the ballroom, located in our larger-than-life home. "Do not embarrass me tonight, Winifred. Your mother and I have invited those I believe will best suit you. Men, I am certain will be able to see potential in a young woman who has not yet been tainted. I should have narrowed the selected few with the other three, however, I allowed them to talk me out of it. Hear me now; I will not be persuaded to do so where you are concerned. If those three haven't locked it down yet, there is no way you have a chance to do so without me stepping in. Do you understand?"

"Yes, sir." I know better than to argue with him.

"Good girl. I don't want to hear any grumbles or groans. I want you to do your best to impress these men. One of them will hopefully end up being your husband. It will be in your best interest to at least show them you have been well-trained, and in a few years will make a suitable partner. Do you understand?"

"Yes, sir." I stick with my go-to response. It's easier that way.

"Mingle with those I instruct you to mingle with. Accept any invitations from them for private conversations, but please do not embarrass me while doing so. It is very important you only converse tonight with them. There will be plenty of time for more after we come to an agreement. Do you understand?"

I have to swallow the bile that rises in my throat before I answer. "Yes, sir."

Even though he did not disclose what more was, I have lived in this house long enough to figure out what that means. If I get my way, more will only take place once a man has made me his wife, not before.

"Good girl. Now smile, and please, don't screw this up. You will be rewarded greatly if you follow those rules I have explained." He pauses and does a thorough inspection of my gown. "I suppose you will do."

I spend the next several hours by my father's side while he introduces me to various men—who are, in my opinion, old. Most of them are in their late twenties, a few are in their thirties. Perhaps if I were older, it wouldn't matter as much as it does right now. Call me old-fashioned, but I've always thought it creepy when a man married a woman a decade younger than him, especially when the woman was in her early twenties—or younger like me.

It became obvious which ones in this selected group were interested in discussing future prospects. Two stuck out in the hand-picked crowd, and both men gave me the creeps.

Lord Ernest Rupert is in his late twenties, I believe. He works in the banking business. His family owns several all over the world, and they are loaded. He is also very homely. Produces an odor that smells of rotting apples in the scorching summer sun. Not to mention his greased back hair and crooked teeth—seriously crooked teeth—which I didn't get since his family could more than afford to correct them. He also believes he is funny. Laughs at his own jokes, with a laugh that is louder than it needs to be. Then there is the fact he is very handsy, always touching me, touching every female who dares to get close to him. A problem I imagine any woman he got involved with would not appreciate.

Lord Hector Colón is in his early thirties. His father is governor of the southern region. He is a solicitor in one of the largest law firms in the kingdom. Many predict that one day he will follow in his father Aaron's footsteps and become his successor. This man is only just a man, as far as looks go. He is very well put together and speaks with an air of certainty. I'd probably not think him odd if he didn't make my skin crawl every time he eyeballs me. Not just how he looks at me, either, but all the younger ladies in the room, some who aren't women yet. For a man in his thirties, it seems as if he is way too interested in me, a girl, still, in the eyes of many. I may be eighteen but I have not yet graduated from boarding school.

Currently, I am standing off to the side with my best friend, Ingrid Lennox. The two of us have been friends since the age of ten. I met her during my first year of boarding school. We were kindred souls who gravitated to the other and have been close ever since.

"Dalia doesn't seem happy," Ingrid points out, fascinated by what is going on with my eldest sister right now.

"I'm positive she isn't. King Antonio hasn't even glimpsed in her direction since he arrived. In fact, he seems to avoid her at all costs, keeping his mother close while he makes the rounds." I scan the room. "Karina is drawing a crowd, though."

At the moment, my second oldest sister has three men surrounding her, all doing their best to secure her attention. She is eating it up, and if I were a betting woman, my prediction is she'll disappear within the hour with at least one of them.

"Are you two ladies hiding over here?" A familiar male voice asks from behind us.

When we spin to face him, we are engulfed in his arms. Not an act that is at considered appropriate for a man in his position.

Prince Lorenzo Reyes is one of our classmates. He is also one of my closest friends. When my sister started dating his brother, I was certain that would change. However, Lorenzo didn't hold her snobby and conniving behaviors against me. Said he could differentiate that we were completely unrelated souls.

"Why aren't you out there showing those men they are interested in the wrong sister?" he asks as he gives my shoulder a little squeeze.

I glance over my shoulder and shoot him my best, *are you serious,* glare? "Like I'd have a chance with any of them. Plus, I've been warned not to interfere with their escapades. My approved collection of men are over there." I point my champagne flute to where that group is currently standing.

"Seriously?" Lorenzo drops his arms, reaching for a flute of his own when a server offers. "Those men are too old for you."

"My father doesn't seem to think so." I groan, totally agreeing with his analysis.

Ingrid sips on hers. "I'm with Lenny. They are old creepy dudes. You can do so much better. Don't you think Fred can do better?"

I should hate that she calls me Fred. Largely, for the reason most call me that is because my sisters once shortened my name as a cruel joke. Introduced me as their brother once they caught me climbing a tree when I was eleven. The only reason I climbed that tree was because I was trying to get a better look at *him.*

Who is *him* you ask?

I'm sure you'll figure that out sooner or later.

Ingrid's faith in my ability causes me to chuckle. "I should hope so. Lord Ernest and Lord Hector seem the most interested when I was forced to entertain them. One smells of rotting fruit and the other, I suspect, is a perv. Both have requested to meet with my father next week, according to him. Which is why I was allowed to join you—give the men a chance to converse without the little lady nearby."

"You can do so much better, Freddie." Lorenzo sounds serious; therefore, I dare to glance back at him.

"Lenny, are you offering to rescue me from the inevitable?" I snicker when he wobbles his head, immediately declining. "That's what I thought."

You need to understand a few details. Prince Lorenzo is an attractive young man, funny, and smells like a man should smell—even after sweating it out. He will one day make a young woman very happy, treat her right, and provide her with an enjoyable life. However, it would never work for us.

I know this and am completely okay with that fact. He and I have been friends long enough now for me to understand that is all we will ever be. And as my friend, he has allowed no one to mistreat me, or at least he has done his best to keep anyone from doing so when nearby. Thankfully, my sisters attended a prestigious boarding school far from me. So, my life at school has never involved them.

"Don't misunderstand, Freddie. If I were in the position to do so, I would. However, I am not, for reasons I cannot reveal at the moment." There is an unreadable expression that appears on his face. "Maybe he can, though."

I have no idea who he is talking about. My back is turned to the majority of the crowd. If it weren't for the wide eyes of my other dear friend, I'd think Lorenzo was just doing what he does best, sidestepping.

A rich, deep voice invades my ears before I can turn and has me melting on the spot. "Glad to see they finally released you to socialize with your own age group. Lovely soirée your family is throwing for you, Winifred. Too bad they felt your time was best spent with those older gentlemen. I was hoping I might be able to steal a few moments with you."

I cautiously allow my body to twirl so I am now facing him. "With me?"

Prince Esteban is standing there, looking as stunning as always. The first time I saw him, really saw him, was when he came to our family home with his father. I climbed the tree in our courtyard so I could appreciate him better while he sat in my father's office. I thought I was being sneaky about it. I assumed no one would notice me.

Except he did.

He stared out the office window and eventually discovered me. Flashed me his perfect smile, displaying his lovely teeth as he dipped his head, gesturing a hello.

Later, when he left, he was friendly with my sisters Karina and Paschal, greeted them like taught. And when they tried to encourage him to ignore the shy, awkward child hiding behind the kitchen door, he slipped right past them. Ordered me to step out from my hiding place and then smiled at me again. Greeted me exactly the same way, except it seemed to hold a distinct significance about it. It was as if he saw me like no one else ever had, and that was the first time I suffered from the fluttering in my belly.

"Is this not your debut soirée, Winifred? I may be wrong, because I never had one, haven't been to very many. Never wanted to attend one until now. I thought those invited, especially the men, were here so they could get to know the young woman being introduced." Esteban displays his perfect smile once again. "Am I mistaken?"

"N-no." I stutter. "I-I mean n-no, Your Highness, not really I suppose."

"So, if I invited you to join me, you'd accept my offer?" He presents his arm.

I stare at it for a few seconds. Not once did I imagine this particular man would approach me and then ask me that question. "I-I guess that would b-be okay."

Leaning in a little closer, granting me a whiff of his perfect male scent, my brain momentarily forgot all the reasons I should decline his invitation. "As the next heir in line for the throne, I insist you join me, Lady Winifred. Are you going to deny your prince?"

"Well, when you put it that way, Your Highness, I don't see how I can. It would be rude and against all those etiquette lessons my mother forced me to attend." I offer Esteban my hand and let him place it in the crook of his arm.

"Shall we take a walk in the garden, where it is quiet and fewer eyes are scrutinizing our every move? I'd like to talk freely without an audience." He leads me toward the door behind us, where a few of his men are waiting, men who are assigned to protect him. "I can assure you no one will bother us and that I will be the perfect gentleman."

I don't argue. Why would I? This may be the only time in my life I'll get to spend time alone with this man. No way am I going to pass up an opportunity like that, no way am I going to turn him down. For once in my life, I am going to go with my gut. Let the object of every fantasy I've had whisk me away like I always envisioned he would.

CHAPTER 2
Esteban

The Royals

I've been waiting years for this moment—seven, to be exact. I know you're wondering why a man in my position would have to wait so long to finally make his move. However, there are several details about the life I live you don't understand, so please allow me to explain.

I am Prince Esteban Carlos Reyes, second born to King Ramos and Queen Angela. (My mother will always in my mind be queen, always. Even though in the eyes of many, she relinquished her title when she divorced her husband, the king, and then he later married another.)

Being the second born is almost as important as being the firstborn, almost. It means I endured all the pre-designed preparations my older brother Antonio went through, even though I was never expected to need the skills they taught me. I was the backup to the heir should something unexpected happen to him.

When I left for university, I chose one in Switzerland, so my life wasn't an exact replica of Antonio's. I wanted to pave my own path, have my own friends. Even make my own mistakes that didn't mirror his. I settled on a business major, chiefly because it was intended I take the reins of the family business once I learned the ropes. I minored in art history, a passion I inherited from my mother, and one I hoped I could use one day.

A little over a year ago, my life changed drastically. My father, the king, was found dead in his chambers. His wife was convicted of poisoning him. Meaning my brother became the new king, and I became the next heir to the throne. All those preparations I suffered through as a young boy suddenly became of use to me.

While I still had so much to learn about my duties as the heir, it wasn't as stressful as what my brother Antonio has had to deal with. My job from that day forward was to be his second hand, pick up the slack. Be an influential face of Hermosa Islas, one who makes his job easier.

I had somehow managed to put my father off—more than once— when he began insisting I consider some of the marital offers being sent my way. Offers from not only those families who resided in our great nation, but a few from other prominent families elsewhere in the world; families with titles equal to the ones mine held. The only difference being our country still honored those titles fully. Saw our family as the leaders meant to rule over them. My father would bring it up, send me a few of those inquires, and then ask me to seriously consider them. I kindly requested he allow me to finish university first. Promised that as soon as I returned home, I would start receiving a few. Go to him so he could help me determine the best fit for me. Knowing I was implying what he thought would be best for the family as a whole, not necessarily just me.

When my father passed, all those promises died with him. I no longer had to wonder how I was going to explain my opinions on that practice. My mother, thankfully, supported her sons completely and didn't pressure us to rush into the sanctity of marriage before we were ready. She openly stands by my brother and his vision of marrying for love and only love. A concept unheard of in the world we grew up in.

Which meant I was free to determine if that was in the cards for me as well. I decided to put off that subject until the woman I am interested in was capable of understanding what I had to offer her, what I was hoping to offer her.

When I first met Lady Winifred Josefina Batista, she was only eleven. It was one summer when visiting my father during the duration of my break. He was conducting royal business as he so often did, and I was accompanying him as instructed to do. There to learn about how politics worked and why it was important to keep your enemies close and content. Justice Ivan Batista had my father to thank for his appointment to the highest court, but that didn't mean they were friends. They were only on the same side of the political spectrum, which meant they worked together better than they did with those on the opposite side of it.

It didn't take me long to realize Justice Batista had his own motives for wanting me to join my father. He was sizing me up, determining if I might be a suitable match for one of his daughters. They didn't specifically mention that, mind you. That isn't how it is done. At that specific time, only one was of age, and as he suggested, already off the market, had her eyes on a prize she was certain to obtain.

The two teenage girls who greeted me shortly after my father and I arrived didn't impress me. They were what my brothers and I referred to as high noses. Those who held their noses high in the air, just so they could glance down at those they now determined beneath them. A habit, I quickly came to realize, they had learned from their mother, Lady Eva.

I swiftly became bored with the topic surrounding me and my future plans, plans I hadn't given much thought to at the age of sixteen. I nodded appropriately, though, while I stared out the large window overlooking the garden.

It took me all of two minutes to recognize there was a pair of eyes spying on me. Had I not been paying attention I might have missed them. They were green and peering behind the leaves of the tree a few meters from the window. Perched on a branch, I am certain was a good four meters off the ground, since the angle had that particular little spy gazing down.

As the conversation turned away from me and onto other national issues, so did my focus. I struggled to determine who could be so brave to climb a difficult tree and then balance their body well enough to keep from falling. But this particular spy was doing a suitable job of not revealing more than the eyes. Until the two previously mentioned teenage girls started screeching at the person hiding. It was clear they were unaware I was watching, taking notes on how obnoxious they were acting. I even watched as they picked up several rocks and then did their best to knock the culprit out of the tree. Luckily for my spy, those two couldn't throw worth a damn. After a while, they gave up long before accomplishing their goal.

Lady Eva finally appeared, hands firmly planted on her hips, where she ordered the climber to come down before shooing the older girls back inside. Which is when I got my first appraisal of the youngest Batista child, a young girl who I imagine would love running around the citadel in Prieto with my younger siblings. She had to be close to the same age as them, possibly closer to Lorenzo's.

Unlike her sisters, who were wearing dresses, this young girl was dressed in jeans and a t-shirt—dirty ones at that. Her hair was drawn back into a braid, a messy braid, most likely that way after getting snagged by all the tiny branches. She brushed her hands off on those jeans, while she displayed a shy little smile at me, before rushing off in the direction the others went only moments earlier.

Ten minutes later, I was officially introduced to her. Not because anyone thought it necessary, they most definitely did not. But something about those eyes sparked my interest, made me want to meet the girl they belonged to.

It has taken that girl seven years to grow into a young woman. During that time, I did my best to forget about her. Reminded myself a few times it was crazy to assume a chance meeting like that was the moment I became obsessed with emerald green eyes. Attracted to women who possessed them, but could never stumble on any that sparkled quite like hers.

So here I am, now leading that young lady to the garden where it all began. Hoping to figure out precisely where I go from here. Wondering if I am as crazy as I feel, or if I made more out of an encounter than I should have.

As soon as we step through the garden breezeway, Winifred releases her hand from my arm and widens the gap between us. I instantly miss the warmth of her touch and want to demand she return.

"Forgive me for being so bold, Your Highness, but this was unnecessary. I appreciate you trying to make me feel special, paying me a moment of attention. However, I am very much aware of where I stand, and the pecking order I am expected to follow," she informs me as we gradually stroll along the stone-paved path. "Thank you for coming."

"First of all, I insist you address me by my name. Better yet, I'd like you to come up with one of your clever little nicknames. I believe Lenny is what you call Lorenzo. He refers to you as Freddie, correct?" I see her nod. "I'm not particularly fond of that nickname for you. Reminds me of when your sisters tried to introduce me to their brother Fred."

A grumble emerges from deep inside her. "Please, don't remind me. I wanted to run and hide when they did that, except you wouldn't allow it. Made me step out and show myself, while they made fun of my clothing and disheveled self."

"All I recall from that day is finally encountering something real. You were the first authentic person I had come in contact with in a very long time. The only genuine person who resided in this very home. The only one who wasn't afraid to show me exactly who she was, instead of putting on some mask to hide behind," I tell her, and am blessed to catch the blush that brightens her cheeks. "May I call you Winnie?"

She nods. "Yes."

"All right, then. So now you need to figure out how you will address me then, Winnie."

Winifred slows her pace to a shuffle. "I'm not sure I am comfortable with that, Prince Esteban."

"Come on. I insist. Brainstorm for me and see what you can come up with. I promise if I don't like it, I'll let you know." I do my best to encourage her, because I want to watch her while she brainstorms.

She shakes her head, frustrated, and then closes her eyes as if she can't believe we are having this conversation. I have news for her; we are going to have many more conversations that will be a bit less comfortable. Not all of them will happen tonight, though. They will occur over time. After all, she is only eighteen and not even close to where I need her to be yet.

"Ingrid is the one who started calling Prince Lorenzo Lenny. Not completely sure why or how it started, but after he laughed at the common name she bestowed on him, that was it for us. We've been mates since. He's sort of like a brother to me, to her as well." Winifred

14

blows out a puff of exasperated air. "You seriously expect me to come up with some nickname on a whim?"

"If you don't mind. No pressure." I shrug and then chuckle when I notice her rolling those lovely green eyes.

"Esteban." She lets my name fall from her lips as if testing it out. "Este sounds odd, doesn't suit you." Winifred tries a few more variations she doesn't like. I get the impression she has come up with something, although I'm not sure if she likes it, either.

"Say it. I want to hear all those fascinating considerations, even the ones you aren't certain of." I roll my hand to encourage her.

"Stan." She blurts out and then scrunches her face as if she's afraid I won't like it.

There are no words that describe how I feel when I hear her utter that name for the very first time. The corners of my mouth turn upwards and I nod once. "I like it. You may call me Stan when we are alone like this. It will be our little secret. Our private way of communicating with each other. No one else will be privileged to it."

Winifred pauses by the tree she once climbed and reaches out to run her fingers along the bark of its trunk. "You want me to call you Stan when we talk? Do you know something I don't, Stan? Because from where I am standing, and my experience to date, this most likely will never happen again."

Not at all appreciating the truth she is revealing, or the fact I know several powers will do their best to work against us, I decide to sway her differently. "Or we could suggest that I've solely been waiting for you to come of age."

Still tracing the bark with her fingers, she whispers, "Is that true?"

I nod, except I know she isn't looking my way. Taking a step closer now, so she can hear my quiet tone. "I believe so."

That seems to grab her attention. "You believe so? The lack of confidence in your response has me doubting the sincerity of your words. Say what you will about the other men my father has selected for me. However, I can assure you they all were bloody confident in their pursuit. Not at all afraid to let those around us know. Especially my father. They seem to understand the best way to secure more time with me is through him, so they confidently went there."

"And if I don't suffer the need to go running to Daddy in order to buy time with you, are you saying I'm wasting mine? Or are you only going along with those traditional methods because you are afraid to rock the boat?" The flash of uncertainty in her eyes, once they glance my way, provides me with her answer.

"I should probably get back before I am missed. I'm sure word has spread that you dragged me off unsupervised into a dark garden. It wouldn't look good for either of us if we stayed."

I don't exactly know what comes over me. I'm not sure if it is her concern or the fact I know she is right. Maybe it is because I am also certain this young woman has always done as she was told. Whatever the case may be, I can tell you I will never regret it as long as I live.

I have daydreamed about this moment off and on over the years. More so, the closer she got to being old enough for me to not feel like some debauched male. I realize I should have waited until she was older, except something inside of me demanded this was my chance to sneak past her defenses essential for her to survive.

The second our lips touch, I wasn't sure which one of us was more affected. I wanted to toss her over my shoulder and take her with me right then and there. I knew at that moment, this woman belonged to me, the one who would stand by my side and bear my children one day.

When I pull back, Winifred sinks onto the bench near us as she brings her fingers to her lips. "Why-why did y-you do th-that?"

"Why do most boys kiss girls, Winnie? Why have other boys kissed you before?" I grin, knowing that little maneuver shook her. "Because I wanted to. Because you wanted me to."

"How d-did you know I-I wanted y-you to k-kiss me, Stan? And no other boy has ever dared to kiss me before. Not that you are anywhere close to being considered a b-boy." Her stuttering is cute and makes me want to kiss her again.

"Are you saying you didn't? That you've not pondered doing just that with me since the first time you sat in this very tree and watched me with those expressive green eyes?" I know I sound cocky, sure of myself, very confident in my assessment.

Isn't that what she accused me of not having? Confidence? I can assure her I have more than enough confidence to go around. I just don't plan on going through her father to win her over. I want her to choose me without the influence of others. Once she has done that, then I will decide how to move forward.

Winifred blinks rapidly, as if I shocked her. "I don't kn-know. I mean, those were girlish fantasies. Daydreams that got me through some tough times, I guess. Reality is different from—"

I press my finger against her lips, stopping her from revealing any more. "Shh. What if I was more than willing to—"

Winifred presses three fingers against my moving lips now, causing me to snicker. "Please, don't. Don't say it. I'm not sure I could handle that kind of..." She stops herself this time.

"Winnie," I mumble behind her fingers. "Do you trust me?"

I'm not surprised when she shrugs. There aren't many people I imagine she has ever fully trusted.

"Understandable. Can I make you a promise? Can I promise to do my best to earn your trust?" I give her chin a gentle squeeze. "Once I have earned your trust, then and only then will we discuss what happens next. Okay?"

"Okay. And maybe you can promise no more unexpected kissing." She blushes as the words leave her lovely mouth.

"You have my word." I reach for her hand. "Shall we head back, before someone comes looking for you?"

I place her hand in the crook of my arm, then lead her to the ballroom. My men are still standing guard, precisely like I knew they would be. I am also aware that they had to run interference for us not all that long ago. One glance from my head of security advises me we came back just in time to avoid a massive scene.

As soon as we step into the ballroom, I snag us both a flute of champagne. Lady Eva spots us and makes a beeline in our direction. Her expression is a mixture between happiness and ire.

She removes the flute from Winifred's grasp and sets it down on the tray of a passing server. "You disappeared."

"I—"

"My fault, Lady Batista. I only wanted to welcome Lady Winifred into the fold. I suggested we go for a walk in the garden, used my position to force her from being able to tell me no. I hope you understand." I grab another flute and hand it to Winifred. "You have done a very adequate job with this one. She is lovely in all ways and will make some *young* suitor very happy one day. Will make a remarkable partner, I am certain."

"Thank you, Your Highness. I just hope we can find one for her."

I have so much I'd like to say to that statement, but refrain.

"Winifred, your father is requesting you join him again. Time to say thank you and let the prince return to those who have been wishing to speak with him."

"It was nice of you to spend a portion of your evening with me. Thank you, Prince Esteban." A small smirk, genuine in nature, crosses her face.

"I'd like to join you if that is okay? I believe I have some business to attend to in the direction you are heading. It might be nice to have a lovely lady with me while I do so." I offer her my arm to take.

"I'm sorry, Prince Esteban, but I don't know if that is such a wise idea. Perhaps Paschal could join you." Her mother suggests, motioning for Winifred to start moving while she waves the aforementioned one over.

"That is not acceptable," I dismiss her instantly and watch her drop her arm in defeat. "Tonight should be about Lady Winifred, therefore I want to keep it that way. I know you understand. Shall we?" I motion for Winifred to lead the way.

There is no way I am allowing her father to make promises to other undeserving men while I am around. No way will I not step in after I made a few promises to her earlier in the garden.

As we walk in that direction, I lean down and whisper, "Did you honestly believe I'd let her steal you away from me, Winnie? Let you suffer through the agonizing stench of rotting fruit."

A joyful giggle sneaks out of her, and I know we are one small step closer to her trusting me.

CHAPTER 3
Winifred

The Royals

W hen I woke this morning, I was certain I dreamed it all. Maybe not all of the previous evening. I know for a fact a fragment of it had to be real. Like those first few hours, when I was forced to endure the company of men I had absolutely no interest in whatsoever. My worst nightmares couldn't top that portion of the evening.

However, I am almost certain the best segments of my evening had to be a dream, my mind playing tricks on me. It wasn't possible the obsession of all my fantasies actually spoke to me on the biggest night of my life. It wouldn't be the first time I'd mixed up my reality with a few fantasies where he suddenly appeared.

For example, when I turned sixteen and a few of my friends threw me a surprise party. Those friends were Lorenzo, Ingrid, and Crispin Oliver. They convinced the dean to allow us to join Lorenzo for a weekend evening away at his mother's home. It was nerve-wracking enough, knowing one of my closest friends was a prince. Then grasping his mother, Her Royal Highness, had personally baked me a cake for my birthday, with the previously mentioned prince's assistance. I often elected to forget my friend Lenny was one of the King's sons.

So, when we slipped out to the barn later that evening with a bottle of his family's wine tucked away in Crispin's jacket and got drunk, my mind invented that the man who escorted Ingrid and me back to our dormitory well after curfew, was none other than Prince Esteban. That he carried my teenage, drunk butt inside, while Lenny and Cris supported Ingrid so she didn't get hurt. It was the same night she acquired her nickname, Dinger. The guys never liked any of the other nicknames they thought up for her, so they began experimenting with all her letters and came up with that. It stuck, even though they had replaced one of her I's with an E.

The only clue I hadn't been mistaken all these years, occurred last night once the party was winding down. Esteban called her Dinger as he wished her a good evening. Ingrid and I both stared at each other for several long minutes before bursting into laughter, knowing my report about what I hallucinated when we were sixteen had been accurate all along.

Several more minuscule incidents, similar to that one, had transpired over the years. Small occurrences where I swore some guardian angel was looking out for me. A very influential one who seemed to have eyes and ears everywhere. And while I couldn't prove he was around keeping watch, I now wonder if he had a hand in it.

An uneasy thought crosses my mind. One that has me picking up my phone so I can send Ingrid a text, asking her if she thinks I am crazy. Except when I finally retrieve it off the charger, I almost drop it.

There's a text from Stan—and yes, it displays that particular name on my screen. Meaning, somehow, he or someone else put that information into my contacts. I read it several times, not sure if I should trust that one of my sisters isn't setting me up. Convinced they somehow overheard our conversation and are now playing a cruel joke on me just because they can.

STAN: Call me as soon as you wake.

The text came in around seven this morning. That was about an hour ago, which is the only detail that has me doubting those first thoughts. My sisters don't get up that early, especially after a night like last night.

Dalia practically glared at every female in the room who spoke with King Antonio. While she glared, her intake of champagne became considerable. One of her male companions ended up escorting her out before she made a scene. My guess is he also took full advantage of her mood, was likely still entertaining her and helping her forget she screwed up in the worst way where the king was concerned.

Karina finally chose an eager male suitor around the same time. I'd watch them sneak off not long after Dalia, using her as an excuse to get it on. She approached my mother, most likely to lie about checking in on Dalia when in reality her only thought was locking this man down. Poor chap had better have supplied his own protection. I wouldn't put it past any of my sisters to trap a man, especially the men in attendance last night. All of those men have large bank accounts, are well-established, and have plenty of influential pull, which make them quite powerful in our social clique.

Then of course there was Paschal. I know for a fact she had ulterior motives. At first, I was worried she'd been pouting because Prince Esteban hadn't shown her any attention. But it seemed my sister had her own idea about who she fancied, and that suited me just fine. The man she'd set her target on was essentially going to cause more strife for her. Not only because he was not on her list of the approved, but also because he was already married. He was here for political reasons and unaccompanied. His wife hadn't been able to attend because she was pregnant with their first child and home on ordered bedrest. My sister zoned in on that man the moment he stepped inside. She hung on his every word and then started hanging all over him. It was obvious to anyone watching he had no issues with that. Would indeed take liberties later before returning to his wife. Which meant Paschal was most likely in some hotel room, getting as much of him as she could before he went back to his life and forgot all about her.

I reread the text for the hundredth time when a new one appears below it.

> STAN: Why haven't you called me yet?
> Call me.

I very likely read that message ten times before my phone lights up and his name flashes across my screen. Even start to smile when I notice a photo of our tree appear behind his name.

After the third ring, I finally press the green button to answer it. "Hello?"

"Are you alone?" His question throws me.

"Yes. I only woke a few minutes ago."

A sound of relief washes over him. "Winnie, we need to talk. Do you suppose you might find an excuse to leave and have breakfast with me?"

"You want me to have breakfast with you?" I ask, surprised by his invitation. "Why did you ask me if I was alone?"

"Oh, Winnie. I would love to have breakfast with you." There is a pause as if he would like to disclose more, but is refraining. "It's just... I was worried after all that was suggested last night... never mind." He's talking about the unexpected segment of my evening I'd much rather forget.

When I returned to my father, he wasn't excited Prince Esteban had appointed himself as my escort. Lord Hector seemed equally irritated about it. My father then inquired if Esteban had any intention of speaking with him, wanted to discuss negotiations, or make an arrangement. I wasn't sure I liked how that sounded.

Esteban tightened his hold on my arm tucked in his, making it very clear he did not wish to do so. He then clarified a few matters where I was concerned.

In his very influential voice, he reminded both men of a case that is receiving a great deal of attention. The case involves an older male and a nineteen-year-old female. She was accusing the man of making an arrangement with her father against her knowledge, not long after she turned eighteen. The arrangement involved a payment from the older male to the young woman's father, suggesting a bill of sale was made. A few days later, the young woman was moved into a townhome that belonged to the buyer. She is claiming to have been held there against her will, threatened violence if she left before the agreed amount of time. Then threatened again after he let her go should she ever consider sharing her story.

I will never forget the displeased expression on my father's face, nor will I forget how Hector seemed angered by the prince's boldness. It didn't go unnoticed he was suggesting they were about to do the same with my young life. That thought had made my stomach churn. I hadn't dared to imagine a situation like that being a possibility until that very moment. Maybe I wouldn't be sold for a period of time like the woman previously mentioned. Something, however, warned me I was being offered to the highest bidder. The one who promised my father he would keep me in line and offer my family something as well.

And that is when I concluded I was nothing more than an object as far as my parents were concerned. One that had been given certain privileges, just so one day I could pay them back in full. I had no choice in the matter, either, unless I wanted to be disowned and left to fight for everything just to survive.

That is where these people trapped you. They understood the lifestyle one became accustomed to would be difficult to give up. While there were those who have walked away, most young women were terrified to do so, of being forced to figure out how to survive on their own. Honestly, I was a little afraid of that myself—why I had always done as expected and let my sisters treat me the way they had. I had no idea how I would survive on my own, not sure I would ever have the guts to even try.

"Winnie," Esteban whispers my name. "Don't be afraid."

"What?" I jostle my head to bring my mind back to the present. "I'm not."

"It's okay to be, you know. You only need to trust me, Winnie. Know I am looking out for you. Will be watching to make sure nothing happens you don't want to happen. This is your life, Winnie, and you should be in the driver's seat, not in the backseat letting someone else drive it for you."

I want to yell at him and tell him I don't know how to drive—figuratively and literally. Someone has always driven me around, told me where I was going and with whom. Never given me any other option than to go along with the program.

"I'll be at your front door in twenty minutes. Make sure you are ready."

I don't let the irony of his words slip past me. "I thought I was supposed to be driving?" The words slip out unexpectedly.

"Touché, senorita. Forgive me. I, too, must learn a few new ways; learn I cannot control everything or everyone. It will be good of you to remind me of that from time to time. Please, will you join me for breakfast if I come and pick you up in twenty minutes? Does that give you enough time to get ready?"

"No. Twenty minutes is not anywhere close to enough time. I need at least an hour, Stan."

He groans into the phone and I can't help but giggle. "I do so adore it when you call me Stan. One hour it is, then. Dress casually. My chauffeur will bring you to me. Don't freak out when he refuses to share any information with your family on where you are heading. I want no one to know where you are going, only because I don't want you to undergo the pressure from those who believe they can control you. Just go along with his explanation and leave the rest to me."

I giggle again, knowing I sound like the teenage girl I am when I do. "Sounds so secretive, which will only perk my family's interest more."

"Exactly, and that, my sweet Winnie, is what will keep them behaving while I do my best to get to know you. I promised last night to convince you to trust me. Now hurry up. I'm hungry, and it seems I have to wait an hour before I will satisfy either of my appetites." I don't miss how he makes all that sound, but I also understand he will keep matters between us simple.

I rush to the shower and do my best to keep it casual. Later today I will head back to Prieto, where I will remain for six more weeks. That's how long I have left before I graduate and leave that place forever.

I am both happy and sad about that for three reasons. I will leave behind three very important people when I ditch the place that has been my refuge for eight years. Ingrid is heading to the United States, where she will attend Princeton, studying engineering. She will also play *fútbol* for them. Something I wish I could do—maybe not for Princeton, but I wouldn't mind continuing competing. Crispin and Lorenzo are both heading to England, where they will study business while competing in lacrosse.

Right now, I'm not sure where I will be allowed to go. My father hasn't approved any of my choices yet. They include Princeton, the University of Melbourne, the University of Edinburgh, and Columbia

University. All great choices and respectable universities where I had been accepted into easily. In fact, with my grades, there isn't a school out there that would deny me admission. Although I'd be surprised if I were authorized to leave the country. Most likely I will be granted permission to pick one of the three great universities here at home.

As soon as I descend the stairs, the drama from last night continues. I can hear my father lecturing Dalia from inside his office. He is not holding back today, laying out his expectations she will be required to follow from this point forward. Clarifying that unless she wants him to cut her off completely, she will start behaving in the way he deems appropriate.

When Dalia emerges from his office, she noticeably appears shaken. I missed the revealing part on why she was receiving such a lecture. However, I don't miss the glare she shoots me. I'm guessing she blames me for her getting lectured by our father, even though I had nothing to do with her behavior last night.

She takes three seconds to prove me right, "This is all your fault."

"My fault?" I point at my chest. "How is it my fault? You're the one who screwed it up with the king. I had no hand in that. You're also the one who drank too much last night and had to be escorted out by one of your many..." I flinch when she starts her advance, knowing that was not the smartest move on my part.

However, the buzz of the doorbell stops her from carrying out her attack. Her entire demeanor alters when a fine specimen of a man swaggers into the vestibule behind our butler.

My father blinks several times before he addresses the man, the one who is staring at me like he knows something I don't. He ignores all the others in the room and struts right up to me, leans down, and whispers in my ear, as he pretends to kiss my cheek.

"Winnie, I presume. Lovely as rain." Then he speaks so everyone else can hear what he has to say. "Lady Winifred Batista, you have certainly grown into quite a woman."

"Do I know you?" I ask, struggling to place him.

My sister gasps as she quickly offers an apology. "Forgive her Your Grace, my little sister has forgotten her manors. What brings the Duke of Falcon to our home so bright and early?"

"Duke of Falcon? You're Darius Falcon?" I bow my head in reverence and blush, embarrassed I didn't recognize him. "Forgive me."

"All is forgiven, but only if you'll agree to have breakfast with me and one of my colleagues." He grins mischievously. "I seem to have overlooked your soirée last night. My invitation must have gotten lost in the mail, no? For that reason, I'd like to make it up to you. Of course, that is, if it is okay with your father? I wouldn't want you to develop a reputation or anything."

Dalia snickers, as if there is something she knows that I don't.

When Karina strolls in from the kitchen, looking like she has had one rough evening, glancing up just in time to spot the duke, she yelps. "You're Darius Falcon. Why is Darius Falcon standing in our foyer at a quarter till nine? Did I miss something?" Then she glimpses down at her disheveled attire and whirls around to escape.

At that moment, her overnight companion enters wearing the same clothing he had on last night. He also does a double-take at Darius, before directing his gaze in my father's direction.

My father is agitating his head in disgust as he groans. "Sir Holcomb, please either leave or step into my office, so we can start the process."

The young man is smart enough to escape while he has the chance, and as he exits, the last of my sisters enters behind Darius. "Whose Rolls Royce is parked out front? Why are we receiving guests so early? Did you find someone to buy...?" She stops dead in her tracks when she notices Darius. "Hello."

A chuckle rolls out of him, as he enjoys the chaos of the morning. "Justice Batista, it seems you've had a very interesting morning so far. Perhaps I can take this one with me, while you handle the others how you see fit? When I return her in a few hours, we can share a drink. I bet you will be in much need of one by then."

My father gestures for us to leave while he takes in Paschal's walk of shame attire. I hear him order her into his office. Then he orders Dalia to go retrieve the other disappointment, so he can handle them all at once. When my sisters grumble, he shouts something I will never forget. "Shut up! Maybe it's time you all take a look at Winifred. Obviously, she understands what she has to do to gain a gentleman's attention without embarrassing all of us in the process. Who would have thought she'd be the one to finally get this right? Now hurry before I..."

I don't get to hear the rest, because we step outside before he finishes. A large Rolls Royce is waiting for us, where the driver is holding open the door. I slide in, and the man who has caused a great deal of ruckus slides in behind me.

Now it's my turn to squeal when the unexpected transpires yet again. I didn't realize someone else was in the car until I am dragged across the aisle to the seat opposite me.

"Good morning, Winnie."

I do my best to straighten and act older than I am; this is not the time to act like a silly teenage girl. "Stan. I thought you said those names were private and only to be used..."

"Falcon will keep our secret. God knows I've kept plenty of his." Esteban reaches for my hand as he addresses the man across from us. "Did they buy it?"

"Hook. Line. And sinker." Darius' smile is one that would make any female shiver, me included. "Now why don't you explain why I just marched into a house of whores to retrieve the only pure thing left?"

"Did you just call my sisters whores?" I should probably be appalled and defend them, but before I can pull that off, I completely lose it and start snorting. "Wow. That was worth putting up with all those insults they've thrown my way. Hearing Darius Falcon sound disgusted, after meeting three women who are the most conniving bitches I know, has made my day. I'll forget none of their faces when they first laid eyes on you, then later realized you were standing there because of me. It was priceless, and I don't even care it was all for show."

Darius wobbles his head as he stares at me. "Honey cakes, you're wrong. I may have been helping out a friend and all, but that doesn't mean it was just for show. Your sisters are living up to their reputations, but let's be clear about something I think you are missing. Those three don't treat you the way they do because they think less of you, they treat you that way because they know they can never live up to you. Your light shines bright and they are jealous of that. They have always known that one day you'd pass them all up, and they'd be left standing in your shadow.

27

"Now please, Stan the man, enlighten me. What exactly is the plan? I do believe after meeting your shining star, I understand why it is important to keep interactions on the down-low. No need to rile up the natives, put them on the attack before the time is right."

I'm not sure what he is talking about, although I think I'd like to hear Stan out as well. What is the man sitting next to me actually thinking?

CHAPTER 4
Esteban

The Royals

I wish I had a plan. That would have been wise on my part. However, when it comes to this young lady seated next to me, I only wish to figure out how I can truly get to know her.

The only reason Darius Falcon is with me at all is because he called me shortly after I hung up with Winnie. I needed to throw those sisters of hers off my scent, while confusing her father long enough for him to agree to let her leave. So, I picked him up on the way. He was not invited to join us, only here as my decoy.

Darius is one of those men everyone finds interesting. He is a duke and a mystery to all, especially females. I know him well. Met him during our days at university. He's Swiss and lived most of his life in Switzerland. His family owns several prominent businesses there that pull in an unbelievable amount of income.

My friend is the youngest of a large family, and doing his best to keep all of them guessing. Most assume he is a playboy, because that is what he wants them to believe. He is very talented at pretending to be living off his family's fortune and not bothered about how his carefree lifestyle comes across. He lets others draw their own conclusion about his adventures and doesn't bother correcting them, even though they are all wrong.

Darius has a very important career. He works for the Royal Family as an investigator. His job is to travel the world as a PI and do undercover work, often using his family name and resources to dig up all kinds of interesting facts. I hired him six months ago when I needed a matter looked into, one I didn't necessarily trust just anyone with. After he proved his worth, it seemed like smart business to retain him permanently. So far, we have not been disappointed, plus it gives the two of us time to catch up and remain close.

"You don't have one, do you?" Darius chuckles when he catches me frowning at him. "I didn't know that was even possible, Este. You always have a plan, backed up by a plan which even has a plan."

"Shut it," I grumble.

"You already had a nickname?" Winifred questions as soon as there is a pause. "Why didn't you just allow me to use that?"

"Because Falcon is the only person who calls me Este. And since I prefer not thinking of him most days, I wanted to hear what you'd come up with." I do my best to maintain my cool, although it's not easy when these two are around.

"Most wouldn't dare talk to him in such a normal manner. However, I dared. I wasn't all that impressed with his prince status, refused to address him by using it when he stepped onto my field that first practice." Falcon's arrogance is reflecting in his eyes. "I still refuse to use it for the most part. There are enough suck-ups in his prestigious life, no need for him to deal with one more. Ain't that right, Este?"

The limo slows down so we can pull over, and my friend doesn't miss a beat. "You kids have fun. I believe this is where I get out."

"You're not staying?" Winifred questions as she peeks out the window to identify where we are. "I thought you were going to escort me back home in a few hours? Have a drink with my father?"

Falcon reaches across the aisle and snags her free hand. "I'm certain your father will be pleased to not have to deal with me again today. I will contact him in a few days just to make the game interesting. Trust me, honey cakes, you don't want a third wheel interfering. And for the record, my man Stan is quite a catch, and it appears he's not such a bad fisherman, either. It was an honor to meet you, Lady Winifred. Now have fun and keep him on his toes." He kisses her hand before climbing out of the car and disappearing into the crowd.

The vehicle is moving again almost immediately so we don't draw attention. It should look like only a drop-off; too many onlookers in this area could easily figure out whose vehicle this was.

"Castile Vicente, sir?" My driver's voice echoes over the speaker.

"Yes, please. Has everything been taken care of?" I hope so.

"It has, sir. Braden has assured me, if we enter through the back, we shall not be disturbed. All staff has been dispersed or sent home."

"Excellent. Pull under the canopy and then leave us." I instruct him.

"Sir?"

"I am capable of exiting a vehicle without assistance, am I not? Instruct the rest of the team on my orders as well. We are not to see anyone until I am ready to leave. Am I clear?"

"As day, sir."

I shift in my seat and glance over at my guest. "Thank you for seeing me this morning."

"You said we needed to talk, yet this entire morning has been downright confusing. What are you up to, Stan? Why do I get the impression you don't want others to see us together?"

I hate what she is insinuating, hate that she is partially correct even more.

"Until I am ready... correction. Until we are ready to go public, I don't want others assuming or drawing conclusions. I don't want them to see us together, because I don't want the powers that be to overreact and push a young woman into something she isn't prepared to handle yet. Do you understand?" I do my best to explain, although I'm not sure it is good enough.

"You don't want them sending out the announcements and planning the wedding." Winifred blushes as she shyly draws her own conclusion. "You honestly believe that is what they would do? I'm not even finished with school yet. I guess that doesn't matter, though, does it? I've seen it happen enough with young girls like myself. I suspect before summer ends, I'll be betrothed too..."

"Not if I have any influence on the matter. You have some growing up to do still, adventures to seek out, a life to live. There is no reason you should not have that like your sisters did. Why do you believe you will not get the same opportunity?" I notice we are getting close to our destination. "Hold that thought."

Winifred nods.

As soon as the car stops, my driver heads for the guard station. I open the door so we can get out, then reach inside and offer Winifred my hand to assist her as she climbs out.

She looks every bit of eighteen today. I mean that as a compliment, by the way. Her youthfulness is refreshing. Not yet fully corrupted by the world we live in, while at the same time marginally aware of the forces that surround us.

I should not be this attracted to a young woman who only recently came of age. It has me questioning if I am more like the man who fathered me than I'd like to be. He had no problem using his influence to get young innocent women, like Winifred, as soon as they were legal. The biggest difference I keep reminding myself of, is that he was only interested in bedding them. I am not at all interested in that, not really. I may not have a laid-out, detailed plan, but I most certainly have very clear long-term intentions where she is concerned.

We make our way through my eerily empty residence. It is not my home. It used to be Antonio's until he moved into the palace. I stay here whenever I am in Aragon, which happens to be a lot this past year.

My home is Esteban Palace located a few hours southeast of here, off the coast. They did not name the palace after me, it is named after the first King Esteban. The structure is the oldest one standing in Hermosa Islas. Constructed in the mid-1600s off one of the highest cliffs that overlook the ocean and mainland. A person can literally see beyond the horizon in every direction. It is my refuge when I can find the time to escape there.

I had my staff prepare a buffet for us in the inner solarium, where we would not be seen by anyone. It is like a miniature garden area that allows fresh air as well as protection from unwanted onlookers. I spend most of my time inside this space because I hate feeling like others can watch me openly when I am outside on the exposed property.

I am very pleased to discover it has been arranged exactly as I instructed. The table is set for two, with several covered dishes. They even added a floral arrangement which contributes a nice touch.

"I hope you are hungry," I tell Winifred as I pull out her chair and motion for her to sit. Of course, she doesn't sit until I do, a habit I wish to break her of one day.

"It all looks so... elegant. Mother would be impressed." Winifred takes her napkin and places it in her lap.

I lift the lids and instruct her to help herself. She does a quick study of the choices offered. Stares at the French toast with powdered sugar generously sprinkled all over it. Eyes the bacon and sausages. Bites her lip when she spots the scrambled eggs with cheese melted over the top of them. After she practically drools over all those delicacies, she opts for the small bowl of oatmeal, a few strawberries, and half a slice of plain toast.

"Thank you. This is perfect." She smiles and begins to cautiously eat.

Then she watches me load up a plate with everything she was just salivating over. Swallows hard when I pour hot syrup over the two slices of French toast and then add a few strawberries. Sighs even as she takes a bite of her chosen oatmeal, which I know for certain isn't what she craves.

When I place the plate next to her, she frowns up at me. "What are you doing?"

"Feeding you." I slide the plate closer. "I didn't instruct my chef to prepare all this food so you could merely look at it. I did so because I wanted you to eat it."

She aims her spoon at the food in front of her. "I am."

"What do you have for breakfast most mornings, Winnie?" I ask as I prepare a plate for myself. "Do you not like the items I plated for you?"

She stares at the plate and shakes her head. "If I eat that, it will all go directly to my arse and thighs."

Now it is my turn to frown. "Stand up."

"Excuse me?" She blinks several times before dropping her spoon and then stands. "Satisfied/"

"Spin for me." I motion with my fork. "Step back a bit and spin, so I can make an observation."

I watch as she lifts her eyebrows, kicks her chair back, and then does as I instructed. Afterward, she grips the arm of her seat, yanks it forcefully closer to the table before she sits back down. She doesn't look at me. Instead, she stares at the water glass sweating in front of her. Her facial expression informs me I may have taken matters a little too far.

"Winnie," I tenderly speak her name. "Look at me."

She directs only her eyes in my direction, keeping that frozen ice queen expression securely in place. If a woman could murder a man with a simple glance, I'd not have survived.

I smile as I shove the plate I prepared even closer. "Seems to me you could use a little more cushion in both. Now eat, before you offend me, and I end up doing something I promised I wouldn't do again."

She snags the bacon and bites into it defiantly while she boldly chews. I watch her and recognize she is soon going to break the ice queen stare. I didn't expect it to turn into one that was as equally damaging to my resolve. A wounded child appears, and I want to kick my own arse for not realizing I needed to be more cautious when dealing with this woman.

I angle my chair toward hers as I slide closer and incline forward, resting my elbows on my knees. "I'm sorry. It's just that I hate seeing you not eating what I know you want to eat. If the oatmeal and strawberries are satisfactory to you, then ignore me. I understand I put too much food on your plate, and that you rarely get to indulge. It's just that there is nothing at all wrong with your arse. Everything about you is perfect as far as I am concerned."

"Nothing about me is perfect," she whispers as she aims her head away from me.

I can no longer stop myself. There is no way I can sit here and listen to her speak like that. I grab her chair and yank it to me. "No more. You will not talk like that. No one is perfect. We all have faults."

"You don't." She blushes and does her best to retreat while I continue to drag her closer.

"Trust me, I do." I reach up, forcing her to look me in the eye. "One of my biggest faults is not being able to resist you. How I ever kept my distance this long is astounding. I'm going to kiss you again, Winnie. If you don't want me to, speak now."

I give her a few beats before I slowly brush my lips against hers. The feel of her soft lips against mine is unlike any other. I know each kiss we share will only stir the perpetual flames, flames that one day will consume us both.

Her giggle is what finally breaks this unplanned kiss. I don't believe a woman has ever giggled while I was kissing her before. It makes me smile and move back so I can look at her.

"Sorry." She giggles again. "I don't know why I am..."

She breaks into a full laugh, and I end up joining her. It is refreshing all the way around to be able to share a pleasant kiss and then express the joy of it like this.

"Never apologize for laughing, not that kind of laughing, at least." I scoot back and start eating again. "So, tell me about your plans after graduation."

After she takes a sip of her water, Winifred begins eating again. I try not to smile when I notice her push the oatmeal aside and pulls the plate I filled in front of her. "Right now, I don't have any."

"Surely you've applied to several universities? I find it hard to believe you would simply assume you would not be allowed to attend." I watch her smile and wish she would do that more.

"I applied to Princeton, the University of Melbourne, the University of Edinburgh, and Columbia University. Father hasn't permitted me to accept any offers as of yet. Keeps putting it off when I ask, says we will discuss it when the time is right." She shakes her head. "My guess is, he means when he has weighed all the other options presented to him where I am concerned. Most likely I'll be forced to attend one of the local universities, so whoever has offered him the best proposal can keep me close."

I grunt in disgust. "There will be no proposals, Winnie."

"How do you know that? I'm pretty certain Lord Hector Colón and Lord Earnest Rupert will contact him later this week to start the process. By the time I graduate, I'm certain..."

"There will be none. Not after my warning last night. I'm not saying those men won't shelve any offers they might have been considering. I'm sure they will. However, until they believe I am no longer keeping watch, they will stand down. That includes your father. None of them needs a scandal right now; they have too much at stake to risk media attention.

I no longer wish to discuss older men who have no business being interested in Winifred. "So, which one of those schools is at the top of your list?"

"Columbia." She doesn't even hesitate with her response.

"Why Columbia?" I grab my coffee and relax back in my seat. "You didn't even have to think about it. Which means you've thought hard about this, and I'd like to hear your reason."

"There are several, actually." She lays her fork down and pushes the plate away.

I'm pleased to see she ate at least half of what I offered her. The satisfied expression on her face tells me she enjoyed it, that it was fulfilling to her.

"First, because it's in the United States. I've never been, and I'd like to go someplace where no one knows me. To a city that is so large, I could get lost in the crowd. Where no one cares who I am or who my family is. I'd be another student in a sea of students, with a diversity of backgrounds."

I nod, perfectly understanding her reasoning for wanting that. It is true that most people in the large city of New York, don't seem to notice foreigners. Probably because there are a vast number of them in that particular metropolis, making it not uncommon for them to encounter one. I have been to that city several times and rarely get recognized. When I do, it isn't a huge deal. I can easily become lost in the vast sea of people who live there.

"Ingrid is going to Princeton, which means she won't be that far away. We can plan weekend outings together. Long weekends, even, if we wanted. If Columbia wasn't an option, Princeton would presumably be my second because of her.

"Plus, it would take me away from my family, harder for my father to keep an eagle's eye on me as he does here. Giving me a chance to do a little exploring into some interests I'd never get the chance to look at otherwise. Get a job maybe."

She hesitates before she blurts out, "There are several bakeries I'd like to work at that aren't far from the university. Each one specializes in unique cakes, and a few of the owners are an inspiration. I would love to learn from any of them."

"A bakery?" I don't mean to sound snobby about it.

She nods warily. "I love baking. Not that I get a lot of chances to do so. I've helped our chef in the kitchen at home sometimes. Secretly joined her when the rest of my family were out for the evening, and they left me home for one reason or another. She's allowed me to assist her, taught me how to make some cool and fun desserts. I even helped decorate my birthday cake one year."

"Would you like to one day own a bakery?" This time when I ask, I don't believe I sound unsure about it. I suspect I sound intrigued. A bright light shines inside of her when she discusses baking.

"Like that would ever happen." Winifred shakes her head, exposing her disappointment.

"Say it could. What would you sell? And what would you name it?" I lift my foot and rest it on my knee.

"I'd sell all kinds of yummy treats. Cookies, cupcakes, muffins, Danish sweet rolls, all those forbidden pleasures I was never allowed to have growing up." She gets this mischievous smirk on her face. "I'd name it Stan's Dreamland, because the only way I'd own a place like that is in a dream you created inside your head."

Now it is my turn to laugh and shake my head. "Dreams, Winnie, are what this world is built on. First, we need to get you to Columbia, so you can take that first step."

CHAPTER 5
Esteban

One year later

I haven't seen Winifred in almost seven months. That was the day I stopped by the apartment I rented for her after she moved in. I leased it the day after her father announced she could attend Columbia University in the fall. As soon as Winnie called me, shrieked into the phone about how she couldn't believe he'd approved her to go, I started my search for a place that was close to campus and secure.

It did not surprise me Justice Batista accepted his youngest daughter's first choice. The week after Winifred's birthday, he called me. Wanted to meet with me, clear up a few issues where she was concerned, had a few questions about my friend the Duke of Falcon.

I cleared an hour on my docket. Invited Darius to join in on the fun. There was nothing more thrilling than throwing a man like Ivan Batista off his game, forcing him to display his true colors.

"Prince Esteban, thank you for stopping by," Ivan greeted as he invited me into his office, also taking notice of the man accompanying me. *"I didn't realize you were also joining us, Your Grace. Please come in."*

"Since I missed our meeting the other day, I thought it would be nice to sit down and talk." Falcon was as brilliant as always. *"You have one wonderful daughter, at least. A diamond in the rough that one."*

"Are you suggesting that you might like to join the list of potential suitors Lady Eva and I are considering?" Ivan didn't beat around the bush, dove right into the heart of the matter.

"May I ask who my competition might be?" Darius took his seat as soon as we got comfortable. *"I'm not sure Lady Winifred is exactly where I would prefer her to be just yet. A little young still. Some world traveling, along with a diverse education, would certainly do her some good."*

We learned Winifred had been correct about her father's initial reasoning for not approving her university choices. He admitted Lady Eva and he were considering proposals by men I believed were entirely too old for her. Men who had underlying drawbacks that kept women at a distance.

"We both assumed those men were about as good as we might expect."

Ivan's nerve to belittle his youngest had me steaming. *"Men, who have no business entertaining such a young girl, is as good as you expect? Have you ever considered there might be a few younger men out there who might step up in a few years once she's completed university?"* I tried hard not to sound disgusted, but it wasn't easy.

"I believe what the prince is suggesting," Darius thankfully took his cue and saved me, *"is perhaps it would be best to let her age with grace first. See what the world has to offer before shoving her into marriage. I personally believe it is good for the soul to experience more before jumping the gun. Don't be in such a rush to force the beautiful young lady into a solitary life. Let her blossom and grow a little. The right man for her will appreciate the fact you did."*

Ivan nodded his head while listening. *"That gives me something to deliberate over. You make a good argument, Your Grace. Perhaps I will do just that. I was ready to make an example out of her after dealing with her disappointing sisters until you showed up. Now, I just might reconsider my approach. It might be better to allow her to show them how to attract a man like you."*

Darius earned an award for his performance that afternoon. He went on and on about how I had suggested taking a thorough look into

Lady Winifred. Mentioned how he was in search of a woman who could fix his tainted reputation, one who could keep him on the straight and narrow. Went so far as to mention how he was very interested in a woman as pure as Winifred, but also desired her to be well-educated, along with being a world traveler. Explained how important it was that his future wife attend one of the more prestigious universities the world offered, naming a few, he thought stood out. Columbia was the second one on his list, named after his chosen Swedish University, of course. By the time he stood to leave our meeting, the Duke of Falcon had the justice eating out of the palm of his hand.

"I do believe your friend might be exactly what Lady Eva and I are hoping for," Ivan admitted as soon as it was just us. Darius had some place else he needed to be, leaving me to finish this meeting without him.

"Then perhaps it would be a good idea to see what we can do to make Lady Winifred more attractive." I had to swallow hard and not give myself away. "I believe he mentioned Columbia University, didn't you say Winifred had listed that as one of her choices?"

I should have felt guilty deceiving Justice Batista like that, except I did not. There was nothing I wouldn't do to make certain Winifred was given the chance to live out her dream, and that was step one. I even offered to help in any way I could to guarantee she stayed on my friend's radar. Explained that the duke felt she needed a few years to mature, although he wasn't against giving her the time to do so.

Winifred had been privy to that information as well. I shared it all with her the next time I visited de la Peña Citadel, the home where my mother resided with my younger siblings. Even had my mother extend an invitation to Winifred and Ingrid for dinner, so I could discuss it with her in private.

And yes, I knew I wasn't fooling my mother, or Lorenzo for that matter. They were aware of my shenanigans. My mother casually smiled and agreed to it without being too obvious. Lorenzo, on the other hand, had not been subtle about it at all. Told me it was about time I stopped pretending she didn't exist.

So here I am. It's been a year since I made my initial move. Once again, it is her birthday, her nineteenth birthday, and I didn't bother letting her know I was coming.

I wasn't sure I'd make it to New York. I've been quite busy doing more than just the job I inherited after my father's death. My brother, Antonio, and I are dividing and conquering the family business, Reyes Capital. He tries to do it all. Run the kingdom he is in charge of, while he remains the CEO of Reyes Capital, but there aren't enough hours in the day to do both. I am as equally equipped to handle the CEO position as he is. That was where I would have ended up had it all gone as it should have.

I've been gone for a month, flying all over the world, checking in on our investments, taking meetings, verifying everything is running smoothly. My plan had been to end the trip in New York, where I intended to spend a few weeks. However, I wasn't sure if those weeks would coincide with Winifred's birthday, even though I'd hoped they would.

Thankfully, my face isn't as recognizable as my brother's. I mean, of course, there are those who recognize me, those who read the tabloids and have discovered me tucked deep inside somewhere. I'm not as interesting as my brother, the unwed king, and I'm completely fine with that, by the way. However, that doesn't mean I can walk around without security close by. Nor does it mean my team doesn't need to do a security check of the establishments I wish to go to. Sweep the place, so to speak. It just means they don't have to be so obvious about it and can often stand down, offer me some distance when we are outside our country.

Which is why, when I walk into one of the local bars, it comes across as if I am with my buddies, more than it does my security team. All three of my guards are with me tonight: Braden, Stew, and Calvin. It isn't just the three of us, though, I dragged Darius with me. He and I have business in the city tomorrow before I can blow off and relax. Not to mention, should I for some reason, get caught visiting Lady Winifred, I can use him as my excuse. Make it appear as if I am performing my best friend duties.

It takes all of five seconds for me to spot Winnie. At first, I smile when I notice her standing around a high-top table, laughing with a group I assume are her friends. Until the guy next to her wraps his arm around her waist and tugs her closer. Quickly, my smile morphs into a frown, and something inside of me rages.

Falcon's chuckle doesn't calm down my rage. Instead, it only eggs it on, forcing me to react. "Rut-row. Easy Este. You have no claim on her."

"Like hell I don't." I stalk up to the table and stop as soon as I am behind her.

It's like she can detect me before I am even able to announce myself. She whirls around with this shocked expression on her face, one that says it all. Her entire body straightens as she does her best to compose herself and act more refined.

I liked it better when she was relaxed and smiling, so that has to be why I wrapped her in my arms and squeeze. It takes Winnie a few seconds to go with it, enfold her arms around my center, and then sigh. Which is when I lift her off her feet and squeeze even tighter. I'd say it is much like when I hug one of my sisters, except it's not, while yet it is. It's undoubtedly an affectionate hug, one that expresses you know this person very well. It also has a nice comfortable ambiance to it, one that warms me like no hug my sisters have ever given me could.

"It's been too long, Winnie. We need to do this more often," I whisper in her ear as I place her back on her feet. "Happy birthday."

"My turn." Falcon shoves me out of the way and lifts my girl in his arms, making her squeal and causing me to get that jealous sensation again. "Honey cakes, you didn't think we'd miss your birthday, now, did ya?"

"Do you know these guys, Win?" The guy next to her once again wraps his arm around her protectively as soon as she is back on her feet, making me want to punch him.

That is, until she reaches down and removes his arm, steps away from him and toward me while she answers. "I do. They—"

I extend my hand to the guy she just stepped away from, as I place my other hand firmly on her shoulder. "I'm Stan. I've known Winnie since she was about eleven. My brother Lenny and she went to boarding school together."

The guy takes my offered hand as he glares at the other one resting on Winnie's shoulder. He doesn't miss it when I slide it down her arm and then place it where his was right before I showed up.

That's right, man, she belongs to me. You may have snuck in, got a little of her time in my absence, but you will never have her. No matter what may happen while we spend these next few years apart. When it is all said and done, this one here will be mine. Enjoy your limited stint, just make sure you don't enjoy it too much, or you'll answer to me.

"Kaleb." He introduces himself. "Win and I—"

"Are friends. Kaleb, Ian, Tanner, Courtney, Lindsey, and Nina." Winnie motions around the table. "This is Stan and Darius."

"Friends? Funny, I thought we decided to be more than just friends." Kaleb shakes his head, a little disappointed.

"Very good friends, better?" Winnie sighs before she steps out of my hold and back toward him. "Don't be like that. I told you it was complicated."

"There is complicated, Win, and then there is obfuscated. Probably best if I don't add to this rather tricky situation." He leans in and kisses her cheek, right before he mutters a few words in her ear.

Winnie blushes and wobbles her head slightly, doing her best to brush him off. I noticed his words did something to her. In fact, they seem to have made her shiver, react in a way I don't care for.

"I'm here. I'll be here later, even. I'm not going anywhere. Think about that, okay." Kaleb grabs one of the other girls' hands and drags her out to the dance floor. I don't miss how he watches us closely when I sit down and encourage Winnie to lean against me.

She also seems a little confused about what she should be doing. It's as if she doesn't know if she should stay here with me, or follow him. Not exactly how I envisioned tonight playing out, not even close to how I pictured it in my mind.

It wasn't as if we hadn't kept in touch all these months. While the lines of communication have been sporadic, mainly because I didn't want to overwhelm her, I wanted to give her some freedom, allowing her to enjoy her time while she spread her wings a little. I hadn't ignored her. I reached out from time to time. Did my best, in my opinion, to express my intent where I believed she and I stood.

"What's his problem?" I ask as I wave down a server and order a drink. "You want something?"

"Can't. US drinking age is twenty-one," she reminds me as she taps the table with her nails.

"Forgot. So that guy, Kaleb. He your boyfriend?" I have a hard time believing she'd have one, but you never know. The way that guy was acting has my radar going off big time.

"Not exactly." Winnie glances over her shoulder, and it seems she sincerely feels ashamed. "I think he was hopeful things would progress later tonight. He's a nice guy. Plus, it's not as if I have anything to feel guilty about, right? You've inevitably been having some fun, figured I was allowed some as well."

"What does that mean?" I don't like how that sounds or what she is implying.

Winifred blinks slowly. "Did you enjoy your time in Rio? Better yet, did you all have fun in the South Pacific?"

Rio. I went to Rio right before the end of the year. Had some official Royal Palace business to conduct. Those who enjoyed putting their nose in my personal life urged me it would be a good idea to spend time with the daughters of those who held an office. After a long week of being stuck in boring meetings and kissing butt, I procured a long weekend. Accepted an invitation from a woman around my age to show me around, one I regretted later. She intended for us to be seen a lot, while hoping to convince me she was the one I had been searching for. The media promptly picked up on the temporary affair and spun it way out of proportion. I haven't spoken to her since I walked away from her and her indecent proposal.

The South Pacific was a trip I took a few months back with Darius and our other pal, Prince Oscar Svendsen of Denmark. A much-needed holiday for the three of us. The media coverage once again made it appear way worse than it actually was—way worse. We hoped to do some fishing, hiking, scuba diving, and all the other guy stuff most ladies hated. Each outing ended up coinciding with a very feisty group of three women, all of whom made sure the media heard about the men stalking them. To be clear, we weren't the stalkers, quite the opposite, although it was hard to prove otherwise, so we ended the trip short by five days.

"Not really." I hold her gaze, hoping she sees the truth. "Don't you dare believe all that crap they print. Both were portrayed in a light that was not at all correct. When have you known me, or those I associate with, to act like that? Have I not made myself clear, Winnie? I will not apologize for others making more out of it than it was."

"Fine. How about the annual Constitutional Ball in January then? Did you and Lady Felicia enjoy the after-party? I don't need to read about that one. Several of my friends captured the two of you dancing, kissing, even." Because I am staring at her, I notice instantly when her eyes tear up.

"She kissed me..." I try to explain.

Winifred yanks her phone out of her pocket and slams it down in front of me. She unlocks it, pulls up the folder distinctly marked "Stan". Then opens it, right before she grabs one of her girlfriend's hands and drags her off to the dance floor where they join the others.

I stupidly open the folder, watch several videos that show my brothers and me enjoying ourselves. I allow myself to let loose once a year—once a year. The rest of the time I color inside the lines and don't give anyone a reason to question my actions. I understand there is certainly no excuse for allowing interactions to be misinterpreted. Giving the impression I could be persuaded to go there, when that is so far from the truth.

"I didn't think you allowed anyone to video those events." My friend's voice echoes over my shoulder. "Wow. Seems like you are having quite the time."

I glare at him.

"I said seemed like. I, however, can read you better than most. While you certainly are kissing her, you aren't kissing her. Know what I mean?"

I do, because that is exactly what it was. It may look like I am kissing her, and I guess in a way I am. Okay, I am, without a doubt, kissing her. However, I'm not kissing her, not like that at least. Not at all like that. The kiss Winnie and I shared at her soirée was more intimate and meaningful than that one could ever be.

"Winnie is a little upset about that, I take it? Can't say I blame her." He flashes me a slight smirk. "If I recall, you nearly came unglued earlier when that Kaleb dude had his arm around her. Imagine how you'd feel if you witnessed that."

"This here is why we do our best to prevent these types of videos from surfacing. Whoever took these was smart to not post them on social media." I rub my forehead and try to think.

Lady Felicia had made her rounds that night. By the time she got to me, she was completely gone. I, unfortunately, wasn't as coherent as I should have been, either. Had let exchanges get out of hand before dismissing her. I thought I'd gotten lucky, and no one had captured my mistake, my horribly regretted mistake.

Seems I was wrong. It also implies someone might be onto the fact that Winifred and I have an attraction. I'm not sure what issue is the bigger one right now. If someone believes something might be going on between us, and word gets back to her family, our relationship could get sticky fast. More importantly, it suggests I need to be more cautious, use better judgment, so this person doesn't ruin all my efforts in getting this woman to trust me, really trust me.

I hear Falcon whistle and then chuckle as only he can do. It has me twisting my head, so I can appreciate what he is witnessing. "Damn. Honey cakes sure has come out of her shell some since the last time I saw her."

"Oh, hell no." I shove back from the table and stand when I catch what he is staring at.

"Hold up. Este, you cannot go charging in like—" He chuckles again as he dashes after me. "Or maybe you can. Just remember to not go overboard."

I nudge my way through the crowd on a mission. My rational brain has dissipated, all that is left is the irrational side. The one that seems to take over whenever I get near this woman.

Winifred is out on the dance floor with her cluster of friends. She is dancing with two guys. Two guys, one in front of and one behind her. They are doing their best to drive her crazy while fighting to claim ownership. One of the guys is Kaleb, and right now I'd say he is winning the game she is permitting both to play with her. Not just because he is currently behind her, with one arm secured around her waist, while the other fondles her left breast. But also, because right before he seizes her face, he catches me advancing with purpose, makes direct eye contact as he drags her mouth to his, and kisses her. He kisses her like I have not dared to kiss her yet. It is the kind of kiss that has me seeing red and wanting to kill him with my bare hands.

Worse—if there is a worse—is the fact that I swear she is kisses him back. I cannot even explain what that does to me, how it makes me feel.

A loud whistle echoes over the music, and I know it is Falcon alerting my men to be ready. Probably a good idea I brought him with me. Otherwise, this could have ended altogether differently.

I don't get the chance to yank either man off of her though. Calvin has the man in front of her removed before I get there. I have no clue how he reached her first, but he did. Two of Kaleb's friends are smart enough to detach him from her as soon as I reach them. I'm guessing they could identify my murderous glare and thought it best to save their friend from himself.

I catch her before she tumbles to the ground after being caught off guard. She was so enthralled in that dance that as soon as both men were removed, there was nothing around to hold her upright.

Winifred protests until her eyes lock with mine, then it seems as if the reality of it all comes rushing back to her. Her eyes shift down to my lips and then back again.

"Did you enjoy yourself?" I growl.

"No," she hisses, as she attempts to step back, except I don't permit it.

"Do you dance like that often?" I can sense the tension in my body building, a tension I hadn't yet experienced in the twenty-four years I've lived on this earth.

"No." Again, she purposely mocks me. "First time, actually."

"You kissed him." Once again, I snarl my words out.

"He kissed me," she counters as pain flashes across her eyes and face.

"You kissed him back, Winnie. I watched you kiss him back." I shake my head, displaying my displeasure. "Was it all you thought it would be?"

"Not really," she grumbles before I yank her closer.

"This one will be," I warn her, right before I crash my lips to hers.

There is no way I am going to allow his kiss to linger on her mind, singeing a memory she will reflect on later. I kiss her, really kiss her, forcing her to open that sweet mouth and accept all I have to offer. I devour her. Consume her, until I myself become unusually lightheaded.

Which also happens to be about the time my men, along with Falcon, are encouraging us to stop and to start moving. Seems we've drawn attention to ourselves, and now it is time to get out of here before everyone recognizes who I am and who I am with.

"Este, I believe it's time we chat about you making some sort of plan. You are not the best at this functioning on a whim thing." Darius laughs as he shoves us inside the waiting vehicle. "Seems when it comes to honey cakes here, all rational thought gets tossed aside. I'll admit, I am enjoying watching the fall, but I don't think it wise to push you beyond your limits. No need to break those hard-earned reputations the two of you have worked to maintain. So, we need to secure a plan that will work and keep you two from breaking protocol."

I agree. I thoroughly agree. This woman is my weakness, and it is time we discuss how to move forward.

CHAPTER 6

Winifred

The Royals

I have no idea what I was thinking, letting Kaleb, along with some unknown male, dance with me like that. It's so not like me at all. If I were smart, I'd blame it on the alcohol—except I hadn't consumed that much alcohol.

Before we all headed to this local university hangout, my friends and I met up at Kaleb and Ian's small apartment. I had one bottle of beer and a shot of tequila—birthday tequila is what they called it. Something to loosen me up a bit, so I could have some fun. Because it was very well understood I rarely allowed myself to have fun. I was too busy making sure I didn't give my father an excuse to revoke my pass. My grades had to be perfect. I do mean perfect, no slacking whatsoever. They had been my motivation that first semester, the only thing I allowed my brain to focus on.

When the semester was over, I expected to be flown home for the break, except that hadn't been the case. My father saw no reason to fly me home for a month when I had a perfectly suitable place to stay here. Plus, according to my sisters, he and my mother were planning to be gone, a cruise, they believed. Not that my sisters cared. With the parentals absent, it gave them the freedom to do whatever they wanted.

If their social media accounts were correct, I'd have to say they roamed freely indeed.

Therefore, I spent that time alone. Just me, my thoughts, along with a city full of foreigners I didn't know at all to keep me company. Instead of sulking and feeling sorry for myself, I decided to see if maybe I could get a job.

Do you realize how difficult it is to acquire a job when you have absolutely no work experience whatsoever? Almost impossible in a city this big, when they had so many others to choose from.

My current visa only allowed me to go to school, didn't permit me to hold an off-campus job unless it related to my field of study. The job I really wanted—the bakery job—technically was in my field, except it wasn't, if you get my drift. It was a business, a privately-owned business, that could teach me so much if I could convince an owner to offer me an internship/apprenticeship. However, I had to wait a year before I could go searching for that kind of paid work. According to the person I spoke with, who was expected to know all there was to know about visas and how they worked, I could accept an unpaid one and not get into trouble.

At first, I wasn't so keen on that idea. However, after a week of doing absolutely nothing but sitting in my apartment, staring at four walls and watching movies, I changed my mind. I went to five establishments I thought I'd like to work at. None of them were interested in working with me. They assumed I was trying to pull one over on them.

I was about to give up when I passed a small bakery/cake specialty shop named Nelson's. The ideal establishment, one I had first considered before I chose to go for the larger bakeries figuring my chances were better with them.

It wasn't dolled up to appear extra fancy like a few others had been. The lobby was small. It had room for a display case that showed off the goodies, larger refrigerated units off to the side where they held the cakes, and a cash register. There was just enough room to walk in and grab what you needed, nothing else.

A middle-aged woman, covered in flour and icing, dressed in a baker's smock, stepped through the doorway smiling like she loved her job. She listened carefully to me as I went through my spiel, that smile on her face continuing to grow the longer I talked. When I was finished, she said one word. Hired. Told me we'd work out the details later. Nonetheless, she would be thrilled to have the help. Free help was even better.

I've been working at Nelson's now since mid-December, almost four months. In the beginning, I assisted her with the books. That's what she hated doing most, where she struggled. Since I was excellent with numbers, understood a spreadsheet and order forms, knew how to write up invoices and make payments, that's what I did. I manned the counter while I got her books in order, made everything easy and simple, all just a click away.

That took up most of my winter break. I spent ten-hour days in the bakery and loved every second of it, taking only Sundays off because she was closed. When February rolled around, she dragged me into that larger-than-life kitchen of hers and taught me how to make heart-shaped cookies, red-velvet cupcakes, and rose petal treats that sold like hotcakes. Basically, if I wasn't in school, I was at the bakery, and when I wasn't there, I was studying so my grades didn't slip.

Somehow, in the midst of it all, I managed to make a few friends. Courtney and I had several classes together. She latched on to me rather quickly once she realized I was smart. Lindsey and Nina lived in the same building as she did, and one night they invited me to join them for a weekend party. Ingrid was coming for a visit that weekend, so I was game because it gave us something to do. That is the weekend I met the guys: Kaleb, Ian, and Tanner.

Now to be clear, this all happened before I began working at the bakery, so ever since then, they have genuinely been on my case. They thought I was crazy for putting in the hours I did while also going to school.

It didn't take me long to realize Kaleb was attracted to me. That became more obvious after the break, mostly because he started showing up in the evenings when he knew I was working the counter at Nelson's. Last month he admitted it, even, and informed me he thought we should give things a go.

I had no reason not to, right? I mean, it wasn't as if Esteban and I were anything more than friends. Sure, he had kissed me a few times, had been the first man to kiss me. How sad was that?

Last summer went by fast. After I returned home from boarding school, I had all of eight weeks before I needed to head to the States. There was a lot to sort out for me to be ready to leave for the United States, not to mention, that a man in Esteban's position had responsibilities. So, the three times I did see him were nice, but not enough for us to build something.

And while we texted regularly—then and now—that was never the same as actually being together. I mean, it is challenging to hold a meaningful conversation in a text.

Even when he called—and he had called me quite a few times, more than my family called me—it wasn't as good as seeing him in person. I enjoyed his calls very much, enjoyed hearing his voice while listening to him go on and on about the little things. We talked about school, Nelson's, life in a foreign country, and how it was different in a good way. There was always something missing during those conversations, though, things we just couldn't say, because we hadn't dared to discuss those matters yet. He'd made it very clear that I was young and should have a chance to experience life first before being tied down. That he wanted me to make my own choices in all matters, to live out my dreams. Which I guess is what I am doing, living my life without the pressure of my family hovering, waiting for them to pounce at a moment's notice.

The only time he has ever visited me here was shortly after I moved into my apartment, the one he helped secure for me. It was nice, in Morningside, only a couple of blocks away from Columbia. It was bigger than what most of my friends had. The apartment had two bedrooms with one bath, a decent-size kitchen, and lots of closet space in one very nice building. I hadn't invited people over, because I knew once they saw it, they'd know I was not just an average student. I was different from them and could afford nice things, really nice things. They were living in small studios or one-bedroom apartments that could easily fit in my spacious residence.

He visited so he could check it out, make sure it was how they had stated, which it was. And even though it was a two-bedroom, he insisted on staying in a hotel. Making our time together less than it could have been if he'd opted to make use of my spare room.

Then, of course, there was the fact Esteban seemed to be living his own life. Dating, even. Women who were older than I. The types of women who seemed to know what he liked and had a great deal of experience with men. The kinds of women my sisters always claimed men like him fell for, the type I hoped to never be.

But then I had gone and danced with two guys at the same time. Let them dance with me like I had watched others dance and always declared I'd never allow a guy to do that to me. Worse, I guess. Not only had I encouraged them to grind their sweaty bodies against mine, I'd allowed Kaleb to kiss me like no other man had ever been allowed to do before.

He'd only been the second guy to kiss me. Our first kiss happened a few weeks ago. Ingrid came to town early for my birthday since her schedule conflicted with my actual birthday. So, we celebrated early, partied it up with my friends at some club she wanted to try. She and Ian always seemed to gravitate toward each other, which was fine. I was happy for my friend, that she had spread her wings a bit and let loose.

The guys escorted us back to my building, tried extremely hard to get us to invite them up. I think if I'd have said yes, Ingrid would have gone along easily, but I was not anywhere near being ready for that. So instead, Ian and she made out on the sidewalk while Kaleb made his move on me. Kissed me softly at first and then went in a little more aggressively. Not as aggressively as he had tonight, but he made it clear what he wanted, hoped maybe I'd let him have it soon.

I hadn't been certain how I felt about it all. Confessed later that there might be another guy, a situation that was complicated and had me confused. He backed off then. Promised he'd let me do my best to figure it out.

It is what I had been in the process of doing. I was considering what he was suggesting, since it didn't seem the other guy was anywhere near as interested in me as Kaleb. So, earlier, I'd told him maybe we could give it a shot, take it slow and see where it led. And that was probably why he'd been more handsy tonight. There was no doubt he was letting the others know where he and I stood as a couple.

And just when I thought I knew what I was doing, what I wanted, Esteban showed up and muddled it up real good. All those crazy girlish sensations took over my brain and body as soon as I sensed him near. Then when he wrapped me in his arms, it was like all that had been missing no longer was. Suddenly, I was back where I was meant to be.

Unexpectedly, I was now caught between two men I respected in very different ways. Kaleb was the guy who helped me learn how to have a little fun and start enjoying where I am right now. Esteban was the man who invaded my dreams, stirred up all those girlish fantasies, said things that made me think one day it could all truly happen.

So, I did what any young woman in my position would do. I decided I had no reason to feel guilty about Kaleb. I had every right to live in the here and now, rather than what might one day be. How dare he inquire if Kaleb was my boyfriend like he didn't believe I could or would have one. I had the right to enjoy my time here as much as he had in Rio and other places. Time to show him I'd kept tabs on his life and knew he wasn't sitting around just waiting for me to come of age. Not come of age. Get a little older, more experienced, even though he never dared suggest I needed to be experienced. I pulled out my phone, then joined my friends and let what happened, happen, while I did my best to profess I'd not feel the least bit guilty about it.

Except that had been one humongous lie. Not only did I feel guilty, but I was also angry with myself for using Kaleb like that. Then I was angry with Kaleb for using me to irritate the man he knew was my complication, the one I had fessed up to. Last, I was furious with my complication for confusing me more by making me go through all these stupid blurred emotions.

Now I am staring at him while he holds me securely in his arms, after I almost toppled over when my dance partners disappeared. I try to wiggle free, but the man is strong for a guy who sits in front of a desk most of the day.

"Did you enjoy yourself?" Esteban growls through clenched teeth.

"No," I hiss as I attempt to step back, except he doesn't permit it, and that ticks me off even more.

"Do you dance like that often?" His entire body tenses, as if he is doing his best to hold back.

"No," I respond mockingly as my hands fist his shirt. "First time, actually."

"You kissed him." Once again, he snarls his words out, letting me know he did not enjoy being a witness to that.

"He kissed me," I counter as I am reminded how many times I watched that video of him kissing Lady Felicia.

It wasn't like I had only one angle to watch from. Seems all those who knew I was missing it wanted to send me proof of how she finally got her target to pay her some attention. None of them knew the two of us had kept in touch after my soirée. Or that he'd made some interesting claims about our future. But everyone knew Lady Felicia had set her eyes on Prince Esteban for a while now.

It is one of those eye-rolling inside jokes that never seemed to end. Which one of the three women who had set their eyes on the three royal brothers would unmistakably win her prize? Dalia laid claim to King Antonio. Lady Felicia proclaimed her undying devotion to Prince Esteban several years back. Poor Prince Lorenzo, I believe, had drawn the short straw in this game, because his obsessed woman was psychotic. Lady Hilda was not about to be one-upped by the others and was always pushing the limits. I believe she may have even been banned from a lengthy number of events in hopes she'd straighten up and fly right.

"You kissed him back, Winnie. I watched you kiss him back." Esteban shakes his head, exposing his displeasure in that. "Was it all you thought it would be?"

"Not really," I grumble right before he yanks me even closer.

"This one will be," he warns before crashing those soft plump lips of his against mine.

The first reaction I intended was to shove him back so I could slap him for stealing another kiss from me. That lasted all of two seconds, if that. Dang if I could even think when his lips brushed mine. Pressed against them, it predestined my mind to completely stop working.

Just when I thought I would pass out from lack of oxygen to the brain, he brings his tongue out to play. Sweeps it along my bottom lip and then forces it inside and goes to town. I'm not even sure I am doing it right at all. It's not as if I've done this before, not like this at least. I can only follow his lead and pray he is enjoying this as much as me.

When he finally releases my mouth with a distinct smacking sound, I swear I've never seen a man look so disheveled before. And knowing I did this to him has me grinning like the nineteen-year-old young woman I am. I've practically brought him to his knees. Lady Felicia's kiss hadn't been able leave him looking like he was about to explode and capable of breaking all the rules.

I don't have a lot of time to study him carefully, because shortly after he releases me, we are moving. Darius Falcon is shielding me on one side. Esteban is on the other. We are flanked by three large men as we step outside and all but shoved into a black SUV that takes off almost immediately.

Now I have an entirely different problem. Did I forget to mention I am claustrophobic?

CHAPTER 7
Winifred

The Royals

The air inside the SUV closes in around me, pressing hard against my chest. I can't breathe. I seriously cannot catch my breath, and no one even seems to notice.

The first time I suffered an attack was when my sisters locked me in a dingy, smelly closest. In the pit we called a cellar, where my parents stored the wine. I don't remember exactly how or why we ended up down in the cellar, however, I will never forget how terrified I was when they sealed me inside that small space.

The room was tiny, big enough for me to sit but not lie down. I know this because they left me down there for hours. When I say hours, I mean it. They didn't let me out until the next morning, once my parents started wondering where I'd disappeared to.

During that time, I experienced several emotional breakdowns. My heart rapidly pounded in my chest so hard I thought I was going to die. My sweaty hands immediately became numb and tingly. My body trembled so fiercely, I had to take a seat on the cold, damp floor. I was shaking so severely I began to perspire, and then I started to chill because of the coolness in the cellar. I couldn't breathe, couldn't see. My voice finally went hoarse from all my crying and ignored screams. Eventually, I curled up into a tight ball and leaned against the chilly damp wall, convinced I would die and no one, not even my parents, would miss me.

From that moment forward, I never stepped foot in that cellar again, avoid cellars and basements all together. I never again trusted my sisters to guide me anywhere, or allowed others to take me some place I was unfamiliar with. That day forced me to avoid cramped enclosed spaces, especially elevators, small public bathrooms, and overly crowded vehicles or I'd end up in a frantic state.

Right now, I am sandwiched between Esteban and Darius. Both are large, broad-shouldered men, leaving me very little space to move between them. Even though this particular vehicle isn't necessarily considered small—compact—it feels like a sardine can. There is no extra room for anyone to shift one direction or the other. No adjacent seat I can dive into. No third-row backseat behind me for me to scuttle off to, frantic, just so I can escape my cramped seat. I am stuck. Unless I figure out rather quickly how to make my escape, I'm going to—

"Pull over!" I order the driver as I lean forward and begin pounding on the back of his seat. I'm sure I sound rather hysterical because that is exactly what I am. "Pull the hell over, now! Right! Now!"

Thankfully, the driver must realize I'm serious, because he does just that. I stretch out and reach for the door handle closest to the sidewalk, which is on Darius' side. Except the door won't budge. I beat on the glass with my fist while I scream. "Open, dammit! Open, you not so good, stupid door! Dammit, open!"

Darius removes my hand from the handle, so he can release the door slowly, or at least to me it seems slow. Before he is able to climb out, I'm diving over the top of his lap and end up smacking into the concrete face first. Then I am clambering to get to my feet, which still happen to somehow be inside the vehicle. I frantically roll over onto my back so I can shuffle backward, and I don't bother to halt until I am free from that confined space. Once I am out of there, once I'm able to appreciate the wide-open space of the crowded city, I plop back onto the sidewalk and breathe. Take several deep breaths and gain some control over my panic.

I sprawl out right there, letting all my limbs spread wide, not even caring right now if someone steps on me. Lucky for me, not that many people are walking around, so the sidewalks are mostly clear. The surrounding trees enlighten me we must be near one of the parks. Riverside is my best guess, although I could be wrong.

"Honey cakes, mind telling me what you are doing down there?" Darius' grinning, yet concerned, face appears above me. "You look like shit, if you don't mind me saying."

"I don't." I reach up and rub my forehead where it cracked against the sidewalk. "Where is Stan?"

"Busy." He smirks and gestures behind him. "His men aren't certain how to handle this. He's about to do something inconceivable."

"Like what?" I blink cautiously as I gather my mind. Before he can answer me, a male body plops down next to mine. "Are you crazy?"

"Seems I might be." Esteban lies down on the path and gets comfortable. "So why are we chilling on the sidewalk, instead of in that nice safe SUV where my men can protect us? I wonder how many princes and dukes have done something similar to this in the wee hours of the morning, all because of a woman. Mind explaining to me why we are doing this?"

"You all can leave, you know. I am more than capable of finding my way back to my apartment." I glance around and realize something significant. "Wait? This is not the right direction. I live that way." I point to the path we were driving away from. "Why are we going the wrong way?"

"Our suite is at The Plaza." Darius plops down next to me and nods at the onlookers who pass, right before he also makes himself comfortable. "Only the best for men of our positions. Not very many luxury hotels in the vicinity of Columbia University."

"I have a spare room, you know." I can't believe I am about to invite them to stay with me. "A bedroom for both of you and a nice comfortable couch I can crash on for myself. I've slept on it a few times when I was too lazy to walk to my bedroom."

"Not sure that is such a good idea. What do they say here often, something like two is company but three is a crowd? Perhaps I'll catch a cab, and you two can figure out this crazy situation transpiring between you." Darius twists his head, so he is looking at me. "Want my personal, non-professional opinion on the matter?"

"No," Stan blurts out loudly next to me.

I, however, grin at him and nod.

"I like her Este. She flies her own kite and lets it soar as high as the wind wishes to take it, not afraid of letting it crash and burn." He shifts to his side and props up on his elbow, looking like a normal male instead of a duke. "My non-professional opinion is this."

He clears his throat and stares at both of us, holds it for a while, letting the suspense build. "Just do it and say screw it."

I giggle. Not exactly the philosophy I was expecting from the duke.

Stan grumbles. "How did I know that is what you'd say? Just do it and say screw it? Tell me, Duke of Falcon, how has that worked for you so far? Aren't you supposed to be working on that rep of yours?"

Darius rolls his eye dramatically. "Este, you need to listen and listen good, my dear friend. Just do it. Meaning stop with this waiting game you seem to be tangled in. Stop with the excuse that she's too young and needs to live it up a little. I believe that is what she was doing when we first saw her tonight. You almost took out an entire bar, because truth be told, this chick has you in knots. And it's no secret that her envisaging you with all those other women is equally maddening. Honey cakes has a dang folder on her phone where she stores all those shams that are only done because you've bought into it all."

"Like hell I have." Esteban protests. "I'm—"

Darius holds up his hand and frowns. "Heard it all before, man. Now is the time to say screw it, screw them. You are both adults, so start acting like adults. Stop letting the powers that be shame you or get in your way. Just do it and say screw it," he repeats.

"Or you could come up with some sort of plan that you are both more comfortable with, I suppose. Either way, you need to do something, my way or yours. One thing I can say without a doubt is that the way you've been doing this is wrong for both of you. If you don't figure out how to do it better, then someone is going to get hurt, or you both are, which is my guess. And what a shame that would be, because I think you all got something special and need to set an example, while shoving it deep down all those bureaucrats' throats."

I giggle, sounding every bit of nineteen. "Correct me if I'm wrong, Your Grace, but aren't you both bureaucrats?"

Darius leans in closer as he flashes one killer smile in my direction. "It's too bad Este and I are such great pals. Hearing your sarcastic mouth call me "Your Grace" sends a wave of heat down my spine and tempts me like no one else has managed. However, we are the best of mates, therefore I know my reaction has more to do with that than anything. It thrills me is what I'm trying to say, to know that one day you'll have him so undone that there will be only one solution to resolve it."

His eyes turn more serious as he continues. "You are correct. Although we were born into our positions, forced to accept this way of life. I always find those who chose the life seem to believe they understand what they can't possibly understand. Given a choice, it differs completely from having your entire life planned and laid out for you. They are the bureaucrats; we are unfortunate executives."

Sadness, a very deep sadness, washes over his face. Darius' eyes shift to Esteban's and I get they have discussed this subject in the past. That they are kindred spirits who are merely doing their best to suffer through the life that was forced upon them. Making me want to do what I can to assist both men however I am capable to give them what they want. How? I have no idea. I sort of feel like we are all in the same boat. Doing our best to bail the water out of it faster than the hole located in the bottom can fill it, striving to drown us.

And just like that, Darius jumps up and brushes his hands off on his trousers. "I'll catch a ride back. Figure this out. If not for you all, then do it for me. How much easier would this life be if one of us were truly happy?"

I sit up and watch him wave down a cab. One man with us starts to join him, but he refuses to allow it and slams the door before there is an argument to be made.

"So, are you going to explain why we are lying on the sidewalk?" Esteban asks as he sits up and begins rubbing my back. "You couldn't jump out of the vehicle fast enough. I thought at first you were going to get sick."

I shake my head. "Panic attack. Tight enclosed spaces freak me out."

"The bar was full of people. We were packed in there. I had to fight my way through to reach you." He brings his hand to my opposite shoulder. "You seemed fine in there, more than fine actually."

I don't miss what he is insinuating, nor will I allow him to get away with it. "First, the bar isn't a tiny, enclosed, tight space. Sure, it was crowded, very crowded, but I don't mind crowded large spaces. Elevators, tiny public restrooms, crowded vehicles where there isn't room to even move. Those spaces send me into a frantic crazy mess. I believe you witnessed it firsthand."

I tilt my head and study him. "And don't think you are going to get away with that other part of your statement. Ever done something out of character before, Stan? Regretted it for several reasons? Tell me, why does it bother you. Why do you care so much? I've lived here since August. You've visited me once. That's more times than my parents or sisters have, so you have that going for you. You confuse me. Bewilder me, really. I have no idea what you want from me, exactly. I guess I'm tired of envisioning you out there living your life, while I seemed to be once again at a standstill. At least where certain aspects of my life look to be going. Know what I mean?"

Esteban nods and rises to his feet. He offers me a hand to help me up off the sidewalk. I perceive the same sadness in his eyes that was in Darius'. Which can only explain why, as soon as I am standing, I do what I do. He doesn't even have time to prepare for it. Probably best, I suppose. I'm sure my lack of experience is the reason he simply stands there dazed and doesn't react when our lips touch briefly.

I begin to step away so I can make my escape. That way, he can take me home and then return to his hotel. It was nice of him to show up and wish me a happy birthday. At least someone from my past cared enough to do so.

Except I don't make it one small step before I find myself whirled around and engulfed in his arms. I think I might have yelped, but I can't be sure really, because his lips, his mouth, swallow it down when he once again crashes those soft lips to mine. The kiss is just as hungry as the one back at the bar, with slightly more finesse to it. It's a good thing he is holding me up. Otherwise, I'm certain I would be a swooning fool. One who once again ends up sprawled out on the sidewalk for a largely different reason.

He pulls back, yet remains close enough for our noses to touch. "My biggest regret, Winnie, is that I..." he trails off and starts again. "You. That I wasn't clear with you on where we stood. Perhaps it's time to rectify that, though."

"D-don't make me a promise you can't keep," I warn as I breathe in his unique scent. It is a scent that reminds me of cinnamon rolls fresh out of the oven.

"Fair enough. How about I only promise to do better? Be clearer about my intentions." He kisses my cheek. "Make an effort, a sincere effort, to get you to trust me to keep my word about all of that. Show you by my actions that no one else is worth my time but you. Visit you more often, so I can do this." His lips brush against mine again. "Winnie, only you have ever been able to jumble my brain enough that I'd risk..."

I don't let him finish. Instead, I lean forward for the second time and press my lips against his. Linger there until he initiates a more intimate kiss. I let him show me how he likes to kiss, while I do my best to remember, so I can satisfy him like the others before me did.

"We should go," he whispers against my lips. "I should take you home, get you off these streets before someone recognizes me."

I nod and allow him to lead me back to the SUV. Now that it is just the two of us back here, I'm much more comfortable. As soon as the vehicle moves, I hear him begin to instruct his men, so I stop him. "No. Take me with you. I want to stay with you."

"Winnie?" I hear an unspoken explanation in his voice. "I'm not that..."

"I know. I mean, that's what I've heard, at least. But earlier, was it not your intention to take me back with you?" I fiddle with my fingers.

He stares at me for a few moments. "Stew, drive us to The Plaza. Tell Calvin to have the hotel bring up a few essentials for a female guest. Make it clear I am not asking for intimate essentials. I only need those items a woman would need to get ready for bed. Perhaps include a t-shirt and a pair of shorts she could sleep in, along with a robe. Anything else, Winnie?"

I shake my head in awe and possibly shock. "You've done this before?"

He reaches for my hand and brings it to his lips. "No. I've put a woman up in a separate suite, on a different floor, after a long evening, when it was too late to send her home. But I've never invited a woman to spend the night in my suite. To be clear, I have a three-bedroom suite. Darius is sleeping in one since he will only be here for a few nights."

"How long will you be here?" I ask, out of curiosity.

"Two weeks." A slow smile takes over his handsome face. "I believe you have spring break the week after next. I thought if you didn't have plans, we could take a mini holiday someplace warmer, perhaps."

I toss my head back and laugh, really laugh. "Wow. You are full of surprises tonight, aren't you? I'll need to talk to Mrs. Nelson. See if she is okay with me taking some days off during that time. I'm sure it will be fine. I have a question, though. I'm simply asking because, well... how are you going to keep these plans, this trip off the radar? Unless you've changed your mind about all that, I guess, I just assumed."

"I would like to keep it quiet for now. Too many noses in our business will not allow you to decide what you want, Winnie. I prefer you to make these important decisions about your life. I want you to choose this life if that is what you want. Not if it is what your family wants. Do you understand?"

I don't mean to cry. Honestly, I don't. But in the nineteen years, I've been on this earth, this is the first time those words have ever been said to me.

My entire life, there has been someone who has told me what I was going to do, how I was going to do it, and when it was going to happen. No one ever asked me or dared to suggest I had a choice in the matter. Not until Prince Esteban stepped out of my fantasies and into my life. It all just seems too good to be true; too fairytale story-like, and I guess I have a hard time believing this is real.

CHAPTER 8
Esteban

The Royals

When we step into the lobby of The Plaza, I recall what she disclosed about elevators. My suite is located on floor seventeen, which is a lot of stairs to climb, not that I am against making the climb. However, before putting us all through that, I need to check with Winnie to determine how honest she was being about not using elevators.

"Are you serious about avoiding small spaces, such as elevators?" I pause in the lobby.

Winnie nods slowly. "I've ridden in them when necessary. Prayed fervently the entire ride, while clenching my teeth and rubbing my hands together frantically. So far, I've been lucky enough to not have a panic attack while inside one. My biggest fear isn't so much the elevator itself, it is getting stuck inside the metal box, not being able to get out. What floor is your suite on?"

I wave to my men and point toward the stairwell. "Seventeen. Looks like we are going to get our exercise this evening."

"That's unnecessary, Stan. I can manage, I'm certain."

But I hear the panic already building in her voice. After already suffering from one attack, I am not willing to send her into another.

"Stew is making his way up, sir," Calvin informs me as we approach him. "I will be one flight ahead, Braden, one behind. Take your time, Lady Winifred. We are all in top physical condition, even the prince here, so this will be easy for us."

Winnie raises her eyebrows as she watches Calvin take off ahead of us. "Is that true? And is he suggesting that it may be difficult for me?"

I motion for her to go first and set the pace before I answer. "I'm sure he was suggesting no such thing. I, however, run with my men most mornings. A few years ago, I was even allowed to participate in my first marathon, the Sparkasse Marathon der 3 Lander, which tracks through Germany, Austria, and Switzerland. These three men ran the entire race with me, trained with me even. Although, I'm pretty certain they were better trained than I was, and that I was holding them back tremendously."

We are a few flights up, and Winnie sighs. "So, this will be a piece of cake for all of you, then. Why, if you don't mind me asking, would you put your body through that?" Three flights up and she is already a little winded.

"Running is relaxing to me. Helps me free my mind, I suppose. Gets me outside in the fresh air. When I was younger, I played sports. Fútbol and lacrosse were my two favorites, lots of running in both."

Winnie pauses on the fourth landing. "I played fútbol, I was a goalie. Not a lot of running involved in that position. The main reason I selected it. Plus, I kind of enjoyed protecting the goal, keeping others from scoring. In my last two seasons, our opponents only scored five goals when I was in, which is why we made it so far, and several of my teammates received scholarships."

I morph my eyebrows into a frown. "Did you receive offers?"

She climbs again as she explains. "Sure. Several, actually. Papa said no. Sternly said no. Fútbol is fine for a young girl to participate in, but not suitable for a lady wishing to secure her place." Winnie alters her voice slightly during that last statement. "Imagine his disappointment if he ever should learn about the bakery job. Probably best I don't get paid for it."

"What do you mean you don't get paid?" This time I am the one stopping halfway up the sixth flight. "You volunteer your time?"

"Yes. It was the only way since my student visa prohibits me from working outside the university. Next year, I might be able to claim it as an apprenticeship that supports my business degree. Not that I need the money, and after all, I am learning so much." She walks again, leaving me standing there bewildered and a little upset.

"If your father had permitted you to play fútbol, would you have?" I ask as I resume to climb.

We make it to the ninth flight when she pauses, again breathing a little harder. "If you had asked me that before today, I'd have said no, mainly because I always knew the answer long before I joined the fútbol team. But after climbing nine flights of stairs..." She takes a few deep breaths and waves her hand in front of her. "Whew. I'm so out of shape. After climbing those steps, feeling like I just might not make it the other eight, that has changed. Fútbol at least forced me off my fat arse and kept the cardio up and pumping. Not to mention I know for a fact, working at the bakery has easily added a few unnecessary pounds to my already plump frame. I think I'm going to have a chat with the girls, see if maybe they are interested in walking some of the paths this city has created."

I hate hearing her disrespect her body like that. There is no way she has added more than five pounds since the last time I saw her. The jeans she has on fit her nicely in all the right spots. The loose shirt she is wearing doesn't hide much, displays her well-shaped chest and a slimmer waist. As I peruse her, I am reminded of earlier and how those other men were all over her. They seemed to agree with me, not at all deterred by her or her body.

"There is nothing wrong with you." I run my eyes over her again. "Nothing."

"Says the man who doesn't possess an ounce of body fat on him." Winnie then lifts her top to display her midriff, where she somehow pinches a section of it. "This, Stan, is what they call a muffin top because it hangs over the waistband and resembles a muffin."

I have to close my eyes so I don't do anything stupid. She has no idea how her words are affecting me. Hearing her say the phrase muffin top makes me want to drop to my knees and taste that particularly non-existent flab. I want to bite it, lick it, and devour it right before I consume her.

"Are you okay?" she asks, sounding concerned. "Your face is a little flushed."

"I'm fine," I tell her as I move again.

"Are you sure? You don't look all that fine. Perhaps you aren't in as good of shape as you thought." She snickers as she follows me.

"I'm fine. Just a little warm." And turned on, completely turned on after that demonstration.

We make it to the eleventh-floor landing when I notice she is slowing quite a bit. "You okay?"

"Fine," she pants, which does nothing to cool me down. "Just. A. Little. Warm."

I wait for her and take a break. "Not much farther."

"Trust me. I know… exactly how… much we… have left. Are we… suddenly racing?" She leans against the wall and fans her shirt.

That motion draws my attention to her glistening skin. A sheen has suddenly appeared on her lovely neck. I also don't miss how her chest rises and falls with each inhale. Or the fact her body is releasing the most alluring scent that transforms my brain into an uncivilized male. A man who undergoes the need to act first and worry about the consequences later.

I stalk my way over toward her and catch Braden rounding the corner. He obviously sees me, understands what is about to transpire between us. Because he retreats as he faintly speaks into his hand, notifying the other men we could be awhile.

"What?" Winifred does a quick inspection of herself. "What are you doing?"

I cage her in and lean forward, allowing myself to take a healthy inhale. Which was a bad idea, because that does absolutely nothing to calm down that unrefined part of me.

Twenty-four years and I have never been remotely tempted to just act. I'm the levelheaded brother who overthinks everything. I was the one who always suggested we think before acting, review all our options first and then decide which one sounds like the best idea.

Last year was the first time I went off course, veered away from my original plan. I stood there those first few hours, watched her father introduce his youngest daughter to men not worthy of such a precious creature. Her innocence was so pure, and she wore it well. It set her apart from three-fourths of the room (and yes, I am speaking of her sisters, mainly). She wasn't a trophy any of them deserved, not even one they had the right to duel over. So, as soon as they gave her a reprieve, I swooped in and decided it was time to win this maiden over.

What I hadn't considered was how dangerously addictive she would become to me. How her innocence would be like a drug I craved, a temptation I wanted to behold. It would awaken all my deepest desires to make this particular female mine, mine alone, and no one else's. I wanted all her firsts, lasts, and everything in between. I wasn't interested in her giving away a few to anyone other than me, which means more than I believe either of us is ready for.

"Stan." That name is like throwing a match on a line of gasoline. Her use of that name, the name only she uses, breaks the last of any control I possess.

I growl like an animal does when he is sending out a warning. Then I drop my lips to her ear and verbally offer her some advice. "Tell me no."

"What?" Winnie questions breathlessly, completely sounding as innocent as she is. "Stan, you aren't making any sense."

"Tell me no." I repeat my words with agonizing slowness before I graze my teeth along her earlobe. "Tell me no, Winnie, and I'll stop."

"Stop what?" She shivers as I begin my downward spiral, one I have no desire to not travel. "Oh. Oh, Stan!"

She mutters those last two words over and over again, while I drag my mouth along her neck and jaw, tasting every inch of her exposed skin. When that doesn't seem to be enough, I drop one of my hands and let it brush against her neck, down her shoulder, along the outside of her breast, until I reach the hem of her shirt.

I pause as I draw back, and then stare into her green eyes, waiting for her to decide if this is also what she wants. When she leans forward to kiss me instead of speaking the words, I kiss her again. My fingers slip under her shirt and come in contact with her soft, smooth skin.

I get lost kneading the area, squeezing it daringly, like I'm certain no one else ever has, not even her. I let them spread out fully so they can memorize the way her skin feels against them. I even drop my other hand; let it begin to manipulate its way underneath while I do my best to savor her.

The entire time, Winifred makes delicious noises that echo inside this space easily. I should warn her to be quiet, tell her that those noises aren't doing a dang thing to halt this unplanned attack. That my men will never let me live it down if this goes on much longer. I have undoubtedly put both of us in a rather compromising position.

The sound of a door opening and then closing, followed by heavy footfall and voices, is what brings me out of the trance. I growl this time, but for a completely different reason. I can't believe I allowed myself to do this while in a stairwell. This woman deserves better. She isn't some cheap date. She is a sophisticated woman. One a man should cherish and treat with the greatest respect.

"I'm sorry." I apologize as I straighten her out and pull her closer. "Winnie, I'm sorry."

"Apologizing, Stan, is what makes it seem wrong." Winifred gives me a slight shove, so she can step back. At that moment, I catch her shaking her head in shame. "Until then, I thought nothing of it."

Then she scrambles up the stairs again at a much brisker pace than before. I hear her say hello to someone as they pass each other. Hear her mumble something to Calvin as well when she reaches him. Even hear him grumble a few quick words, as if giving a direct order, followed by a huff I am certain is hers.

Braden is climbing the stairs again now and joins me where I stand, right as the other couple passes. He is unmistakably trying to not smile or show his amusement about the entire stupid act. Once I am more composed, we begin traveling toward our destination.

When we reach Calvin, I ask him the obvious. "Where is she?"

He points to the steps behind him as he once again climbs. I don't miss his exchange with Braden, nor do I miss the smirk he aims at Winnie when he steps past her.

Winnie is sitting there with her elbows resting on her knees. "Are all your men always this bossy?"

I reach down and grab her hand to help her stand. "It is their job, Winnie, to make sure everyone stays safe."

"I walk around all the time without someone hovering. Just like everyone else does, and surprisingly nothing has happened," she reminds me as she ascends the stairs.

I don't bother responding.

When we reach the sixteenth-floor landing, she spins around and glares at me. Her hands are firmly placed on her hips and there is a fire in her eyes that makes me want to grab her all over again.

She waits for me to get a little closer before she points that finger at me. "I am alone, correct? You wouldn't."

I can't help but chuckle as I slip an arm around her, while I encourage her to keep moving. "Not yet, Winnie. I promise when the time comes, where I feel you require a few shadows, I'll let you know."

"You promise. Swear you aren't lying?" She glares at me.

"Winnie, one thing I will never do is lie to you," I tell her as we reach our designated floor.

We walk down the hall and then step into the suite, and I make a beeline for the decanter of dark amber liquid. I need something to take the edge off. What I didn't realize was that I was going to need more than one drink to get through.

"May I ask you something? Will you promise to be honest with me?" Winnie strolls over to the bar area and leans her elbows against it while she watches me. I give her a nod, and she takes no time to get right to the heart of the matter. "Do you treat all the women who have somehow found themselves in your company, the way you have treated me?"

I drop a few ice cubes into the tumbler before I open the decanter. "I don't think I understand your question, Winnie. No other woman has found themselves in my company the way you have."

"Don't treat me with kid gloves, Stan." Winnie scolds, and I know I unintentionally smirk. "You've dated more than just one woman. While I know the tabloids exaggerate matters, I am aware that a few of those women were real, genuine dates."

"I've dated more than one woman, yes. Taken my share of women to events when I required an escort. There have been a few I've spent my precious free time with. I don't get a ton of free time, so when I do, I like to not waste it. So, if a woman isn't doing it for me, holding my attention, I don't see the point in giving her more of that precious time." I lift the amber liquid to my lips and take a sip.

Winifred is processing all I have just shared. I can identify her mind mulling it over in her head, much like mine does. It is a real spine-tingling sight to behold, and I soak it in while I enjoy my drink.

"Are you saying you've never done what you did to me in the stairwell to any other woman?" she blurts out without warning.

I end up choking on my drink, coughing hard as the liquid slides down the wrong pipe. "What? No. No, I have never mistreated a woman like that before."

Mortification takes over her face as if my words strike her hard and am blaming her for my behavior. She straightens, so I reach out to stop her.

"Please, Winnie, don't misunderstand. I'm only saying that no other woman has tempted me the way you do. I've always been in complete control, never lost my tight grip on it and allowed something like that to happen."

"Always?" She crosses her arms as if she doesn't believe me. "Were you in control when you kissed Lady Felicia?"

I drop my head in shame, knowing that kiss was going to haunt me more than it already has. "Not completely. I may have had a little too much to drink that night. However, what you think you saw on that video wasn't precisely the same as what transpired earlier with us. Did I kiss her? Yes. I shouldn't have. It was wrong of me to do that for several reasons."

"What reasons?" she asks blushing as her voice grows soft.

I lean back against the small counter behind me. "First, because I am not at all interested in feeding her obsession where I am concerned."

A smile plays on her lips. "Aren't you afraid of feeding my obsession?"

The laugh that emerges surprises us both. "No. That obsession is one that doesn't at all scare me. It's not a *Fatal Attraction* kind of obsession like I'm afraid Lady Felicia's might be."

"What?" Winnie giggles. "I don't understand."

"*Fatal Attraction* is an old movie from the 1980s. My mother often referred to it when my father and she were going through their divorce.

So, it sort of perked my interest and I watched it. The main character's lover is a little off her rocker. One day we will sit down together and have a movie night. That one will be at the top of our list of thrillers," I tell her and am rewarded with a slight blush.

"My other reason I shouldn't have allowed it to happen, is because it wasn't her I was thinking of while we were kissing." I make sure she is looking me directly in the eyes when I explain. "Not that she reminds me in any way of you. She most certainly does not. All night, while I socialized with all those women so eager to secure my attention, there was only one on my mind. Except she couldn't come, because she was away doing what she needed to do so she can hopefully one day have the life she wants."

I pause for a beat and notice she swallows with deliberation. It is no surprise to me that her hearing me verbally offer my support gets to her a little. Winifred Batista isn't accustomed to that sort of gesture; it will be up to me to make sure she gets used to it.

"I'd pretended all night long. Drank a little more to help numb the mind, so I could suffer through. I'm not sure why I finally danced with her. I knew it was a mistake not all that long after we got started. I closed my eyes and envisioned she was you, so I could just get it over with and move on, but then she kissed me. At first, I was so engrossed in my own mind, I forgot it wasn't real. It didn't take me long to remember, because it felt wrong in every way."

Again, I pause while I punish myself a little here. I can identify the hurt in her eyes. It doesn't take much for me to imagine how she felt. I know firsthand. Not so many hours ago, I was suffering from that very feeling, and I hate I put her through that unnecessarily.

"I'm sorry, Winnie. That will not happen again. If I must take someone with me to an event, I'll get your approval first, or take my sister, or one of my cousins. And the reason I said I was sorry earlier wasn't because I wanted you to feel bad. I only meant that I shouldn't have allowed it to materialize in a stairwell like that. You shouldn't be treated like some cheap date, ever. But when I'm with you, there are times I feel like I have absolutely no control."

She nods slowly. "I probably shouldn't feel good about that, huh?"

Again, I laugh as I rub his forehead. "Probably not."

Winnie shrugs as she rests her chin on her fist that is propped up by her elbow. "Guess I better work on that, then, because honestly, I sort of do feel good about it. In fact, I feel rather victorious about it, and most likely will do my best to break that control as often as I can."

I slam the remainder of my drink down because I know before this is all said and done, I am going to be apologizing regularly for my actions.

CHAPTER 9
Esteban

The Royals

These last nine months, I've done my best to make it back to New York as often as possible without raising suspicion. It hasn't been easy keeping matters between Winnie and me private. In fact, it has taken some real finessing on my part. I've had to involve two of our closest friends to assist us.

We almost got caught right away, shortly after Winnie's birthday. It was the weekend before her spring break when first required to put our heads together. Thankfully, we decided it wouldn't be a great idea for us to go somewhere alone. It was clear that being unaccompanied—as unaccompanied as one can be, with security always lurking around—could get us into trouble. Mainly because it would be five full days without a break or a way to escape the other person.

Since Ingrid also had spring break that very same week, we invited her along. And because Winnie was inviting a friend, I invited one as well. That had worked out better than we'd hoped, for several reasons.

Falcon and I were on our way to pick the ladies up when I received a text from an unknown number.

UNKNOWN: Just go with it.

"What do you suppose this means?" I showed Falcon as we climbed out

of the car.

"Not sure." He shrugged, and we almost ignored it.

We were immediately buzzed up and then greeted by a pale and wide-eyed Winifred, who ignored me while bestowing my best friend with all her affection. "Your Grace, please come in."

I nearly grumbled out my complaint when she placed a kiss on his cheek before she reached for his hand. I thought we'd come so far in the last few days that I nearly shoved my friend aside to demand what game she was playing.

"Your Highness, it's nice to see you again." Winnie finally addressed me, although she refused to allow her eyes to meet mine.

Thankfully, I took a moment to take in my surroundings and noticed her parents standing just inside her living room. Had I not taken that time our cover would have been blown.

"Lady Winifred." I'd forced a smile on my face. "We didn't know you were expecting company."

"Neither did I," Winnie softly mumbled. "Seems my parents thought it was time to see how I was getting along."

Imagine how very surprised we were to see them. They hadn't bothered to call Winifred on her birthday, nor had they dared to inform her of their plans to visit the following weekend.

Leave it to my friend to know exactly how to wing it when he had to. If he weren't my best mate, a man I thought of as another brother, I'd have decked him more than once before that dreadful weekend was over. Darius was one of the best at playing the deceit game. We'd been successful at pulling the wool over her parents' eyes, even granted permission to go on with our original plans.

As if any of us needed their permission, especially not Darius or me. However, I understood why Winifred felt like maybe she did. Her parents had always directed her, and it was difficult to break away from that. I had to remind myself that she was only nineteen. At her age, my parents still had some influence on my life—okay, my father had a great deal of influence.

The reason it worked so well was because her father was now more confident the Duke of Falcon was actively pursuing his daughter. Meaning he was willing to hold off the others who were still interested in her. Because a duke, even one as notorious as Falcon, involved with his daughter, was in his mind worth more than an earl or viscount. It became even clearer at that point that he wasn't concerned about what Winifred wanted. His concern had everything to do with which man could assist Justice Batista the most, who could he profit from more. Proving my point on why I didn't want to put myself on his radar.

Instead, I had unexpectedly added my name to Lady Ingrid's list of potential suitors. Not that I had anything against the other young woman. I most certainly did not. She was a lovely, pure soul, very much like the one I was captivated by. It was that I didn't wish to deal with all of that, answer stupid questions, or flat out lie about my interest in her.

Funny thing—if you can find any of it truly funny—is that little did any of us realize where all this would eventually lead. (I'll get there if you'll give me some time.)

Gossip travels fast, and it took no time at all for Lady Eva to share with her socialite friends about Falcon and Winifred. Expressing how she was so certain they were going to work out. Nor did she keep it quiet about how she suspected I had my eyes set on Lady Ingrid.

Which only made interactions between us harder. I had to make sure I planned trips around business, so there were legitimate excuses for me being in the city. Drive to the city, instead of flying in when I was stateside. Use an alias, Stan de Manna—Darius came up with it, imagine that—whenever I booked a hotel room in a less exclusive hotel. I learned that if I dressed down, looking more like a university student, or even a regular everyday person, I could blend in and not get noticed. This was one positive fact about living in a country whose royal family wasn't as well-known as England's royalty was.

And I made sure I kept a very close eye on the justice and his household. My team kept tabs on each one of them, to ensure when I was anywhere near Winifred Batista, they were all accounted for far away from us.

I was very disappointed in Winnie's family and their disinterest in their youngest member. It was as if they had sent her away and never thought about her unless it was beneficial to them. In the long run, it worked best for me, because it also meant they weren't keeping tabs on her, didn't see a need to do so.

And that is how I was able to fly her back to Hermosa Islas with none of them catching wind of it. They were too wrapped up in their own unimportant lives that they had once again left her to spend her winter break in New York alone. If I could have gotten away with it, I would have flown to New York and spent Christmas with her. That, however, wasn't an option. My family always got together for the holidays. No excuse that wasn't a catastrophic one of major proportions would be acceptable.

To be clear, I'm certain my family would have gladly invited her to spend the holiday with us. Might have even been okay with me joining her in New York. They weren't the issue. It was a well-known fact that all business ended for the royal family on the twentieth of December and didn't resume again until the fifth of January. Therefore, flying out of the country would have drawn a lot of unwanted attention.

So instead, I sent an itinerary with a flight plan that transported her home without alerting the masses. Her plane from New York landed in England. She would then switch over to a private jet, one that would fly her to the small airport just outside of Cabrera. Which also happens to be the small town where my home is located, right off the coast. Esteban Palace is on a secluded plot of land that is only accessible using the very guarded and remote highway, or by helicopter—which was usually my chosen form of transportation.

On the day before she was due to arrive, I made sure to make it known I was leaving Cabrera, by flying my recognizable helicopter back to Aragon Palace. Which is also where I left it, and where it will remain until the day after Winifred flies back to the States. I also visited with the king and my sister Isabel before making a pit stop at my home in Aragon.

Then I did the unthinkable. I sent my decoy car to my mother's residence in Prieto. Requested some assistance from her, because if anything, my mother understood all too well about privacy and how important that was. She respected the fact her children wanted something different from what had always been. An hour after I supposedly arrived in Prieto, I escaped in one of my men's vehicles—I'm not sure whose exactly—and drove myself to Cabrera.

Don't worry, I was perfectly safe. I had my tracker with me. And while it's not ideal and often frowned on, I am allowed to do things without my security team hovering when I am home. Surprisingly, it is very safe for me here in my homeland, not all that many wish to do me harm.

It wasn't uncommon for my security to come and go from the residences I kept in Cabrera. I'm sure it was a regular occurrence and happened a lot more than I was even aware of. And since no one expected me back at Esteban Palace, I'd given the staff a paid holiday and told them to not report back until a few days after the New Year. Again, something that wasn't unheard of. We often sent our staff home around the holidays, so they could enjoy time with their families.

Winifred's plane was scheduled to arrive later this evening, when the airport will be predictably less busy. I arrive in that same vehicle I drove earlier and greet her as soon as she steps off the plane. The smile she flashes once she recognizes I am her chauffeur, the man she's been on countless dates with these last several months, made all the trouble I went through worth it. It is even better when she approaches me, wraps her arms around my neck, and kisses me like I imagine other normal couples kiss after spending six weeks apart.

"Hi," she sighs. "It's wonderful to be home."

I don't mean to growl my approval after hearing her say that, but I do. Listening to her disclose that while wrapped in my arms is music to my ears. "Home is glad you are here as well. It isn't nearly the same when you aren't around."

My sweet Winnie smiles as she shakes her head. "Why do I feel you are speaking metaphorically? I missed you, Stan. I also missed all of this." She steps back and twirls in a circle, smiling as she takes it all in. "No place else is quite like this secluded piece of land we live on. I'm not sure I appreciated it before."

I grab her hand while I encourage her to get into the car. Once she is settled, we head back down the coastal highway that will lead us to my sanctuary. I try to focus on the road, but find it challenging with her sitting next to me. She has this special smile on her face as she takes in all the sights that are unique to the area.

"What?" She glimpses my way and laughs. "What?"

"I don't know that I've seen you smile so big before." I reach over and take her hand. "It looks fantastic on you."

I can't see clearly because it is so dark, but I am certain she blushes. "As I said, I'm happy to be back, even if only for a few days. It's nice to breathe in the fresh air and scents that remind me of Hermosa Islas. Smog is not as cleansing to the soul. Know what I mean?"

Thirty minutes later, we arrive at my larger than necessary home. All the homes the Reyes family own are larger than most, much larger than her apartment in New York. The room she will call home these next five days is probably equal in size.

The only other staff with us will be Stew, along with a few guards posted outside the perimeter. Making it my responsibility to make sure her luggage gets placed in the proper room, and that she has everything she needs before we turn in for the evening.

I know Winnie has to be exhausted. She's been in the air most of the day. Jet lag can be tricky if you aren't used to dealing with it. I want her to adjust as swiftly as possible so we can spend our days together while we have them.

"I can't wait to appreciate this place in the light of day." Winnie yawns from behind me. "Sorry, I tried not to sleep on the plane. Wanted to be tired, so I'd hopefully sleep tonight."

When we reach her room, I open the door and signal her to step inside. "Bedroom is through there with an en suite bathroom. There is a large tub, feel free to use it. All the bathrooms have separate water heaters, so no one has to fight for hot water. Would you like me to start a fire in the fireplace? It heats both the bedroom and sitting areas."

I notice her shiver and almost kick myself for not thinking to do so earlier. These rooms can get drafty when shut off. Even though I adjusted the heat in here yesterday, it is still unpleasantly cool, which is why we keep a fire burning in most of the livable spaces. The extra heat helps ward off the chill.

"Go put your things away, and I'll start one. I should have done that earlier. I'm sorry." I set her bags by the door to the bedroom. "Then I'll get out of your hair for the night so you can get some sleep."

Winnie stands in the middle of the room for several long seconds, like she is debating something over in her head. Finally, she crosses her arms and rubs them.

"I don't know if..." she shakes her head and waves her hand, dismissing her thoughts. "Never mind. I'll go put my things away."

"What were you going to say?" I step in front of her and notice she has this frightened mien about her. "What is it, Winnie?"

"Nothing." Her voice fluctuates, telling me she is lying. "I'm not a child any longer, so it's rather stupid, and I'd..."

I secure her face in my hands, making sure she understands a few things. "I know you aren't a child. Trust me, Winnie, I am very well aware of the fact that you are a woman."

"Is that so?" She grins as only she can. "Good to know."

I lean forward and kiss her smart mouth. I don't linger, because it has been way too long since I've spent time with her. If I'm not careful, things could get out of hand, and I've been really good at not letting that happen again. So, I end it quicker than I'd like and brush my nose against hers. "'Tis the truth, and I am delighted about that. Now tell me, so I can see if I can do something about this frightened expression hidden on your face."

"It just that this home of yours is enormous. I'm guessing it most likely makes strange funny noises at night as well." She grunts as if she can't believe she is about to admit this to me. "I'm scared of the dark, okay? I hate all the noises that emerges when it gets quiet. I sleep with a nightlight, leave the kitchen light on, and sometimes I even turn on the stereo to drown out any unwarranted sounds."

There is no way not to chuckle about something so incredibly adorable. Gabriela hates this creaky old palace. She swears it is haunted and refuses to sleep alone in one of its many suites. She and Winnie are not all that different in many ways, and I should have thought about that.

I lean forward and kiss her forehead as I wrap her in my arms. There is no way I can stop the next words from escaping from my lips. They pop in my head, and I don't even bother not speaking them. "If you wanted to sleep with me Winnie, all you had to do was simply ask."

CHAPTER 10
Winifred

The Royals

I can hardly believe I heard him correctly. He is very aware of the innuendo, and I know I am as red as a tomato. It has nothing and everything to do with that statement.

These last nine months there have been some ups and downs. Most of it has been positive and extremely refreshing. However, like every relationship, there have been some adjustments, and a few were difficult. I'm sure you are confused, so just give me time to see if I can help you understand.

After the almost disastrous incident that involved my parents, we spent the next week discussing how we wanted to handle them moving forward. It didn't take me long to understand his concerns after my mother went a little loopy and all but claimed Darius Falcon was courting me.

Not once had Darius made that claim. Not once. He's stated that Esteban and he were in the States and stopped by to visit me. As soon as they discovered Ingrid and I had a break, and since they were planning a mini-holiday around that time, they felt it would be fun to show us a good time.

I believe his exact words were, "*We thought, or perhaps I thought, it would be enjoyable spring breaking it with the young ladies. See if they can keep up with us. Determine if I still have it, or if I've finally aged out and need to hang up my party card."*

He certainly didn't need to hang up his party card. I believe it was Ingrid and me who had trouble keeping up with him. We had one exciting week, where I got the chance to know and understand both men much better than before.

It seems Esteban isn't as serious as I always assumed he was. He definitely has a little of Lorenzo inside of him, can let loose, and gets a little crazy when no one else is watching.

One fact we both agreed on was to do our best to keep what was materializing between us quiet. We promised not to feed the rumors or gossip about Darius and me. Let those who wanted to assume they knew more than they did, continue to do so. We would not pretend to be in any relationship we were not in. Meaning, Darius and I wouldn't make appearances as a couple just to please the parentals. Nor would either of us discuss any blooming relationship just because others wanted us to do so.

One interesting fact I discovered about Esteban was that he'd never actually had a girlfriend before. Not even as a teenager, which I found hard to believe. I had been certain I'd heard his brother reference a few girls as Esteban's girlfriend when we discussed our families over the years. Of course, I'd paid careful attention whenever Lenny brought up that particular brother, asked follow-up questions, even. Something that hadn't slipped past Esteban's focused mind when I explained it in detail.

I obviously hadn't ever been a girlfriend before. I wouldn't give him the real reason for that, I only expressed it was because the boy I was interested in hadn't asked me out. Meaning there was only one who held my interest, one I'd been obsessed with since I was eleven. That part I left out for good reason. Even after he, in a roundabout way, suggested something similar to that.

The first time he visited me after our week together was right after the semester ended. We'd celebrated a successful first year. He took me out to a nice dinner where I had to dress up. Then the next evening he'd gone out with my friends and me. I reintroduced him to them—not that he needed an introduction after what occurred the last time he was in town. This time, however, when I introduced him as my friend Stan, he corrected me and introduced himself as my boyfriend Stan de Manna. As you can imagine, I nearly choked and had to take a drink of water in hopes they wouldn't catch me laughing. Seriously, I had not expected him to have such a crazy made-up last name, nor had I expected the boyfriend statement.

So, my boyfriend, Stan, visited me every four to six weeks. His visits lasted at least three days. Sometimes those days were busy with school and work, and sometimes they were free of both. However, our evenings were always open during his time with me, since he made sure to always alert me when he was coming.

I am going to assume our time together was much like other couples who were starting out. We spent a lot of time getting to know each other. There was a slow progression of comfortable physical affection, no more unexpected attacks in stairwells. He held my hand almost all the time. Even had an arm around me whenever we were sitting or standing close enough for him to do so.

We also kissed.

I'm not sure if I am disappointed about the kissing part, I don't believe I am. I mean, because I knew it was not in either of our characters to kiss like we had on my birthday. My guess was that several unexpected factors played into things getting out of hand. The kissing had indeed been toned down, mostly.

Stan knew how to kiss and kiss well. I was new at it, so I did my best to follow his lead. He always kissed more affectionately when he first arrived or when he was heading out. Those kisses seemed to be the only kisses that got extremely hot and a little wild. The rest of the time, he kissed me with controlled finesse. Mind-blowing kisses that made my heart beat faster and got me a little lightheaded. Which in all honesty, I believe is what we both needed, so we didn't get ahead of this long road we were heading down.

This is why his words throw me off a bit. I am not going to lie and say I haven't fantasized about sleeping with Esteban. Granted, I have very limited knowledge about what transpires between a man and a woman in the moment, but I've watched enough romantic movies to vividly put a few images together. I imagine him losing that well-managed control of his, much like he did in the stairwell. Kissing me passionately because he was no longer capable of holding back. Words would become unnecessary. Our eyes would speak for both of us, revealing we were both in agreement and not at all ashamed about what was about to transpire between us.

Which is when my mind usually remembered how his large hot hands felt against my sensitive skin. It was able to take that memory of when he first touched me and then place those masculine hands all over my body. Heating it, as he caressed my skin gently, while he continued to kiss my lips. Then it would recall those lips trailing down my neck and conjure up how it might enjoy those lips exploring other sensitive areas. It was quite the vision. One I'd found myself having more and more often the better we got to know each other.

That is where it ended, though. It never went further than him doing his best to drive me insane with his lips and hands.

Okay, so I may have also envisioned his half-naked perfect body. I have been privileged to appreciate it firsthand when we took that trip during my spring break. Stood within a meter of him, where I could watch the water droplets run down his defined muscles, as they got lost in the hairs that scarcely covered him. Studied how the sinew on his abdomen dipped and moved when he laughed, walked, or shifted, just so I'd be able to enhance those fantasies. Noticed the trail that disappeared under his board shorts, which sometimes appeared tighter than others, depending on how he was sitting. I tried not to stare at that particular region, because I honestly was a little unsure about my thoughts on it.

"You have turned a lovely shade of red, Winnie. It makes me wonder what kind of thoughts are running through that beautiful mind of yours." Esteban draws back and smiles victoriously down at me.

I have no words, really. It's not like I'd dare admit I was imagining him half-naked while he drove me insane.

"Come on." He steps back and grabs my luggage again. "We need to get you settled so you can get to sleep."

I follow him down the corridor and to the main area of the palace he calls home. There are so many passageways that veer off this wing; I imagine it would be easy for one to become lost. After I do a spin to take in the large vestibule, I don't remember which one we just exited, and almost miss him heading down one of the others. How horrible would it be if I got lost and panicked, all because I couldn't find my way out?

I trot to catch up to him, right as he ascends an enormous staircase, one that spirals up before it disappears. It reminds me of one of those movies set back in an era when a place like this was built. If I weren't with Esteban, knew his character, I might be leery following him up them. Afraid he could lead me to a tower, one he will lock me in, so I cannot escape.

A shiver trails down my spine at that thought. It has nothing to do with the fact I am frightened about being locked in a mysterious tower. I once again allowed my fantasies of the man to take over. Consider how I wouldn't mind being hidden away, as long as he visited me often to do unthinkable lovely acts to me.

When we reach the second landing, he steps into the long stone corridor and glances back. He is wearing a beautiful smile, a smile that has me wondering what he might be thinking, although I don't dare ask him.

"We are almost to my lair," he informs me when I catch up to him, with this playful hum in his voice. "Don't be frightened, I promise to protect you while you stay with me. There are no ghosts that haunt these particular hallways."

I smack his arm before he starts walking again while chuckling. "Thank you for adding to my anxiety. I hope you are prepared for me to..." I stop there because... well, just because.

Esteban halts in front of a set of large double doors before pushing open one of them. The dang thing creaks, echoing throughout the long dark hall, giving it a very eerie ambiance. Then he snickers as if he understands exactly what I might be thinking.

"It is not as scary as you might picture, I swear." He nods for me to enter first. "These are my private quarters and..."

I miss what he says next, as I step inside and get my first view of his accommodation. The fire is roaring in the fireplace, making it feel very homey. There is a large rug covering the stone floor. He set the living area up much like the one in my apartment. It even has a larger than required television, arranged just to the left of the fireplace, so that one can enjoy both if they desired.

Esteban steps up behind me after he shuts and locks the large creaky door. "Well?"

"Nice and cozy." I glance over my shoulder.

"Thank you. I spend most of my evenings here. There are several spacious rooms in the palace, much like this one. When I have guests, we hang out in the drawing-room, I arranged it much like this but it is bigger. I like the ambiance of the old palace, but I also enjoy the luxury of modern technology. No reason one cannot have both I say." He nudges me forward. "You will sleep in my room tonight."

"What?" I can hear the uncertainty in my voice.

"Move. I meant alone, Winnie." He snickers as he encourages me to move my feet. "I will take the other room that has been set up for my sisters. They also don't enjoy sleeping alone when they visit me here."

"Oh." I sigh out of relief. "I can sleep in there, Stan. If it is good enough for a princess, it is surely good enough for me."

"You will sleep in my room. The only bathroom in here is off of mine. The other space was originally designed to be a personal library or perhaps a nursery. It is not as big and doesn't even have a fireplace or a door that closes. Therefore, I will take it and you will sleep in my bedroom, no arguing."

I start to argue, anyway, because it is in my nature to do so. Except I don't get the words out before he puts his lips on mine to prevent them from coming out. Those lips are my downfall, and I imagine I will never tire of them or him.

"No arguing. I know where there is another bathroom in this monstrosity of a palace. You do not. Should I need to use the facilities in the middle of the night, it would be no problem, although that usually isn't an issue for me." Esteban breathes faintly as he releases my lips. "Plus, the idea of you sleeping in my bed..."

I blush again, like always when he makes those sorts of suggestions. I'd be lying if I didn't admit I also like the idea of sleeping where he sleeps. "Okay."

"Winnie." He whispers my name, letting his breath heat my lips. "One day."

Oh, for the love of all that is forbidden. I swear silently to myself, as I take a step back and pretend to survey the room. I refuse to allow my mind to ponder on what one day may refer to and do my best to remain in the present.

His bedroom is large. There are high ceilings to make room for the hearth and several tall windows with floor to ceiling curtains hanging next to them. Masculine furniture dominates the space, the kind I envision a prince like him would own. The colors that accent the space are equally masculine; a shade of forest green and gold. Should this man ever inherit the throne, these colors would be perfect to use in his coat of arms.

The family crest is proudly displayed above the hearth, as a token of his importance, a reminder to encourage him to never forget. Not that I imagine he could forget, but perhaps seeing it regularly keeps his mind focused.

"Very lovely, Your Highness." The words slip out of me, as I am reminded of just whom I am sneaking around with. "I'm still not at all comfortable sleeping in your personal space."

Esteban leaves my luggage next to the bathroom door and then leans against the frame. "Then let me make a decree you will not be able to protest. As your prince, I mandate you stay in these very quarters so I might keep you safe and close. Since it is just the two of us who will reside in this large establishment, I don't feel comfortable allowing you to sleep elsewhere. There are many hidden passageways, and you might get lost or frightened. If that should happen, I would feel extremely guilty. You don't want your prince to feel guilty, do you, Lady Winifred?"

"No, Your Highness," I respond a little worried I've offended him.

"Good." He pushes off the frame and struts toward me, displaying all his authority with each step. "It is no secret that I am an important man, one who holds a title that can be very intimidating. But you have no reason to be intimidated, Lady Winifred. If anyone should be intimidated, it shall be me."

I take a step back. "I am the least intimidating person in this very room."

"Not true." He keeps advancing until I have no more room left to retreat. "You hold a threat that only you can possess. It's one that could devastate me, should you decide I am not worthy of your companionship. You don't appreciate the kind of power you have over me. It is far more powerful than any I might have at my fingertips."

My entire body seems to heat at those words. Power is not something I've possessed much in my life. Knowing I have some sort of spellbinding power over a man like Esteban, is sort of empowering and frightening all at the same time.

"As your boyfriend—you haven't forgotten that I am your boyfriend, have you?" he asks as he rests one hand against the wall behind me. "As your boyfriend, however, I would appreciate it if you'd allow me the pleasure of sharing my personal space with you. Let me offer you some comfort that is less intimidating than the room I first offered you. I would get absolutely no sleep whatsoever if I thought you were frightened and alone."

His eyes grow darker. "I'm going to kiss you now, Winnie. Then I'll leave so you can get ready for bed. I'm so glad you're here with me, so very glad."

He leans in and kisses me in a way that is both devastating and precious, all at the same time. I wonder if maybe there is more transpiring between us than just a fondness or an attraction. I wonder if perhaps I might be falling for this man, and that terrifies me the most.

CHAPTER 11
Winifred

The Royals

I 've been here a few days now, after my under the radar return to my homeland. Esteban gave me a very personal tour of his lovely palace during that time.

In the light of day, the palace is beautiful, exposing the history of the place that can not only be seen but also felt. The open balconies looking down onto the main entryway, on each of the five stories, are like nothing I've ever laid eyes on before. It gives his home a museum-like ambiance. A true palace atmosphere that provides you with the foresight of how those guarding the royal family living here had advantage points if attacked.

Each chamber also has separate balconies that are unique to them. And the rooms considered the private quarters of the family, all have connected passageways hidden behind the walls. Those passages are not accessible through the many others traveling through the palace walls. There are escape routes, which merge, all extremely complex and difficult to follow unless you are familiar with each route.

Thankfully Esteban is, and we never became lost when we explored them. Of course, he also explained they are now monitored by his security team to ensure no one got lost inside. His sisters enjoyed playing in the passages when they visit. He was afraid his youngest, Isabel, might become confused and then frightened if it took someone too long to locate her.

The nightfall brought a completely different ambiance to the old palace. The corridors are much darker once the sun goes down, eliminating the natural light the day carried with it. Then, of course, there are the sounds that echo when the wind picks up and whistles down those passageways you can't see. It makes the walls sound alive as if they are breathing, whispering a few secrets. The kind only a place like this held, secrets that were never to be shared without suffering the consequences. I was more than thankful Esteban insisted I spent my nights locked in his quarters, where he was only a room away. Knowing he was close made me sleep better than I would have if I'd been left in one of the many other suites.

I woke up this morning to discover it snowed during the night. That would explain why the walls howled last night. The view from his bedroom was breathtaking as it was. However, today, it was just a little more so, with the white landscape that fell away when it met the cliffs. I could even make out the ocean waves beating against the shore below as I watch the whitecaps roll in.

My mind drifts off all on its own as I began imagining a different life from the one I currently enjoy. In the garden directly below me, I envision children rushing around dressed in their winter clothing. They are running from a man flinging snowballs at them. Laughing like only children who are truly happy ever do. The youngest trips and lands face-first in the snow. Instead of leaving her, so he can catch the other two who are faster, the man stops and scoops her into his large arms. He swings her around once before he props her on his broad shoulders so that together they can bombard the others for leaving her behind.

The scene alters as I picture myself joining in on the fun. A family of five, all playing happily together in the snow, laughing loudly. Not at all caring that we are covered in the white stuff blanketing the ground. When the kids run off to do what kids do, the man turns his attention on me. He struts forward, targeting me with authority. He is ogling at me in that way of his as he approaches. Reaching up, he brushes off the snow covering my head, right before he leans forward and kisses me. Which is when we are bombarded by snowballs thrown by the children the two of us created. Although that doesn't prevent the kiss, it only makes it that much more intense.

I give my head a good jostle as I drift back from a way too authentic daydream. I refuse to dwell on it too long; afraid if I do, I'll get hurt when I come to realize how very fictional it ends up being. Instead, I grab my clothes and head to the bathroom so I can clean up for the day.

I step into the sitting area where I first notice the bowl of grapes and strawberries on the side table. Underneath it is a note that reads: *I'm in the gym. Join me if you dare. If you, however, are not daring enough, then please make yourself at home in my kitchen.*

I snatch up the bowl and carry it with me as I head for the kitchen a few floors below. So far, I haven't had the privilege of cooking for him. The man has either beat me to the punch or produced an already fixed meal—which I still haven't figured out how those meals suddenly materialize from thin air. Obviously, someone is cooking for us in a hidden galley, then delivering those meals when instructed to do so.

As I enter the kitchen, I am pleased to discover nothing has been prepared. Therefore, I rummage through the pantry and fridge until I have everything for me to construct Belgian waffles.

Thirty minutes later, I am elbow deep into the process and loving every second of it. I sense him long before I see or hear him. I can't explain it, but it's like I've always been able to detect Esteban whenever he is nearby. Like we have developed some special connection not long after that first encounter when I was eleven.

He doesn't say a word or make a sound. Instead, he stands in the doorway, staring at me with an unreadable expression pasted on his face. About the time I am close to inquiring what he is thinking, he leisurely advances my way. I was just about to pour more mix into the waffle maker, except he seizes my hand in his and twirls me around to face him. We exchanged no words before he leans down and kisses me as if he has been waiting his whole life to do so. I swear my entire body shivers and I nearly forget my own name.

"I have never seen anything so lovely before. Such a stunning view, and I wanted to take it all in before interrupting you." Esteban rubs his nose against mine as if there is more he'd like to reveal, but then realizes now is not the time to do so. "Breakfast smells and looks delicious. You didn't have to cook for me."

I clear my throat as I gently shove him back so I can finish. "I enjoy cooking, Stan. It relaxes me and allows me to express myself, revealing how much I appreciate you. I believe there is a saying that declares the way to a man's heart is through his stomach."

I have no idea what possessed me to announce something so personal. It isn't like me to bring up those types of sentiments. I would normally avoid articulating how I desire to one day own his heart, in the same way, he already owns mine. Again, not that I'd ever share that with him, not yet at least.

Esteban reaches up and closes the waffle iron before he spins me around again. The fire displayed in his eyes warns me he is very close to losing some of his precious resolve. "You desire to get close to my heart, Winnie? Have you not been paying attention these last several months? My heart—"

My phone rings, as does his within seconds, interrupting us. I notice Ingrid's name flash on my screen when I glance down to check. He takes a step back. Stares at his with a sour expression as he spins and walks away before answering it. Since the conversation we were having is not going to continue, I answer mine to get my mind off what he was about to reveal.

"Hello. Are you enjoying your holiday?" I ask my friend as soon as I press the button.

She is sobbing hysterically and unable to speak.

"Ingrid?" I panic. "What's wrong?"

"There was an accident," she finally sputters out. "They don't know if he will make it, Freddie."

I am confused. "Who honey?"

"Darius." She sobs out his name. "Someone shot him. We were... we were... oh, Freddie, I don't know if I can."

My friend breaks down again. I can only offer her my silent support until I understand what is going on. I try to console her, except right now she isn't making any sense and I feel helpless.

Esteban steps back into the room wearing a very somber face. He motions for me to hand over my phone, so I do.

"Dinger, I need you to calm down. Better. We will be there as soon as we can. Switzerland is a short plane ride away. I've instructed my head of security to contact Darius' top man, to make sure he immediately notifies you of his condition when he hears anything. Put your name at the top of his list. No problem, honey. Just hang tight and know that Darius is one stubborn SOB and doesn't give up easily. He clearly has a reason to not do so now, doesn't he? Keep your thoughts positive and try not to envision the worst."

I dig out the waffle as soon as it is finished, so it doesn't burn, while I listen to him talk her off the ledge. I can hear Ingrid's voice subside moderately as he encourages her.

When he hangs up, he stares at the wall in front of him for a few seconds. Then, out of nowhere, he picks up a glass and throws it hard against it. I've never seen Esteban so messed up before, and I'm not sure how to deal with this outburst.

"Sorry," he grumbles as he drops his head into his hands, ashamed. "Dammit."

His eyes meet mine, and I detect the pain he is suffering in them. He is truly devastated over the news of his friend, and I completely understand. I am very fond of Darius, or at least I consider the other man a very good friend, so I follow how hard this has to be on him. Those two are as close as I am with Ingrid. If something had happened to her, I'd be a mess right now.

"What happened?" I question as I reach over and cover one of his hands with mine.

"Darius flew Ingrid out to be with him during a portion of her break. As you are aware, they have become rather close since our excursion last spring." He starts there.

It was no secret something was transpiring between those two, at least not to either of us. It started the week the four of us spent some time together. Darius took one look at my shy, moderately stunning friend, and it was as if he no longer possessed eyes for anyone else. He visited her as often as he could, much like Esteban did me. The only difference was that Darius refused to use an alias, not his style. He openly made regular visits and somehow no one caught on to why that might be. Not that I'd cared or would have outed them.

"He was planning on introducing her to his family," Esteban reveals next and glances up at me. "He bought her a ring."

"What?" I am utterly surprised by that news.

"Darius told me so I'd be prepared for when it became public. He planned to ask her on New Year's Eve, when the clock struck midnight, start the year off right, then introduce her the following day."

"Oh, my..." I cover my mouth when it hits me. "That would have been tonight."

"Yeah." He sighs and I understand where he is coming from, or I thought I did. "Someone shot him outside his home when he was collecting the mail. His team believes he was targeted because as soon as he stepped out the door, he was hit. They believe he was shot because..."

Esteban pauses there, and I have to wonder what he is going to tell me. "Why Stan?"

"Because word spread he had company with him, female company." His fists tighten by his sides. "They said the guy they caught and questioned told them he was hired to take out the man involved with a certain female companion."

"Why would someone want to kill him because of Ingrid?" I am so very confused right now. It makes no sense to me whatsoever.

"The female this person believed he was involved with was you, Winnie. Someone took a shot at Darius because someone didn't want him to be involved with you." Esteban's words seem to stir up a deep anger inside of him. "No one knew about Darius' relationship with Ingrid. They only overheard the rumors he was supposedly with you."

I feel all the blood leave my face while I listen. Darius could die because someone didn't want him dating me. Why me? What could I possibly possess that was important enough they would take a man's life? Why would anyone risk killing another person because of me?

Those are the question I continue to ask for the next several hours. I am numb inside. I can't figure out any of this. I have no clue why someone would want to hurt anyone because of me.

I'm nothing, no one. I am the last person anyone would find interesting enough to decide they had to kill someone else over.

WE ARRIVE at the hospital where Darius was taken. Ingrid is frantically standing by to hear how he is. I locate her in the waiting room pacing back and forth, looking like I imagine I would look if Esteban were the one in surgery after being shot. As soon as she spots me, she comes running and I open my arms so I can offer my support.

After several long minutes, she whispers into my shoulder, "I love him, Winifred. I love him and I may never get the chance to tell him that. If he survives this, I am not letting a second pass before I share that with him. I can't lose him, I can't."

"Shh." I rub her back, and as I do, my eyes land on the man who brought me here.

We haven't talked much since this morning's phone call. I'm sure he is worried about his friend. Right now, he is doing his best to put the pieces together about what Darius' men shared with him. However, the way he is watching me, expresses he is thinking exactly what I am.

While it would be harder to get to a man like Prince Esteban, because he has men constantly keeping eyes on him, it wouldn't be impossible. Nothing is ever impossible.

Ingrid pulls back and wipes her eyes as she smiles up at me. "So, you were with...?"

She doesn't mention his name because she doesn't need to. It is clear who she is talking about for two reasons. The first being the fact he spoke to her after taking my phone earlier when she called. The other is that he is standing not very far from us now, as if he is my protector.

"Yes." I guide her to the chair. "So, you and Darius. Ingrid, I'm so sorry this happened."

Tears fill her eyes. "I didn't plan on it, you know. I did my best to encourage him to give it up and forget about me."

I laugh because I know how very true that is. Ingrid was okay with the two of them being friends, even the kind of friends that kissed occasionally. But as far as letting him suggest they were more, was something Ingrid tried to deny relentlessly. Darius, however, was not the type of man who allowed her to deny what he wanted. He was relentless and used his suave techniques to convince her otherwise. It would be difficult to ignore a man like the Duke of Falcon, much like it was ignoring Esteban, the Heir Prince of Hermosa Islas.

"A man like Darius Falcon doesn't give up without a good fight." I squeeze her hand, hoping to remind her how they got to this point. "I'm certain he loves you as well."

Ingrid shuts her eyes and smiles with this sadness behind it. "I hope I get the chance to find out."

Right then, a doctor steps into the waiting area, very close to the same time an older couple enters. There is no mistaking the couple is most likely his parents; the man looks like an older version of Darius.

"Are one of you ladies Ingrid Lennox?" The doctor is staring directly at us.

Ingrid stands rather rapidly. Her entire body is shaking. "I am."

"The Duke of Falcon wanted me to let you know he will be fine." He smiles at her with fondness. "I promised to deliver that message to you before I rushed him off to surgery. He said you were to be the first person I should notify because you were the light that would bring him back."

Ingrid stumbles forward. Thankfully, Esteban is there to catch her. "He said that?"

"Yes, miss. He was very clear about that, very adamant actually." The doctor takes a seat as he glances around the room. "You must be the duke's parents."

"We are." The woman speaks over the man standing next to her. "I am the Duchess Geneva Falcon Blomquist. This is my husband Earl Horton Blomquist, he is Darius' stepfather. I'm sure his father—"

"Is right here." A man struts in, and there is no mistaking he is somehow related to the other.

"Brother." He addresses the Earl.

"Doctor. Marquees Julius Falcon. Please tell us how our son is doing."

I glance around the room and notice that this family seems a little off. I had heard they had their issues, but I wasn't completely certain what they were. When Julius leans down and kisses Geneva's cheek— like it is his right to do so—I have to wonder.

"Don't try to figure it out," Ingrid whispers. "It's way more complicated than one can fathom. Darius is very ashamed of so many of his family's practices, which is why he has refused to get involved in the family business."

The doctor begins as soon as everyone is seated. "He lost a lot of blood. We had to give him a transfusion. Luckily for him, he kept a supply of his own blood on hand. Apparently in his line of work, he always felt he might need it, so he made sure to make regular deposits."

His mother gasps. "Thank God. Mixing his blood with someone else's would have been unthinkable."

That seems like a rather odd statement to make. Why would something like that matter? Who would care as long as it saved his life?

The doctor shakes his head as if he expected the duchess to say something so absurd. "The bullet missed his heart, as well. However, it nicked one of his major arteries. I was able to repair it with no issues and don't expect it to slow him down much once he has fully recovered. I predict that to take at least four weeks. He should refrain from any form of strenuous activity during that time. That includes stress, exercise, and sex."

He glances at Ingrid and tries not to smile, but fails. "I need you to make sure he understands how important it is he follow my orders. He claims two out of the three are feasible, but the third will happen as soon as he is well enough to leave the hospital."

"I don't know why he..." Ingrid is severely blushing now. "I'll make it clear that you said four weeks and not a moment sooner. Surely, he can wait four weeks, he's waited this long, so four more should be a walk in the park."

The doctor reaches inside his coat pocket and hands a sealed envelope to her. "He wanted me to give this to you. You are not to open it, but you are to keep it safe for him."

Ingrid accepts the envelope and clasps it carefully in her hands. Tears fill her eyes as she stares at it and the detectable lump. "He's going to be okay?"

"He is going to be okay." The doctor informs her. "A nurse will come when we get him settled in a private room."

I take a deep breath, thankful Darius didn't die for something that had to do with me. Now if only I could figure out what is going on.

CHAPTER 12
Esteban

The Royals

The remainder of our time together has been spent in Switzerland. Not at all how I hoped to spend these days with Winnie, not even close. We stayed with Ingrid at Darius' home so we could escort her back and forth from the hospital daily. I did what I know my friend would want me to do, what he would have done if the tables were turned. And of course, Winnie does the same thing for hers.

Thankfully, Darius woke up after being transferred into a private room, where the two of them had a quiet moment. During that time, he instructed Ingrid to open the envelope she had in her possession, then asked her right then and there to marry him. Naturally, she accepted without having to think about it. After staring death in the face, my friend would not let another moment pass without his woman by his side. Can't say I blame him. It's too bad Winnie and I aren't ready for that kind of commitment.

Ingrid hadn't wanted to leave his side; however, the hospital staff was very strict about visiting hours. So, it was either go back to his home and rest like he needed her to or camp out in one of the waiting areas. Since we happened to be with her, she opted to go home. I was afraid I'd have to drag her out kicking and screaming.

Winifred and I haven't communicated much since arriving. I mean,

99

of course, we've talked, but not about the important issues that had to do with us. I knew she was stressing about the information I'd shared, suggesting someone had shot Darius because of her.

I guess I could've lied or chosen not to disclose that information to her, however, I felt she had every right to hear about it. It affected her as much as it did Darius and me. Actually, I believe it affects her more in the long run. Her understanding that he was shot because of her was extremely important and meant we had to take action.

Winifred was scheduled to fly back to the States this afternoon. A private jet would fly her to England. Once there, she would catch the commercial overnight flight, which would land bright and early the following morning in New York.

That meant we only had a few hours left to hash out a few very significant details. I'm uncertain how she is going to take what I have to share with her. Nevertheless, the only detail that matters to me, the only situation that will ever matter to me, is her safety. There is nothing I wouldn't do to ensure Winifred Batista remains safe from any threats made against her. While she may not see this as a threat against her, I've come to the realization it most definitely is. Therefore, I have no choice except to act on it, in a way that I can guarantee she will remain safe until I am able to bring her under my personal protection.

At this very moment, we are seated in a very nice restaurant in Zürich. A private establishment where only those who are members or of an elite, select group are permitted to dine. I needed a location where I could take her and not worry about us getting photographed. Drawing unwarranted attention at the moment would only alert whoever is keeping tabs on Winifred's life. Not something I am willing to do until I know what I am up against.

As soon as we are seated, Winifred stares out at the view before us, although I'm not sure she is seeing it. "They are going to announce their engagement as soon as Darius is released from the hospital. Ingrid has decided not to return to Princeton for the spring semester. She will remain here with him while they organize a very quick wedding. She is expecting it to take place in a few short months. March, I believe, is her target. She's hoping to schedule it around my spring break. That way I can be her maid of honor."

"I know," I tell her because this is not news to me.

I was there, just like she was when Ingrid revealed her plans. She wanted Winifred to stand next to her, share in the most important day of her life. Neither Darius nor Ingrid blames her for what happened. They blame the person who thought shooting someone over a rumor was acceptable. They are as equally worried about her as I am—maybe not just as worried, but they are concerned about her safety. Darius vowed to put his investigative team on it until they uncovered the person responsible and then take them down, make them pay for all the trouble they've caused.

"I know you do." She slowly lets her eyes slide my way, and the sadness I witness breaks my heart. "I also appreciate what you are going to say."

It is hard for me to believe she truly does. "I doubt that."

Winifred blinks several times before she reveals she is way smarter than I have given her credit for. "I agree, by the way. There are a few ways we can handle this, I suppose, but only one solution that will work."

"There are several options I believe that could work." I hate there is only one that will give her what she needs, though.

"One, if you plan on keeping your promise about giving me a choice in how my life will actually play out." She glimpses back out the window and sighs. "I understand you are stuck between a rock and a hard place here."

"Do you?" I reach over and seize her hand that is ice cold in mine. "Do you really understand? Because if I am being honest, Winnie, I do not and it is killing me."

"You cannot risk your life, Stan. The best way to ensure you are safe is to make sure we do not draw any attention. Not give this person a reason to target you." She doesn't look at me as she reveals my early thoughts, with her own twist, obviously. "I care about you too much to bring what happened to Darius to your doorstep, your family's doorstep. Until it is safe..."

"Winnie," I whisper her name when she stops abruptly. "Please, look at me."

Her eyes shift gradually, and I am gutted deep when I connect with them again. "I will be fine. I'll figure out a way to get through this."

"I will make sure of that, Winnie. This..." I motion between us. "This is not over."

Her eyes drop as her head tumbles forward. It doesn't take a genius to realize she is crying, that she isn't at all in agreement with what I am communicating to her. Clearly, she doubts we will be able to recover from this, that she doesn't completely understand how much she means to me.

We eat our meal in silence. I don't let go of her hand. I hold on to it, memorize how it feels in mine. I'm not positive when I will see her next. Not sure if I'll speak to her regularly for a while, if it is safe to even do so.

Right now, my team is working overtime, doing their best to figure out the connection between Darius' shooting and Winifred. There is a connection, that is a fact, but so far, they are unable to determine who ordered the hit. A mystery I am beginning to understand, with this nauseating awareness, will do a great deal of damage to all the hard work I have put in these last several months.

Since her flight out of Switzerland is private, and the airstrip she is departing from is secured, I insist on escorting her. My limo can drive on the tarmac and drop her off in front of the plane, given that I am a diplomat with special privileges.

We arrive early enough she doesn't need to jump out as soon as we park. My driver, however, does, that way, he can retrieve her luggage and get it checked in while granting us our privacy. Winifred tries to follow him, except I refuse to just let her go without making my thoughts very clear to her.

"Do not doubt my determination to fix this as quickly as possible. This last year, Winnie, if anything has shown me why I need to..." I am unable to finish my declaration because Winifred flies into my arms and kisses me, like it will be the last one we will ever share. And because I am not positive when I'll get the chance to kiss her again, I want to make certain I cherish it.

I grab her waist and haul her into my lap, forcing her to straddle me while I wrap my arms around her. She is the only woman I have dared to let matters get out of hand with, and I plan on her being the only one ever. It's definitely a good thing she is wearing jeans instead of a skirt. Since my hands seem to roam all over her body at the moment, memorizing it the best they can in such a short amount of time.

I should be ashamed to admit this, except I'm not. When I am with this woman, I let my mind stop thinking. I allow my body and the desires I feel for her to take over. There isn't a lot of shame involved during those moments.

She is wearing a sweater with a low neckline, one that is also a little loose. Meaning when I permit my lips to roam away from hers, they travel down her jawline to her neck. I explore her collarbone with my tongue, where my chin discovers the crevice between her ample breasts. At that point, I become an obsessed man.

I pull back, so I can look at her and those lovely breasts that are now eye level. My hands react all on their own, snaking up her soft sweater to land on the outer half of ample chest. Which explains how my fingers manage to manipulate the neckline of her sweater, tugging it down just enough to reveal the lace on her bra. Black lace, I discover, is much softer than it appears. I stare at her soft creamy skin making my mouth water, appreciating the contrast of her skin tone against the color of her bra.

"Stan." Winifred mumbles my name as she digs her fingers into my hair and then lets her nails scrape against my scalp.

"You are *espléndido*, Winnie." I kiss the flesh exposed very carefully so I don't get carried away. It would be so embarrassing to do something completely out of the ordinary for a man in my position. "A *Princesa*, my *Princesa*."

I allow my fingers to caress her tender skin for a few moments before I let her sweater cover them again. My hands roam to her backside as I bury my face into her neck and I nibble on it, making my way back to those gorgeous, plump lips of hers.

While I am kissing her intimately, I tug her forward so she understands how vulnerable I am. I want her to appreciate what she does to me, what only she does to me.

"Feel that," I growl against her lips, pressing my hard length into her. "You, *Princesa*, caused that. You have affected me like that so many times these last several months, that sometimes when we are apart, just thinking about you gets me all worked up. No other woman, none of them, has ever stirred me the way you do. No one has had me in knots, as you have me, Winnie. No one ever will."

"Please don't." I hear the desperation in her voice as she pleads for me to drop it. "Please, I can't hear that, knowing this could—"

I ignore her pleas and kiss the last words right off her lips. I kiss her like I have never dared to kiss a woman before. I give her everything I have inside of me, all I am capable of giving her at the moment.

I want to shout the words that are on the tip of my tongue. There is nothing I desire more than to say them to her, so she understands this is not our final goodbye, not even close.

The only consideration holding me back from speaking them is that I understand how powerful those words are. I know if I disclose them, I will never be able to let her go. I'll have to forbid her from returning to New York, where she lives. Where her life is hers to live as she sees fit and also happens to be the one she needs right now. Her freedom to have these next few years is important; it will allow her to grow and become the woman I need her to be when the time is right.

The light taps on the window, followed by a male voice notifying us it is almost time, has me dragging her away, so I can stare at her again. I grab her face and hold it between my hands, using my thumbs to wipe away those tears streaming down her cheeks. I hate seeing her like this. Hate it so much that I am frantically trying to figure out how I can fix this.

Winifred leans in one more time and kisses me eagerly. She scuttles off my lap as she grabs her small purse without hesitating. It is clear she refuses to say another word or even glance back as she climbs out of the vehicle. The accelerated pace she is determined to take toward the stairs conveys she is doing her best to just get this over with as quickly as possible.

I wasn't planning on exiting the car, revealing myself to those who may be in the vicinity. However, I couldn't care less if anyone sees or hears me tell this woman what I need to tell her.

"Winnie," I shout her name right as she reaches the top of the stairs, forcing her to stop and spin. "Do you trust me?"

She nods with the same sad expression on her face. "Yes, Stan, I trust you."

"Do you remember what I stated would happen once I got you to trust me?" I lean against the limo and study her carefully, so I can recall this moment forever.

"Yes." She wipes a tear off her cheek, still not fully understanding what I am revealing.

I wink at her, as I give her the sincerest smile I can at this surreal moment in time. "Good. Finish school for me, *Princesa*. Earn that degree you are so determined to acquire. When you return to Hermosa Islas, I will expect you to run my newest investment."

Her face contorts in the cutest way, a way I am going to miss while I do my best to protect her, us. "What investment is that, Stan?"

I relax totally, knowing this next statement should get her to understand what I am suggesting. "I believe the name of the establishment will be Stan's Dreamland. Do you think that might be something you'd be interested in?"

Her entire face lights up like I knew it would. "I might be."

"Good, because I was thinking it would be the perfect place for someone who enjoys baking wedding cakes to design her own dream cake. I hear wedding cakes are very important and all. I imagine a baker might want to be in charge of her own, especially one as talented as you." I watch the realization of what I am suggesting wash over her face and I laugh. "No more tears, Winnie. Time to trust me as you promised."

CHAPTER 13
Winifred

The Royals

Two Years Later

The ringing of my cellphone wakes me before the alarm does. Since I am usually up before the crack of dawn, so I can help Melody at the bakery, my phone ringing so early surprises me. There aren't many people who call me anymore. My friends gave up after I stopped answering and declining their invites to go out. I've sort of become a recluse since my return to New York after the incident. The only things I am interested in these days are school and the bakery; everything else seems pointless.

I know I shouldn't be so down about what happened. The fault doesn't fall on the shoulders of those I am punishing. It doesn't even fall on mine, or my friends, or the man I try really hard not to think about —an impossible feat, by the way.

I mean, I tried to pretend I didn't care that I was struggling to move forward after a tough breakup. Did my best to smile and put on a happy face so I didn't make others around me uncomfortable. The problem was I've faked it so much throughout my life, I just wasn't interested in returning to that girl. I'd been living the life I'd always wished of one day having with the man who walked out of my dreams for almost a year. To have it ripped away without warning, broke me inside.

The only places I was marginally at ease were school and Nelson's. Therefore, I finally decided the best way to get on with my new life was to focus on those two things, because they made me forget, mostly. Not the empty space inside, though. It was a constant reminder that I was alone in this world once again. It reminded me often.

As did my mother, she took all of five seconds to ring me after Ingrid and Darius' engagement was announced.

"I don't know why I ever allowed your father to deviate from our original plans. There was never any doubt in my mind you'd mess it all up where the duke was concerned. A man of his distinction could never truly be interested in such a plain girl. Now we have to establish if we can salvage your reputation with any of those men he will once again be negotiating with. Such a disappointment you have always been Winifred, always a disappointment."

"Mother, did you ever once suppose that Ingrid..." I hadn't gotten the chance to say more.

"Oh, for God's sake, Winifred. Your friend is no better of a catch than you are. She simply understood how to better attract the duke's attention. Knew the best way to do so was by offering him what I'm sure you never did."

Her hateful words about how my friend—who she didn't believe worthy of a man like the Duke of Falcon—on how she stole him right out from under my nose, irritated me. Her claim for the relationship— our fake one—falling apart, occurring because I was not giving him what he needed, ticked me off. It proved Esteban's point on why my mother should be kept in the dark about our affair.

I wanted to shout that she was right, that Ingrid was giving Darius her love and commitment, true blissful happiness. However, I couldn't disclose the truth about it all, because if I did I would out Esteban, and I respected him too much to put him in her spotlight.

My mother would do more damage than good if I revealed there was never anything between Darius and me. That the duke had been covering for his friend as a favor. I can't even imagine the hatefulness she might have vomited about the mess I was in now. I'm sure it would have been on how foolish I was believing a man like the prince would ever be interested in a girl like me. That I should have locked it down when I had the chance. Commented on how I was just as obtuse as she always expected me to be, since I had let Esteban slip right through my fingers.

There wasn't an exchange between us that didn't end with my mother reminding me how I messed up my future. Lucky for me, she rarely calls or visits, therefore I don't have to listen to her go on and on about it. Being an ocean away from her has its perks where this minor issue is concerned.

Since I spent all my free time at the bakery, and no longer have friends, I wasn't sure who could be calling at such an odd hour. So, when I retrieved my phone to find his name displayed, I stare at it in disbelief.

I've heard from the man twice since the day I jumped on a plane to return to my life thousands of miles away. He called both times on my birthday. Given that it is close to that time of the year again, my first thoughts are that has to be the reason for this call as well. Unfortunately, I stare too long at the screen before it automatically goes to voicemail, making it impossible for me to find out why he is phoning.

I miss him more than words can express. My mind likes to pretend he misses me as well, although I'm not naïve enough to genuinely believe that. A man like Esteban doesn't have the time to ponder on a silly girl like me. I'm certain he has moved on by now. Two years is an awfully long time to put his life on hold. There is no way I plan on holding him to all those promises he made, suggestions he felt he needed to reveal. They were done to make it easier for me to walk away, a gesture that our time together had at least held some minor significance in his memory bank.

It's not as if I see myself ever returning to my homeland after graduation, not if I get a say in it, at least. My time with Esteban had given me some courage to admit I had input about my future, as did my experiences here. I wasn't worried about disappointing my parents anymore. If nothing else, they'd shown me these last four years how little I truly mattered to them. I was easily forgettable when I wasn't around, always have been. So, my plan was to apply for a permanent visa, granting me permission to stay and work with Melody, until I saved enough money to open my own bakery.

My phone rings again with the same name flashing across my screen. I find it strange he is calling again almost instantly. Which is why this time I answer it on the third ring.

"Winnie." His rich voice casts the same spell on me, the same way it has for as long as I remember.

"Your Highness." However, I refuse to use the nickname he insisted I come up with. It is too personal, and because we no longer have that sort of relationship, it is best I keep my sentiments to myself.

"I wish you wouldn't call me that. It wounds me deeply when you treat me like an acquaintance when we are so much more." His disappointment reflects in his voice, and I might give a damn if I thought he was being sincere.

"Are we? Seems like if we were more than acquaintances, I'd hear from you more than once a year. Seems like the only time you think of me is when my birthday rolls around and you suddenly undergo the guilt to reach out." I know I am not being as polite as I should be, but the truth is what it is. There was a time I might have let it go. But I've changed these last couple of years, become a more outspoken person.

"Point well-made, Lady Winifred, as always." He expresses, and I swear I can picture him smiling at my unwavering nerve to call him out when he messes up. "I am, however, calling because I didn't want you to hear this news from the media. I'm not sure your sisters will think of notifying you, therefore I thought I would take care of it."

I sit up, not liking the theories running through my head. Is he about to tell me he has moved on?

"What is it?"

"I wish I were there to... that I could have jumped on a plane and gotten to you before I had to share this." His voice is so serious now I am really worried. "Your parents and Dalia were in an accident, a serious one. Your father is currently undergoing surgery. His status is extremely critical. They are unsure if he will survive, and if he survives, there could be complications."

I stop breathing. My father and I may not be close, but he is still my father. I'm not sure I am ready for him to be taken from this world just yet.

"Your sister suffered some significant injuries that also required surgery. She is in recovery now and expected to be fine. She'll have to spend the next several days in the hospital. She suffered a concussion, so they will need to monitor her closely."

I am also glad to hear Dalia is going to be okay. We may not be close, but then again, she is my sister, my blood. "I'm sure the nurses will be ready for her to be discharged by the time it is all said and done. A few might even call in sick, just so they don't have to listen to her or my mother's demands."

There is a long silence that has an eerie quality to it. When Esteban speaks again, I can hear the dread in his voice. "I hate having to tell you this over the phone. Winnie... Winnie, I'm sorry to inform you, but your mother did not survive the accident."

"What?" I know I must have heard him wrong.

"Lady Eva, along with the driver, didn't make it. According to my brother's sources, she died on transport. Her injuries were too severe. They believe she bled out before they could get her to the hospital. I'm so sorry I have to do this over the phone."

I have no words right now. While my mother was certainly not my biggest fan by a long shot, I'd have never wished her dead. Not even when she was doing her best to belittle me, or worse yet, punishing me for not following her rules. I loved her the best I could, I suppose, the way a child always feels affection for a parent.

"Winnie." Esteban's voice echoes in my ear. "I'm sending a member of my team to collect you and then escort you back in one of my planes."

I swallow, even though my mouth is dry. "That is unnecessary, sir."

"Dammit, Winnie. There is more and I don't have time to explain." He sounds angry with me, while sympathetic. "They will be there within the hour. I want you to be packed and ready to go by the time they get there. This wasn't just some unfortunate traffic accident. It was a targeted one. Someone opened fire on the justice's vehicle. It happened shortly after the three of them left an event and were heading home. As of right now, we don't know all the details, but I am not taking any chances with your life. It is too important to me; you are too important to me."

"I'll be fine. I don't need an escort." I scoot to the edge of the bed and place my head in my palm. "I've not been in any danger since that dreadful day, so I don't imagine I will be now. A commercial flight will get me home just fine. This way, I won't have to experience any guilt about using you or your resources. Thank you for calling."

"Winifred Josefina Batista, I hate to be the bearer of more unfortunate news when you are already upset." His tone is direct and has me sitting up straight again. I can't believe he used my full name as if I am a child. "But if you thought for one second that you've been on your own these last two years without a team to protect you, then you are sorely mistaken. I don't take threats lightly, especially threats made against the woman who holds my happiness in the palms of her hands."

"Excuse me." I know I heard him incorrectly. "I'd know if I had a team following me."

"Not if they didn't want you to," he arrogantly enlightens me. "Those who work for the Reyes family are the best at what they do. They don't make mistakes and follow orders to the T. You've had personnel on you since the day you stepped off that plane after returning from Switzerland. I believe I told you to trust me."

"What does you putting staff on me have to do with trust? You also once promised you'd warn me if something like that ever became necessary. Since you dumped me abruptly after your friend's life was put in danger, linked somehow to me, I guess I assumed..."

His voice cuts me off, and is loud, with a tone of authority that shuts me right up. I've never heard him sound so determined to get his point across while clarifying he is a man who gets his way in all things.

"I did not dump you. I was protecting you like I promised I would do. Sometimes, in order to protect the person you would gladly lay down your life for, it means you take a step back so you can evaluate the situation better. I should have enlightened you about assigning them to you, I suppose, but I will not apologize for ensuring your safety. There are certain details I'm not willing to negotiate on. That one, *Princesa*, is top on my list."

The only sound after his little rant is us both breathing harder than is undoubtedly healthy. I swear if he were standing here in front of me, I'd slap him so hard he'd have to take a step back.

How dare he think he has the right to interfere with my life when he stepped out of it so easily? So instead of responding to his over-the-top explanation, I hang up on him. I sit there with my phone secured in my hands, listen to it ring, but have no energy to care. I stare at it as my emotions bounce all over the dang place.

There is a young desperate girl inside of me, one who wants to do a little dance. Realizing her dream man basically revealed there was still a sliver of hope. I hold her back, though, because I refuse to let myself go there again without absolute proof and a promise to accompany it.

That little girl is also doing her best to process the news he called to share. One of my parents is dead, my mother. The woman who wasn't kind to me from a very early age, all because I didn't look or act like the other three girls who lived in the same home. They punished me for stuff I had no control over. Withheld food when I put on a few extra pounds and was given smaller portions that weren't adequate for a child who was growing and active. Even though my mother could be cruel and make me feel unimportant, a part of me loved her. I made excuses for her behavior, claimed she had learned it from her own mother and was doing what she thought was best for me.

That little girl only ever longed for her mother to be proud of her just once, which is why she always tried her best to not upset her. But that never would be. I would never get the chance to make mother proud, and that saddens me deeply.

Tears I didn't know I had inside of me fall for her.

They fall for my father as well. I know the man isn't perfect, that he has his share of faults and allowed my mother to treat me cruelly. But there were a few times I encountered a different man, one who seemed to appreciate the fact I wasn't like my sisters. It wasn't as if he came right out and said it, or even showed it openly to me. It was that he had stood up to my mother when I reported I wanted to play *fútbol*. Told her it would be good exercise for me while helping me maintain that weight she was always complaining about. Or when he would call me into his office during my school breaks to analyze my marks. He never said "I'm proud of you, Winifred, for being an exceptional student." Instead, he'd go over the classes he thought I should take next, ones that were always challenging. He'd warn me not to disappoint him for recommending me to take them. While he did that, there was always a plate of cookies on his desk he would push toward me. I had obviously inherited my sweet tooth from him. It was our little secret that he snuck them to me, making certain mother wouldn't freak out.

I believe he also allowed me to attend Columbia as a sign of good faith. He knew I would be successful, make a name for myself here, bring some pride back to the Batista name. My sisters certainly hadn't gotten into prominent universities on their own. They had forced my father to use his influence to get them admitted into the ones they'd chosen. So even though we might not have the greatest relationship, I believe it is better than the one he has with any of them.

I don't have the energy to reflect on Dalia, really. I suppose the reason I hold any sentiments to her at all is the fact she is my sister. Out of the three, she is by far the cruelest, which isn't saying much about the other two. She is the ringleader. Her constant need to always put me down in the long run has taught me how to stand up for myself. I might even declare she empowered me to want to be a completely different type of person, the opposite of what she was. And I can only imagine the trouble she is stirring up right now, how she is spinning this to benefit her.

My phone has been ringing off and on for the last half hour. The number is the same one that has been calling all morning. I, however, refuse to answer it, because I don't have the energy to fight with him over all of this right now. I need to pack, contact my boss, inform someone at the school that I will take a leave of absence and why. Then book a flight home so I can be there for my family. I don't even have time to consider why no one—other than the man I refuse to acknowledge—has called to tell me about my mother and the accident.

My phone rings again at the same time the buzzer from downstairs sounds. This time the number is Melody's. She is probably wondering where I am. I answer it as I make my way into the living room, so I can also answer the buzzer. It's most likely someone who has the wrong apartment. It happens. Or it could be someone hoping I am dumb enough to just buzz him or her in without asking who it might be.

"Hello Melody," I say into my phone. "I..."

"Your boyfriend called and told me, dear. He said you'd be gone for several days while you made arrangements. Wasn't exactly sure when or if you'd be returning," she interrupts me.

"I'll be returning no matter what. I have a little over a month left of school, and I don't plan on blowing it off after working so hard. My family wouldn't expect me to. I'll be back sometime next week," I inform her. "And for the record, I don't have a boyfriend."

"Well, whoever he is to you, that is not my business. You take all the time you need, honey. Your job is safe here," she informs me, and after I thank her, I hang up.

I press the intercom button, so I can send whoever it is on their way. "How can I help you?"

A female voice responds. "Lady Batista, my name is Hillary. I've been instructed that as soon as you are ready to leave, we can head out."

"Hillary?" I shake my head, annoyed no one ever listens to me. "Do you work for Prince Esteban?"

"I do, miss," she replies. "Do you need any assistance with your bags? Would you like Vincent or me to make a few phone calls for you? We are here to be of service. Nothing is too big or too small, my lady."

"I'm not getting rid of you, am I?" I pound my head against the wall, feeling defeated.

"No, miss. We have our orders and, as you know, our loyalty..."

"Is to the man I'd like to slap, right after I shoved my boot up his fine arse," I grumble. "You might as well come up and wait with me while I finish packing."

Five minutes later, there is a knock on my door. Before I open it, I check just in case. Not that I have any idea what Hillary or Vincent look like. I mean, they could be impostors, I suppose. But the official Royal Family Security badges they freely expose, along with their credentials that include photos and everything I imagine might declare them legit.

I open the door and motion for them to enter. They are dressed in everyday clothing, blending in well with the patrons of this city. If I saw them daily, I'd not have thought twice about it. They could pose as a married couple who lived in the area... wait.

"I know you." I point my finger at them and scowl. "You come in for a pastry almost every morning around the same time. I've seen you both. Talked with you even a few times outside this very building. You told me you lived in the neighborhood, a few buildings over."

I then direct my finger at Hillary and feel like a complete idiot. "We have several classes together this semester. You sit in the same seat, three rows back, two over from me, in almost all of them. Dammit."

"Don't feel bad, miss." Hillary at least has the audacity to appear guilty for misleading me. "We were to watch and observe. Do our best to not interfere with your life, so you could maintain a sense of freedom. Hoping that you didn't always bear the need to look over your shoulder."

"Are there more of you?" I am pretty sure I already know that answer.

Vincent flashes that dimpled smile I noticed the first time he walked into the bakery. "Of course there are, but you won't be able to pick them out, any better than you could pick us out. It is better that way. Not only because we don't want you to give anyone away, but also because it allows us to do the job they have assigned us to do. Protect the future..."

I hold up a hand to stop him from disclosing more. "Do not say it. I am not what you were about to suggest, not by a long shot."

"If you say so, miss." He obviously disagrees. "This is for you."

I glance down at the phone in his hand. Notice that whoever is on the other end has most likely been listening to us. "I have no interest in speaking with him."

"Doesn't matter." Vincent jiggles it at me. "He'll only keep calling me until you do."

"What does he want?" I take a step back and put my hands behind my back.

"He didn't tell me, exactly." Vincent is now smirking. "Should I put him on speaker?"

I shrug as I turn around. "You can do that, I guess, if you wish to. That doesn't mean I'll speak with him. Right now, speaking to him is the very last thing I desire to do."

"Then you can listen to me," Esteban's supercilious voice fills the air, and hear the irritation in it. "At least you let my people in so they can do their job. I appreciate that."

"I wasn't given much choice about it, was I?" I roar from the kitchen, as I start some coffee so I can think. "I do believe a man I once cared for reported I should always have a choice. I trusted him to keep his word. It seems like I was foolish in doing so."

Vincent whistles at that statement, and I do believe I already like him.

"I'd rather not have my staff privy to this conversation, Winnie. Please pick up so we can speak in private." Esteban does his best to not sound as if he is giving me an order.

"Nope. You made this bed, now you must lie in it." I grab the sugar and cream and set them on the counter. "I'm mad at you."

I swear I hear him chuckle, as he repeats my words in a form of a question. "You're mad at me?"

"Yes. I'm mad at you. You can't call my employer and tell her you're my boyfriend when you are not." I hear him start to say something. "Nope. You don't get to interrupt me just because you are accustomed to always getting your way. You will not get your way this time, Stan. I'm mad at you and I don't plan on getting un-mad for a long time. We can't simply pick up where we left off, not after all this time has passed. Plus, I refuse to be your secret. That didn't work the way you had hoped it would, so you can forget about me agreeing to that again." I take a deep breath.

"I will finish school soon. Once I'm done, I have a few things to figure out. While I do that, you can decide what it is you want as well, I suppose. You should also understand that I won't settle for less than all of you this time. You also have a choice, Stan. Now I need to go, so I can catch a plane back home. Stop bothering me."

I don't wait for him to respond. I take off for my room and shut the door. I hear Vincent speaking to someone very formally. I imagine he took Esteban off speaker and is now explaining how I left.

My text tone dings, so I glance down only to see it is from none other than him. I have to stop what I am doing so I can read it. I'm glad I did.

STAN: I choose you. Simple as that.

CHAPTER 14
Esteban

The Royals

They alerted me the second my plane landed at the Royal Airport just outside of Aragon. The passenger onboard is the most important person in the world to me; therefore, I've been keeping tabs on the plane's location all day.

Calling her first thing this morning had been a no-brainer. I wanted to phone her as soon as I heard about the accident, except I knew there was nothing she could have done except worry. So, I opted to wait, which ended up being best, because by then I had updates on the three members of her family who were involved.

Informing Winnie her mother had passed was difficult for me to do over the phone. I so badly wished I'd jumped on a plane last night as soon as I was notified about it. But by the time I'd have reached her, she was sure to have heard the news stations reporting about it. That was no way to learn your mother had been killed, or that your father and sister were critical.

These last two years had been very challenging for me. It drained me of the joy I felt during those months when we were in constant communication. I hadn't aspired to go cold turkey on her like that. The threats my team uncovered, warning me if I continued our secret affair would put her in danger. In order to ensure she remained safe, I backed off.

The only time I was able to see her after we suffered through our heartbreaking goodbye was at Ingrid and Darius' wedding the following March. Ten weeks had passed since I'd watched her fly away from me. It took everything I possessed to not say screw it the second I saw her and deal with the consequences as they emerged.

During that time, I pretended the best I could to display we only knew each other through Darius. Kept a safe, respectable distance, or as far as the best man could be from the maid of honor. Thankfully, I wasn't forced to escort her down the aisle before or after the ceremony. The wedding party was quietly dismissed, while the bride and groom greeted their guests. It was clear my friend understood more about why that was important, and I greatly appreciated that fact.

At the reception, I couldn't help but notice how Winifred picked at her food, food I knew she would normally love to have eaten. I wanted to blame it on her mother's hovering, eyeing her closely, making her self-conscious. Except there was no mistaking she'd lost weight, and I hated to think it was because of me.

The most surprising event that occurred at their wedding was when Lady Eva approached me. I hadn't expected that, and I'm not sure why. No one ever accused that woman of not sticking her nose where it didn't belong or seizing an opportunity when it fell into her lap.

"It's such a disappointment to realize my daughter wasn't able to lock down the duke when she had the chance. That she allowed her tramp of a friend to weasel her way in and steal away what was rightfully hers. If you ask me, that is not how one treats someone they claim as a friend." Lady Eva accused with so much spiteful anger behind it. *"May I ask how you allowed that to even happen?"*

"I did no such thing. Darius is a man with a mind all his own. I suffered no need to interfere when it became evident he was falling hard for Ingrid. Your daughter and I saw no reason to not encourage something so true. A love so pure that most can only wish to discover something like it," I told her while watching the devoted couple dance. *"Then again, it wasn't as if either of them asked for my opinion. I can assure you, had I been in the same boat as them, I'd not ask for theirs."*

"And here I thought all those trips the duke was making to the States

were because of my daughter, not that little tart. He seemed to make a number of them over the past year. I was very hopeful, you know?"

It surprised me how she seemed so on top of his comings and goings. It also confirmed that it had been wise of me to use an alias and fly into less noticeable airstrips. Scheduled my visits to the States around the family business, alongside my duties as the prince.

"You two seem to travel together a lot as well. Met up occasionally, I believe when he was there, correct? Maybe I have been focusing on the wrong man all along. Are you interested in my daughter, Prince Esteban?" Lady Eva was quick to get to the point, even though I remained silent, determined not to provide her a reason to believe that to be true.

An evil snicker finally escaped as more vile words followed. *"That is absurd, I know. Why on earth would you ever be affected by someone so plain as our boring Winifred? One could wish, but truth be told, she has always been less than pleasing to the eye.*

"You know, now that she is back deep in negotiations, we would be willing to make a very friendly agreement. It could benefit both our families. We have some very influential connections. Not to mention, I can assure you that my daughter is still a virgin, a rarity for a woman of nearly twenty. She is also very well-trained in keeping matters quiet, knows when to speak and when not to. Understands her place and would not embarrass you. It would be easy to train her should that interest you, allowing you to focus on more important issues. Winifred has never given us trouble, well besides maybe with her inability to resist sweets; nothing a strict diet cannot tame."

I remained quiet, afraid if I opened my mouth, I might say more than I should.

"If you offer us the appropriate amount, Your Highness, say..." she mumbled an exact number that had my blood boiling. *"If you were to do that, then I can promise to bump you to the front of the line. Think about it and get back to me before her fate is sealed and someone else claims her for himself."*

Consequently, I felt the need to remind her of the case that had recently settled in our highest courts. I stated that the outcome had favored with the young lady, allowed criminal charges to be brought up against her family, along with the man who had exchanged money for her.

"I was so disappointed when our courts failed us there. Disbanding the practice of arranged marriages will only put so many young women at a disadvantage. The benefits outweigh all the negatives. I should know. It was how Ivan and I came to be. My Winifred will never land a decent man without her father and myself stepping in and arranging it for her."

Thankfully, she had walked away immediately when she finished, long before I responded, saying something I'd have regretted.

I'd placed my team on alert right away. These last couple of years, they have been keeping close tabs on the finances of the Batista's, which wasn't as easy as one might believe. Families like theirs knew how to manipulate the system, move money around to make transactions appear legit. Meaning they hadn't been able to uncover anything that appeared suspicious or out of the ordinary. And I hated that, because I knew from that conversation, things were not as they seemed.

So, I'd done my best these last two years to maintain my distance from the one person I so very much wanted close. I did so because I was trying to protect her from the powers determined to keep her in line. And so far, it appeared my efforts had worked out in her favor. She could go on with her plans for school while continuing her job at the bakery, both without interference from her family. They'd continued to all but forget about her, or at least ignore her for now. Giving her time to learn her craft and grow into the woman I wanted her to become. An independent one who didn't need anyone but herself to survive in this world.

When I got the call that Winifred was back on the same soil as me, the first thing I wanted to do was go to her. And that is exactly what I would have done if I weren't currently in an important meeting with my brother and the members of his council. When something like this occurs, the first matter that needs to be considered is if the threat made goes beyond the target and affects others of equal status or higher. So far, that has not been determined. A strategy is being constructed to keep the king and his next in line protected, indicating that extra protection will be assigned until it is resolved.

My brother seems to agree with them for now, although he has made it very clear that his life will not come to a complete halt. He dares to remind them of the woman he is involved with, one who isn't on the list of the approved where most of them are concerned. Even puts them on notice that he intends to keep his promise to her by having dinner with her family tomorrow night. While he will take the necessary precautions to ensure everyone remains safe, he is not canceling. He goes so far as to stand and walk out when those who disagree with this affair voice their objections. As he exits, he shouts over his shoulder he is not in the mood or frame of mind to have this argument again.

Of course, that leaves me sitting there amongst the sea of hungry sharks, all who intend to get their pound of flesh one way or another. When my phone buzzes again, with a notification from my team, alerting me Winnie is visiting her family at the hospital, one particular shark attacks.

"Are we boring you, Prince Esteban? Seems your phone has gone off more times than I can count." Governor Aaron Colón grumbles from his seat across from mine.

I pick up my phone and read the message, the complete message this time. "I can assure you I am not bored, sir. I am, however, a very busy man and life doesn't stop moving forward just because—"

"Nothing right now is more important than what we are discussing here. Perhaps if you would take this job more seriously, take your role more seriously, you'd be able to see that. You'd also be of use to the king, by helping the rest of us, supporting your people, by not sitting there ignoring his outrageous behavior. Nothing can come of this silly affair he is having, and someone close to him needs to remind him it is time to take his responsibility—"

"Stop! Stop right there." I warn him as I tighten my grip on my phone. "Do not tell me what I need to do where my brother is concerned. I know precisely what I need to do, and I am doing it."

"Are you?" Governor Saul Lyles leans back and crosses his arms. "Your father would not have allowed this to continue."

"My father is not here now, is he? And just because he wouldn't have doesn't mean a damn thing to me. My brother is very happy, happier than I have ever seen him. He has made his choice, and I can assure you that I fully support his choice." I glare at all the faces scowling at me, all because they don't like my answer.

"He is going to disgrace the throne and cause a revolution," Governor Cristopher Hanson gripes as if it truly upset him about Antonio's behavior. When in reality, he will be the man leading the revolution, should one occur. "Mark my word. If he continues, the people will rise up and demand he step down. When that happens, will you be ready to take over? Or will it be the first time in the history of our great nation that the third in line be granted that right? A young man like Prince Lorenzo could be exactly what this country needs. He is still young enough to be groomed in our traditional ways."

I cannot help but scornfully laugh at that statement. That is the most ridiculous statement made to date. They obviously don't know my little brother at all. Lorenzo is the least of the three of us to lie down and play nice, to follow their rules of tradition. A bitter woman had done her best to give my brother as much independence as possible since the age of four, when her marriage fell apart. She permanently moved her children to de la Peña Citadel. Around the time my sister Gabriela turned two, then refused to allow my father to dictate how those two were to be raised. Therefore, my youngest brother was in complete support of Antonio and his woman, Larkin. He'd even provided them refuge not that long ago, when it was needed, so they could work out some issues privately. Training him would be like going into the wild and expecting a ferocious lion to be as gentle as a house cat. It just wouldn't happen.

"Are you making threats, Governor Hanson? Do you honestly believe the crap that spills out of your mouth?" I begin to gather my possessions. "My brother is the most popular king to date, more popular than any of those who have come before him. He has the full support of his people. And if you were up to date on all that, you'd realize how ridiculous you sound. I suspect the people who are most threatened by him are seated in this room with me. I presume you hate his choice because it means the power you once held, when a spouse was handpicked for the current monarch, allowing you to maintain a certain ounce of control, is being ripped away. Hence, should he continue down this path, and end up marrying this wonderful woman, you'd lose that power and even your seat, wouldn't you?"

My phone buzzes again, and I am not at all pleased with the message that flashes across my screen. Seems Winifred isn't being welcomed in the manner she should be by those who are supposed to be her family. Indicating it is time for me to do what I should have done and take care of this before it gets out of hand.

"I need to go." I stand and begin to leave.

"Where do you think you are going? We still have a great deal of business to deal with here. Nothing has been solved, and we need to get to the bottom of this." Governor Colón slams his fist against the table.

"Not that it is any of your business, but I need to put a few fires out before we have a much bigger issue. Lady Winifred Batista has returned, and there is a matter that requires my immediate attention. Unless you want to deal with this?" I cross my arms and wait. When no one speaks, I continue. "That's what I thought."

"Why do you believe this is your responsibility?" Governor Lyles asks with bitterness in his voice. "Since when is it the royal family's job to settle disputes?"

I have to gather my thoughts and not allow myself to speak out of turn. Keep my mouth shut about the real reasons I feel the desire to step in. It's not that I have an issue alerting this crowd about my true motives for caring so much. But right now, is not the time or place to make such an announcement. I need to speak with Winifred first before making that sort of proclamation. She made it clear we couldn't just pick up where we left off two years ago, so I need to respect her opinion.

"She is a family friend. My brother Lorenzo and she were remarkably close growing up, still are I believe. Therefore, it is my duty as a member of the family, to offer her some support while going through such a difficult time. Surely you can respect that." I hope they are buying what I am doing my best to sell. "And as her prince, it is my honor to extend to her how sorry we are that she and her sisters are dealing with this loss. Along with the uncertainty of where her father is concerned."

Governor Ruth Niles speaks up for the first time since my brother walked out. She is one of two in this room who has shown her full support where the king is concerned. Taking a stand against several traditions she believes are barbaric. "Please offer them our condolences, Your Highness. I am positive we can continue without you and the king for now. We can put our minds together and formulate a plan on the proper manner on how to deal with this sensitive situation. Let us know if there is anything that we can do to make things easier for Lady Winifred and her sisters. Your mother, our once gracious queen, did her best to install compassion inside each and every one of you, and for that, I am most grateful."

"Thank you, ma'am." I nod toward her. "She did her best, I can assure you. Now if you'll excuse me."

I don't wait to find out if any of them object again. I hightail it out of the palace while I send a text to my men, notifying them of my intent. I am pleased to see my car waiting for me like I had requested when I arrived. My men are very good about following my orders and knowing which ones are not to be questioned.

"Any news?" I ask Stew as I climb in the back.

He spins around, and there is a gleam in his eyes that cannot be hidden. "Seems Lady Winifred has learned a few tricks since we last encountered her."

"Meaning?" I'm not sure if I should be pleased to hear that or if I should be worried. "Don't hold back."

"Just that, I don't imagine her sisters will give her as much grief as they once did. She is quite the force to be reckoned with, I hear, and put those two in their place within seconds of arriving. Took over and is now dealing with matters as they should have been dealt with from the very beginning. Braden mentioned something about how we should probably be prepared for what is sure to transpire once you arrive." He clears his throat, then gives me this expression that states he can't wait for the showdown. "You should probably say a few prayers and get ready as well, sir."

I chuckle, because what else can I do? Sounds to me like my woman has found her voice and is not afraid to take charge. I always knew she had it in her, always suspected there would be a day when she'd shine.

Two years isn't a terribly long time, but then again, a lot can happen in two years. I can't wait to verify all those changes and witness them firsthand.

"Thank you for the warning, Stew. I think I'll do just that." I inform him as I press the button to lift the window separating us. After all, I need time to prepare, and I don't need him witnessing me grinning like a dang fool, knowing this could get rather interesting.

CHAPTER 15

Winifred

The Royals

A s soon as we landed, everything morphed into one gigantic whirlwind that swept me up inside of it and kept going. I haven't had a second to process any of it, because that is precisely how my family drama enjoys playing out. Nothing has changed since I've been absent.

I arrive at the hospital within twenty minutes of stepping off the plane. I shouldn't have been surprised to stumble upon my sisters putting on a winning performance for anyone interested in watching. They hadn't even bothered phoning to notify me about the accident, so as you might have imagined, were shocked to see me standing there.

"Fred." My blubbering sister Karina comes running. Her hysterics are about as real as the heartfelt hug she offers me. "Oh. Thank God. Who called you?"

I refuse to return her fake affection and remain stalk still with my arms hanging down by my side. "Not you or Paschal."

She releases me straightaway when she hears my hostile voice, taking a step back. Hands firmly now on her hips, allowing those true colors of hers to shine. "Well, excuse me. I've been a little busy dealing with—"

"Whatever." I roll my eyes when she starts. "How is father?"

Paschal has obviously been drinking, possibly still is. I wouldn't be surprised if the stainless-steel tumbler she holds in her hand contains some sort of alcohol. She has been concealing her beverage of choice inside her multitude of cups since she was sixteen, claiming it was only juice when it was laced with so much more.

"How did you get here so fast?" She waves her tumbler at me, stumbling as she moves.

"I caught a flight shortly after noon. I would have been here sooner, but the weather in New York kept us grounded."

I had to wait three hours on the private jet before they gave us the all-clear. Making my wait on that plane ten hours total. A bumpy first couple that had me wishing Esteban were there to help me get through it.

"Father, how is he?" I ask again.

"He'll live," Paschal reports, using a tone that rakes over me the wrong way. "Or at least that's what the last doctor reported a few hours ago. Not quite sure if that is good or bad since they declared it could be a long recovery. Meaning we could be left with having to deal with all of that. Like I have time or the desire to..."

"Shut up!" I yell at her. "Just shut up!"

Karina giggles.

I can't stand any more of this. Along with the fact I have had a very long day, I'm certain I might break if they continue. Therefore, when she opens her mouth as well, it takes all I have inside of me to hold it together.

"She told you to shut up. When the hell did Fred grow a pair?"

"She's always possessed a pair." Paschal chuckles before she takes a sip of whatever she is hiding in her cup. "Apparently she's finally accepted them, and they have now given her some kind of false assurance that I won't kick her arse like I have done plenty of times before."

I genuinely hate my sisters.

"Oh yes, you were always very good at that. Remember the time you held her down and chopped off all her hair so she'd look like the boy hiding inside of her. That was priceless, and it suited her so well, made her look like a Fred." Karina is now full out laughing. "Mother was so pissed."

"Not really." Paschal seems to recall something. "Mother had to punish me because Father put up such a stink about us always tormenting his precious little Winifred. Later, however, we had quite the laugh about how Father had finally gotten the son he always dreamed of. She considered maintaining the short hairstyle and dressing this one in clothes that were more gender appropriate."

I remember my mother dragging me down to the stylist a few days after my sister tormented me. She ordered her to cut it like she would if I were a boy. Said that it served me right to have to suffer others thinking I was a boy since I acted more like one than I did a girl. Threatened to keep it so she didn't have to explain why her daughter was always climbing trees, wearing filthy clothes, and chunkier than the other girls. Claimed I'd be more accepted if I were a boy and make her life so much easier as well.

Thankfully, the stylist had refused to cut my hair the way Mother suggested. Instead, she threatened she would ban Mother from her salon if she ever heard her speak to me like that again. I had expected my mother to yank me from the chair, while she informed that woman just how she planned on bashing her to all her friends.

Except that isn't what happened. I learned an important lesson that day from the woman who cut my hair, doing her best to even make it look cute. She informed me that those who thought like my mother often forgot where they stand, who they depended on to take care of them. Power wasn't in the grips of the women like my mother. The power was in the hands of those who helped those women maintain a certain status and paint the right picture. Slapping the hand of the person who feeds you, clothes you, makes sure those wrinkles disappear, that those gray hairs are dyed perfectly, suddenly you aren't able to maintain that falsehood. No one wants to deal with a bitch.

I giggled at the woman and resolved to be more like her than my own mother.

"Mother always took pleasure in seeing this one suffer." Paschal laughs and then makes a face that makes me want to slap her. "So, are you sad, dear Fred, that you will no longer have to deal with her? I for one am not. I believe she got exactly what she deserved, and hope she suffered tremendously as her pungent soul departed this world."

That was all it took for me to have my fill. I yanked the container out of Paschal's hand and tasted the potent drink she was consuming. I was standing very close to the waiting room sink and dumped the remainder down it.

"What the hell do you think you are doing?" My sister screeches as she claws at me. "Bitch, I'll take you—"

I drop the cup in the sink as I spin to face her, seizing her hand like I had been taught to do in those defense classes I've been taking. Since I had believed I was on my own, with no one around to look after me, I decided I needed to take care of myself. Two nights a week I attend a self-defense class offered by a local community center. The instructor took it upon himself to find out why I kept showing up and relearning the same moves over and over again. I think he expected some sordid story about how I'd been a victim and was there because I was determined not to ever be one again. I guess in a way that was why I was there. I told him I was alone in the city and required to know how to not become a victim. That's when he invited me to join a different class; one that taught me more than defensive moves, while sharpening those skills, giving me even more confidence. I also believe he was hoping to coerce a date out of me but learned rather quickly that dating wasn't something I was interested in, so eventually, he gave up.

"Stop!" Karina is slapping my shoulder screaming at me. "Stop Winifred. You are going to break her arm. What is wrong with you?"

I release Paschal's hand after I've made my point. "I wasn't going to break her arm or even her wrist. It was the safest way to stop her from getting injured. I'm not the same defenseless little girl you two used to torment. I've learned a few things while I was off finding a life separate from this one."

"You had better sleep with both eyes open." Paschal is holding her arm like she is really hurting. I know she isn't, though. Sure, it is a little achy and numb, but in a few minutes, she won't even remember I brought her to her knees.

"And you are drunk, so I'm not all that worried about your idle threats. Go home. Sober up before returning. If you show up here like this again, I'll have security escort you out. Have a little pride, for Pete's sake."

I direct my attention to the other one, who is gaping at me like she doesn't even recognize me. "Take her home, Karina. I know I shouldn't be surprised, but for some reason I am. I thought perhaps this would wake you both the hell up. However, I guess when your only concerns are yourselves, that just isn't plausible. Don't return until you can show a tinge of respect for the people who raised you."

"You've lost it." Paschal points her finger at me. "Gone off to some other universe and forgotten the reality of where you came from. Your reality is all mixed up in that small brain of yours."

"I wish. Reality is not so easily forgotten, unfortunately. What I've done, is decided that the only person who can make me happy is me. I refuse to blame those around me any longer. And it saddens me that something so tragic happened to those I am obligated to call family. If you two want to continue down the same path set before you, that is your choice, but I've pursued a different route. I'll make the best of the cards I've been dealt." I don't know why I even bother sharing any of that with them. They will never understand because they are perfectly content with the lives they live.

"Delusional," Karina mumbles as she steps away. "You have no idea what the hell you are talking about, Fred."

I watch them proceed through the doorway and make their way to the elevator. I don't miss the snickering that occurs when they push the button and mock me as they step inside. They are very well aware of my fear of tight spaces and never let me forget why whenever they get the chance.

I know about as much as I did when I arrived. Those two were more interested in stirring up trouble than they were in giving me any real answers. So, after I gather my composure, I make my way to the nurse seated at the desk just outside the ICU.

"May I help you?" She glances up, and I don't miss that she seems to have been listening in on the commotion that took place moments ago.

"I hope so. I'm Winifred Batista. I was wondering if you could tell me anything about my father, Justice Ivan Batista?" I sigh, because I feel completely drained and defeated at the moment.

"Would you like to see him?" She stands and heads for the security doors. "I can have the doctor come and speak with you if you'd like."

"That would be great." I nod as I follow her. "Thank you."

"Your sister is also a guest with us tonight. If you'd like, we can stop by her room as well. She is..." She pauses and gives me a sympathetic look. "I believe her pain medications have kicked in by now, so..."

I can't help but snicker at how positive she is striving to be. "I take it she's been a handful."

"Understandably." The nice nurse defends her. "She's been through a lot since her arrival. Along with her pain, she has suffered a loss, and I'm sure is concerned about your father as well."

"Are you certain about that?" I blurt out and then cover my mouth, ashamed by my response. "Sorry, it's been a very long day."

"I understand." She stops outside a room and lays one of her hands on my arm. "I want to warn you before we go inside. Your father is touch and go. We don't know if he is out of the woods yet, and probably won't for several more days. He is unconscious and could remain that way for days or hours, only time will tell. His brain suffered a great deal of trauma, as did his spine. He broke both his legs and has several lacerations on his face that appear worse than they are. He will not look like the strong, brilliant man he is. I just want you to be prepared."

"Okay." I take a deep breath, not sure I will be able to do this alone, but knowing I don't have any other option. "I'm ready, I think."

I was not at all ready for what I encountered. The man lying in that hospital bed was broken in ways my mind wasn't prepared for. His skin is so pale it looks like death is close. The machines in the room are beeping loudly, proof it has not taken him yet.

When I reach out to take his hand, it is as cold as ice. That is when it all hits me like it hadn't yet. I drop into the chair next to him and sob for the man who had a hand in giving me life. I feel a mixture of emotions for him that is unexpected.

"Take all the time you need, dear. He's not had a visitor yet, and I believe you might be just what he needs." The nurse rests her hand on my shoulder, doing her best to comfort me.

"Does he know?" I whisper as I glance at the woman standing above me. "Has anyone told him?"

"No." She pats my shoulder, understanding what I am asking her. "It isn't our job to share news like that unless the patient asks."

"My sisters haven't been back to see him, have they." It wasn't really a question.

"No." Her hand tightens on my shoulder. "They visited your other sister, though. Had quite the reunion and were asked to step out so as not to disturb our other patients in this ward."

"Of course, they were," I mumble. "I'm sorry."

"Don't apologize for actions you are not responsible for. They are grown women, who should know how to act in public." Again, I notice the smirk on her face.

"But don't," I stutter out, doing my best not to get angry again. "I wish I could say they aren't normally like that and that this is all a result of what happened. I wish that were the case."

"Honey, we all have crazy people in our families. Every single one of us has to deal with that at one point or another." She moves away and begins messing with my father's machines, checking them. "I believe the saying I once heard is that if you don't know who the crazy one is, then perhaps you should look in the mirror."

That makes me laugh, really laugh. "Oh, I know who they all are, actually. I require no mirror for my dysfunctional family. I think my sisters have been competing for the drama queen title all these years. Still trying to determine which one of them will wear that crown before it's all said and done."

"Not. You." A mumbled gravelly voice interrupts us. "Not. You."

"Papa." I blink back tears when I hear his voice. "Shh. I'm here. Winifred. I'm here, Papa."

He squeezes my hand slightly, as his one good eye opens, and he strains to look at me. "Not. You."

"Justice Batista." The nurse shines a light in his eyes as she smiles down at him. "Hello, sir."

"Not. Her." He heavily mumbles again, and I can tell it takes a lot of energy for him to say those two words.

"Your daughter wanted to visit you. Glad you decided to show us some signs of life." She ignores his repeated words and continues checking him while she talks. "I'll let the doctor know you seem to be waking."

"You are going to be okay, Papa." I pat his hand. "Dalia too."

"Eva?" He blinks slowly. "Gone?"

I can only nod as the tears flow. I can't bear to speak the words right now. I know my parents' marriage wasn't perfect, and love wasn't really a part of it, but that doesn't mean they didn't care for one another.

A tear streams down my father's cheek, as he closes his eye and fades back into the darkness. I wipe it away and don't miss that more continue to fall. No matter what kind of relationship he shared with my mother, I suppose he loved her in his own way. She was his partner in crime for many years, and they seemed to have some sort of arrangement that worked for them.

I'm not sure what he was struggling to say by repeating, *not you*. I may never know, I guess, and that is okay. I'm just glad I was able to speak with him briefly, let him know I came home as soon as I heard.

I have a tough time figuring out why my sisters hadn't visited him when he needed them. Sure, the man was tough on us, expected a lot from us, lectured us when we continued to disappoint him. But I didn't doubt my father loved each of us in his own way. I had to believe that, to ensure my childhood wouldn't seem so heartless and depressing.

"He'll likely sleep the rest of the night," the nurse informs me as she messes with the sheet covering him. It is clear she takes great care of all her patients, and I am very grateful for her kindness. "You are welcome to stay, although it would be best if we let him rest. In a few days, he is going to need you more than he does right now."

I bring his cold hand to my lips and kiss it. After a few moments, I stand and follow her out and to another room. I don't miss how she pauses before opening the door, nor do I miss the groan that escapes her as soon as my sister starts in.

"It's about damn time one of you came to check on me. I've been suffering for several minutes now because I can't seem to get comfortable. I need to use the bathroom." Dalia practically shouts the second the door swings open.

"I've told you, you have a catheter, so..."

"I don't need to pee, you stupid bitch." Dalia has never been a patient person.

"I can offer you a bedpan." The nurse spins around with a forced smile now on her face. "I'll return shortly."

"I don't want a damn bedpan." And that is when she spots me, standing just outside the door, and directs her attitude my way. "Fred? What the hell are you doing home?"

"Nice to see you too, Dalia," I say as I step inside and walk over to her bed.

My sister is lying flat on her back with all kinds of tubes attached to her. She has a nasty bruise on her forehead, and one of her arms has a brace on it. There is no mistaking her body has been through a lot. Even though I can't see everything, I can judge by her face alone she is in pain.

"I didn't..." she waves her good arm at me. "Mother is dead."

Her bitter words send a chill down my spine. "I know."

"Who told you?" She rubs her head and winces.

"Doesn't matter. What can I do to make you more comfortable?" I ask, taking a step closer.

"Not a damn thing." She spits out with a ton of hatred behind it. "It was Prince Lorenzo, wasn't it? He called you. He's always had a thing for you."

Not true at all, about him having a thing for me, that is. Lenny and I were no more than friends. Neither of us was interested in the other person in that way because we both knew where my attraction lay. Not to mention he had no desire to get involved with anyone remotely close to resembling a proper relationship. As far as I knew, my friend pretended very well about having certain relationships, maintained a good front.

At one time, I had assumed he swung the other way, but learned that not to be true. He just wasn't interested in being used as a pawn in this game, so instead, he chose to do a little magic and fool them all. Sleight of hand is what he referred to it as a few years ago when I asked him why he dated so many girls. He stated the key was to get those interested to glance one way while distracting them from the truth of what you are up to.

"Not true, Dalia. Lenny is a friend, one that will remain strictly in that zone, by the way." I have expressed this many times before. "And it wasn't him who called me, someone else did. It doesn't matter who it was, or why this person even called. It only matters that they did, because they wanted me to know before I heard about it on the news. I'm very grateful for that, by the way.

"I just spent the last half hour with Papa. He woke for a few minutes, briefly spoke, asked about Mother, then fell back to sleep. He isn't doing all that well, and I guess that is to be expected. I imagine it will be a long road ahead to get him back on his feet."

Dalia, in her truest form, doesn't seem at all concerned about any of that. "Yeah, so I've heard. Most importantly, though, is that I will go home sooner rather than later. Perhaps this is my chance at getting King Antonio back where—"

"For heaven's sake, Dalia, just stop. Stop thinking about you for once in your life." I wish I could say I'm shocked at how selfish my sister is being, except I'm not, not really.

"And who do you suggest I think about? Father? Or is it Mother? Do you think either of them would give a second thought about me? Did the old coot even ask about me? My guess is no. He only thought of her, and I doubt he cared much either way about either of us." Dalia's scowling only makes her look a tad worse than she already does.

"He didn't ask, because I explained you were okay. And when I told him about Mother, he actually cried," I inform her with a few unshed tears of my own, remembering how sad he looked.

"Those were not sad tears, Fred. Those were tears of relief. He was relieved that he was finally rid of her miserable arse." Dalia directs her finger at me as she erupts with such hate.

My mother and Dalia did not have the best relationship. It turned shortly after she failed at locking it down with King Antonio. As I have pointed out more than once, my mother can be—could be—rather cruel. Those two have been at war ever since it all went down. Many times, I've wondered which one was going to survive when it got bad. And may I remind you it got very bad the second Mother heard the king had a new woman. What made it worse—if that is even possible—was learning this woman was not even in the same social class as Dalia. In her mind, she was a commoner, a person who didn't understand the way it all worked, or even how to be the wife of a king. Although I didn't have a front-row seat to the war brewing since the other woman showed up, I've read all about it on my sister's social media accounts. Heard my mother's displeasure when we talked last month.

Thankfully the nurse returns, giving me an out from this conversation. I leave Dalia's room, listening to her giving this kindhearted woman her opinion on what she thought should be done, and how she believes the woman should perform her job.

I step out of the ICU ward, ready to get out of here. Not that I want to go home, where the other two will be waiting to pounce again, but I could definitely use a reprieve and sleep. If I'm lucky, I can sneak in and then hide out in my room until morning.

And that is exactly what I tell the two private security personnel, who have been by my side since this all started. I guess they have been there longer, I just didn't know. I notify them I am ready to leave and then follow them down the stairwell to the garage where a car is idling, as if waiting just for us. I think nothing of it, mainly because I'm too exhausted to process anything at the moment.

Vincent opens the backdoor, and I swear he has this almost pleased expression on his face as he motions for me to get in. "Perhaps this will help."

"Nothing, I'm afraid, will help me right now, Vincent." I enlighten him as I climb inside.

I swear I jump out of my skin when I realize I am not alone in the back of the large SUV. I don't know if I want to slap him, yell at him, or lean into him while I let him do his best to comfort me after this day from hell.

Thankfully, he doesn't give me a chance to ponder too long on any of those options. Instead, he wraps me in his arms and secures me against his large warm chest.

I do my best to not react, not give him a clue how much I need this, need him. Except the sound of his voice, along with his sturdy hold, breaks down all my resolve, and has me falling apart for the second time since it all began. I give up trying to pretend I don't need this or him and let myself fall into the only person who has ever shown me compassion.

"Sir." I hear Vincent's voice address us from the front seat.

"Take us home," Esteban instructs him. "I am taking Lady Winifred back to Castile Vicente with me."

"No," I object. "Take me to my parents' place, please."

"Ignore her." He rubs my back. "Do as you're told and take us home."

I want to argue with him, but what is the point? Right now, he is in charge, so arguing will be futile when these men work directly for him. Instead, I close my eyes and let go, I let go and for the first time in two years and allow this man to hold me while I do.

CHAPTER 16
Esteban

The Royals

I know the second she falls asleep next to me. Her breathing slows to a steady pace as her body relaxes completely against mine. That slight snore of hers clues me in as well, and I cannot help but chuckle. We've bickered a few times over that when she would fall asleep during our time together. She'd expressed I had heard my own snore, not hers.

My lips brush the top of her head as I breathe in her unique scent. It's different than I remember. Before there was a coconut fragrance to her hair, tropical, I suppose maybe is what it was. Now she smells of cinnamon and sugar, like a bakery after a fresh batch of goodies recently taken out of the oven. It's not overwhelming, more like the delicious aroma has been embedded into her pores after spending so many hours inside a place that bakes those treats.

While she naps, I enjoy this uninterrupted time we are sharing. I realized, as soon as I saw her exit the hospital, how weary she was. I may not have laid eyes on her since our friends' wedding, but I can still read her body language. Every muscle in her face was tight, her shoulders were hunched, her posture defeated. Which was why I hadn't hesitated to haul her into my arms and offer her a reprieve from it all. I suspect she hasn't leaned on anyone since I abandoned her, and I hate myself more now for not figuring out a better way to deal with it all.

Forty minutes after we leave, we reached my home in Aragon. I've spent more time here these last two years than I care to admit. It was too depressing returning to my home in Cabrera, since that was the last place the two of us had created happy memories. A few of her forgotten items from that trip remained where she left them, simply because I liked the reminder she had once been there. I kept reminding myself that when she returned, they'd be right where she put them, because I was determined she one day would return, prayed for it daily.

I know I need to wake her so we can get out, except I don't want to. I'm truly afraid she will wake with a protest. Demand I take her to her parents' place on the other side of the city.

"Sir." Vincent turns around and I don't miss his smirk.

"Did she sleep on the plane?" I ask, stalling.

"No. She stared out the window in a daze. Barely touched, the meal offered her." He clears his throat. "Would you like me to take her bags inside or are we..."

"Take them inside," I instruct him. "Tonight, she will stay here. Tomorrow may be another story, but tonight, I am not accepting an alternative."

I do my best to sound as if I am completely in charge. That my ultimatum will not be questioned and my orders are to be followed, no matter what. Even though I know deep down, I would not force her to stay. If she put up a fight, I would escort her home, no matter the time.

"Set her up in the room Isabel uses when she stays with me." I realize that isn't the best idea, since that room is connected to mine.

Isabel is used to the closer quarters Antonio lives in at the palace. That residence is like a large penthouse, and not as spacious as the homes I inhabit. Not to mention that when she stays, it is typically just us. I always give her au pairs the night off since I don't have her full time. Many times, my little sister ends up crawling into my bed with me because the sounds and ambiance of my accommodations are different for her. I don't exactly mind.

I hear Vincent relay my orders to Calvin when he jumps out to open the backdoor. Meaning I don't miss the chuckle that escapes the other man, or his comment about being prepared to make a run to a twenty-four-hour chemist later.

My guards know that the woman passed out cold in my arms is my weakness. They've witnessed me more than once get carried away until it required me to distract myself, so I didn't break those rules I've lived by when it came to her. My brain, the part that often warns me about slowing down and thinking first, often misfires and shuts down around her. And it has been way too long since I have spent time with her. I have no doubt that I may do something hugely reckless.

"Winnie." I nudge her and she barely moves. "Winnie, we are home, love."

She nuzzles in farther and then shivers. My actions and voice don't wake her, nor will it. I know this because I've had to carry her to bed a few times in the past. Once this woman is asleep, really asleep, she doesn't wake easily. That means there is only one way to get her inside.

I manage to maneuver her into my lap while scooting across the seat so I can climb out without dropping her. There is no mistaking that more than her scent has changed during that exchange. Her body has gone through a transformation as well. I do my best not to dwell on it, but having her in my arms makes that nearly impossible.

My men, along with Hillary, lead the way toward the main entrance. Each one of them has had a front-row seat to the relationship developing between Winifred and me. Vincent and Hillary's team maintained eyes on her and then reported to Braden daily. I counted on him to alert me if there was an issue that required my immediate attention when he read them. It is clear he did his best to not share everything. That he took her privacy to heart, and only let me know she was doing as well as could be expected. I could have read the reports, but didn't believe I had the right to after I stepped away to keep her safe. Meaning, I had no idea what her daily life consisted of—her routine— or even if she was doing her best to stay healthy.

Hillary takes the bag from Calvin, then follows me down the hallway to the room I will settle Winnie in for the night. She opens the door and places her items next to the large bureau. "Do you need anything else, sir?"

I shake my head. "No. I have this."

She turns to leave, but before she can go, I stop her with a question. "How long has it been since she has had a proper meal?"

"Excuse me?" Hillary spins to face us. "I don't believe I understand."

"She's lost a considerable amount of weight," I explain as I place Winnie gently down on the bed. "More than I imagine is healthy."

When I glance back at the other woman, she is doing her best not to laugh at my reaction. "I suppose the fact she runs several miles, five times a week, might have—"

"She does what?" I whip my head around and gape at the woman spread out before me.

"She runs in the morning before she goes to the bakery, then again in the evening when she can. Sunday afternoons are when Lady Winifred runs until her body demands she stops. I've seen her catch a cab home many times because she literally couldn't take another step." I don't miss the respect in the other woman's voice. "I believe she does it so she can sleep at night. She pushes herself to the point she wears herself out, allowing her brain to shut off as her body demands a break. Her days mainly revolve around school and the bakery. The remainder of her free time, she stays as active as she possibly can. It's as if she understands it's the only way for her to get through without falling into a deep depression."

"You may go." I dismiss her because I don't know how to deal with that information.

I kneel on the bed and remove the white trainers and socks off her feet. There is no doubt that I should refrain from removing her jeans, except I can't imagine sleeping in a pair. Without giving it a second thought, I unbutton them and drag the loose material down her legs. I do my best not to stare at her exposed skin, not to mention those curves that drive me crazy once they are uncovered.

Standing next to the bed, I study her.

When I escorted her to the garden during her soirée, a few days after she turned eighteen, there was no mistaking she was very much a young girl still coming into her own. There was a hint of the woman she would one day grow into in a few years. I often caught sight of that woman off and on during the time we spent together before it all fell apart. Each day, I witnessed her changing slowly into a stronger, more independent woman, a woman who would become confident in her own skin.

Now that young girl is the one hidden somewhere beneath this shell. There is a suggestion of innocence about her that still shines. A purity that radiates off of her, warning a man to be careful when scrutinizing her, so as not to mistake her as also being naïve. This woman is far from naïve. She has fought for her independence and somehow made it on her own, after those she counted on deserted her. She's figured out how to become strong and grew up without anyone holding her hand.

I stare and wonder if maybe she has somehow even outgrown me. Did our time apart damage any chance I once had? She still emits everything I once found attractive about her, but in a way that is now intimidating. There is no way this woman is even in my league. No man will ever be good enough for her.

"You realize you are staring at me?" I hear her voice and startle.

I jerk my eyes off her body and find her eyes blinking sleepily at me. My hand lifts and rests on the back of my neck, and I know the smile on my face has to be a wolfish one. "Sorry."

Glancing down at her bare legs, Winifred gives her head a shake before she crawls under the covers, somehow shifting to her side, all while watching me. "Are you?"

I agitate my head, knowing she isn't stupid. "Not really. You've grown into a very beautiful woman, Winnie."

The roll of her green eyes occurs right before she sits up and leans her back against the headboard. I can't help but watch in wonder as she reaches under her shirt. It takes her a few seconds, and before I realize what she is doing, she has already done it. I nearly swallow my tongue when she drops her bra on the floor next to the bed.

"Not to mention sexy," I blurt out as I stand there and know she can't miss that I am becoming aroused.

"It's been a very long day, Stan." She yawns, dragging her fingers through her wavy hair, which appears silkier than it once was.

Dropping onto the bed next to her, I bring one knee up to the mattress so I am facing her. "How are you?"

"I've been better."

Reaching for her hand, I take it in mine and squeeze. The zing of electricity that passes between us almost stops my heart and has my brain firing off all those mind-blocking endorphins. I have to repeat over and over in my head that we cannot pick up where we left off. She is not the same person she once was and needs time.

As if reading my thoughts, Winifred tugs her hand from mine, then folds both of hers in her lap. The blush that takes over her cheeks informs me she felt what I did, but her body language confirms my earlier thoughts. She may still have feelings for me, but refuses to give into them, because, like she expressed hours ago, she is mad at me.

"What do you need? Whatever it is, all you need to do is ask, and it shall be yours." I mean that too; right now, I'd do whatever was in my power to do for this woman.

There is an expression behind her eyes I am having a tough time ignoring. She is doing her best to conceal it from me. The problem is, when it comes to us, Winifred struggles just as hard as I do. Right now, her struggle with all the other issues surrounding her is winning. It allows me to perceive more than I imagine she would like at the moment.

"I'm still mad at you." And the tone of her voice makes that very clear. "But right now, I'm willing to shelve that because I have no one else who understands."

I nod once to let her know I understand all of it. "Go on."

"I need you to hold me." Tears well up in her eyes as she admits she cannot deal with this on her own. "All night. I need you to hold me all night."

I stand and offer her my hand. "Your wish, my lady, is mine to offer, but not here. Isabel sleeps in this bed. If I am going to hold you, I am going to do so in a place I will be able to cherish the memory until it becomes a permanent reality."

She hesitates for only a moment before accepting my hand. I grab the handle of her suitcase and drag both through the connecting door that leads to my bedroom. I release them both in front of my bathroom and offer her a suggestion. "Why don't you wash the day away before we settle in for the night? While you do that, I will change into something more comfortable and be waiting for you."

Winifred tugs her suitcase through the door and shuts it behind her. I hear the shower start while I am rummaging through my closet for a pair of lounging pants and a t-shirt. I am about to slip into them when I hear her crying.

If I told you I paused and thought this through, then I'd be lying. The only thought that runs through my mind is that she needs me to hold her; therefore, I am going to comfort her no matter the cost.

The steam is thick when I open the door, but not so thick that I don't miss the discarded clothing on the floor. Again, I don't give my mind time to ponder about how very wrong this is right now. Instead, I strip off my clothing as swiftly as possible, then yank open the shower door so I can step inside.

Winifred is seated on the floor, with her head buried against her knees, sobbing uncontrollably. No sexual thoughts are clouding my brain at the moment. All I see is a woman who is suffering and needs someone to hold her up while comforting her.

That is, until she lifts her head and runs those beautiful green eyes over the length of my body and gasps. "W-what are you d-doing?" She hiccups in that soft, sweet voice of hers.

Doing my best to keep this as amicable as possible, I lean down and pull her to her feet. I notice she retrieved her hygiene products before stepping inside and make a mental note to stock up on them so they are always available for her. After, I spin her around so she is facing away from me. I squeeze some shampoo into my palm and begin massaging it into her hair. I rinse and repeat the process with her conditioner, but leave it in to do its job as I reach for a washcloth and apply body soap to it. Then I scrub her, much like I would Isabel when she was younger and required assistance in the bath. I do my best to not focus on the fact that the body I am washing doesn't belong to a little girl—ignore that it belongs to the woman who holds a very special place in my heart.

My body isn't able to control itself. It knows whose body it is currently standing so close to, with nothing between it and hers. Therefore, it gets ahead of me. Forgets about being polite and not scaring the beautiful woman trusting both of us right now. And because it has fantasized about this moment many times, gotten off on those fantasies, it is eager to attract her attention anyway it can.

"Ignore it," I grumble, disgusted with myself for not thinking before jumping. "He has a mind of his own and will be punished later for not being polite."

Winifred attempts to spin around, but I stop her. So instead, she glances over her shoulder and immediately detects my predicament. "He isn't easy to ignore."

Those words make him twitch, which causes her to giggle, which provokes him to twitch again. A never-ending vicious cycle. Hence, the reason I reach up and swat her behind. "Not helping."

She squeals and giggles, which only causes me to become more aroused as the seconds tick by.

I stand straighter and back away, so I don't brush against her, and then shove her forward under the water. While she tilts her head back, allowing the spray to wash all the soap off, I take the time to rinse myself by flipping on the second showerhead behind me. Turning my back to her, I allow the water to help me gain a segment of control. I am about to step out and grab us some towels so we can move past this. But right as I reach up to turn off the shower in front of me, soft hands slide down my back and fondle the globes of my arse. Her nails rake a path that puts all my nerves on alert, bringing me right back to where I was seconds earlier. My hands end up flattening against the cool tile walls to hold me steady while she explores.

When her nails scrap across my hipbones and land on my stomach, I feel my knees buckle. She must as well, because she tightens her hold, doing her best to support me, so I don't end up on the floor of the shower. That, unfortunately, doesn't help, probably because it presses her curvy body firmly against mine. And then, of course, there is the fact that her hand slips and lands centimeters from my growing problem.

Both of us gasp at the same time.

I reach down in an attempt to remove her hand, except she is way quicker than me. At that moment, I discover just how much this woman has changed. No longer shy about taking the initiative, apparently, since her hand is now tightly gripping me in the most unexpected place.

"Winnie." Her name is forced from my lips as my head tumbles forward, and I glance down at her small hand. "That is the most stunning sight."

Her lips brush my back as she tightens her grip on me. Those nails on my stomach dig in as well, and my lucky member begins to cry.

"Tell me how to assist you," she speaks into my back. "I've never..."

I grab her wrist and stop her, or I try. "This is not... damn."

Who knew that the caress of her small hands moving up and down my shaft would feel so good? "You don't have to do this."

My little nymph drags those nails down over my hipbone, then along my thigh. All my resolve to end this has now dissolved. I loosen my hold on her wrist so she can finish what she started.

I don't guide her or instruct her on how to continue. I do my best not to encourage her, nor do I order her to stop. No, I only watch as she moves her hand up and down my flesh until my hips follow her lead. It takes only a few ticks before I am exploding all over the shower wall and growling like some animal.

"Impressive." Winifred kisses my spine before releasing me. "I'm going to step out and get ready for bed. Give you time to clean up."

If she thinks I am going to just let her step away after that exchange, she is crazy. My brain cells stopped working the moment I exploded all over my shower walls. I reach for her as she steps toward the entrance. Bring her body to mine and crush my lips against hers.

The last time we kissed seems like a lifetime ago, and there is no doubt that this kiss is about making up for all those years we've spent apart. Not sure it is possible, but I swear it's like we are doing our best to put those lost years into this embrace. Struggling to bring us back to where we might have been had we been allowed to enjoy them.

I jerk back and hold her face in my hands so I can appreciate this new woman standing in front of me. "You amaze me."

A sly smile takes over her face. "Hurry up in here."

She rises on her toes and brushes her lips against mine one more time before she steps away. I stand there and strain to figure out what that was all about, except I don't know I will ever be able to do that.

By the time I am finished, she has vacated the bathroom. I hurry and get dressed so I can join her in the bedroom.

I find her seated on the bed, staring at her phone as if waiting on me.

As soon as she spots me, she places it on the nightstand and slips under the covers.

I crawl in on the other side and reach for her, dragging her into my arms and then tuck her securely against me. "Okay?"

"Yes," Winifred whispers against my chest.

"About earlier." I lift her chin so we are looking at each other. "That shouldn't..."

"Consider it forgotten. Write it off as a reaction to you being so caring, and me wanting to do something just as thoughtful for you." Winnie kisses my lips. "Now can we please move on?"

"For now, we will drop it." I kiss her as well. "But there is no way I will ever be able to forget it."

She nuzzles into my chest and sighs. "Me either. If this is awkward, I can sleep—"

"Nope." I tighten my grip on her. "You've been trying to sleep with me for years now, therefore you should enjoy it while you can."

She giggles and shakes her head. "Stan?"

"Yes, dear." I love hearing her call me Stan.

"What happens now? I mean, I don't expect you to go out tomorrow and announce to the world about us and all. Especially with all the stuff I will deal with while I am home. My sisters obviously can't be counted on to take the lead or be expected to make arrangements. That will fall on me. I'll need to do that first thing tomorrow; those responsibilities will take up most of my time." Winnie voice is stressed and I understand.

Looking up she continues. "I plan on returning to New York as soon as logically possible. I guess that will depend on the status of my father. He is going to need me since it is clear the other two have no idea how to handle any of this. If I don't make arrangements for his aftercare, there is no way any of them will do so."

There is a brief pause before she switches gears. "After everything is handled, after I am finished with school, I'm not sure what I want to do next. I thought about staying put, procuring a work visa, and starting over there since..."

I squeeze her against me when she leaves me hanging. "I thought I explained this to you once."

"Words proclaimed across a tarmac are not ones that can be taken seriously. I would never hold you to those, Stan. I'm not the same woman I once was, either. I have come to appreciate how to survive this world on my own. I don't need someone to hold my hand any longer. Nor do I want someone to give me a handout. I want to earn it all on my own, make my own way in life, my own choices about the life I decide is mine to live."

To hear her proclaim her independence warms my heart. Winnie is not at all the same woman who left here four years earlier, certain her future had been laid out for her. She has grown into a woman who has discovered how freeing it is to have a say in being independent, what it means to earn it.

"Then you shall be allowed to do just that. If you choose to return here when your time is finished, it would please me greatly. If you prefer to restart somewhere else, then I suppose that is when I will have to figure out how to proceed. Either way, whatever choice you make, know that I will support you and do my best to be there with you if that is what you want. Understand that no matter what, you are the only woman I desire a future with. It has only been and will always only be you." I whisper against her hair.

"I can't think about that now, Stan. I guess time will tell." I hear the doubt in her voice but don't argue with her, not tonight.

We fall asleep holding onto each other. I'm not sure what will happen next. I'm sure it won't be as simple as I'd like it to be; nothing about this has been simple.

When I wake the next morning alone, I know for certain that the journey is going to be rough. We may have shared a moment unlike any before, but there is still so much standing in our way. Until we can figure out the best way around these obstacles, I get this sick feeling in my gut I will not enjoy the next several months ahead of us.

CHAPTER 17
Winifred

The Royals

I spent two weeks in Hermosa Islas. During that time, I was the responsible family member who dealt with all those details that needed to be handled. My sisters were of no assistance. They were preoccupied by the attention they were receiving from anyone willing to give it to them. Accepting visitors when they stopped by offering condolences and then permitting as many gentlemen who offered to soothe their grief.

My mother's funeral took place three days before I was scheduled to return to The States. I held it off as long as possible because my father had stated his desire to attend. I was determined to give that to him, since he seemed to be the only other member of my family mourning her death.

Vincent and Hillary stuck by my side the entire time. I introduced them as friends who insisted on traveling with me, and no one seemed to question that. They stayed at my parents' home in one of our guest rooms, chauffeured me around, so I could multitask and not have to worry about much else. Most of the time I don't believe anyone even noticed them. They easily blend into the background. I understood why I hadn't spotted them before now; they were very good at their jobs by not drawing attention.

The only time they stepped in and took over was when I was doing my best to focus on my father. During my mother's funeral, I was responsible for him. He was bound to a wheelchair and required assistance getting in and out of the vehicle. Vincent stepped up to the plate and dealt with a man who wasn't necessarily being easy. Grief-stricken and stubborn arrogance aren't great combinations. My father was both, and that meant his temperament that day was not pleasant to swallow. Somehow, we struggled our way through, survived, and were able to get him back to the rehab facility with no one else losing his or her life.

I've been back in New York for a few days now. It was nice to leave the stress of my family behind. Dalia was an absolute nightmare to live with. She was so certain King Antonio would come to her during her time of need. After he left her alone in the hospital and then dared to bring his new woman to our mother's funeral, she went off the deep end. Her behavior was embarrassing, and I was more than ready to get away from all the drama she stirred up.

Thankfully, I'd kept up with most of my classes. My professors sent me links to their video lectures, even gave me time to make up any missed work assigned while I was absent. Meaning, I spent every single free moment these last few days catching up while getting geared up for the week we were about to enter.

The good thing, if there is one, I guess, is that spring break transpired during my second week away. So, I only missed one week's worth of classes, although, at this stage in the game, those classes were difficult, and missing any put you behind.

My front buzzer sounding has me taking my first break since I got up this morning. "Yes?"

"Buzz me in." I stare at the intercom because there is no possible way that voice is his. "Hurry it up, Winnie."

I press the button again. "Why are you here?"

"Buzz. Me. In. We can have this conversation inside your cozy dry apartment," Esteban suggests, sounding vaguely irritated.

I buzz him up and then begin pacing.

That last time I spoke with him was that first night when he dragged me back to his place. We all know how that night ended. When I woke that next morning, my earlier, bolder self disappeared. I couldn't believe I'd been so forward in the shower and touched him as I had. After suffering his gentle, caring caresses, hearing his shaky voice while he apologized for his body's reaction to it, something inside of me stirred. I tried to put it out of my mind and let the water cool me off, as it washed away the suds sliding down mine.

However, when I spun to face him, and was blessed with the perfect vision before me, I grew bold and reached out, only planning to touch that area of him. I ran my hands down his back, so I could recall how he felt when I was once again alone. I only wanted to burn that image in my brain. So, I'd be able to close my eyes and bring it to mind when I found myself getting low.

The problem was, as soon as I touched him, I couldn't stop touching him. My fingertips burned, and it was as if they moved all on their own, knowing exactly where they were heading. I hadn't meant to touch him like that, not really. His body shifting downward had thrown me off-balance, and my hands did what came naturally at that point to steady my feet. Landing on the coarse hair next to his impressive package had been unexpected.

What happened next was as much of a surprise to him as it was to me. I wasn't the type of girl who made the first move; I didn't take the initiative because I lacked confidence. Once I had my hands on him, though, it was as if I became someone else entirely. I wanted to bring him to his knees, partly because I could. I craved to give him something no one else before me had, so he wouldn't forget me as he had before.

Listening to him mumble out all those sounds and words was empowering. Feeling his body growing harder beneath my hand, as I stroked him in a way I prayed he enjoyed, watching those muscles tense on his back as his hips shifted in rhythm with my manipulation, was powerful. Hearing the roar that escaped him as soon as his member jerked in my hand, and creamy white liquid shot out of it, landing on the wall in front of him, was satisfying. My body was reacting in ways it never had before, and I tried my best to escape, so I could process what just happened.

I knew I would only have a brief window to flee before he recovered and reacted. That window was way shorter than I had predicted, though, because he had spun me around and crashed those soft, luscious lips against mine before I could object. He tasted so much better than I remembered, and I couldn't get enough. I wanted to crawl up him and offer more before I changed my mind.

Thankfully, he ended the kiss and brought me back to the reality of it all. Reminding me we were both naked and vulnerable, not at all considering what we were doing, only falling further down the rabbit hole we had dropped into. One of us had to climb out, and right then it was clear he wasn't capable of rational thought; it was up to me to put an end to it.

The loud knock against my front door brings my thoughts back to the here and now. I glance down at my sweatpants and hooded sweatshirt, believing them to be a suitable shield to protect me from him. After giving myself the proper pep talk, I march toward the door and unlock all the security between us before I yank the door open.

Esteban is standing there in a pair of jogging pants, an old sweatshirt, and dripping wet hair. He has obviously been out running; the sweat trickling off of him reveals that to me. My heart beats faster as I scrutinize him, recalling what he looks like without clothes on.

Suddenly, I don't feel like I have enough layers between us at all. If I can easily recall what he looks like, I know he can do the same.

"Invite me inside," he orders in that voice that offers no other alternative.

I take a step back and motion for him to come in. Then I retreat and head to my kitchen to retrieve a bottle of water from the fridge. He obviously needs one, and I need to get as far away from him as possible.

The front door closes, and I hear him engage the locks as I am getting him that water. When I see him approaching me, I toss it to him and step back, so there is a counter separating us. I watch him twist off the cap and then guzzle down the cold liquid. Damn, that image is breathtaking, and I am growing warm just watching him.

"What are you doing here?" I grip the counter, hoping to keep from launching myself at him.

He swallows the remainder of his water and wipes off his forehead with his sleeve before he answers. "Queens Marathon is tomorrow. I'm here as a participant. I arrived yesterday. I would have told you, but it seems you've been avoiding me since I left Hermosa Islas merely hours after your mother's funeral. How are you?"

"Busy," I fidget. "Very busy."

He flips the empty water bottle between his hands as he stares me down. I can see the wheels in his head spinning wildly, while he strains to figure out what he should do next.

We speak at the same time.

"So, you should go, because I'm busy."

"Are we good, Winnie?"

Once again, we are at a standstill, staring at each other; afraid to move, knowing the first flinch could bring us to a place that will be impossible to get out of. The sexual tension in the air is so thick, I can feel it like a dense fog surrounding us.

My eyes move on their own accord, down his torso slowly. They stop at the obvious bulge behind those loose joggers he is wearing. I quickly return my gaze to his face and am knocked back from the heat blazing in his eyes.

He tosses the empty bottle over his shoulder and begins strutting toward me. It is the kind of strut that warns me everything between us will change if he gets his hands on me.

"Please stop." I raise my palm to him.

He does as I have requested, although it is clear he is not happy about it. "Why have you been avoiding me?"

I close my eyes and shake my head as I take a much-needed breath. "I'm not ready."

Esteban drags a hand over his face and tilts his head back. "For what exactly?"

"I have three weeks of school left." I begin there. "My visa is valid until the end of August. My lease here ends around that same time. I told Melody I would stick around and help her train my replacement."

"You're coming home, then?" I hear the hopefulness in his voice.

"My father asked me to." A smile overtakes my face. "So did this guy I sort of like. He said he'd be rather pleased about it if I did. Something about me being the only woman he was interested in. I'm sure it was just a line he spoke after I gave him a hand job in the shower."

Esteban grunts and clenches his teeth, until the cords in his neck become visible. The sexiest thing I believe I've seen in a very long time. Okay, so not true. How about the sexiest thing I've seen with my clothes on?

"Most definitely a line." He finally speaks after he gains a portion of control. "You should be careful around him."

"Kind of why I've been avoiding him. Something about him melts all my defenses and brings out this crazy woman who cannot control herself. For that very reason, I thought it best to maintain a safe distance until we were both ready to do something about it." I cross my arms and hope I don't sound like some lust-driven nutcase.

"Most men like crazy women who cannot control themselves." He grins and I swear my panties melt. "He probably wouldn't object to you losing control. Perhaps you should recall that he has lost his mind a few times as well. Done stuff that he has never once considered doing with any other woman."

"Such as?" I can't help but ask. "Maybe he should refresh my memory."

"Kissed you in the garden where he first saw you, all because he wanted to see if those lips of yours were as soft as he imagined they would be. They most certainly were." He licks his, as if remembering.

"You caught me off guard that night for sure." I will never forget how shocked I was when he stopped me from speaking with my very first kiss.

"Attacking you in the stairwell nearly a year later, was in all honesty, the first time I got carried away. All I remember thinking while it was happening was how I wasn't sure if I ever wanted it to end. I'm not sure you are aware of this. I don't recall sharing this information with you, but I experienced my first spontaneous erection that night."

His words are like a magnet that force my eyes to travel southward and focus on that region of his body. "I don't believe you."

"I'm not saying that part of my body had never been awoken. I am a man, after all, who was a teenage boy who would get a woody in gym class for no particular reason at all. Talk about embarrassing, no guy wants other guys to get the wrong idea." He reaches down and moves things around. I don't miss why he needs to do so, since I am staring at that region like it is the most interesting part on him.

"I'm admitting that for most of my adult life, I've maintained a portion of control so I didn't suffer any embarrassing moments. Imagine how awkward it would be, standing in front of a crowded room where several attractive women, all dressed in outfits to grab a young man's attention, with your soldier saluting everyone."

I burst into a fit of hysterics. Several of those events he is talking about, I have had the privilege of being an attendee. I know how those women dressed in hopes to snag the Reyes boys' attention. The older they got, the lower the necklines dipped, revealing developing breasts they hoped became a focal point. It was a common topic amongst my small group of acquaintances when the dancing started. We wondered if the brothers chose their partners on cleavage reveal, or if they weren't influenced by the bosoms on display.

"You have no idea, Winnie, how difficult that can be for a hormonal teenage boy, whose little soldier only needs a warm brush of wind to affect it. Lots of practice focusing on blood and guts, lacrosse, doing extremely difficult mathematical equations in one's head..."

"Stop. Please stop." I slump over laughing, now understanding why they always looked so serious when greeting all those eager maidens. "Does it still work when you ponder on blood, guts, sporting events, or those mathematical equations? Are you able to maintain that control and keep him at ease?"

"Most of the time it does. Lately, I've not had much of an issue with him acting out unless a certain female is in the vicinity. Now I hate to admit this, because honestly it is rather embarrassing, and I'd hoped to keep this private." Esteban shuffles his feet in my direction until he is only a few steps from me. He leans forward and inhales as if recalling a memory.

I straighten and lean my hip against the edge of the counter, so I am facing him. "What are you doing?"

"You should know that you have ruined me." His eyes lock with mine. "Now, whenever I catch the slightest whiff of cinnamon or sugar, things get cloudy, and I have trouble performing the simplest math problems in my head. All the blood that delivers my brain with the food it needs to function correctly, seems to want to travel elsewhere. Do you know how many times a day I am bombarded by that aroma?"

I shake my head slowly. "No."

"So many times, that I'm certain members of my staff are going to start filing harassment charges soon. I swear Braden glared at me the other morning when he was eating a Danish while sipping his coffee. Wondering if he was going to have to deck me for thinking dirty inappropriate thoughts about him and his delicious treat—and I got the impression he thought the treat I was interested in was attached to him." How he maintains a straight face while sharing his thoughts with me, I have no idea, because I certainly could not.

"Braden is an attractive mate." I snicker and know my smile gives away how funny I believe the story is. "I'm sure he has a very sweet treat."

I squeal when I am suddenly encased in large arms and trapped against the counter. "Shame on you, Winnie."

"You are the one who brought up his sugary cinnamon treat, not me." I giggle, trying not to let my mind focus too hard on the fact I am wrapped up in a delicious treat of my own.

"Have dinner with me." Esteban leans forward and presses his forehead against mine. "I'm here, therefore I want you to have dinner with me."

I want to, I really want to. The problem is, I know that dinner will lead to me wanting more. He will want more, invite me to his hotel suite, or even invite himself back here to my place. If either of those happens, then it will move to other things, things that will have both of us fighting urges we have already succumbed to once. Therefore, I do my best to let him down as easily as I can. Or that was the plan. Before I can get the words out, the door to my apartment opens, revealing a group of my friends as they enter, carrying several containers.

"Chinese okay, Win?" Kaleb shouts over the others.

I push against Esteban's chest and force my body to step away from his.

"We voted on the way over," Nina explains. "Kaleb said it heated up best if we didn't..."

"Hello." Lindsey is grinning like some sappy lovesick puppy. "You forgot to mention Stan was stopping by. When did you two get back together?"

Kaleb glares at the man standing directly behind me. "Are we interrupting? I thought you said we should bring dinner and hit the books. Wanted our assistance so you were—"

"I did." I move in their direction, leaving Stan behind.

I was surprised to hear all the messages they left me as soon as they heard about what happened. Courtney offered to help me catch up when I got back, as did Lindsey and Nina. Before I returned to the States, Ian, Kaleb, and Tanner had left me messages as well, letting me know they would be there for me once I returned.

I cried in my childhood bedroom, knowing that this group hadn't ever stopped being my friends, even though I had done my best to push them away. They'd found ways to stay in touch. Stopped by the bakery regularly and chatted with me. Forced me to have lunch with them a few times a week when they spotted me in the cafeteria or library. Invited me to join study groups, since most of us were in so many of the same classes.

The only other people in my life who I considered true and devoted friends, were the three I went to boarding school with, Lenny, Cris, and Ingrid. We have remained surprisingly close, even though we live on different continents now. The guys are in England and Ingrid is residing in Switzerland with her husband.

I hated I had pushed these new friends of mine away when my life took an unexpected turn. It would have been so much easier to get through had I allowed them to be an active part of my life, while they distracted me.

Esteban glances around and I can sense his disappointment. "I should—"

I whirl around and blurt out the only thing that will make me feel better, "Stay and have dinner with us. As you can see, they have brought more than enough food."

"You sure?" He eyes Kaleb like he doesn't trust him. "I don't want to get in the way."

Nina wiggles up close to Kaleb and wraps her arm securely around him. "Babe?"

He directs his eyes down towards her. "Yes, dear."

"Stop glaring at him. Winifred is a big girl. We all know that whatever happened between them, was bigger than what we could understand." She glances at Esteban. "Plus, I believe there is that little matter of him being a prince that added to the issue."

I spin around and gape at them all. "When did you..."

Lindsey pops a dumpling in her mouth. "Girl, we read the tabloids. He may not be front-page worthy, but it's not like we don't know who he is. He's hard to miss. Not to mention his brother has been hogging all the attention lately. How do you feel about your brother's American girlfriend?"

Esteban shrugs. "I think he is a smart man. Able to make the right decision and should not have to worry about what everyone else thinks."

"How old are you?" Courtney is plating up some food when she asks. "They never mentioned that in any of the articles I've read."

"Twenty-seven." Esteban reaches in his pocket and growls at his phone. "I need to take this."

We watch him step into the hallway for some privacy.

"So, you two..." Courtney motions between us.

"I don't know." I sigh, not ready to share everything with them. "It's complicated. Why didn't you guys say anything?"

"Figured, if you wanted us to know, you'd have said something. It was clear that you were escaping from something." Ian wraps an arm around my shoulder. "You okay, kid?"

"Yeah." I nod, meaning that.

"Family isn't always easy to deal with. Lord knows I'd run far away from mine if I could." Tanner slides in next to me and grabs my left hand. "So, no ring yet. I was certain he'd put one on it so no one would miss the fact you belonged to him."

I blush and yank my hand away from him. "I barely saw him while I was home. I had other stuff that was more critical to deal with."

Tanner bends at the knee and stares directly into my eyes. "Something happened, though, between the two of you. A man just doesn't jump on a plane and show up for no reason."

"He is running in the Queens Marathon tomorrow," I announce, praying they don't keep pushing for more information I don't have.

"Impressive." Nina passes me a plate. "You going to tell him you signed up as well."

"No." I shake my head. "Definitely no. I plan on being in the back since it is my first. I don't need him witnessing me passing out when I reach the finish line."

"Or he could be there to encourage you. Standing just on the other side, in his sweat-soaked little racing shorts and tank. Now that would be an incentive to finish strong." Tanner fans his face, and I can't help but chuckle. I still haven't figured him out yet. I assume he might swing both ways, but he's never come out and said it, and I've never asked.

Kaleb rolls his eyes. "Tanner, I sometimes worry about you, dude."

Nina and Courtney pretend to swoon against each other as they fan their faces. "Totally agree."

Large hands grip my waist and tug me against him. "What are those two doing?"

I glance up and almost swoon at the sight of Esteban hovering above me, looking very swoon-worthy. "Who really even knows? Tanner made some comment, and they had to make him feel important and all. So, are you staying?"

He waves his phone at me. "Can't. I need to head back to my hotel and deal with this. Sorry."

"As you can see, I've got plenty to keep me busy." I shrug. "No big deal."

Esteban glances around the room and gives them all a nod before he takes my hand and drags me to the front door. "So, we good?"

"Yeah."

"Winnie, these next several months are booked solid for me. Lorenzo will transition into the family business, taking over some of my accounts and learning the ropes. Meaning, I'm going to be traveling while I train him and get him ready to take the reins. That along with my duties associated with the crown is going to keep me notably busy.

"Antonio is taking a holiday while Isabel is on summer break. Therefore, I am going to have to step into a few of his roles, so he can enjoy that well-earned break." He runs his fingers through my hair and then holds my face in his hands.

"Perhaps it is best that you will not be back until early September when things hopefully settle. I'd like to see you regularly then if you are interested."

"How about we—" I start to suggest we just wait and determine what happens. But he doesn't allow me to finish before he crashes into my lips and kisses me until I lose my train of thought.

"Finish strong here. Come home when you are ready. Know I'll be counting the days until then." He kisses me again before stepping back and heading for the stairs. I've noticed he takes them more now after hearing how I hate elevators.

CHAPTER 18

Winifred

The Royals

I return home later than originally planned. After the summer, where I spent hours working and training my replacement, I decided a holiday would be an excellent way to clear my mind. So, these last three weeks I traveled to places I always wanted to see. Took some time to get myself ready to face the obstacles awaiting me once I returned home.

A lot has changed since the last time I stepped foot on Hermosa Islas soil. Not just with my family, but the entire country is on edge at the moment. Seems the king has taken a stand where his personal life is concerned and done the unthinkable. A few months ago, he announced his engagement to the American, Larkin Cross. It has caused several ripples, upsetting those who believe he is breaking tradition and making a huge mistake.

As you might imagine, my sister Dalia is right there with them, speaking out about the outrage. She has thrown herself into the charity work my mother was always involved in, taking over those responsibilities while also promoting her own agenda. I guess the positive is now Dalia has an outlet for all that excess energy, along with ears willing to listen to her complaints while she earns a few bucks. She moved out of my father's home. Not by choice, since he sold it within weeks after being released from the hospital. Said it held too many memories. Dalia now lives in Aragon, in the heart of the city, in a very swanky condo. She is now paying her own bills and getting on with her life.

Karina began working at my father's firm a few months ago. After a long debate with him about his expectations for her to use that degree she earned and then passing her boards, he put her to work. I hear she is making a name for herself. Not necessarily a good one, but as a solicitor who deals with the clients she has to deal with, I understand it is driving her to excel exactly the way she wants. She has always been an excellent intimidator, and I'm sure the court loves her. I even believe she will one day be one of the top solicitors in her field. She resides in the same building as Dalia, not at all a shocker. Those two have had certain plans I'm convinced I don't want to know about. I always got the impression she was just as infatuated with King Antonio as Dalia was, so I've refused to ponder on why that might be.

It was a known fact that Dalia and she often went after the same men, shared them even at times. Karina enjoyed playing the field, and not dealing with the commitment it took to form relationships, while Dalia enjoyed both. I got this unsettling sense that eventually Karina would have gladly stepped into being a mistress to the king when the time was right. It seemed like she and Dalia had discussed it. Those two were a pair. One day, it would indisputably explode in the worst of ways.

Paschal seemed the most shocked when my father sold the estate. She made the biggest stink about it and wanted him to reconsider. That didn't change my father's mind, but it had put her in a predicament that forced her to make a few choices about her life. It was no surprise to hear she accepted a job with the man she had been involved with these last four years. Allowed him to set her up in a condo where he could keep an eye on her, while he continued to live a life separate from her. The life he shared with his wife and two small children. It was no oversight to realize how disappointed my father sounded about the choices she made. Neither was it a surprise that my sister made such an unwise decision.

My father is recovering gradually. After selling the estate, he bought a much smaller home closer to his office. Soon he will return to his post as one of the justices, relieving the man who had been appointed to take his place while he recovered. Ivan Batista was not a man who gave up so easily, he was a fighter and wouldn't let much defeat him.

For now, I have decided to live with him in his new place. He made it clear to me I was welcome to do so until I figured out what I was going to do next. I wasn't surprised by the offer itself, but his suggestion surprised me. I had things to figure out? I always assumed my father had it all figured out, and once I returned home, the two of us were going to need to come to some sort of understanding.

I've been home for a few days now and have put this off long enough. My father is sitting in his home office. He has had his morning coffee and taken a few phone calls. I spent my morning in the kitchen, baking a treat I know he will enjoy, hoping it will soften him enough to hear me out.

I knock on the door and wait for him to acknowledge me. Taking a deep controlled breath, I offer a prayer before stepping inside, carrying a large cinnamon roll fresh out of the oven.

"I wondered what that delicious smell was coming from the kitchen. I see Sue Ellen has been busy this morning." My father waves me over to his desk and motions for me to set the dish down and take a seat. "Thank you for bringing me a treat."

"Sue Ellen isn't the one who made this." I set it down and then just blurt it out. "I did."

"You did?" I hear suspicion in his voice. "When did you learn how to make something as yummy as this?" He rips off a portion of it and shoves it in his mouth. "Damn, that is good. So, when?"

I take a seat and fold my hands in my lap. "Sue Ellen first taught me when I was younger, piqued my interest."

My father raises an eyebrow and motions for me to continue.

It's now or never, I suppose. "While I was in New York, getting my business degree, I also did an apprenticeship at one of the local bakeries. Melody taught me everything she knew about running a business. She also allowed me to get my hands dirty while I experimented with a few recipes of my own. I loved every second of it."

I watch as my father deliberates over what I just shared with him. He points at the cinnamon roll and asks, "One of your creations?"

"Yes. It's a basic recipe that I added my own flair to." I shift nervously.

"So, the entire time you were meant to be learning about business, studying marketing, along with spreadsheets and how it all worked, you were also playing around inside a bakery?" I hate how he is making it sound.

"I was getting some hands-on experience while working my arse off and keeping my grades up to the standards you always demanded." I do my best to defend my actions. "It taught me more than the books ever could have. I was able to apply all the knowledge I was studying and determine how it worked in the real world. Bookkeeping was one of my main focuses while working for Melody. I set her up on a system that made it all so much easier and only a click away. Trained my replacement, so that Melody could continue to focus on the portion of her business she most enjoyed."

A rare smile nudges the edge of my father's lips. He leans back in his large chair and stares at me for several long minutes. "You graduated with honors, Winifred. Don't sell yourself short. It sounds like you did that while holding down a full-time job. That my dear is very impressive, and exactly what I have always expected out of you."

"Thank you, sir." I let out a lung full of air I didn't realize I'd been holding.

"Don't thank me just yet." He clears his throat. "I assume we are discussing this because you have some sort of interest in this type of business."

"Yes." I nervously shift my hands around in my lap. "It's been a dream of mine, since I was a young girl, to one day own a bakery."

He taps his finger against his top lip while he thinks. I know that means he is about to let me know a few details I am not going to want to hear. "Before I can allow you to do that, we need to clean up a few matters. Negotiations have been in the works with a few gentlemen. Your mother had been handling them."

I start to object, but he stops me with a raised hand.

"Hear me out, before you inform me you are not interested in any of that."

"Fine." I cross my arms and I know my body language reveals my thoughts.

A smirk takes over my father's face. "As you know, there are some stipulations laid out in the terms of your trust. One of those terms states you are not eligible to touch it until you have reached twenty-five or completed a list of requirements. Those that your mother and I predetermined."

"One of those being that I marry a man you two have chosen for me." I cannot believe what I am hearing.

"I believe that was once stated in the terms, yes. Your mother and I revisited those terms a few years ago when it became clear this country was moving away from those types of arrangements." My father seems rather pleased that he has shocked me.

"Excuse me?" I hear myself ask. "No way mother agreed with that."

"You're right. She didn't agree with me changing it at all. However, since I am the one who has always made most of the important decisions in our family, I insisted on it. I agreed to allow her to have a slight influence on how to reword those terms, providing her a chance to convince you her way was best for your future."

"What does that mean?" I am so confused right now; I don't dare try to figure out what these new terms entail.

"You are no longer obligated to marry a man we have chosen. You only need to consider those we have selected, by taking some time to get to know them. If you don't agree with any of our selections, after proving you've given them a real shot to win you over, then you will have fulfilled that particular stipulation." He shoves a folder at me and waits for me to take it. "Inside are the three men your mother felt best suited to you. I have met with each of them regularly and find them all applicable choices as well."

"You can't be serious." I retort as I study the names on what seems more like a résumé.

Lord Hector Colón is the first man I come across, and I want to throw up. The other names are no better, Lord Ernest Rupert and Lord Mitchel Dewar. Dewar was a surprise, since he was closer to my age and not as influential as the other two men.

"Lord Dewar is no longer interested in moving forward." My father surprisingly laughs. "Seems he was only doing so to please his parents while pursuing a woman that better suited him. He has apologized for wasting my time, but is now married to his very pregnant wife, one of his mother's friends, who is quite a bit older than he is."

"Holy shit." The words slip out before I can stop them. "Wow."

"My thoughts exactly," he laughs. "However, the other two gentlemen are very much still interested. Both willing to move forward as soon as you are."

I hate I am even considering this. "How long is considered a reasonable amount of time before I may dismiss them?"

Again, my father laughs. It is a sound I haven't heard a lot of over the years. "I will let you be the judge of that. After you meet with each man at least once, if you choose to dismiss him afterward, then that is your choice. Keep in mind, however, that the money will remain untouched until you turn twenty-five unless you marry."

"Are you suggesting I marry one of these two men just so I can get my hands on my trust?" I have to ask. I wouldn't put it past my father to suggest that, hoping I will fall in line like I always have.

"Absolutely not. I'm simply pointing out, that if you are expecting to use that money to start a business, like the one you mentioned earlier, then perhaps it would be worth giving them a shot." He rests his forearms on his desk.

"Do you believe either of these men would allow me to work? Start a business like the one I mentioned?" I have my doubts about either.

"I guess that is something you should ask them yourself." He nods towards the cinnamon roll. "Perhaps you should entice them by displaying your skills. It worked on me."

"You really wouldn't object to a daughter of yours opening a bakery?"

"Surprisingly, no." He shakes his head, displaying his own shocking revelation. "I am honestly impressed you know what you want and are willing to take a chance. I've had some time lately to figure out what is important in this life."

We stare at each other in silence.

Then my father surprises me once again. "My guess is that you already have a plan. I believe it would be in your best interest, to put this all behind you so you can move forward with that plan. Fulfill your mother's last wishes by doing this in the way she wanted, but don't allow her wishes to impede those plans. Once this is all behind us, you will be free to live your life the way you have always dreamed of, with no objection from me."

I tuck the folder under my arm and stand. My father has thrown me for a loop, and I'm not sure I trust him. If what he says is true, after I dismiss these gentlemen, I will finally be free from the hold my family has always had on me. If he is lying, then I have nothing to lose, because I was planning on walking away from it all, anyway. There was no way I was going to allow anyone, other than myself, to decide the direction my life was heading.

I'm not sure I'd have been able to say that and mean it four years ago. My time abroad had provided me with enough freedom to know I could never be satisfied with that kind of life. Not to mention the man who has invaded my life, seems to want me to be exactly who I am while I take charge of how I get that life. Now I just need to be brave enough to reach out and grab it with both hands, and then pray that once I do, everything I have ever dreamed of will follow.

CHAPTER 19
Esteban

The Royals

I've done my best to not push Winifred before she was ready. After my trip to her apartment in New York, I once again backed off but no so much she thought I was ignoring her.

For example, as soon as I heard about her running in the Queens Marathon, the same one I was there to run, I didn't intrude on her desire to do it all by herself. I'm not saying I didn't keep an eye on her, because I most certainly did. I delayed my start until her designated group started and then maintained a safe distance.

The pride I felt watching her finish was overwhelming. Which is why I couldn't stop myself from wrapping her in my arms once I crossed the finish line a few seconds behind her. I'll never forget her words as long as I live.

"Don't think I didn't notice you, Stan. You weren't fooling me by staying a respectable distance behind me."

"I just—"

She raised her fingers to cover my mouth.

"I know and appreciate it. I admire the fact you allowed me to prove I could do this by myself... well, sort of." Her head dropped to my chest as she wrapped her arms around me. "It's refreshing to know you always have my back, even from a distance."

We spent the rest of the day recovering. I made sure she rehydrated properly, ate the right kinds of food that would help her body regenerate faster. I even scheduled her an appointment with a masseuse the following day to work out all those aches and pains.

The next time I saw her was on the day she graduated. No way was I missing that. Once again, I found myself proud to discover Winifred Batista graduated with honors, which I know is no easy feat. I took her to dinner later that evening, along with all her friends, since that had been their original plan. At the end of the night, I hadn't allowed myself to ask what the future held for her. I didn't want to make her feel obligated to do something she wasn't interested in doing. Although I was comforted by her words once again, held them close to my heart.

"Thanks for coming. It means a lot you are here."

I squeezed her hand. "No place else I'd rather be."

She leaned in and placed a sweet kiss against my lips. "Which is why it means so much to me. I'm thinking of taking a mini-me holiday after I finish here. I just want you to know so you don't worry."

"I'd be glad to join you." I had to try.

"I need some time to sort out a few issues alone, Stan. Have one last hurrah, so to speak, before I find myself so busy, I won't have time to think." She let her eyes find mine and smiled. "But not too busy for you."

Not long after that, I found myself very busy, almost too busy. Between training Lorenzo to take over the family business, and me stepping in so Antonio could have this time, I barely had time to sleep. But none of that stopped me from doing my best to keep the lines of communication open with Winifred. We talked on the phone at least once a week. Texted almost every day, multiple times each day. I even sent her a few long emails, where I did my best to express how much she meant to me.

I returned to Hermosa Islas only hours ago. Since Winifred's holiday, where she requested time to sort things out, I haven't once been in communication with her, except through a few emails. So, I'd been planning on contacting her almost immediately once my day wound down and I was free to do as I pleased.

Expect I didn't get the chance to do that. My brother Lorenzo informed me we were meeting Antonio and his fiancée at the opera house later. My first thought was it would be the perfect opportunity for me to invite Winifred to be my date, get a read on what everyone thought about it. Again, I wasn't awarded the chance to do even that. Lorenzo had already taken care of my date for the evening, one that was a friend of the date he found himself indebted to. I couldn't argue. Not once he explained how he had promised the young lady who was his date, to take her the next time he went. It seems he lost a bet with her, one he wasn't necessarily sad about losing, although he refused to share what the bet was. And because I knew Lorenzo would never set me up with a woman who misunderstood why I was helping my brother out, I went without arguing.

We'd arrived early and met our dates there, saving us the awkwardness of making small talk longer than necessary. And because the ladies were friends, it made the conversation flow smoother between us. These two women are very good at not needing assistance in discovering subjects they liked to discuss. Which meant Lorenzo and myself could sit back and relax while those two chatted it up. I have no desire to be here. It has been a very long summer. I was ready to put it all behind me and hunt down the woman who was crowding my thoughts.

As soon as we take our seats in our family box, I allow my eyes to search the crowd for familiar faces. Directly across from us is a man I have been keeping a very close eye on for the last four years. He is one of the men who at one point expressed interest in my Winifred when she was barely eighteen. A man ten years her senior, with a reputation that suggested he was not worthy of her time.

Which explains why I almost drop my drink the second I spot her entering his private booth. "What the hell?"

"Something bothering you, Your Highness?" My date, Lady Bella asks when she hears my objection.

I turn to her and do my best to smile. "Just saw something I don't entirely appreciate. How old are you, Lady Bella?"

That question causes her to blush. "Twenty-two."

"Tell me something. Would you date a man ten years older than you?" I know it's an odd question, but I don't understand why so many often do.

"I suppose if he were the right gentleman, I might consider it.

Although I don't believe I would. Seems like a man ten years older than me should either already be settled down, or interested in a woman closer to his own age. I'm not sure we'd have a great deal in common." She answers me honestly and then follows my line of sight and giggles. "Awe. Now I believe I understand."

"What do you believe you understand?" I ask, perplexed she sounds so confident.

"I'm not so sure Lady Winifred is interested in a man like Lord Ernest. If what her sisters have been suggesting holds any truth, then it seems she is here with him because her father asked her to consider him as a potential husband." She sounds a little disgusted by it all.

"Excuse me?" I realize I am about to show my hand.

"I heard Karina and Paschal making a big deal out of it earlier. According to them, their mother was negotiating with a few men, where her youngest daughter was concerned. They suggested that after matters with the duke went south, Lady Eva wasn't willing to take any more chances with Winifred. Those two seemed to find it quite humorous while doing their best to make it sound as if their sister wasn't capable of doing better than a man like Lord Ernest."

"Bullshit," I blurt out before I can stop myself.

"My thoughts exactly, Your Highness. Out of the four Batista sisters, I believe Lady Winifred is the one most likely to attract a man with some class." I don't miss the grin that says she is seeing more than I might be comfortable with. "Don't worry, sir, your secret is safe with me. I'm not one to go spreading rumors out of school. She is one very lucky woman, to have a man such as you so concerned about her well-being."

Lorenzo has suddenly joined in on our conversation. "I swear brother, I will hurt you something fierce if you don't correct that very soon."

"Correct what?" Lady Ceria perks up as if thirsty for information.

"I was just telling Prince Esteban that I believe Lady Winifred could do so much better than Lord Ernest. Told him what her sisters were so eager to share with us before they arrived. Explained how I suspect she was only doing her best to satisfy her father's request and meet with the men her mother and he had approved of. I was about to disclose that it was clear to everyone earlier how she was not interested at all in him.

And that several of us suspected her to dismiss him before the night is over."

Lady Ceria glances across the opera house and smiles. "Or perhaps she will dismiss him sooner after that little move."

My head spins around so fast I will probably suffer from whiplash later. I all but leap from my seat when I spot the man pressing his mouth to hers. It is obvious she did not encourage him to do so.

After she recovers from his boldness, Winifred gives him a solid shove and then slaps him harshly across the cheek. She then stands abruptly and points her finger in his face. I'm not sure exactly what she is saying. But it is clear she didn't appreciate his little move, and will not be sticking around to suffer his company for one more second. As she starts to storm off, he stops her and appears a little remorseful. He urges her to sit back down, even motions to the empty seats that are currently unoccupied behind him.

When another couple joins them, I watch her huff as she takes one of those seats far away from him. She then turns to talk with the woman who joined them. It doesn't take long for Lord Ernest to pardon himself after glancing down at his phone, clearly making up some excuse that will allow him to bow out gracefully.

"I'd say he just got dismissed and will not be back, or even pursuing her any longer." Lady Bella nudges me with her elbow. "Breathe."

"If he knows what is good for him, he'll not show his face in my company," I grumble.

The lights dim, indicating it is almost time for the opera to begin. Although, it is not so dark that I don't miss Winifred making a quick exit.

I can't let her leave. "I am going to order a refill. Do you want anything?"

Lady Bella shakes her head and smiles. "No, thank you. Perhaps you should check out the other bar. I do believe I heard this one stopped taking orders at curtain call. Maybe that one will still be open."

I don't miss what she is suggesting, just like I know she didn't mistake my departure had nothing to do with me needing a drink. "I might do that."

As I step out to leave, the usher offers to get me whatever I might desire, so I don't miss anything. I wave him off as I walk into the mostly empty hall, then wander to the opposite side of the opera house, where Winifred was seated moments ago.

She is pacing the corridor nervously, glancing back toward the bar area, where one bartender is mixing a drink. I stroll up to the counter and receive attention immediately.

"Your Highness, what can I get for you?"

"The drink is for Lady Batista?" I ask as I glance at the woman still pacing.

"Yes, sir." He finishes it and places it in a glass with just the right amount of olives.

"I'll make sure she gets it. Thank you." I slap a large bill on the counter and snag the drink.

Winifred was oblivious to me until I stepped around the pillar and am now standing directly in front of her. At that point, she halts her pacing and stares at me with a tinge of shame displayed on her face.

"I believe this is for you. I'm guessing it is essential to aid in the disinfecting of your mouth after Lord Ernest dared to put his lips where they do not belong." I pass her the martini while I maintain eye contact.

"It's not at all what it looked like." She takes the glass and shivers when our fingers graze. "Tonight was supposed to be about me putting an end to an arrangement I never agreed to. It seems he misunderstood."

"That is saying it lightly." I notice a door to my left marked private and step toward it so I can determine if it is locked. When the knob turns, I smile, knowing I am taking full advantage of this mistake.

"When did you get back?" I hear Winifred ask as I release the doorknob and take a few strides toward her.

"This afternoon. I was planning to call you, but your good friend Lenny needed a wingman, and I was elected to be his." I place a hand on the small of her back and encourage her to just trust me. "I will be refusing all other wingman obligations from this day forward."

Winifred allows me to guide her while she tries to figure out what I am talking about. "Does that mean you are on a date, then?"

I don't answer her. Instead, I reach for the handle, as I shove her inside the room with the private sign visible on the outside. I assumed it was some sort of office or perhaps a preparation area. I was wrong on all accounts. It seems I have just shoved us both into a small closet where they store everything necessary to clean the opera house once closed.

I don't even notice right away, because I am more interested in kissing the woman I shoved inside. Eager to erase all traces of him from her lips while putting my taste on them instead. It isn't until I come up for air, reach for her glass so she doesn't spill it, then finally locate the light switch, that I realize my mistake.

Winnie is still blinking slowly when I laugh at the irony of our surroundings. We are literally in a closet where I am stealing kisses from her, so no one will be the wiser about us. Reality slaps me in the face and shows me how utterly ridiculous this entire fiasco between us has become.

"Why are you laughing?" She asks me as she touches her lips and shakes her head. "Oh. So, I guess we are in a closet."

I point at her martini at her and nod. "A metaphor, I do believe, that shouts at the irony of what we have become. While I know the phrase usually means something entirely different, it is fitting at the moment."

"Because from the beginning, we have been hiding in a proverbial closet in hopes to keep those who felt they knew best out of it all." Winifred glances around and lets the space we are standing in speak to her. "It's even a little messy, much like the one I believe we've found ourselves inside of more than once."

I set her drink on the shelf and take her hands in mine before I speak my next words. "I'm finished hanging out in the closet with you, Winnie. I want to come out of it with you secured to my side."

"I'm game for that. I have another matter I need to take care of first. Once I have put it behind me, clarify that I will be making my own choices from this point forward, I think we should do just that." I don't miss that she put a contingency on my desire to take this public.

"How long until that will be a reality? Am I expected to wait another four years for you to get your house in order?" I know I sound like a bitter man who has reached his breaking point. "I'm sick of waiting, Winnie."

"I know, Stan. One more order of business before we can do just that. It is important that I handle this on my own. There are reasons I am not ready to get into at the moment, but I need you to trust me."

She removes one of her hands from my hold and reaches up, caressing my face with her soft palms. "I am doing this, so I am completely free to make all those choices where my life is concerned. Free to make you a part of that life should you decide it is what you want."

"Do not doubt that you are exactly what I want, what I have always wanted," I inform her as I tug her closer. "I hear there is a party at the palace tomorrow night, an engagement party."

"Please don't." Winnie blinks with deliberation. "I'll be there, of course, but that is not the time for us to come out, even if I were ready to do so. I imagine this mess will be cleaned up soon, but not that soon. Plus, I think your brother, and his fiancée should be the focus at their party. It is their turn to make whatever statement they need to for others to hear. Not have someone steal their thunder and possibly create even more storm clouds that will dump on their relationship. Our time will arrive soon enough."

"Promise?" I press my forehead against hers.

"One way or another, Stan, I promise you that my plan involves us having the ending we always dreamed of having." She presses her lips against mine. "Nothing could change my mind about that."

I want to believe her.

Forces have been pulling us in so many different directions all these years, I have my doubts. It seems like something always gets in the way and throws us off the direct course to where we hope to end up.

CHAPTER 20
Winifred

The Royals

I'd planned to attend tonight's celebration alone. I certainly didn't want to show up with a date that would rub the man who held my heart the wrong way. That being said, I also wanted to desperately put everything behind me so I could begin focusing on my future.

When Lord Hector Colón showed up to accompany me without my knowledge, I almost declined his offer. Found it rather presumptuous of him to assume I would not have an escort and therefore required one. My father encouraged me to let the man do his best to prove himself. So, against my better judgment, I obliged both men and joined him for the evening.

My father heard how awful my previous evening had ended and didn't seem surprised about it. He accepted my decision that Lord Ernest Rupert and I were not going to work. He didn't raise a stink about me not giving the man a second chance, but instead agreed I hadn't written him off before he had the chance to ruin it himself.

It made me wonder if perhaps the accident had truly given him a new perspective on life, or if he was simply playing some sort of game with me. Since returning, I hadn't seen the man he once was, had only been witness to the one he appears to be now. I was still skeptical about such a drastic transformation, although I have heard about how traumatic events often bring on an entirely new perspective, changing a person's view on life. I hope that is the case where my father is concerned.

We enter the palace and join the long line of guests where King Antonio and Madam Larkin are expected to receive us. I still have to chuckle when I think about how the king first introduced his new woman to my sister, why she possessed a title above hers. Not that the future queen allowed him to use that title. She insisted everyone refer to her as miss. That didn't stop most of the kingdom from using the once declared title out of respect for their king.

As we get closer, I am surprised to discover the king standing there with his mother instead of his fiancée. Several murmurs are traveling down the line. They are discussing how is it obvious a common woman, such as her, has no knowledge of how vital it is to properly receive her guests. Now giving those who wish to discredit her more firepower.

Hector is one of those complaining. "This is why it is essential one maintains protocol in these matters. A woman such as her has no idea what it means to hold such a significant title. There should be a law erected to prevent this kind of behavior. He should have chosen a woman who was more suitable for the title and role. There are plenty of lovely acceptable ladies willing to accept such an offer."

"Wow. Just... wow." I have no words at the moment. "So, duty over love is the one true and only way."

"Precisely." He places his hand on the small of my back, and I step forward to escape that unwanted contact. "I'm glad to see you agree."

I see no point in informing him I do not agree because my words will only fall on deaf ears. He has proven that more than once tonight when I said something that contradicted what he had already made clear. He either ignored me completely, or alerted me I did not know what I was talking about, and therefore should not worry my little head about important issues.

The second I catch Madam Larkin stepping up behind the king, then appreciate how she touches him in a way that displays so much, I want to cheer. No other woman in this room would dare lay her hands on him like he was only a man. They could never forget that he was a king first to them.

Last night, it was made clear more than once this is why the king fell so hard for the woman he is now staring at with adoring eyes. She sees him as a man first and foremost, one who has obviously captured her heart. While she understands he is also a king, his title does not define who he is. It is simply the role he was born into and one he takes seriously. Being king is his job, and one's job should not be the only role a person takes on in life. She even dared to state that it is important he also be allowed to be a man, a friend, a lover, a husband, and hopefully one day a father. All who also happen to be a king when called upon to do so. Which is when I decided I liked her so very much and would give her my full support moving forward.

After an exchange of words with my sisters, of all people, King Antonio and Larkin excuse themselves and head down a hallway that is very well hidden. I can't help but wonder what they might be discussing, or even plotting. Her fancy dress has my mind doing a little speculating about what sort of event this might end up turning into before the night is over.

We are about to shake hands with Her Royal Highness Angela when I spot Stan approaching from the long hallway just behind her. No man should look so stunning in a suit; a suit I don't miss seems a little formal for such an occasion. I am staring, because I cannot help myself. Then I am blushing the moment I feel his mother grab my hand and draw me closer.

"Lady Winifred, I believe I understand what has you so captivated," she whispers in my ear as she places a kiss on my cheek. Not everyone gets a kiss from Her Royal Highness. "How are you managing? I do so hope I will get the pleasure of seeing you again for a family dinner soon. Perhaps once things settle, Prince Esteban will bring you with him. He misses more than he should and needs a good woman to encourage him to visit his mother more often."

Esteban steps up next to his mother and takes my hand from hers. "I think that is a lovely idea, mother."

He then tugs me closer, so he too can place a soft kiss on my cheek, before he mutters his thoughts in my ear. "You seem to have picked up a leech since the last time I saw you. I do so hope you will get rid of him rather swiftly. He seems to be holding you back from your true potential. A woman such as you needs a much more sophisticated escort, one who would allow you to shine like the diamond you most certainly are."

I don't have time to respond, because Lord Hector is on me quickly, urging me forward and away from the prince. "Prince Esteban, I see you are once again disturbing my date. Are you not capable of getting your own? That really is a shame."

Esteban growls as he offers Hector a very clear warning. "I have a date. Right now, I am trusting her to look out for herself. But don't think should I get any intuitions that matters are not going so well, that I won't step in and claim her for all to see. You, Lord Hector, have been warned."

I want to do a little growl of my own after he all but staked his claim on me like that. Except I can't help but appreciate he felt the need to not sit back and watch me with yet another man that isn't him.

"Did he..." Lord Hector doesn't sound at all pleased. "Are you two?"

I should deny it. I should refute it until I am blue in the face because that seems like the proper thing to do, the way others would have handled this minor incident. However, I am not capable of denying it any longer, pretending that nothing is going on between us. So, for the first time since it all began, I decide it was time to come clean.

"We started as friends who were very attracted to one another. After I had been in New York for almost a year, interactions between us changed. They changed again when his friend got shot, and there were implications that it somehow had to do with the rumors surrounding our involvement. Two very tough years later, he has re-entered my life. And right now, we are negotiating the terms." I figure it best to speak his language.

"Your father never mentioned another party had entered negotiations. It is in our agreement that I be made aware of any changes," he grumbles, and then all but stomps the remainder of the way to the Throne Room. "This is unacceptable. I will be making that very clear later when we sit down to finalize it all. I expect to be compensated for him breaking our arrangement."

I roll my eyes following him, grabbing a flute of champagne off a tray when it passes. I am going to require a great deal more bubbly liquid to get through this evening. "Perhaps you should explain this arrangement you believe you've made with my father."

"One does not discuss such matters with a woman," he informs me as he sips on the flute he grabbed for himself. "It has been taken care of, and that is all you need to know."

I raise my eyebrows so high, I am certain they reach my hairline. "Perhaps you can at least explain to me how you struck such a deal with him, then."

A sly smile crosses his disturbing features, and I shiver for reasons I don't like. "I believe we met the day after your soirée to begin negotiations, but those were halted when the duke displayed some interest. Once that was resolved, I quickly took advantage and made certain I would not be denied what I was promised. As I stated, it has all been taken care of, and soon, Lady Winifred, we will make it official. Prince Esteban, I'm afraid, is too late and will—"

"I'm not entering into anything with you, Lord Hector. I only agreed to allow you to escort me tonight so I could clarify that this was never going to go any further." I down my drink and place it on a tray when the server walks by.

"Then you will do so with nothing but the clothes on your back." He grins and I want to slap him. "I'm afraid your mother and I made certain that should you dare refuse me, you would be left with nothing."

I slowly blink as a few realizations settle in my head. "You hired someone to take a shot at Darius, all because you believed it was me with whom he was involved."

He shrugs and wobbles his head. "Proving that would be impossible. And I'm not about to admit something like that to you. It's a shame, though, that he suffered something so tragic when it seems he was not the one overstepping into another man's territory."

"I am not your territory. Now or then. Nor will I be anytime in the near future." This man is crazy. I should tread lightly so I don't upset him, forcing him to do something even more outrageous.

I leap out of my skin when I feel a hand wrap around my arm from behind. "Is there a problem, Lady Winifred?"

I spin to find a member of Esteban's personal security standing there, looking rather concerned.

Behind Lord Hector, I notice Hillary and Vincent approaching, dressed as one of the many guests. They blend in, like always. I have never been so happy to see them.

Hillary steps around Lord Hector and places a friendly kiss on my cheek. "It is so good to see you again, Lady Winifred. Why don't you join my husband and me, so we can catch up and hear all about your adventures in America."

"She's with me," Lord Hector objects, while staring at the woman he is doing his best to place.

"I was with you," I boldly state, desperate to get away. "I am no longer interested in keeping your company. I would love to join you, Lady Hillary."

Vincent flanks my other side when Stew releases my arm. "I believe you heard the Lady. She will no longer require your company for the remainder of the evening. Perhaps you should have heeded Prince Esteban's warning and realized he has eyes and ears everywhere."

"This is not over," Lord Hector announces with determination. "I always get what I want in the end. It will be no different this time."

Stew steps in front of him as a warning to back off and let me go, which he does. I am led immediately away from the seething man, who at least is smart enough to know not to react here, where he will not get away with it. Instead, he watches me with am ire in his eyes that has me grateful we were not alone when this all went down. It makes me wonder if my father realized it was safer for me to deny him in a public location rather than in a more secluded one where I would have had to deal with him on my own.

"Are you okay?" Hillary questions me as she guides me to the front of the room.

"Yes. It was him who hired the man who shot Darius." I then explain what he said and watch her eyes widen. Not in disbelief, but something else. "You already knew that, though, didn't you?"

"He actually told you that?" I don't miss how she neglected to answer my question.

"In so many words, yes." I grab another flute and take a healthy gulp. "How long has he been a suspect?"

"About ten minutes." She smiles and I roll my eyes. "We've had eyes on him for quite a while now. We've been tracking his assets for over a year. Several months ago, he seemed to have come into a great deal of money that no one could figure out precisely where it originated from."

I pause and glance back over my shoulder where we left him standing. He has moved along and is now chatting with a distinguished group of aristocrats. His father is amongst them. I watch as they scowl at me with disapproving eyes and know the answer to my next question before I even ask it.

"How much money, exactly?" I maintain eye contact, not about to let them intimidate me in the least.

The number is precisely what I had expected, but what I didn't expect was to hear what follows.

Vincent steps into my line of view and forces me to glance up at him. "We believe your mother paid him off to have your father killed. Used the court ruling as an excellent way to cover her tracks."

My knees buckle and I feel Hillary's arm wrap around my waist. "She paid... why?"

I don't get an answer, because the formal announcing of the royal family interrupts us. I try extremely hard to pay attention to what is going on around me. Except my mind has blocked most of it out, while I try to process the overload of information. It does, however, come back when it hears the man making the introductions, announces the King and Queen.

"Did he say, queen?" I whisper in Hillary's ear.

She smiles widely and nods. "He did."

I watch as King Antonio and Queen Larkin proceed down the aisle, wearing the colors and unmistakable crowns. They look divine and united as they march together for the first time. A sure sign that they have duped us into believing this was a simple party, when in reality it is anything but.

I bow out of respect as they pass and then glance up to find Prince Esteban eyeing me with concern. Does he know?

"Prince Esteban would like for you to join his party," Vincent begins.

"Can you take me home?" I have no desire to be here right now.

He shakes his head. "I'm sorry, Lady Winifred, it is safer if you stay."

I nod and listen as the king and queen make their announcement and decree. I don't take my eyes off Prince Esteban while I take in every word. Doing my best to not lose my composure that will surely have him acting out. It is in my best interest to keep a level head and let those in charge investigate.

Tonight is a celebration, and I will not ruin it. So, I do what I have done most of my life. I pretend all is well.

CHAPTER 21
Winifred

The Royals

I am unable to escape the inevitable once they relocate the party into the dining hall. Even though I attempt to convince my escorts to relay my trepidation about joining the royal family, I am ignored. In front of the entire room full of already surprised guests, I am ushered forward to where I am, then passed off to the man making demands.

"Your Highness." I give the appropriate curtsy out of respect when what I really would like to do is cross my arms and show my disapproval.

"Lady Winifred." He takes my hand and places a kiss on the back of it, sending all kinds of crazy heat through my veins.

"I shouldn't—" I start to deliver my objection, but his mother's voice stops me from continuing.

"So glad you could join us, Lady Winifred. I didn't like the company you were keeping earlier. Therefore, I requested the Countess and Earl intervene on my behalf." Her Royal Highness sidesteps up next to me and slips an arm around my waist. "I do believe I was informed you only accepted his invitation so you could make a few matters to him clear. Plus, it seems my son would not be capable of truly enjoying tonight's festivities with you not close by his side."

I am at a loss for words, momentarily at least. Stunned by the open

185

affection of a woman I have admired most of my life. "I don't know what to say, Your Royal Highness."

Esteban has released my hand and is patiently waiting while he listens.

"First of all, it's Angela." She nudges me to proceed, and we walk around the table toward the empty seats.

Esteban steps in behind us.

"I couldn't p-possibly," I stutter as my nerves get the best of me.

"You can and will." She pats my arm. "After all, I do believe one day soon we will—"

"P-please d-don't." I lift my trembling hand as a signal I insist she not finish.

The joyous snicker that resonates from her explains she is way ahead of us and has probably been aware for a long time. "As you wish. She is all yours now, son. Please take proper care of her and make sure she enjoys herself."

Esteban bends over and kisses his mother on the cheek before he answers. "It will be my absolute pleasure, Mother."

I am astonished and very aware we are drawing attention. So, I close my eyes and bring my hands to my face in an attempt to do my best to calm my nerves.

Then I shiver again when I feel his warm breath tickle my ear, as he instructs me to take a seat and breathe. How am I expected to do that when I am certain we have become the center of attention?

"Lady Winifred." I drop my hands when I hear my name spoken in a clear American accent. Which is also when I realize I am going to make a complete fool of myself.

The beautiful queen reaches across the table and offers me her hand, wearing a huge smile on her face. "Larkin Cro... Reyes. I'm Larkin Reyes, and it is a pleasure to meet you."

King Antonio agitates his head, displaying a large smile on his face as well. "Queen Larkin, she meant to introduce herself as Queen Larkin. Hello, Lady Winifred. I'm so glad you joined us this evening. Perhaps you will be able to keep Prince Esteban out of trouble and occupied, so he leaves us be."

"Not a chance, brother," Esteban replies as he reaches for the queen's hand and brings it to his lips. "My beautiful sister-in-law and my queen, you are causing lots of chatter, looking undeniably divine and outshining them all. Allow me to make the proper introductions. This stunning creature next to me is Lady Winifred, my intended."

My head jerks around so I can gawk at him. He has lost his mind introducing me in such a way. I was prepared to give him a piece of my mind until I hear Queen Larkin snickering.

"Wow. I see boldness runs in the family blood. I do believe you should have run that one by her before making such a declaration." Larkin reaches out and takes my hand, giving it a gentle squeeze. "Word of advice, don't allow him to get away with that. Unless you are in complete agreement, that is."

I sigh, displaying my frustration. "Agreement or not, Your Majesty, I have come to learn that Stan says and does as he pleases when it best suits him. If I am being honest, and I believe I probably should be, I'm only bothered by it because we've not openly come out as a couple."

King Antonio is now chuckling. "I believe you sitting at the royal family table, during such an important event, has outed you."

"Not my intention, Your Majesty. I apologize for stealing away some of the attention that should be directed toward the two of you." I am blushing; I know this because I can feel the heat rising.

Queen Larkin leans forward as if to share a secret with me. "I hope you don't mind me saying this, but honestly, I am thrilled to have some it off of me. I'm not a fan of being in the public eye. I know what you are thinking, why become queen, then, where you will be in the spotlight always. Simple, really. In order to be with the man I love, I had no other choice but to embrace it. I am counting on him to guide me and teach me all I need to know, get me through all the public scrutiny I am not fond of. A sacrifice I am willing to make after he stole my heart and refused to give it back."

I glance up at the king, who is standing proudly behind his wife. I refer to her as his wife, because that is what she is to him. It is written all over his face that she is it for him, and that he married her because of the love he feels for her.

I want that. I want a man to look at me the way he looks at her. Love me so much that it is written on his face by a simple glance for all to witness. Which is when I peek over my shoulder at the man next to me and nearly lose my balance when I catch him staring at me. His eyes have that same glow and rake over me, making me weak in the knees.

We make it through a delicious dinner. I am stuffed, and at the same time, a bundle of nerves. Esteban has moved his chair as close to mine as humanly possible without sitting in my lap. He reached for my hand between courses and only released it when I was required to use it to eat. He carried on conversations with his brothers and sisters, along with the other guests who joined us at the table, acting as if this was normal.

We even talked about my thoughts the moment I heard the royal couple announced. He wanted to know if I had been shocked. Then he shared with me how it all came to be, and that it wasn't prearranged, as some speculated. It wasn't until my sisters and their friends stirred up trouble last night that they got married; their behavior had set it all in motion. I was ashamed and hoped Queen Larkin didn't think I was anything like those three.

Once the meal is over, all conversation stops as everyone watches the couple mix it up a bit with some wedding cake traditions. While we are eating a delicious slice, they enjoy their first dance, and I am blown away watching them. Witnessing such a powerful man let loose with his lovely bride brings a genuine smile to my face. They are making the best of this and having a blast just like they should be. Several whispers are traveling throughout the room. I'm certain they are emerging from those who wish to voice their disapproval of the entire event and show.

They then open the dance floor for everyone else, once the featured couple has finished their second first dance. I hear the chair next to mine scrap against the floor soon after the announcement.

"Join me."

"I'd rather."

He ignores my words and drags me to my feet, forcing me onto the dance floor.

I am thankful the song playing when we get out there is more of a fun tune. One that doesn't encourage him to draw me in close or even touch me. We are allowed to dance with a distance between us for now.

Lorenzo and a few others join us, so I begin to loosen up and have some fun. I'm dancing much like I have in the past when attending events like this, with one very noticeable exception; I am not alone on the dance floor. A very possessive man is keeping a close eye on me; ready to pounce should any other male think he can move in on what is his, and his alone.

When the music slows, a song I have heard a few times plays. One that immediately has my mind focusing on him. It is also when I sense him moving in behind me moments before I feel his hands capture my hips. He squeezes them as he slides in close, then sways our bodies to the beat.

My hands lift instinctively to the back of his neck, authorizing us to get as close as we can with my back to his front. Every nerve in my body is firing off, completely aware of the man grinding against me, reminding it of all those moments we spent together over the years. We've danced more than once during our time together, not quite like this, though. I'd not allowed matters to get carried away as they had once with two men. Afraid if they did with him, then we'd both not be able to prevent the inevitable.

He leans forward until his lips brush against my ear and repeats a line in the song. It's about letting go and not playing it safe. Stan spins me around so we are now face-to-face, so close I swear if we were any closer, we'd sink into the other person's skin. Our eyes never disengage. We get lost in each other and forget about everyone else around us.

Song after song plays, and we continue to sway to the beat as it changes, remaining in some sort of lover's trance. Putting all those years of turmoil behind us, while sanctioning our true emotions to surface.

"Winnie." He whispers my name as he lets his forehead pressed against mine.

"I know," I whisper back as I sense his hands tighten against my backside. "I know, Stan."

"I'm not letting you go." He does his best to tug me closer. "Never letting you go."

How is a girl meant to respond to that, exactly? If any other man said those words to me, I'd be freaking out. "Please don't."

"Never. Letting. You. Go." Esteban repeats them slowly with meaning, and that has me wondering if he misunderstood the implication in my words.

"Promise." I try using a word I don't think he'll misunderstand.

Esteban lets me go, only so he can seize my face in his hands and hold me there. "Forever."

He then crushes his mouth to mine and kisses me so hard, I have no doubt that it bruises my lips. It's a possessive kiss that leaves no skepticism to anyone watching to whom I belong.

When he draws back, I swear my body gives way, only being held up by his tight hold on my face. I have to tighten my grip on him so I don't become a pool of messy goo all over the floor.

"I'm taking you home with me," Stan informs me. "I'll make you mine tonight. I hope you understand what that means."

He doesn't give me a chance to respond before his lips crush mine again. And this time there is something different about his kiss. I have no objections to his statement, though. I am more than ready to be his in every sense of the word and in every way. I know him well enough to appreciate he won't disrespect me by doing something that goes against everything we believe. Although, I am curious about his intent and meaning behind those words. How, exactly, will he make me his?

We are interrupted when the music changes to a song that requires us to switch it up. *Let's Get It Started* has everyone around us shouting and bopping. Esteban brushes his nose against mine before he takes my hand in his and puts some distance between us. We join everyone else laughing when we notice Queen Larkin dragging a young boy with her. As she encourages him to join in, we all make room.

My hand remains in his while we dance to several more enthusiastic songs. I have no doubt that he meant he wasn't letting me go, not physically or otherwise, now that he has made his sentiments clear to everyone.

When the king and queen leave to escort the young boy back to his family, I notice my sisters watching as well. I also catch Lord Hector's displeased face in the crowd as he stares at Esteban and me with scornful intent. And I don't like it.

"What's wrong?" I hear him ask as he leans in.

"Nothing." I do my best to deny anything is bothering me. "I need to use the loo."

"Okay." He drags me toward a private door behind the dance floor.

"Where are we going? I believe the ladies' room..." I quit speaking when he shakes his head and points at the door. "I don't understand."

"If you think I'm letting you out of my sight, even to use the loo, you are mistaken. The royal family's exclusive lavatory is this way." He reaches the door where I notice one of the king's guards is standing, keeping watch.

I can't believe him. "I'm not a member of the royal family."

We step through the door, which has now been opened by the guard, into a quiet corridor. I am pressed up against the wall in no time next to the door as I watch it close slowly.

Esteban is glaring down at me with a fire in his eyes that burns me in a way I can't even explain. "Did you misunderstand what I said only moments ago?"

"No." I swallow the lump in my throat. "You were serious?"

He reaches up and brushes his knuckles against mine. "Deadly. Do you not want that, Winnie? Are you expecting something grand and public?"

Oh, wow. He is serious. Which means I have to gather a few nerves, so I can give him an honest answer. "A profession might be nice first. Then a proper proposal, where I can at least provide you with a response. One that allows me to have a say in the matter, might also be nice."

I watch a crimson color take over his cheeks as a mischievous grin emerges on his face. "Forgive me. I suppose you are correct."

"Suppose?" I giggle nervously, not believing we are having this conversation.

"Use the loo while I come up with a plan." He points to a door across from us.

I nod, and when he steps to the left, I walk through the door. This most definitely is a private bathroom with all the bells and whistles—a vanity that shines and has a gold-plated faucet, even. I use the toilet first, before stepping up to the sink and checking out my reflection in the mirror. I wash my hands, then reapply my lip-gloss after I powder my glistening face, just like I have been taught to do.

I refuse, however, to let my mind go there. I'm certain he was only metaphorically expressing his thoughts and got way ahead of himself.

There is no way he could have been serious about what he was suggesting.

The man often gets carried away and has to be prompted to slow down and think. I suppose when you are raised in an environment where those surrounding you do as you say—always—then it is to be expected. Now that he has had a few moments to consider his words, I am certain he will apologize for his hastiness, and we will move on with our evening.

I step out to find him propped against the wall, looking every bit the confident man he is. "Ready to do this right?"

Perhaps I am the delusional one. "Do what right?"

"Do you trust me?" Esteban pushes off the wall and offers me his hand.

I stare at it for a second before I take it. I've trusted no one the way I do him. "Completely."

CHAPTER 22
Esteban

The Royals

I hadn't planned to do this tonight, although I had intended to make my move quickly once her affairs were in order. Perhaps I am rushing things between us, even though it doesn't feel that way to me. It feels like I have been on stand-by for four long years. I've put a good portion of my life on hold while waiting for her to mature into this woman, one who could deal with the life we would share.

When I left for university, she was hardly a teenager, thirteen. I wasn't certain why I held deep concerns for such a young girl, why I cared so much about her well-being.

By the time I was twenty, I understood. The day I carried her drunken sixteen-year-old body back to her dorm room at the boarding school was when I came to accept that one day I hoped to make her mine. Of course, I hadn't dared reveal that to her, I knew neither of us were ready for anything so serious.

When she turned eighteen, I hadn't meant to approach her and then share so much. I'd only intended to wish her a happy birthday while I charmed her a bit. But once I'd gotten a taste of her, it was over long before it ever began.

We'd had one year together shortly after she turned nineteen. It was then that I fell for her fully, although I never shared that with her.

Afraid once I admitted it to her, I'd not be able to walk away, leave her to finish her schooling. I walked away to not impede her accomplishing all those dreams she once expressed she had.

Now she is twenty-two, and we've put this off long enough. After my trip to New York in April, I started my search for the perfect ring. It had taken me a few months to come across it. During one of my many trips to our business associates in Italy, I roamed the more exclusive jewelers. When I saw it, it reminded me of her eyes, and I knew it was the one designed exclusively for her. A large oval cut emerald stone, set in a sea of diamonds, making it glisten so it would stand out on her hand. Declaring boldly that she was spoken for. So, of course, I bought it and have been holding onto it ever since.

I wasn't sure what possessed me earlier to grab it and shove it in my coat pocket before I left for the palace. I'd done that a few times when I wanted to remind myself I was going to eventually make Winifred mine now that we were both on the same page. Having the ring with me kept me from becoming overanxious and storming the castle like some deranged madman.

As soon as we step back into the dining hall, my little sister Isabel, who is beaming, approaches us. "Time to catch the mouse."

I glance down at the woman standing next to me and see a glimmer in her eyes. She has played this game before and understands it is one tradition we all enjoy.

I spot my other cohorts already spreading out, hoping to prevent the couple from escaping before we can drag them back to the party. I wave my mother over, who drags Triana, my brother's secretary, with her. I explain briefly what is going on and then send Triana and Isabel to the garden to guard the exit that leads back to the residential section of the palace.

We then spread out and join the others, although I keep Winnie's hand in mine. I'm not about to misplace her during this game. If I let her go, it is possible her sisters might try to drag her off. Or she might decide on her own to make her escape before I can carry out my plans. So, I tug her along with me as we stroll the perimeter and watch carefully. The others have dispersed elsewhere, and we are one of the few left inside the dining hall to catch them.

I spot a group run out of the kitchen and have this gut-tingling suspicion they may have missed them while doing so. Right as I tug Winnie into the prep area, I see the door to the garden bounce closed, so I jog over to shove it open.

"Brother," I holler over the darkness. "Isabel and Triana are guarding the garden passages. You will not make it out that way."

I try to watch for movement, but don't see or hear anything.

Winnie, however, must, because she points in the direction of the large oak tree we used to climb as kids. And when the door opens behind us, she grins and shakes her head.

"What do you see?" I ask, trying my best to locate what she is staring at.

"Oh no." I hear her cackle. "No, you don't need to not look right now. The queen is disrobing... oh my."

I close my eyes, so I don't see something I shouldn't. "Oh my, what?"

"Well, it seems... wow... your brother has given her his shirt to cover her." I hear her giggle, as if impressed by it all.

"Don't look." I reach up to shield her eyes.

"Are you worried, Your Highness?" She tugs on my hand to remove it. "They are scaling the large oak."

Gabriela must spot them because she screams the same thing.

"Bugger!" Lorenzo shouts.

"Is this her dress?" Sonia, my brother's best mate's wife, asks as she picks it up.

I drag Winnie behind me as we watch Antonio and Larkin scale it in record time. "This will be one to send the guards over the edge for sure. When Isaac or Sir Edward hear you climbed that tree, they'll chop it down. Didn't know the queen had it in her, or I'd have posted someone here too. I am glad to see she at least covered herself."

I laugh as Larkin expresses her competitiveness and then displays her skills of tree climbing. We watch as she takes Antonio's hand, and he assists her onto the balcony.

Fernando joins his wife's laughter at the sight of his mate dragging his wife close to his side. He congratulates them on a job well done and then sends them on their way.

Everyone goes back inside, except for Winnie and me, that is. I watch them tread up the pathway they came running down, as I take her hand and drag her off in the opposite direction. I know we won't be missed right away, and I believe I know the perfect spot out here to take care of business.

"Shouldn't we head back inside?" She sounds a bit nervous.

"No." I glance over my shoulder. "We should not."

"Okay." She sighs and slows her feet, so I am practically dragging her now. "Are you going to defile me?"

I don't answer her right away. Instead, I continue to drag her behind me until we are under the vine-covered stone pavilion. I release her hand once we are inside and spin around to face her.

She is admiring the beauty of the area and almost misses it when I drop to a knee so I can present the ring I had hidden in my suit jacket to her. "What... w-what are y-you doing?"

"I thought that was obvious?" I grin up and watch her eyes fill up with tears.

"Perhaps y-you sh-should explain." She covers her heart with her left hand.

"I'd be honored to do that." I take a deep breath and begin. "First, I should let you in on a little secret."

"W-what secret?" She hiccups.

I hold her gaze and wait until I have her full attention. "I love you."

Winnie stumbles forward and ends up taking a seat on the concrete bench just to her left. "Wh-What?"

"I said, I love you." I smile like I don't believe I ever have before. "You are the only woman I have ever loved. In fact, the only one I ever plan to fall in love with."

She blinks as she nods. "I love you, as well."

"That is a huge relief," I tease, as I shift a little closer. I love hearing those words. "Because when two people fall in love, they should do something about it. I've not said it before now, because I was afraid I'd ruin all those ambitions of yours that you had set out to accomplish. I know you haven't finished accomplishing those yet, and I still want you to have everything you set your mind to. I'd love to watch you achieve all those dreams you have inside of your head. Be there, standing next to you while you do so. I never wish to hold you back, prevent you from opening your own bakery. Nor would I allow others to tell me I should not encourage the wife of a noble to do such a thing. If the queen can maintain her job as an architect, then surely the *princesa* can own a bakery, and be allowed to provide delicious delicacies for others to enjoy."

Winifred takes both her hands and wipes off the moisture that has been leaking from her lovely green eyes.

I reach out and take her left hand in mine and bring it to my lips. "Lady Winifred Josephine Batista, it would please me greatly, if you'd agree to become my wife. I love you; therefore, I am kneeling, begging you to agree to marry me. Will you? Will you marry me, Winnie?"

She whimpers and nods.

I remove the ring from the box and place it on her finger. "I need to hear you say it, love."

"Yes," she chokes out before falling forward into my arms. "Yes."

"Thank God." I wrap her in my arms and hold on with all that is inside of me.

"What now?" I hear her hiccup out against my neck.

"I meant what I said earlier. I don't plan on ever letting you go." I turn my head so I am gazing down at her. "I believe we've waited long enough, and I'm not sure—"

"I agree." She sits back down on the bench in front of me. "We are only asking for trouble if we wait. I believe we have proven that fact a few times already. And now that we have declared our feelings, there is no way we can be trusted to be alone."

While I have an idea, one I am onboard with, I'm uncertain she will agree to something so unconventional.

"Just tell me." She takes my face in her hands. "I've already said yes."

"I don't want you to think I'm only suggesting this because..." I feel the heat rise in my face. "I love you, Winnie. I've loved you from the moment our lips first brushed against each other."

"And I love you as well, Stan. I've sort of secretly been since before I understood what it was." She runs her thumb over my bottom lip. "Just say it."

"Did you know that as the prince, I am not required to apply for a marriage license? As a member of the royal family, certain laws are below me. I only need to declare you as my wife to make it so." It is an old law written long ago. Adopted from a time when most of the kingdoms surrounding us were at war, and the nobles took what they wanted without a care.

A cheeky grin takes over Winnie's face. "So, you are just planning on declaring me yours and that will be that?"

"It had crossed my mind." I kiss the pad of her thumb. "But I thought it best if I had a witness or two when I did my declaring. As a royal, it is also one of my privileges to anoint clergy or give a person certain honors."

"You aren't making any sense, Stan," she huffs.

"I'm taking you home with me," I inform her.

"So, you've said."

"To my home in Cabrera. We will take the helicopter, so we can be there before the break of dawn. I will arrange for a member of the local clergy to meet us there, and he will perform the traditional ceremony. It will be recorded on the books and sanctioned, that way it cannot be questioned or declared unlawful. No one will be able to break it without the approval of the king himself." I stare at her, begging her to understand.

"Someone like Lord Hector or my father, you mean." She is a very smart woman, indeed. "What do you know, exactly, Esteban?"

"That they have been conspiring for a while now. I wasn't certain of how they planned on convincing you to proceed. I still am not. All I know is that Darius has been keeping a very close, watchful eye on the Colón family accounts this last year. I've had my team also keep an eye on your family's funds. Both haven't been easy to track, which makes one wonder what activities they could be involved in." I hate dropping this on her like that.

"My father? He's been different since my return." She appears hopeful, and I'm not sure I want to upset her.

"Governor Colón and Madam Kamilla visited him shortly after you departed this evening." I watch the color drain from her face. "They stayed for about an hour. Had their driver come and retrieve two large suitcases and place them in the trunk."

"Which suitcases?" She already knows the answer; I can see it in her eyes.

"Yours." I squeeze her hand, hating how that must make her feel.

A tinge of anger crosses her face that overrides the hurt. "When were you planning on sharing all this information with me?"

"Hold on. First off, I was only made aware of most of it while you were using the loo. Given a quick brief."

Braden approached me when he saw I was off alone with her. Thought I needed to be made aware, so I could keep a very close eye on her. He'd not said anything, because he didn't want to draw attention. But he assured me his team, along with the king's, had been keeping eyes on all aforementioned parties.

She isn't buying it completely, and I guess I don't blame her. "Is that why you said you weren't letting me go? Why you suggested earlier you were taking me home with you? I want the truth."

I stand up and take a seat next to her on the bench. Once I am seated, I grab her hand, her left hand where my ring proudly now rests. I stare at it, touch it briefly, before I encase her hands between mine.

"When I saw you with him tonight, I panicked." I knew he visited the Batista home, that they seemed closer than I liked.

"Because you knew he was a dangerous man. Don't you think that is something I should have known?" She is shaking her head and I don't blame her. "I was alone with him in his vehicle."

Guilt.

That is what I am experiencing now. "Not exactly."

Her eyebrows lift, demanding I explain. So I do. "His driver is one of Darius's men. A plant. You were never alone with him. There is no way I would have allowed that. Eyes have been on you constantly."

"What about when I was with my father?" I hear the hurt in her voice, and it essentially kills me.

"Someone was watching and listening," I assure her. "I did my best to stay clear of it, so I didn't do more damage and get in the way of their investigation. Any sign of a threat concerning you, and you would have been evacuated and brought to me."

"Is this how it will always be between us? You only telling me when..."

I cut her words off. "No. Early on, there wasn't much to report. While you were living in New York, I honestly believed you were safe. My team never once got the impression you weren't, not once. But I refused to pull them, because, Winnie, if something had changed, if someone thought for one second they could... I wasn't willing to risk it. I wasn't willing to risk your safety.

"Moving forward, if you want me to fill you in on every little minute detail, I promise to do just that. I only want you to trust me, know that I am always thinking of you and your safety, that you have a say in all matters. Although, there will be times when I might overrule you if I suspect it puts you in harm's way."

"You should have told me this. I could have—"

"I know. However, I didn't, because I know you well enough to appreciate that you would have done something, and it could have put you in danger. Please understand and know I could never do that, never." I reach up and cup her face. "I love you. I need you safe and with me. I was afraid if you suspected you'd have... stormed the castle, so to speak."

A determined expression grows on her face. "I probably would have. I believed my father had changed, that the accident had somehow reformed him. He knew all the right words to say, knew what I wanted to hear. Do you suppose he ever suspected us? My father is a smart man, after all."

I kiss the bridge of her nose. "I do not. I believe if he had, then Lord Hector would have been dismissed. I am a member of the royal family, Lady Winifred. I outrank him and hold more power than he could ever dream of."

"Next in line for the throne," she whispers as if it is news to her, and is just now realizing what that means for her.

"Only until our new queen gives birth, then I get bumped back again." I chuckle, certain within the next year they will demote me. "Does that make me less desirable now?"

She rolls her eyes and shakes her head. "Slightly, I suppose."

I tap her new ring. "Marry me so we can put all this behind us. I believe I told you once that I wanted it to always be your choice and no one else's. Didn't want others closest to you to influence your decision about us. If we do this as I suggested, then we don't give them a chance to butt in and make demands. We can shock them all, proving that you are in control of your life. We remove the power they believe they hold."

"I told Lord Hector about us. He knows we have a history. He wasn't happy about it. Threatened to make my father pay for not informing him." Realization washes over her face. "He knew as soon as you approached him, warning him off, that he was going to lose. He wasn't about to let that happen. He instructed me I needn't worry, because all would be taken care of soon and that you were too late."

"Seems he was wrong." I press my forehead against hers. "He will not get in my way. I don't care what sort of contract he made with your father. They never made you aware of it. You signed nothing, or even accepted a proposal from him. Seems I've trampled in and done the negotiating with the one person who is more than capable of making her own choices about how she wants her life to go."

Winifred grins in a way that knocks me back a few. "You should know that I'm penniless. Lord Hector all but admitted my inheritance was given to him as insurance that I make the right decision."

"I don't want your family's money. I'll gladly take you penniless, homeless, and disowned. It would be my honor to offer you everything that is mine. You will not only be richer than before, but I will cherish and care for you as you deserve. I promise you will never again want for anything, or feel as if you are all alone in this world. I will forever love you and stand by your side like no one else before me ever has. I will make you rich in life and love if that is what your heart so desires." I lean forward and kiss her, expressing I mean every single word I said.

CHAPTER 23
Esteban

The Royals

"Excuse me, Your Highness." Calvin is standing at the entrance looking guilty for interrupting us. "Your mother would like a word."

I nod to let him know it is okay to allow her to enter. Winifred frantically begins messing with herself, as if she is a disaster and not put together well enough to receive company. I, however, believe she looks beyond beautiful and perfect, so I tell her so. "Stop fidgeting. You are perfect, and she is only my mother."

"Only your mother?" Winifred screeches at me. "She is more than that and forgive me if I am still trying to wrap my brain around all this."

I shake my head as I watch her dig in her small clutch and pull out her compact, so she can do what women do. While she is busy reassembling herself, I stand to receive my mother.

I lean forward and kiss her on both cheeks as I greet her. "Mother. What is so urgent it couldn't have waited?"

"Don't be rude, Stan." I hear Winnie scold from behind me as she approaches. "Your... I'm mean Angela, it's good to see you again."

My mother smiles as she steps toward Winnie and wraps her in her arms. "Let me see."

When we appear a little taken by her comment, she rolls her eyes and takes hold of my fiancée's left hand. "Wow. No one will mistake the meaning behind this lovely, generous rock. I assume you said yes?"

"I did." Winifred softly admits, wearing an unmistakable smile. "It is rather, *in your face*, isn't it?"

My mother laughs and pats her hand affectionately. "Not at all, dear. It simply makes a statement that you are loved and appreciated."

"So now you've seen it. We were just about to say our goodbyes and then carry on with our evening." I slip an arm around Winnie's waist so I can feel her close to me. "Was there anything else?"

"Actually, yes. Lord Hector is making quite the scene. Spreading the word that you have intruded all over his date enough this evening. Demanding you now return her to him, so he can take her home."

"I believe I left him on my own accord after he all but tried to put me in my place," Winnie inserts, sounding put off.

"He also seems to be letting those interested in listening know that Lady Winifred has already entered into an official arrangement with him."

"Not true," Winifred boldly proclaims. "I dismissed him. Told him I was not at all interested. I have witnesses to that. I've never once discussed any arrangement with him personally."

A smile forms on my mother's face as she reaches out and pats Winifred's arm. I recognize it as her offer of comfort, knowing the information is upsetting and isn't about to get any better. "That within the next month, he expected her to make it known and then begin final preparation. He claims he has proof of it and, therefore, has threatened to take action against you if you continue to meddle and confuse a very vulnerable young woman. Claims you are only interested because you enjoy throwing your birthright in everyone's face; that all the Reyeses' do. And now you are attempting to prove a point after this evening's unexpected events." I can hear my mother's disgust in her voice while she explains.

"And what point is that exactly? That I can convince a competent woman to spend the rest of her life with me instead of him?" My voice is calmer than I had expected it to be after hearing his fabrications. "What do you want to do, Winnie? I've already pleaded my case, so I don't feel I need to explain further. No matter what you decide, understand that moving forward, you will be in control of your life. I will only be a voice of support and offer advice when necessary."

I hate watching Winifred struggle with the reality of all the issues she thought were behind her. She spins and paces quietly behind us as if she is gathering the strength needed to make the right decision. It is so hard not to go to her. To engulf her in my arms, to do my best to influence her, by giving her a gentle shove toward my suggestion.

However, I keep my feet firmly planted and wait. I need her to choose me because it is what she wants. I want her to decide the direction she wishes to move. And I desperately prefer it to be with me, standing right beside her from this day forward, united as one.

I shove my hands in my pocket and inhale deep, controlled breaths, and wait.

As soon as she halts her pacing and cautiously spins, I know by her expression she has decided. I close my eyes, waiting to hear what it will be.

"I choose you." I hear her tenderly proclaim and my eyes fly open to find hers. "I choose you. Us. I choose a life that includes you, and I want it to begin now."

I don't dare stand there one second longer. My feet are moving rapidly until I gather her in my arms and drag her to me so I can devour her lips with mine. "You won't regret this."

The most joyous giggle escapes her lips as she draws back and stares into my eyes. "I do not doubt that. I've not regretted a single moment we've spent together."

My mother has obviously been deliberating about this because she makes a few suggestions. Winifred and I listen to her. We both agree her proposal is sound and the best way to get the results we desire.

I kiss Winifred one more time before passing her off to my mother and two of her most trusted security personnel. We will meet up again within the hour.

"This is the best way." My mother assures me when she detects uncertainty in my eyes. "If others witness her leaving while they see you enjoying yourself at the party, then you cannot be blamed for her sudden disappearance. It will force them to make their departure, so they can track her down; except we are way ahead of them, and tracking her down is going to be impossible. By the time they figure out it was a diversion, it will be too late and you two will be long gone."

If it weren't for my mother, whom I trusted completely, I'd demand a different strategy altogether. But I know she will not let Winifred out of her sight, place her with the best security team possible, and make sure Winifred makes it back to me within the hour.

I watch them hurry off to one of the less used entrances—or, in this case, exits. Once they are out of sight, I head back to the party the way I disappeared. The crowd has disbursed considerably, although there are still a countless number of influential dignitaries left.

After I grab a flute of champagne from one of the passing servers, I join my brother Lorenzo on the dance floor. He glances up and does a double take, as if searching for my missing link. I shrug, as I do my best to act as if I am not at all bothered that she is not currently with me. I even dance with a few of the ladies who have joined him while I was absent, two who happened to be our dates from the previous night. They should help me sell that I am here having a good time since we are all laughing and chatting it up as if we don't have a care in the world.

I feel a hard tap on my shoulder, so I spin and come face-to-face with Lord Hector. "Where is she?"

"Where is who?" I squint as if I have no idea, or even care, that he is asking about Winifred.

"Lady Winifred." He crosses his arms, displaying he is certain I know more than I am letting on. "You've taken up enough of her time and I'd like to leave. Now tell me where she is."

I lean forward as if I am a little intoxicated, pointing my drink at him, spilling a little of it, even. "I believe the last time I saw her..." I shift as if I might lose my balance. "Lorenzo? Have you seen Lady Winifred?"

My brother grins and shrugs before he responds. "Not since we all played our little game of cat and mouse. I believe I lost track of her around that time. Perhaps she finally made her escape, while we were distracted chasing after the king and queen. I do believe I may have seen her conversing with Madam... Madam Cosette. They appeared to be partaking in a deep conversation, and she seemed rather upset about something."

My brother has always spun a story better than anyone else I know.

"There you have it, Lord Hector. Have you seen Madam Cosette lately?" I ask, staggering and then dumping the rest of my drink on his shoe.

"I believe she has already departed," he growls and glances around the room as if checking to see if he spots either of them.

"Perhaps she offered her a ride, then." I spin back around, suggesting I am bored with this conversation.

"I'm onto you." I hear him express as he walks away.

Lorenzo laughs as he leans in toward me. "He is onto you. Now tell me you know where she is, so I don't have to hurt you."

"Mother is entertaining her for the time being," I reveal, only loud enough for him to hear. "I'll need a distraction soon if you think you might manage."

My brother shakes his head at me. "Antonio and you have always competed against each other. I should have known you'd not let him procure all the attention without stealing a portion of it. All I ask is that you take care of her and let her fly."

There is a commotion across the room. I notice Lord Hector is in the middle of it all, as are his parents and a few others from his chosen alliance of comrades. It seems they've just received word that Lady Winifred has vacated the grounds without alerting anyone or drawing a great deal of attention. If all went as planned, he will hear that she disappeared with another man, which should surely get his boxers in an uncomfortable twisted bunch.

My mother re-enters the room and gives me the signal.

I nudge my brother and offer him a farewell. As soon as the Colóns have left, I depart through one of the designated palace doors, which happens to be visible but guarded. Stumbling my way through, like I am about to pass out, while I make certain to bump into a few of those who will be delighted to spread the word.

As soon as I am clear, I make my way to the library where my mother has stashed my fiancée. I don't take my time getting there, either; I move as quickly as my legs will allow me without running. I burst through the doors and find her there, pacing, looking as equally anxious about all of this as I am.

"Shall we?" I huff out as I approach her with open arms.

Winnie flies into my arms and buries her head into my chest. "Get me out of here."

I gladly take her through the hidden passages that lead to the helipad. My pilot, along with several members of my security team, are waiting for us. The benefit of doing this covert operation, on the same night the king announced he has now acquired a queen, is that no one will suspect a thing. They will probably assume the adoring newly married royal couple are leaving to get away from it all. It won't be until the morning after I have made my own announcement when it will become crystal clear who made their escape in the chopper.

"I've never been in a helicopter before," Winifred admits as I strap her in, noticing how apprehensive she appears. "I hope you remember I am absolutely terrified of tight and confined spaces. You should probably be prepared for me to have a complete freak-out moment not long after we take off."

I do a quick glance around the crowded space and nod. I had not taken a moment to think that this might not be the best idea. "Sorry about that. It is one of my favorite ways to come and go from my two homes. It will take us about forty minutes tops."

"All right."

I notice her mentally preparing herself for what is coming.

"Do they serve alcohol on this flight?"

I chuckle and shake my head. "I don't believe so. I could request that in the future, though."

She waves her hand at me as if to dismiss that suggestion. "Probably best they don't. Drunk and full-blown panic attacks, don't mix well."

As soon as I am strapped in next to her, I signal to my men we are ready. I deposit a headset on her head, so I can speak to her as we lift off. "I love you."

"I love you as well." She does her best to offer me a smile, but I catch the fear rising inside of her.

I squeeze her hand and then bring it to my lips. "Seems like you've once again figured out a way to sneak into my bed. You have always been good at figuring out how to do just that, although I believe this one is your best scheming plot to date."

There is a little turbulence, and the chopper does a little drop.

"Oh, God!" Her hand forms a fist and I sense her trembling. "Are you complaining about that, Your Highness?"

"Not at all, Lady Winifred. I'm simply stating a fact." When the chopper wobbles a bit, I seize her face and force her to look at me. "Or maybe this time it is I who has figured out a way to make you a permanent fixture in my bed. I've had a small taste of what it was like and discovered that I enjoyed it very much."

I watch her cheek blush. "I liked it as well."

"You should know that this time, however, I don't plan on either of us doing a lot of sleeping." I lob it out there and then grin when I notice she is no longer focused on being cramped inside this confined chopper. "I believe I owe you."

"Owe me or own me?" She whimpers and swallows hard as if both sound rather interesting.

"Owe you." I lean in and brush my lips against hers. "Seems like the last time we found ourselves alone and naked—"

Winnie covers my mouth with her fingers and glances around to see if the others with us have overheard. "Shh."

I notice Braden holding back a snicker across from me. He, too, is wearing a headset, as are the pilot and co-pilot. All of which are on the same frequency, and I know they've heard every word of our conversation.

"I just thought I'd give you something to consider," I express as I once again kiss her lips.

I feel her nails scrap against my cheek. "We are really doing this?"

"Yes." I stare into those emerald green eyes that have mesmerized me for so long now. "I can hardly believe it myself."

"If this is a dream, Stan, promise me you won't ever wake me."

I brush our noses against each other. "If it's a dream Winnie, I want to remain in this dreamland for the rest of my life."

CHAPTER 24
Winifred

The Royals

S urprisingly, we made it to Cabrera's airstrip without me having a full-blown panic attack. I was outright distracted by the man who never once took his eyes off me. Kissed me constantly, doing his best to keep my mind off the small cramped space and focused on him, along with all the promises he brought with him.

It was almost one in the morning when we landed. The airstrip is abandoned because of the late hour, making it much easier for us to get in and out of there without being noticed.

As soon as they shuffle us into the waiting SUV, the helicopter immediately takes off again and heads north. It will land in Sevilla and remain there until further notice. A ploy designed to not give away our location should someone try to figure out where the prince has disappeared to. It is a well-known fact, that when he comes to Cabrera, he always uses the chopper and keeps it handy, so he can return on a moment's notice. With no chopper in sight, they will believe he is not here, keeping all attention far away from us.

As soon as we arrive at his home, Esteban dismisses his security team. We enter a very dark and quiet palace that instantly brings back several blissful memories. The last time I was here was right before it all took a nasty twist, and we ended up spending the next two years apart.

I am so lost in my thoughts I don't hear Esteban at first when he speaks. It isn't until he lowers his face right in front of mine and makes a funny face I realize he said something.

"Sorry." I smile at him and then yawn.

"That answers my question." He kisses my forehead.

"What was your question?" I yawn again and want to kick myself.

"I said it was getting late. That perhaps we should postpone this for a few hours so we could get a little rest." He runs his thumb along my jawline and stares at me with so much love behind it, I nearly melt.

"Not a chance, buddy," I warn him. "You promised to marry me before the night was over, and that is exactly what you are going to do."

"Are you giving me orders, Lady Winifred?" He chuckles. "I believe I'd like you to remember the vows you declare and be awake while doing so. I prefer you alert and completely—"

"Is the vicar here?" I am determined to get my way.

"He is."

"Then instruct him we are ready to do this." I do my best to give him a direct order, although I'm not sure it is working. "I want this to be finished so no one will ever come between us again. Please, Stan. If you think I won't remember promising my love and life to you forever, then—"

He leans in and kisses my moving lips. "I'm sure you've dreamed of having a big ceremony."

I reach up and take his face in my hands. "Actually, no. I never allowed myself to have dreams about a wedding ceremony because I was always certain I'd not have a say in it. All I have ever wanted, since this began between us, is that somehow, I'd end up with you forever by my side. I never dared to dream of how that would materialize, I only allowed my mind to hope that it might."

"I want to give you everything you deserve. Fulfill every girlish fantasy that has ever crossed your mind," he whispers, and I can hear the sincerity in his voice.

"Stan, you are my girlish fantasy." I blush as I admit the truth where he has always been concerned. "All I have ever wanted, since that first day when you were kind to me, was to one day become the person you loved."

"I do love you, Winnie."

"I know you do. So, fulfill that fantasy by marrying me in a simple but very legitimate ceremony. I don't need a big wedding, where everyone in attendance feels the need to critique my dress, hair, and the decorations I've selected. A wedding my sisters are sure to sabotage and make it all about them. Nor do I need my father to give me away, as if I require his approval to marry the man I have fallen madly in love with. All I need, all I require, is for you to be there willingly, while we pledge out loud to each other we are entering into this marriage freely and voluntarily. I promise I will not regret marrying you like this, and will share our story many times over to the children we will one day hopefully have."

I hear a throat clear from the corridor. "Well said, my lady."

We both glance up to discover an older man, dressed in a very formal robe, holding what looks like a Bible in his hand. He is smiling as if he has been listening to every word we've said.

"I heard you all pull up. I was in the library preparing, asking God to show me his intentions for the two of you. I'm sorry if I intruded, but I do believe the lady has a point, Your Highness. Sometimes a simple ceremony, between those making a lifetime commitment, is better than the larger-than-life ceremony often practiced. After all, this is between you two and God, no one else needs to be present besides the person guiding you to ensure you do it right." He motions for us to follow him.

Esteban must like what he heard because he offers me his arm, which I gladly take. We both follow him out to the stone platform built into the cliffs. It gives us a perfect view of the palace and the ocean below us. The moon is large, and the sky is full of stars. I don't imagine there could be a more perfect night.

The vicar recites a passage as soon as we are standing in front of him. He directs us to hold each other's hands while facing the other person as he does.

I stare into Esteban's eyes and don't once consider that what we are doing is a mistake. All I think about is how we finally have gotten here, and after this is all said and done, we will never be apart again.

We repeat the traditional vows. I promise to uphold my royal duties, should I be called upon to do so. And when it is time to exchange rings,

I should have known Esteban had taken proper care and possessed one for us both. His ring has a beaten copper overlay around a shiny titanium band. It fits him, one that seems very appropriate for a prince with a great deal of clout. It has an old ambiance about it that makes a statement. Mine, of course, matches perfectly with the emerald ring he presented to me only a few hours earlier, making it that much more noticeable.

As soon as we have completed all the required components, the vicar announces, "What God has ordained as good, let no man deny or attempt to separate. I proudly pronounce you husband and wife. Prince Esteban Carlos Reyes, you may now seal the vows the two of you exchanged with a kiss."

My husband seizes my face with both his hands and hauls me in close. He then deliberately lowers his head and places a kiss on my lips, one that most certainly seals the deal. It isn't over the top or overly intimate. It is the perfect kiss; respectful while displaying how seriously he takes what we just entered into.

"My work here is done," the vicar announces proudly, wearing a genuine smile. "It has been an honor to perform such an authentic ceremony. I do not doubt that this marriage will be able to withstand a lifetime and grow deeper each and every day. God bless you both. Prince Esteban, Princess Winifred, I bid you both a goodnight."

I am in a daze. Not at all positive, I'm not dreaming, and that very soon I will awake and realize none of this is real. I know it has to be extremely late, or early, I suppose would be the correct term to describe the time. As we stand there, I draw in a lung full of the fresh open air and stare out over the dark ocean spread out before us. This view will linger as a memory for the remainder of my life and become one of my most favorites. Every time I stand here, or even look out over this view, I will recall the night I married the man I fell in love with, in our own very secret and private ceremony.

Large arms encircle me and tug me against his solid frame. "Mrs. Reyes, you have made me a very happy man."

"Am I Mrs. Reyes?" I peek over my shoulder and find him smiling.

"You are my missus.," he whispers in my ear. "Officially, however, you are Princess Winifred Josephine Reyes. It will require others to address you as Your Highness. Quite a leap you have made in society's mind. You now hold a title very few before you have. Young girls will look up to you because of it. A princess is only one step below the title of queen, although in my eyes, my love, you will always be looked upon as my queen and treated like one."

"All I want is for you to love me, to love you back," I tell him, right before I yawn again as the weight of the day takes over.

"And you will be." He spins me around so I am facing him. "Time for bed. You are exhausted. It has been a very long day for us both."

He seizes my hand in his and tugs me gently, encouraging me to follow him. Of course, I don't fight him. I would follow this man anywhere. I completely trust him to take care of me and never lead me into harm's way.

As soon as we reach the back entrance, he stops and scoops me into his arms. I don't miss the delight in his eyes as he carries me over the threshold and through the palace to his private quarters. Not once stumbling or taking his eyes off me, moving fluently and with ease, while holding me securely in his arms.

I am laid down on the bed gently as he collapses down beside me. His eyes remain locked with mine, allowing me to decipher every thought floating through his mind. Eventually, I reach up and caress his face, feeling the course whiskers that have grown after a very long day. My emotions suddenly take over, tears of joy fill my eyes and slide down my face. I never believed that one day I would indeed be this man's wife. That he would be my husband. That we would make it to this point, without someone interfering and stealing it away before it could become my reality.

"Why are you crying?" He lifts his hand and uses his thumb to wipe my tears away.

I don't answer him. Instead, I lean in and kiss his soft lips. As you might imagine, that kiss spins into something more rather quickly. Within a matter of seconds, we are frantically doing our best to disrobe the other person. Neither of us is willing to slow down until we have reached a point where we require breaking the kiss so that items can be removed.

Once we pull apart, our eyes dance around wildly. Every button on him has been undone, leaving his clothes hanging open. Mine are no better. The zipper to my dress has been lowered, leaving the fabric now hanging as far as possible off my shoulders.

One look at our disheveled selves has us bursting into hysterics.

"What a sight we must make?" Stan shakes off his shirt, still laughing. "I've never been so desperate to get to someone until I had a taste of you, love. Never imagined I'd act like some deranged maniac, who felt like if he didn't hurry things along, it would all disappear."

I sit up, so I can remove my arms from the sleeves of my dress. And then yank it over my head and toss it behind me. It no sooner hits the ground, than I find myself trapped under him, with his hands on my exposed skin while he stares down at me.

The only clothing that remains on my body, is my matching set of French knickers and full figure support brassiere. Not something a woman slips on when she imagines she will be with her man for the very first time. They are all about comfort and support, absolutely nothing else. I believe I might die a slow embarrassing death the second I remember I have them on.

"Please don't look too closely." I seal my eyes and whisper, knowing they are not at all attractive.

"Open your eyes, Winnie." He nuzzles his nose against mine.

"No." I try to shift out from under him. "I am so embarrassed. I never imagined you'd see me in these."

I feel his fingers trace the large comfortable gel straps, and then down the top of my brassiere that covers my breasts completely. He moves to the dip between my breasts and then back up the other side. I cannot for the life of me pry my eyes open, afraid his face will reflect how horrified he is to catch sight of something so non-sexy on me.

He runs them down the outside next until he reaches the peak of my left breast. The lined cup prevents him from noticing how they are reacting to that move, thankfully. I don't miss that he does the same to the other. And is now straddling me, resting his bum on my thighs, while his hands are firmly planted around my encased breasts.

"Does it fasten here?" His voice is deep and dang sexy.

That is also when I become aware of his fingers tracing the seam, and then slipping underneath, as he tries to figure out how it all works. "I've never had the pleasure of…"

I snap my eyes open, and then nearly melt at the sight of him above me. He is gnawing on his bottom lip, concentrating while bent over me, inspecting how it all comes together. I've never seen a man look so delicious before, and I must moan.

His eyes shift up to catch mine as a sinful grin appears on his face. "I believe I see how this all works now. May I have the pleasure?"

What am I expected to say to such a question?

"Sure?" slips out, sounding more like a question than an answer.

Thankfully, he gets to work, and within a few seconds has successfully unfastened it. Quickly, he yanks it open, allowing my girls to spill out all over the place.

Heat, as I have never experienced before, floods my body. Not to mention the fire that seems to burn in his eyes as he stares at them.

"More spectacular than I remember. You have nice breasts, Winnie." He then leans over and kisses them tenderly at first with his lips.

"Oh, God," I whimper. "That feels nice."

What feels even nicer is when he runs his tongue all over them, while kissing them. Right as I thought I just might combust, he slips my nipple between his lips and sucks on it with his warm mouth. I lift off the bed as I arch my back, shoving my breasts toward him.

"I take it you like that?"

His fiery breath tickles against my now damp breast, only adding to the sensation.

"I do as well. I'll come back to play with them more later. Now let's talk about these lovely bloomers you have on." His hand slides down my stomach, where he snaps the waistband.

I swear I want to escape out of shame. "I would have picked something sexier had I realized—"

Stan crashes his lips to mine, which presses his moderately hairy chest against mine. The feel of that begins affecting my sensitive nipples again. "Anything sexier than these would have done me in *princesa*. Everything about you is sexy as far as I am concerned. A burlap sack would, in my mind, look sexy on you. There is nothing wrong with your choice in undergarments, as you can see."

Right then he grinds his hard length into my thigh, causing me to shiver. My hands recall what it felt like holding him in them. Which explains why they rise off the bed and land on his hips. Then shove the waistband of his trousers down, hoping to free that hard member from its restraints. Thankfully, Esteban receives the message and kicks them off.

I will never get the image out of my mind, the moment when I first saw him naked that day he stepped into the shower. It was burned into my brain, and I have been able to bring it to mind whenever I desired to do so. However, the sight of him now is even better than I recall, and I swear I find myself drooling as I blatantly check him out.

"You are one spectacular male, Prince Esteban," I inform him as I rise, so I can touch him, all of him.

"I'm glad you think so." He grabs the waistband of my knickers and tugs. "Since you will be forced to look at me in my truest form, many times throughout our marriage. Daily, in fact, especially these first twenty years, while I do my best to get my fill of you."

I lie back down and lift my hips, laughing. "And after twenty, will you cover up and deprive me?"

"No." He shakes his head, almost laughing. "After twenty, I suppose I might be satisfied with every other day, although I could be wrong. I might realize by then, that I haven't nearly gotten enough and double my efforts."

I shiver and watch as he stares at the triangle of hair between the apex of my thighs. His body shifts once again, as he grips my knees and pushes them open, so he can slide in between.

I become mortified again, at the sight of him scrutinizing my most private area as it opens up to him. I want to throw my hands down there and cover it up, so he cannot look.

"Incredible," he whispers as his hands slide from my knees to my inner thighs. "A beautiful sight a man dreams about getting lost in for hours on end. I can smell you, love."

I want to die again by his declaration. "Perhaps I should clean up, then."

He brings my leg up to his mouth and nips it. "Not a chance. It is the most alluring scent ever. May I have the pleasure of exploring your body, so I can learn how to satisfy you? I believe I owe you a monumental orgasm, to repay you for the one you once gave me."

Right there, with this gorgeous man between my legs, admiring me in such a way, I melt from the inside out. All my insides spill out of me for him to witness. And I believe that I just might not survive the night.

CHAPTER 25
Esteban

The Royals

There is nothing more pleasurable than watching a woman wither under your ministrations. I've fantasized about this very moment several times over the years. Now that I have her in my bed, this time for real and to stay, I plan on taking it slowly and enjoying every part of her.

She nearly combusted when I asked permission to give her what I believe will be her first orgasm. Or at least the first one administered by another person's hand. If she was as weak as I was—especially after our shower fun—then I wouldn't be surprised if she indulged in a little self-love. I'd gotten off more than once, just recalling that moment. It came to mind each and every time I stepped inside my shower back in Aragon.

I've kissed her breasts several times now since I slipped her brassiere off. I have no idea why she thought her undergarments weren't sexy. I almost exploded at the sight of the dark silk covering her most intimate regions. I suppose they make rather revealing undergarments for such an occasion. But for the life of me, I can't imagine being anymore turned on than I was admiring her in the ones she'd selected.

My fingers are soaked in her sweet nectar that invaded my senses the moment I confiscated her knickers. It was very cute watching her blush while declaring she could clean up, misunderstanding the meaning of my words. It just goes to prove women don't understand the way a man's brain works. That he in no way would find the scent of her arousal repulsive. It took all I had in me not to lift my fingers to my nose, so I could give them a proper sniffing before licking them clean. I'd most certainly do that one day after she has gotten more comfortable with my barbaric male ways, understood that I was only doing what came naturally to me.

At the moment, I have buried three fingers deep within her soft wet cave. Doing my best to get her accustomed to having something with girth inside of her. Stretching her the best I can, so when the time is right, I won't hurt her.

She is about to explode again; I can feel her inner muscles twitching. As soon as she has recovered, I am going to suggest we give it a solid attempt.

"Stan." My name is whispered out in a pleasant cry, as her entire body breaks out in a sweat. "How many do... d-do you plan... p-plan on... g-giving me before... Oh, God."

I let my fingers slide out of her and then watch her wither again as her eyes struggle to open. She is peering up at me with hooded eyes that express I've done a proper job satisfying a need deep within her.

"How about we work up one more before calling it a night? This time I'd like to be deep inside of you, spilling my seed, marking you as mine."

"Yes, please." She lifts her hand slowly to caress my face. "I can't feel my legs."

I watch as she giggles after her confession. Believing what she is disclosing is that most likely there will not be a lot of pain, because I have thoroughly shattered her.

"Are you ready, love? I will go as slow as I can." I position myself between her thighs.

Looking down, so I can align my tip, I then work the head inside her. Immediately, I sense my groin tighten as a flood of heat travels down my spine. There is no way I am going to last long this first time. I'm liable to explode while working my way inside her.

"Oh, wow." Her weak voice squeaks.

I pause and gaze down at her. I've only gotten the head inside. There is still quite a bit left to go before I am completely in. I can already sense her muscles rippling.

"Oh, wow, good? Or oh, wow, bad?" I grit out, trying not to lose it.

Winnie places her hands on my shoulders and blinks her hooded eyes slowly at me. "Not sure, honestly."

Okay.

I slide in a little further and encounter some resistance. As I attempt to push forward, I come to realize that it's going to take a little more pressure on my part to push through. "Shall I continue or—"

"Don't you dare stop now." She moans as she digs her nails into my shoulders. "Just bloody do it already."

I love this woman so very much.

Leaning down, I kiss her mouth as I deliver a solid thrust. Capturing her yelp, that soon turns into a moan and then a war of tongue tango. Her nails drag down my back, leaving behind a fiery trail and most definitely moon shape indentions along the way, halting once they reach the curve of my arse.

"Okay?" I breathe against her lips as my hipbones bump hers. "Oh, wow. This... this is... this, Winnie, is where I want to be when I die."

"No dying." She nips my bottom lip and tugs at it. "You are not allowed to die any time soon. Oh, wow. Move."

Of course, I do as she suggests. I draw back and then slide back in, gyrating my hips each time. Listening to her whimpered sounds in tempo with my drive forward as I grind against her. Surprisingly, I am able to get a good ten thrusts in before I explode like a volcano, erupting as I strive to get even deeper, not feeling like I am inside her enough.

Then I collapse on top of her, losing all ability to hold my tired body above hers. I am certain I have smothered the life out of her before I recover enough to roll us onto our sides. If it weren't for her moans of disapproval, I'd have had to check for a pulse soon and then revive her if necessary.

"Don't move," she warns me, as she does her best to shift closer. "Stay."

"I'm not going anywhere, not ever." I kiss the top of her head, loving having her in my arms.

"Good, because I'm never letting you go." I hear her sigh, right before those soft little snores begin.

I don't bother moving or disconnecting us. My arms are long enough to snag a corner of the soft sheet and tug it over the top of us. I soon join her in her slumber. This right here, is how I want to fall asleep every night for the rest of my life.

IF YOU'VE NEVER WOKEN in the exact same position as you've fallen asleep, then you are missing out. Because when I wake several hours later, I find that neither of us has moved. Winnie's naked body is still smashed against mine.

I'm even surprised to discover that I am still buried inside of her. I start to question if the dreams I had off and on during the night were dreams at all. Perhaps they were my subconscious enlightening me about what my body was up to while I was sleeping.

"Again?" I hear her moan and then snicker. "Doesn't he need sleep or at least recovery time?"

My semi-erect member grows harder, stretching her as it does, reaching deeper until it runs out of room. "He does as he pleases when he is this close to you, love."

"He's been doing that all night." She tilts her head back and places her lips against my neck. "I'm not complaining, to be clear. Orgasming in one's sleep unquestionably leads to some pleasurable dreams. Waking up to a slow, pleasant thrusting that sends you on a nice relaxing high is a very gratifying way to wake. I must admit, I never imagined something like that was even possible."

I lean down and kiss her lips. "Me, either. I slept through most of it, I believe. Why don't you do your best to give me a demonstration?"

Winnie yelps as I flip over onto my back, positioning her body above mine. She is straddling me now and shifts into a better sitting position, giving me the most alluring view. The sight alone makes me grow harder and longer. When she wiggles those hips, shifts her weight, while attempting to get comfortable, I swear I slide in even deeper.

Her eyes roll back as her mouth drops open, making that perfect O shape. I watch her with hooded eyes as she lets her head topple forward, and all that lovely hair of hers curtains her face.

Rising enough so I can capture her lips with mine, I slide my hand behind her neck and haul her closer. Kiss her like I haven't kissed her in ages, making every nerve in my body wake.

"Good morning, wife," I whisper against her lips, smiling. "I believe this is how we should wake every morning for the rest of our lives."

Those green eyes of hers sparkle as she stares straight into my eyes. "Good morning, husband." Her hips gyrate in a slow, circular motion. "Sleep is overrated. Who needs sleep when they could do this?"

I groan against her mouth as my left hand cups her breast and plays with it. "Definitely overrated."

She shoves me back onto the bed as she descends forward, resting her hands on my shoulders to hold herself above me. Then she does her best to slowly send me to an early grave. Those gorgeous breasts are just out of reach of my mouth when I lift my head. That, along with the manipulation of what her body is doing to mine, has me acting out of instinct.

Time to turn the tables on her, so I am back in control. In one swift move, I have her on her back, hair spread out around her, those breasts exactly where I want them. I lean forward and capture one between my lips, while I begin driving my hips in and then out. Slow at first, until slow just seems to not be enough.

Her legs wrap around my hips, and she squeezes me, making the muscles inside of her tighten even more, sending me right over the edge of no return. I nearly blackout and end up collapsing onto her again. I bury my face in her neck while I do my best to catch my breath.

"Do you imagine it will always be like this?" I hear her pant underneath me.

"With you, yes." I withdraw gradually and hear a whimper escape her, so I shove up to my elbows and glance down. "Sore?"

The wicked grin that emerges gives me a semi all over again.

"I suppose that is to be expected, after hours of you buried inside of me."

"I'm sorry, love." I kiss her. Not really at all sorry. "Would you like me to run you a warm bath?"

"That would be appreciated," she replies against my lips. "You will join me, won't you?"

I nod as I climb out of bed and get a very good look at the mess we've made last night. "If that is what you want. Don't move. I'll come back to help you."

She sighs sweetly, and I don't miss how she is watching as I stroll towards the bathroom. When I return, I am glad to discover she listened and is still lying there waiting. I amble over to her side and scoop her into my arms, then carry her into the bathroom. The bathtub is sunken into the floor, making it easy for me to step in with her secured in my arms. I settle us both into the hot water and then arrange her where I want her, between my legs, facing away from me.

"Feel good?" I ask as I nuzzle her neck.

"Divine." Winnie's head lobs back against my shoulders as she relaxes into me. "Am I expected to go without clothing for the remainder of our time here? I only ask because I think I'd like to get out later and explore the grounds. Stretch a bit. Possibly go for a run."

"While I do believe, I like the idea of you running around our estate in the nude, I do not want others seeing you, appreciating what is for my eyes only. I'm certain they will soon deliver your wardrobe." I snag a washcloth and begin washing her.

"My clothes?" She lifts her leg and runs her toe along the edge of the tub. "Or new clothes?"

"For now, new ones. I instructed my staff what to get you need. I included comfy clothing, which I suppose you could run in if you so wish." I wash her breasts. "Although I might need to have them acquire you a better support brassiere, I'm uncertain, though. I guess it depends on what my mother and Hillary instructed them to send."

"If they didn't send something adequate, a pleasant walk would suffice." She shifts, so she is now sitting and can look at me better. "When are you going to announce you've kidnapped me and forced me to marry you?"

"When do you want us to announce it?" I lift my hand and shove her hair behind her ears. "I thought it would be best we do it together. Let the people see for themselves how blissful you look. Allow them to ask their questions before others spread rumors. I have instructed my staff to keep tabs on any gossip surrounding you, so we can get ahead of it before we find ourselves on the defensive."

Winnie sinks back down into my embrace and rests her cheek against my shoulder. "Let's do it after breakfast, then. Not hideout at all, now that the day has broken. I want the entire world to know I freely and willingly married you because we fell in love. That we've been seeing each other off and on for the last four years. After the accident that took my mother's life, decided then that we wanted to make a lifelong commitment."

"Will you explain why we waited? Why we chose not to make it public?" I tilt her head so I can see her eyes.

"If they ask, I will tell them I knew where my family stood. That had they been aware of your interest, it would have become a negotiation, where my parents would want to be more involved than necessary. Explain that from the very beginning, you suggested it be my choice about the man I ended up with. That it was you who didn't want others making that decision for me. You have always given me the right to step away or end things if I chose to do so. We both wanted the freedom to make a choice without the influence of outside parties. Therefore, we did what was necessary to keep it private and between us. Then, once it became clear, we were ready to make a lifelong commitment, it seemed only appropriate we marry in a private ceremony that only involved the essential parties. It wasn't because we preferred to be sneaky about it, or even afraid of what others might think. It was because it seemed fitting, one that made the most sense to us."

I have never been prouder of the woman settled in front of me. To hear the confidence in her voice come out loud and clear warms my heart. All the turmoil we have been through during these years seems well worth it. It all played a part in forming her into the woman she is today, the one who will forever stand by my side.

This woman is my wife, my partner, who will always be there when I need her to be. The one I will get to stand by and support as she goes out into the world and makes them take notice of her. I should have known she was the one God had designed for me, and I am glad I listened and waited for her until the time was right.

CHAPTER 26
Winifred

The Royals

T he last two days have been incredible. Somehow, we surprisingly stayed off the radar, allowing us to postpone our announcement. I guess when you run off and get married, the same evening the king announces his queen, the world is more engrossed in how that came to be than they are about some absent fourth daughter of a justice.

Not that my absence had been broadcast. It was as if no one— especially my family—had even noticed I'd gone missing. Which is why Esteban and I gave the king and queen their due, while we enjoyed the peace and quiet as long as we could.

We returned to the capital early this morning, to the home my husband maintains in Aragon. He requested a family meeting, a dinner, to be exact. Extended an invitation to his family as well as mine. It became clear upon the arrival of our guests, which ones knew—or at least hoped they knew—why they had been invited.

His mother and sister, Gabriela, were the first to arrive. The welcome I received from both was exactly what I needed. I was wrapped in arms that displayed so much love, I couldn't prevent the tears that took over and began spilling down my cheeks.

I'll never forget the words Angela spoke as she welcomed me into her family. "I am so very pleased my son listened to his heart. You truly make a lovely princess. It is so nice to know that my Esteban will be loved like he deserves to be. Welcome, my dear. You are a wonderful addition, and I have no doubt what kind of example you will be to all those watching."

"Mother," my husband's voice reflects his concern about how those words might affect me. "Don't scare her off."

I, however, end up laughing as I draw back and swipe my tears away as ladylike as I can. "Afraid it is too late for that, Stan. I believe I vowed to be yours until the end of time."

Gabriela studies us carefully. "How long?"

I smile fondly at the man standing next to me and then give her the honest truth. "Your brother cornered me at my soirée when I was just old enough to be considered legal."

"Don't tell her that." Esteban gathers me in his arms, almost as if he is embarrassed about that very fact. "She'll get the wrong impression."

"It is the truth," I reply as I glance up, completely taken by the mere sight of him. "He even kissed me for the first time then. It was my very first kiss, and I all but fainted. Then he began trampling all over the men my father had invited. He did what men in his position often do, and used his influence to help me escape, so I could get away from it all."

I can see the wheels in Gabriela's brain spinning. "Was your time away beneficial? I mean, did it give you the time to—"

I reach out and take her elbow, pulling her in close. "It gave me the freedom I needed to grow. Had I been forced to stay here, it would have been more difficult for me to discover myself. Away from it all, both physically and mentally, I was allotted some time to learn what this was, without others influencing me."

"He let you do that?" Gabriela glances over my shoulder at the man hovering. "He didn't trample?"

"A little, maybe," I recall what happened on my nineteenth birthday and snicker. "But in the end, he allowed me to decide on my own. Of course, he did his best to persuade me as only a man can."

"So, all this time you two have been together, behind everyone's back?" She shakes her head in disbelief. "I find that surprising. Mainly because it is not the kind of situation I imagined Esteban to be part of.

Lorenzo is the sneakier brother, the one who only shows the cards in his hand he wishes for others to catch sight of. Esteban has always been the rule follower, the one who preaches about why it is so important to not get caught with one's hand in the cookie jar. And then to find out he's been keeping secrets, sneaking cookies and getting away with it."

"My dear sister, perhaps one day you will understand why I didn't want the entire kingdom's noses in my personal business." He leans forward and places a tender kiss on my temple. "There are times when a few secrets are important, necessary, even."

"I've always wondered why Lorenzo never snagged you up for himself. I guess I have my answer now." Gabriela kisses my cheek. "You were always very kind to me. I often wondered how you could be related to the rest of them."

There were so many times I wondered the same thing. While I in many ways resembled my father, very few traits connected me with the others. I had often assumed the reason my mother hated me so much was because I wasn't hers. Although I could never imagine my mother agreeing to raise a child who was a product of an affair, so I always wrote it off as wishful thinking on my part.

Lorenzo was the next to arrive, and he arrived in a style only he could pull off. After greeting his brother and sister, and then, of course, giving his mother an over-the-top embrace. Reminding her how he was her favorite son, and the only one left for her to offer all that advice she had about choosing a proper woman. He circled to face me, with his hands firmly on his hips, and smiled.

I didn't wait for an invitation. As soon as I saw that smile, I took off and ran into his arms. Those arms were my reprieve for many years growing up. Arms that always made me feel safe. Where I never had to hide or pretend, I was always just accepted as I was and then expected to open up and let it spill out.

Wrapped up in that safe place, I hear his voice resonate in his chest. "My dear Freddie, it is good to see you glowing. Tell me he is treating you well. That he didn't unleash on you like the Neanderthal he seems to turn into whenever you are around."

I giggle. I cannot help myself. "Some specifics, Lenny, are private and not at all acceptable dinner party conversations."

"Ruining all my fun, as usual, my dearest Freddie." He chuckles as he grips my shoulders and tugs me back. "It is quite obvious that you have been well taken care of, loved properly."

"Enough." My husband engulfs me from behind. "No more questions on matters that do not concern you."

"I beg to differ, brother." Lorenzo gets that playful glee in his eye I know all too well. "I do believe, if I am to be an uncle, it is important you all get it right."

I turn beet red and shut my eyes. That possibility had not crossed my mind until Esteban had finally asked me if I wanted to make an appointment with Dr. Wilson once we returned. We'd never once discussed the topic of children, yet we'd had unprotected sex many times over the weekend. Funny how something so important can get overlooked when your mind is distracted by the man determined to love you beyond all bounds.

We'd met with the good doctor earlier and suffered through that conversation. Until she could confirm I wasn't already with child, there wasn't much she could do. So, we were playing the waiting game for now. In a few weeks, if my always on-time monthly doesn't come, then I'll be tested. If it shows up as scheduled, then we had several choices she spoke with us about.

I'm not sure I'm ready to be a mother yet. I guess I should have thought about that before I allowed him to ravish me several times over. And should something so miraculous come about, I at least know the man I have chosen will not let me down. So, for now, we were going to take our chances and let what will be, be. Deal with it when we must and not worry. There are so many other issues to worry about at the moment.

"Who wants to place a wager?" Lorenzo juggles his hands as he turns his head to welcome our newly arriving guests. "Which royal couple will produce an heir first?"

Our nuptials aren't news to this couple; we informed them early the next morning what we had done. Esteban wanted to give his brother the king a heads up, so our unexpected coupling did not catch him off guard. He was very supportive and offered his congratulations. Ribbed his brother in that way only he is allowed to do, about not wasting any time to haul me off before I changed my mind. Then thanked him for taking a portion of the heat off of Queen Larkin and him. Proving to the rest of the world that when a king gives a decree about the future being in the hands of each one of his siblings, that the moment it left his mouth, it was not up for debate.

Although, that doesn't mean I'm completely at ease with my new role. I'm still very insecure, fearful that I will not be suitable enough to do it correctly. Esteban has promised to not throw me to the wolves, to stand by me every step of the way, and make certain I don't make a fool of myself.

I glimpse up at the queen, who has not been raised in this culture. She does not understand all the traditions they will expect her to uphold, or even fully aware of how cruel those opposed to their union will certainly be. I notice her smiling at me, with these eyes that are so welcoming, as she takes a step in my direction. All I can do is pray I don't make a complete disaster out of it and begin stuttering like I often do when I get nervous.

Larkin leans down to kiss my cheek as she holds both my hands in hers. "Promise me you will help guide me through when we are forced to attend all those social events. It will be nice to have someone equally new to this, but with a little more experience under her belt. I might drive you insane with all my babble, and you might have to slap me to shake me out of it if Antonio is not around." She glances over my shoulder and smiles at her husband like I imagine I do mine. "He has other more effective methods to stop me when I get started."

"I could never slap you, Your Majesty. Something like that would make headlines, and not the kind I believe either of us would appreciate," I inform her, being completely serious. After I blink, I decide to be honest with her. "Although you might be forced to talk me off the ledge should we ever be shoved into an elevator unexpectedly. Or worse yet. You might decide how much better off you'd be on your own when you are walking up twenty flights of stairs because I refuse to use said elevator."

She tosses her head back and laughs. "We are a pair, that is for sure. Together, we shall divide and conquer. I look forward to determining what kind of trouble we can get into. Shake things up a bit and get all those high noses talking about how we wormed our way into these positions. Now I hear you will be opening a business, one that is sure to force me to start working out. I'd love to hear all about it."

Now it is my turn to laugh. The queen has the most perfect body I've ever seen. I don't imagine she has ever once worried about her weight. I imagine she rarely thinks about it all, unlike me.

During our little exchange, it seems we've accumulated a few more guests. I know this because I hear my sisters gasp when Esteban's butler announces them. "Excuse me, Your Highness, Lady Karina and Lady Paschal are here as requested. Are you and the prince ready? If not, I can stash them in the library until you are."

I can barely see my two sisters standing behind him, although they are trying their best to peek around the large man, blocking their view. "Is Lady Dalia not with them?"

Paschal shouts her response to my question. "She won't be attending. Protesting all royal invitations until further notice."

Queen Larkin mutters her thoughts next to me as she releases my hand. "Pouting, no doubt. Probably best. Sorry. I know she is your sister and all but..."

I lift mine to stop her. "You are absolutely correct in your declaration. She would have caused a scene like only she can. Actually, I'm confident she'll be disappointed she refused after she hears why we invited her."

Turning to my husband, who is keeping a watchful eye on me, I ask for guidance. "Shall we invite them in, or would it be better to wait until my father arrives?"

"Father's coming as well," Karina loudly announces with a tone of shock in her voice. "Invite us in, dear sister. Seems you have been keeping secrets from us long enough."

Esteban motions for me to invite them inside, but doesn't speak. I get the impression he doesn't want to give himself away until he can appreciate watching their reaction. He has been around long enough to understand it will be epic and one for the record books.

They step inside, carrying themselves with extreme confidence as they take in the crowd before them. It becomes clear they think they know more than they do. I watch them stare at Prince Lorenzo and then smirk.

"We are just friends," Paschal blurts out sarcastically. "Nothing to report about, because I don't have those types of feelings for the prince."

Karina crosses her arms and glares at me. "All this time Fred, you have been lying through those crooked teeth of yours."

Prince Lorenzo is standing closer to me than my husband at the moment. Being the troublemaker he is, and because he loves stirring the pot just enough to mix things up a bit, he steps closer and places a platonic kiss right next to my lips. "Make them pay for every nasty cruel word they have ever said about you," he whispers, drawing back and walking over to his mother, who is on the opposite side of the room.

My sisters, at first, were ready to make a bigger scene after that brief peck. That is, until he walked away and left me standing there alone.

Queen Larkin has joined her husband as well, leaving me in front of them with no one close by, although I don't remain alone for long.

Esteban strolls up behind me and wraps an arm around my waist, drawing me securely against him. He then reaches down and takes my left hand with his, luring their eyes to the lovely ring that screams its meaning clearly. They both pale as their jaws drop, and for the first time in my life, they become speechless. It is the best reaction I could have ever hoped for, one I will hold on to and cherish.

"Excuse me, Your Highness." The butler is standing at the door again. "Justice Batista is here, sir. As requested, he has brought Lord Hector with him. Shall I send them in?"

"Yes, please." Esteban answers and glances down at me. "Are you okay, dear?"

"I wasn't aware you invited Lord Hector." I suddenly feel a little ill. "Why would you do that?"

He leans forward and kisses my lips delicately before answering. "I wanted to make it very clear to all parties interested. Witnesses, in this case, I believe might benefit us while keeping tempers under control."

Before the butler leaves, Esteban instructs him to inform the staff that we will all be convening in the dining room soon. And then he straightens and watches as my father and Lord Hector step through the door and get their first look at the room and us.

"You believe this will delay me from moving forward." Lord Hector boldly proclaims as he stares at the man next to me. "I don't care who you are, or what you believe you can do to prevent it. It has all been arranged and there is not a damn thing you can do to block it."

Esteban ignores the man and addresses my father instead. "Justice Batista, it is good to see you getting around so well. I'm glad to see you've made such a speedy recovery."

"Thank you, Your Highness." I've never seen my father appear so uneasy before. He properly addresses everyone in the room, even the queen. It becomes clear he realizes something is amiss and the jig is up.

"Seems we are intruding on a family dinner party. Care to explain why we have been invited?" he asks finally.

"Not at all." Her Royal Highness Angela steps forward. "I believe my son has forgotten his manners. Please forgive him. It has been a rather interesting and busy weekend; one we are still coming down from. Go ahead dear, after all, I do trust this is why you called us all here."

"Forgive me." My handsome husband once again takes my hand in his so my ring shines brightly. "I don't believe I've properly introduced you all to my wife, Princess Winifred Josephine Reyes."

"What sort of game are you playing here, Prince Esteban?" My father grabs a hold of Lord Hector's arm when he makes an aggressive move.

"No game, Justice Batista." Esteban drops my hand before he enfolds me in his side. "I've been courting your daughter since I approached her at her soirée the night she was introduced to *all* eligible bachelors. We continued to see each other off and on during her time in New York. When she returned home after Lady Eva was killed, and you and your other daughter suffered serious injuries, we made an even closer connection. I made it clear to her then what I wanted, what I also hoped she wanted."

My father nods, confused, or at least he is doing a fine job of giving us that impression. Although I don't quite buy his act, something informs me he knows more, or suspects there is more than he is willing to display.

"This is not possible!" Lord Hector roars, and I swear I am a little worried about him at the moment. His face turns a nasty purple color that doesn't look healthy at all. "I was promised!"

"Did my wife make such a promise?" Esteban makes a point of calling me his wife. "I don't believe she was aware of any such agreement."

"I will protest this so-called marriage." Lord Hector points his finger angrily at us. "You will not get away with this."

"Seems I have." The ever-bold prince, standing loyally next to me, states the obvious. "I can assure all of you that this was recorded properly, and in all ways, legal. I proposed to Winnie in the garden at the palace, during the king and queen's wedding celebration. After much discussion between us on how to best assure no one interfered, we mutually decided it best to get married in my home in Cabrera, a place that already held some very special memories for us. The local vicar, who was waiting when we arrived, married us. What is done, is done, and there is nothing you, Lord Hector, can do about it."

"You are all okay with this?" Lord Hector directs his anger at the royal family standing behind us. "You have no problem with him kidnapping a vulnerable woman, who is evidently confused and not in a right state of mind."

I've heard enough. "Excuse me. No one kidnapped me. Although I do believe had I left with you that night, that statement might be different. Tell me, Lord Hector, were you planning on returning me home once we left the party?"

"Of course." He retreats slightly and loses a little more coloring.

"To my home? The one I shared with my father? Or perhaps you thought I'd not protest being forced to accept a new one." I can see the shock of my statement as it registers on his face.

He had no idea I was aware of his plans. That he had intended to make it clear where I would live, and exactly what arrangements had been made for me.

He has the audacity to straighten his spine and then pretend what he was intending to do that night was perfectly acceptable. "I had worked it out, Lady Winfred. The groundwork had been taken care of, and the dowry paid and accepted months prior to your return. A legal and binding contract, that not even your precious prince can break, not even with this farce declaration of a marriage."

"Princess Winifred or Your Highness. That is how you will address my wife, Lord Hector," Esteban growls.

"How can it be binding if I never signed or agreed to such an arrangement? And I do believe nothing is final until the ceremony has been performed and the marriage consummated." I shiver when I feel my husband tighten his grip on my hips, reminding me how they feel against my bare skin.

"Damn," Paschal mumbles. "Who would have guessed that our little Fred would be the one of us to figure out how to weasel her way into such a prestigious title. Dalia is going to explode and need to be committed when she catches wind of this."

Karina whistles and then dares to ask the question I know they both want to know. "Did you consummate it with Prince Esteban?"

I cannot help but blush from head to toe. Not that I have any reason to be embarrassed or ashamed, but I react nevertheless and even smile.

"Well, look at that." Karina proudly shakes her head. "I take that to be a yes. Well-played, Winifred. Perhaps you have been paying attention and even learned a few important tricks from us. Seems you, Lord Hector, are going to have to bow out and accept defeat. Our little sister has outsmarted us all."

Lord Hector has one last temper tantrum before he retreats and storms out of my home. "This is not over. You can count on that. The court of public opinion will stand by my claim and will force you to give her back to me."

Esteban is not about to let this man get away with that. He stalks after him and blocks him at the front entrance. "Are you threatening my wife?"

"You mean your whore? That is what you've made her. That is what she—" His words are cut off, when Esteban's fist crashes into his face, knocking him back a few. Blood instantly begins spilling from his nose.

"How dare you disrespect the princess?" Esteban lifts him off the ground, ready to give him another blow. You can almost see the steam rolling off him, before King Antonio and Lorenzo step in. They are holding onto his arms, while he lunges forward, making him look like a madman ready to rip the other man apart. "Get out!"

"Gladly. No need to waste more time here. You will be hearing from my solicitor, Your Highness." He accepts the handkerchief his driver offers him as soon as he steps outside. "You can keep your... her. I am no longer interested in something that has been used and defiled."

I'm uncertain what his last departing statement was meant to do. Did he believe I'd be mortified or ashamed by it? That I was somehow embarrassed because I'd freely made a choice and let this man hovering angrily in the entryway, use me in the best of ways?

I had nothing to be embarrassed about; therefore, I stalk next to my husband and stand there proudly. I might still be blushing. But that has nothing to do with me being ashamed, and more to do with me recalling all the delicious ways I was defiled and used.

While I watch Lord Hector stagger to his car and climb inside, I boldly make a declaration. "I suppose that was meant to offend."

"Ignore him." Stan reaches out and grabs my hand, a gesture that offers me support and comfort.

"He wasn't wrong. I allowed you to defile and use me." I smirk and blush even more. "For hours, in fact. While I was sleeping or attempting to, at least, all night long. It was quite impressive and more than satisfying."

"TMI," Lorenzo grumbles from his spot just behind us. "I could have gone a lifetime without hearing your bedroom confessions."

The four of us walk back inside.

Three familiar pairs of eyes are staring at me when we return.

"Please give us a minute," I request and am pleased to see the others file out.

Esteban leans down and kisses my cheek. "I'm going to clean up. I'll be back in five to escort you to the dining room. Until I return, Calvin will keep watch." He glances over his shoulder at the man hovering in the corner.

Taking a deep breath, I look at my father, "Will you be joining us?" I know my sisters will, but he is another story.

"Are we still welcome?" my father asks, not at all the confident man I have lived with my entire life.

"Paschal and Karina, why don't you follow the others into the dining room? I'm sure you will have no problem locating it." I need to speak with my father without an audience.

As soon as my sisters scamper away, ready to devour as much information as they can, so they can report it to anyone within earshot, I give my father the time needed to explain.

When he seems at a loss for words, I decide it is time to just ask the one question that has been on my mind since I first learned of his betrayal. "Why?"

CHAPTER 27
Esteban

The Royals

I stand behind the old stonewall that is between us, listening to Winnie and her father. Or at least that was my plan. Although, so far, there is only silence. It is the kind that draws out and becomes uncomfortable.

I have to strain my ears when I hear the rumbling of a male voice echo in the large empty space. It is not at all the powerful voice which has always been associated with the man known as one of the toughest justices who has ever sat in one of those seats. Instead, it sounds defeated and unsure, almost regretful.

"There isn't an excuse good enough that will make you understand." Ivan Batista starts there. "My hands were tied."

"You lied to me. Flat out lied to me." I don't miss the crack in Winnie's voice, and I want to join her, offer her my support.

I don't, though. I don't because I know this is important to her. She needs to do this without me hovering, looking like a man ready to destroy anyone standing in the way. It is essential she gets the answers she wants, needs, all on her own.

"Yes." He doesn't deny it. "It was the only way."

I can practically envision Winifred rolling those green eyes of hers in disgust. "No. Not the only way, Papa. You could have come clean. You had the perfect opportunity to do so that day in your office."

"Like you did, you mean?" He fires back, sounding just as annoyed right now. "Perhaps had you been honest—"

"Don't you dare." She cuts him off with a harsh tone to her voice. "Don't you dare turn this around on me. I had my reasons for keeping my relationship with Stan quiet. You and Mother would have gone crazy. She would have seen a crown, not the crown, but one that represented power and prestige. I'd have never been given the chance to genuinely get to know him. It would have all been put under her microscope and handled. So, I kept something as special as him to myself, until I was ready to deal with it all."

"Making it impossible for me to step in and figure out the best way to handle your mother. Instead, I was forced to allow her to... to make a deal I'm afraid may have cost her, her life." Ivan's voice stumbles, displaying he is raw and on edge. "She was determined that one of her daughters was going to do this her way. Fed up with the other three, who somehow sabotaged all her hard work and always failed to seal any deals. You were not going to be permitted to do just that. No matter my protest—and yes, I did protest against how she was managing it all— your mother was under the impression she knew best, that there was only one way. Hers."

"So, you essentially sold me to a man I made clear I wasn't interested in?" I hear the pain in her voice again. "Like some piece of furniture, a useless heirloom that had been forgotten about, until the time was right and then sold to the highest bidder."

"It wasn't like that, Winfred." Her father sounds insulted by her accusation. "Not for me, at least. I stepped in. After I learned what she had done, promised, I stepped in and—"

"But by then it was too late, wasn't it?" I can hear Winifred has reached a conclusion, one she always knew to be true. "She wasn't about to allow you to interfere, so she... she figured out a way to prevent that from happening. Paid the right people to take care of it all, so you wouldn't be around and I wouldn't be the wiser. Instead of informing me about her plans, you tried to handle it, tried to deal with her. What if she had succeeded? I'd have walked into a trap and then what?"

Silence.

It is so quiet in that room that the silence speaks volumes.

"Did you know?" Winnie once again seems to believe he will understand her question, even though I am having trouble following.

"I became suspicious." Ivan's voice takes on a different tone. "Your prince, however, is very good at feeding false information to those watching. I knew I could never put a person on you or him without attracting attention. If my suspicions were correct, he'd have been onto me long before I was ever onto him."

"So, you risked my freedom—"

"What choice did I have?" Ivan cuts her off. "Lord Hector and his little group of conspirators knew things. I had no other option but to pray I was right and that he would smell the stench and step in."

"And if he hadn't done that?"

Ivan Batista surprises her—and me—with his response. "Then I was prepared to go to him and demand it. Risk exposure. Let all my wrongdoings come out. Do whatever was necessary to give you a chance to get out while you were still untouched.

"I know you have no reason to believe me. In fact, I wouldn't blame you for calling me a liar and sending me on my way. The truth is, Winifred, that I am not a perfect man, that I have made more than my share of mistakes and don't deserve a second chance with you. But I'm asking that you take pity on me and give it to me, anyway. Let me do my best to prove to you I am not the same man I once was, that I have changed. Please."

"Why should I believe you? Why should I give you a chance?"

I know skepticism has been a factor in her life for so long where her family is concerned, she can't let it go.

"You shouldn't," he advises her. "I've given you no reason to trust me. The only reason I can offer you is..."

"Is what?" Winifred asks when he hesitates.

"Is because if you don't, then how am I ever going to prove otherwise? How am I ever expected to make it up to you? How will I ever get the chance to prove it, unless you allow me to do so? Let me show you, by being the grandfather your children will be proud of and want to hang out with." His voice grows weaker and weaker.

"Please, Winifred. Give me a chance to at least disappoint you one last time."

Words are not exchanged after that heartfelt plea. I can detect the heels she is wearing, clicking against the marble flooring, as she advances towards his voice. Then I hear her fall into his arms, wonder if he has ever held her like that before, if so, I am certain it didn't happen often.

I've waited longer than I said, so I step out from my hiding place. They are just now stepping away from each other, and Winnie is dabbing tears from her face.

"Are we ready?" I try to act as if I heard nothing, know nothing.

Ivan Batista offers me his hand, a gesture not typically done to a man in my position. I recognize it, however, as a sign of a desperate man wanting to make a few things clear. "Thank you, Your Highness, for making sure my daughter has remained safe all these years. It is good to know someone was there to look out for her."

"It has been my pleasure." I accept his hand in good faith.

He places a hand on my shoulder and grips it tightly. Again, not something typically allowed, but right now it is clear I am being treated with respect and like a man rather than a prince.

"Now understand that I expect you to continue to take care of her. Keep her safe. Allow her to shine in all things. I suppose if the queen of this great land can hold down a common job and pursue a career she has worked so hard to get good at, then there shouldn't be a problem with the heiress princess also being allowed to chase a career. One I know will become a favorite. And it will have nothing to do with who she is, it will be because the delicacies she serves are simply the best offered." I do believe I notice a tinge of pride as he speaks about his daughter's talent.

"I couldn't agree more. That is on my list of things to take care of this week." I release his hand and reach for Winnie's. "Shall we join the others?"

We step into the dining room and I can't help but smile. My mother has strategically placed herself and Gabriela between Antonio, Larkin, and Winifred's sisters. She has also used my brother Lorenzo as a buffer on the other side of Larkin, who is across from her. Leaving three chairs open on the side opposite Winifred's sisters, placing my brother the king and me in the end spots, the two heads. Ivan is next to his daughter and Lorenzo, a safe zone that should help maintain the peace.

It is a talent my mother has always possessed. And considering everyone is smiling and both Paschal and Karina seem in awe of her, I have never been more pleased to have her on my side.

I instruct the server pouring drinks, that we are ready to begin and then promptly serve the starter.

It was Winnie's job to meet with the kitchen staff and select the menu. Not exactly a task she was comfortable with, even after I assured her my head chef would gladly make suggestions. Later I did my best to make it clear she only needed to finalize those choices.

The first thing I notice is that she has gone with two selections. Allowed for there to be options, making it clear she was unsure if her sisters would eat the heavier options. I am pleased to see she chose the dish she desires, not the one she was most likely always instructed to select.

"These were an excellent idea," I make sure to tell her as I devour a stuffed mushroom cap. "That also looks delicious," I point my fork at the fruity dish served to her sisters.

They must agree because I notice they clean their plates faster than the rest of us.

Larkin decided to eat the fruity dish too and confirms my suspicion. "Delicious. Is this a dish you created, Winifred?"

My wife pauses mid-bite, glances past her father to my dear sister-in-law. "No. It was the chef's suggestion. I take it you liked it? I'm not a fan, so it's difficult for me to get my palate on board."

"What do you mean you are not a fan?" Ivan lays his fork down. "You always selected those courses when offered in the past."

"Not by choice," she whispers, barely loud enough for him to hear.

Karina speaks next. "Mother always insisted. Winifred choked through many of our meals."

"Or picked through the earlier courses," Paschal adds.

Plates are cleared, and we are offer the second courses. This time I notice everyone but my sister picks the pasta dish with sundried tomato sauce. She asks for an alternative and is offered an apricot squash dish that looks delicious.

Ivan this time initiates the questions we are both wondering. "Not a fan of that dish as well?"

"Actually, it is one of my favorites. Just not in the mood for it tonight. It goes well with the courses being offered, and I'm pleased to see Gabriela is enjoying it."

I notice my wife only eats half of this dish; it is rather rich and filling. "Are you finished?"

"What?" She shoves her food around. "Sorry. I guess I know what is next and I want to save room."

"Never be sorry about food, Winnie. Eat what you wish, as much as you wish." I reach for her hand and squeeze. "You've slimmed down more than I suspect is healthy. Wouldn't hurt to add back some of it. I believe I once expressed how I appreciated all of your curves."

"You did not just say that." Winnie's eyes widen and then scan the table frantically.

"I believe he did." Paschal leans back in her seat and begins studying me carefully. "Why don't you enlighten us on how this relationship developed, exactly?"

"Yes, Prince Esteban, please do share." Karina is equally interested. "Perhaps begin with how you procured the nickname Stan."

"Ignore them," Winnie instructs me. "They are only being nosey so they can report back to the one who refused to attend. I'm shocked she hasn't yet crashed the party. I was positive, as soon as they got the chance, they'd have notified her."

"True," Karina smirks. "Except that delicious security man confiscated our phones. Something about it being a security risk, and upon our departure they would be returned."

Lorenzo is now laughing as our plates are cleared. "After all the hoopla you ladies are known for, I do believe that was wise. It's no secret that trouble follows you two."

They gasp, although it is done playfully.

"You know them well." Ivan elbows Lorenzo. "I blame their mother. She encouraged that type of behavior. Winifred, on the other hand, never liked the attention they attracted. She was always satisfied letting them have it all, while she would stand back and observe."

"Papa." Winnie shakes her head. I can see she's afraid he is about to shame her other sisters, and doesn't what that. "Please don't."

"I only meant…" Ivan glances at his other two daughters. "I should have done better by all of you. I didn't mean it was completely your fault. You all were following the example your parents set before you. However, you are adults now, therefore it is your responsibility to decide how you want others to perceive you. It's not too late. These last few months you've gone out there and taken important steps. Karina has taken her job seriously and not let anyone get in her way."

My mother reaches over and pats Karina's hand. "I've heard you were born to do the job you are doing now. Perhaps in some unconventional way, you were training to face those who can be rather ruthless."

Winnie suddenly begins laughing, and I don't mean a normal sort of laughing, I mean she laughs so hard she is having trouble catching her breath. Paschal seems to catch the laughter bug and joins in.

Karina, at first, doesn't find it funny, but when her sisters can't seem to get it together, she finds herself falling with them. Which as you might imagine spreads to the remainder of the table.

"I'm sorry." Winifred finally recovers enough to speak. "Oh. I needed that. Karina, please don't misunderstand."

"Why were you laughing?" Her sister asks as she takes a drink. "I mean, I believe I detect the irony and all."

"You certainly never took anyone's crap growing up." Winnie laughs again. "You were possibly the best at letting no one intimidate you. Dalia, I remember, would get so furious with you. You'd stand nose to nose with her until she stomped off."

"And she was the best at getting me all riled up." Karina reaches for her wineglass and stares at the dinner in front of her. When she looks up again, I believe I observe what one might call respect.

"You also were not easily intimidated, little sister. No matter how horrible we all were to you, it was a rarity for you to allow us to witness how it all affected you."

"She's right, you know." Paschal clears her throat. "I realize you think we hated you."

"You did." Winnie's laugh this time is more sadistic. "I'm not sure what I ever did to you all, but it was clear I was always an outsider looking in."

"That's because no matter what it was, it always seemed to come easy to you. You outshone the three of us, and it was very irritating." Paschal points her fork at her sister. "Everyone loved our Fred. They loved you even more after the incident we won't speak off. How adorable you looked in that pixie cut, infuriated me."

"Dalia hated that you got so many compliments. That it was the talk of the party Mom and Dad threw. It was why she convinced us to lock you in the cellar, to teach you a lesson you'd never forget." Karina looks very guilty. "It killed me to listen to you cry out like you were. If it weren't for Dalia threatening to do the same to me if I saved you, I'd have let you out."

I growl at them, totally exasperated about how that incident impacted her. "You do realize how that little stunt affected her, don't you?"

"Stan, please don't. The past is the past, and none of us can go back and change it." Winnie reaches over and grabs my hand, shaking her head.

Then, as a way to change the subject, my wife gives her sister what she asked for earlier. "He acquired his nickname in the garden the night of my soirée. Insisted I give him one, one that I found fitting. Adamant I use it whenever it was just us."

I smile at her fondly, and I swear I hear her sister sigh. "I wanted to form a bond with you that night. Make a memory that stayed with you so you'd not forget me."

Paschal spits out the wine she was sipping and coughs. "Excuse me. I'm sorry, Prince Esteban, but you are not the sort of man a woman could easily forget. None of you are." She glances around the table and shakes her head. "I'm just stating the obvious here. Not only because you are who you are, but have you looked in the mirror?"

Gabriela clicks her tongue. "Lady Paschal, may I request you not point those details out to them. It isn't as if every woman in the kingdom has never mentioned that before. They already possess big heads."

Ivan aims his eyes at my mother. "It's good to distinguish you've dealt with some sibling adversity as well."

"You have no idea, Ivan. These boys kept me on my toes and gave me most of my gray hairs. This one," she nods to my sister, "she was very proficient at learning how to use those brothers of hers in her favor. Played them against each other and had them running interference with me. I've always declared, even behind all this nobility, they are still men who act like every other man out there if ever given the chance."

Gabriela rolls her eyes. "I'm not a man, last I checked."

"No dear, you are most definitely not." My mother blinks slowly. "You are a young woman who is sure to put me in an early grave. I thought it was grueling keeping those three out of trouble while I made certain they kept it in their pants."

"Please shut up!" Gabriela shrieks.

"I feel for you, Ivan. Raising boys means you only need to teach them about the one penis—or in my case, three—that is attached. But with girls, you have to worry about all those young men who have not been taught to keep it tucked away. It amazes me how these young gentlemen seem to be on a conquest to establish how many young ladies they can bed. I cannot imagine the worry you must have endured dealing with four." Mother dares to scan the table and shrug as if what she just verbalized was proper dinner conversation.

Lorenzo has always been the one to know when it is time to move a conversation along. "So, we were making wagers before you all showed up. Since my brothers no longer have to keep theirs tucked away, and I'm predicting they aren't wrapping it either, I thought it'd be fun to bet on which one is going to make me an uncle first."

Winnie scolds my brother. "Lenny, I thought we discussed dinner conversation etiquette earlier."

He leans forward and grins. "Sorry, Freddie. By all means, I assumed you'd appreciate me attempting to change the subject. But if you'd rather my mother continue discussing our penises, and all the ones she's hoping to warn off, then I guess I was mistaken."

"No, yours is safer. My money is on our king. I believe he has more incentive to produce an heir. I'd like to wait a few years before starting a family. Sorry, Larkin, I hope you are on board with that." I watch

Winnie rub her forehead in disbelief that she's taking part in such a discussion.

Larkin reaches over and takes Antonio's hand. "It will happen when it happens. We are leaving it in God's hands."

"Are you as well, sister?" Karina is on the edge of her seat. "I'd not mind being an aunt. I have no desire to birth children, but it might be nice to spoil a few."

Winnie takes a deep breath and swallows. "Dessert? Who wants dessert? I baked it myself."

"Nice evasive way of... oh my." Paschal stares at the cobbler that is still bubbling and licks her lips when the server sets it down in front of her. "You made this?"

Her father smiles and breathes deeply. "Your sister is quite talented. Dig in."

Thankfully, that is what they all do. All previous conversations halt, as everyone enjoys the treat my lovely wife baked specially for them.

CHAPTER 28

Winifred

The Royals

The next three weeks were mostly a blur. So much has transpired since we revealed our marriage to our families. While we did that, and before Lord Hector could do his best to sabotage our announcement, we released a statement to the press. It was quick and to the point. The plan was to do a live interview in a few days, where we would offer them more details.

We knew it was a risk to not do the press conference first, but it was one we were willing to take. What we discovered was that it gave us time to prepare for all the accusations the Colóns were behind. They were doing their best to drag my family and me through the mud.

However, it backfired on them once the country could see for themselves the love Stan and I shared. Once we revealed our love story and provided as many details as we were willing to expose, that's when it became clear we had more supporters than we did enemies.

And that only infuriated Lord Hector so much that he turned to the one person who probably hated the Reyes family as much as he did. Forcing the other members of my family to decide which side of the fence they wanted to be standing on. I had expected to be left standing on one side alone. Except it turned out my other two sisters had witnessed something that night we got together. So, when Dalia started in on her little rant, with Lord Hector close by her side, they surprised me and told her she had it all wrong. My father quickly dismissed her and her allegations as well. Then advised her it was time to stop acting like a spoiled brat and start acting more like the woman he knew she could be.

Now that they were a united front, an odd pair with one goal in mind, Hector and Dalia were determined to make the Reyes family pay. Apparently, the best way to do so was to join into a union that undoubtedly was built on revenge and scornful emotions. Not the ideal way to enter a marriage, because when things turned ugly and difficult, there wouldn't be a solid foundation to stand on. It was a disaster waiting to explode, and once it did, there would be severe damage left behind.

That all occurred in the first week.

So, as you might imagine, I was feeling the stress of it all. Not sure we'd made a very wise decision, acting so hastily. Plus, I still hadn't gotten a chance to decide what I was going to do with that dream I had floating around the back of my head.

During that second week, it was our privilege to be in charge of Isabel. I'd spent little time with the youngest Reyes until then. We'd not invited her to the family dinner because her maternal grandparents had come to visit her. It had probably been best since I hadn't been certain my family would act civil. So, when we got the pleasure of inviting her to stay with us while the king was on the beginning of an extensive tour, I was ready for the distraction.

It didn't take long for me to fall completely in love with Isabel. She was a ray of sunshine, and very excited about having another sister. Had all kinds of inquiries about my relationship with her brother. She also shared with me how Antonio had met Larkin, how he was immediately captivated by her. To hear how it all transpired through the eyes of an innocent eight-year-old, awarded their romance with that fairytale ambiance.

I knew her own story was tragic, but establishing how well-adjusted she was, how close she was to each of her brothers, stirred something deep inside me. I got a firsthand perspective on the kind of father

Esteban would be one day by watching him with Isabel. He wasn't as strict with her as I'd seen Antonio be. Of course, he didn't have to deal with her day in and day out. He only stepped in when he needed to or when he wanted to.

We'd had to cool matters down during her extended stay with us. Every night she started off in her room that was connected to ours, but before the night ended, she often found her way in between us. Meaning we had to make certain we were clothed. Kept the door between us locked—before we were ready for her—so we didn't teach her more than she was ready to learn. I figured she has a few years left of innocence before that topic needed to be broached. Therefore, I had done my best to put off my new husband, or at least made sure we were quieter and then redressed, before falling to sleep.

Once we returned her to the palace, so she could spend time with Larkin, I was not allowed to see daylight for an entire weekend. I was left in two states once it was over. Sated and exhausted.

If I'd not known the type of man Esteban had been prior to us getting together, I'd in all likelihood be a very jealous woman. Fortunately, I had nothing to be jealous of; there had been no one else. He was just that talented and willing to take his time, so he could learn how my body worked when he did very wicked delicious things to it.

So, when I woke up sore and achy, I wrote it off as being overused and well-taken care of. That was until the cramping and bloating began, followed shortly by that tell I always get, one that had me making a quick dash to the bathroom.

I'd not even packed anything and was thankful I'd caught it before it turned into a horror show. I was going to need to make a run to the chemist to acquire the supplies required to get me through these next few days.

I turn the shower on so I can clean up. If I am lucky, I have time to get there and back without any supplies.

"What are you doing?" Esteban walks into the bathroom naked, scratching his chest and blinking at the bright lights. "The sun is just now peeking over the horizon."

"I need to make a run to the store," I inform him as I step into the shower. "Go back to bed."

I should have known he was not about to listen to my request. He opens the shower door and steps inside and then stands there while steam surrounds him. "What store? I'll send one of the guys to get whatever you think you need this early."

"That's unnecessary." I shake my head as I let the water soothe my sore muscles. "I rather do it myself."

I hear the other showerhead turn on, and then am blessed with him standing directly in front of me, looking as tempting as always. I tilt my head toward the ceiling above me and do my best to not think about him. It is an impossible problem because as soon as I open my eyes, I find him staring at me with hooded ones. I know exactly what he is contemplating; I don't have to check the lower half of his body to appreciate what I will uncover.

"How are you not..." I don't even get the words out before he seizes me in his arms and kisses me.

"You are the battery that recharges me instantly." He groans as he works his way down my neck. "I just can't get enough of you."

Esteban's hand slides down my body and I know where this is heading.

"Stop." I realize I didn't sound serious, so I say it again. "Stop, Stan."

"I can't." He skims his fingers over my belly. "And you know—"

"I started my period," I blurt out, hoping to put an immediate halt to this attack. "That's why I need to make a run to the store. I don't have any supplies."

He draws back little by little, letting his hand slip around to my back. "Check the spare bathroom next door. Gabriela keeps stuff like that under the sink."

I'd not thought to check there. She hasn't stayed over since we got married. I had forgotten she sometimes crashed here when she was in Aragon. Currently, his sister was in Sevilla, attending university.

"So, I guess that means it's safe to assume..." He kisses the top of my wet head. "How are you feeling?"

"Stan?" I shove him back so I can look up at him.

His eyes shift so we are now staring at each other, which is why I can recognize the disappointment in his eyes. It isn't there long, but it is there long enough I wish I were ready to give him what he wants.

"I'm not ready for that yet, Stan," I whisper softly as he nods and smiles down at me.

"I know. Sorry." He pushes my wet hair away from my face. "We have plenty of time. In a year or two, when we are both ready, then we will discuss it."

I love this man more than words could ever express. "You sure you are all right with that? I just... everything..."

My husband leans down and kisses my lips. "When the time is right, Winnie, we will both know. Right now, it is not the right time."

We wash up. He helps me like he always has since we started bathing together the morning after our nuptials. When we are clean, we get out and I make a quick run to the bathroom next door to retrieve some emergency supplies. Then dress and start the day way earlier than originally planned.

I am sitting at the table, looking over my neglected business plan. So much still needs to be done if I am serious about getting it off the ground. Real estate is difficult to come by, the kind I am going to require at least. I have an idea of where I'd like to set up a shop, but I know it won't be easy finding a place that has exactly what I need in the area.

Of course, there is also the fact I need to revise my business plan. Originally, I was planning on using my inheritance to help me get started. That money no longer exists, thanks to my mother and her determination to make certain I didn't veer from her design for my life.

My father stresses he didn't know she had done that. Claims he knew a portion of it had been used, but he thought he'd stopped her before she made such a foolish error. I'm not sure how that much money disappears, or how a man in his position doesn't notice, but I'm doing my best to let it go.

I am also doing my damndest to forgive my mother for all the truths I have recently learned about her. Because she isn't here to explain or answer the million and one questions I have on the matter, there is no reason to hold a grudge. That will only make me bitter. Therefore, I'm pressing forward and trying to leave it in the past. I need to figure out where I am going to get my startup money now, since I no longer have the funds I was counting on.

It's not just the real estate or expensive rent I will be forced to pay, because the area I am interested in isn't cheap. The high traffic in the neighborhood will help offset it all and draw in more business. It's also all the equipment I'm going to need to buy to get started. The renovation of the space to bring it up to code, is going to not only cost money but also take up a tremendous amount of my time. I'll also need to hire and train staff, because there is no way I can do this alone. A couple of extra hands will be suitable enough to get me started, and if the business takes off, then I can hire more when required. Everything is so overwhelming now that I have to deal with money issues, too, I don't foresee how any of this is going to get off the ground.

As I close my laptop out of frustration, Esteban strolls into the inner garden wearing jeans, a Henley, and darker pair of trainers. "Ready?" he asks, holding my purse in his hand.

"Aren't you working today?"

Antonio is still gone. Esteban will join him in a few days and is then taking over the remainder of his tour. He will be gone for two weeks, so I know there is a lot of preparation that needs to get done these next couple of days so he is prepared.

"Nope. Unless some unforeseen crisis occurs, I have other business that requires my attention today." The grin on his face sends warm heat throughout my body.

"Have you so quickly forgotten, Stan, that I'm unavailable for such business?" I stand slowly for several reasons. My body is tired and achy for one, plus the bloating makes me sluggish and irritable.

"I've not forgotten. Our first stop, after we go to the store, will be to see Dr. Wilson. I believe she requested to see you when the time came."

She did. I mentioned how heavy and uncomfortable my monthly was, so she wanted to examine me. I hadn't intended to follow her orders, because I wasn't comfortable making a visit like that. Evidently, I will not get the chance to blow her off.

"I'm fine, Stan. I don't need to—"

"You do and you will." My husband will not let this go. "She thought it might be something she could help with. And after I've gotten a firsthand understanding of what you were trying to explain to her, it is clear you need—"

"Please just stop," I grumble as I take my purse from him, not wanting to discuss those matters.

Like always, my lovely monthly roared her ugly head not long after we sat down for breakfast. Cramping so hard that I barely touched my food, and downed three pills for the pain. Not to mention, I had to go and change outfits when the gusher started, since Gabriela's supply was for a normal woman and not one who experienced extremely heavy cycles. And because I'd not thought to double up, thinking I'd be okay until I could get to the store, an embarrassing accident had occurred.

Then, because my husband is so aware and beyond concerned, it did not go unnoticed when I dashed out in a panic. He checked on me, walked in while I was attempting to clean up. While I was mortified, he was not. In fact, he instructed me to shower again while he took care of everything else. Returned with my granny panties and clean comfortable pants, before he washed out the soiled ones I'd left in the sink to soak.

Talk about initiating him into the world of what it was like to be a woman.

He stops and spins me, so I am facing him. "Winnie, there is no need to be embarrassed."

"Says the man who has no idea what he is talking about," I grunt, as I roll my eyes. "You men have it so easy. You don't have to deal with cramps, bloating, or sore, bloody vaginas. Until you've dealt with that, you can't even begin to understand."

Wrapping me in his powerful arms, so I am tight against his delicious chest, my husband does his best to sympathize with me. "Women certainly drew the short straw when it came to the reproductive organs. If a man had to go through all that once a month, the world would come to a halt. Nothing would ever get done, and we'd still be living in the stone ages. It is very clear to me now which sex is stronger, and why all men should worship the women in their lives. Women deal with so much more than us men ever could and do it like it is nothing to fret about."

I want to cry, stupid hormones. This man has no idea how rare he is, and I give most of the credit to his mother. She instilled some amazing traits in all her boys, from what I've experienced, and I am very thankful for that.

"Now let's go get this done, so we can move on with the rest of our day. We have so much to do and I want you at your best." He leans forward and kisses my forehead before he releases me. "Come on, *princesa*, we've got a lot of ground to cover today."

CHAPTER 29
Esteban

The Royals

I wanted to go with her into the exam room, except my wife was not having that. So instead, I am forced to wait it out in the good doctor's office while those two discuss her body.

In no way do I consider myself an expert on this issue. Anything I'd learned about a woman's cycle before this morning was notably limited. I knew mood swings often occurred more when it emerged. The term walking on eggshells fit well when my mother and sister were experiencing theirs. Tears flowed more easily, tempers surfaced faster, and you were taking your life into your own hands if you didn't approach with caution. When my parents were married, my father always seemed to go MIA around that time. Scheduled late-night meetings or out of town/country trips, just so he didn't have to deal with it.

What I didn't understand or even know was why it affects women that way?

My father was of no great assistance in discussing the reality. He only avoided my mother when her time came. Called her bitchy and moody, along with unreasonable and unable to think clearly during that week. Warned us boys to read the signs and then be on our best behavior or suffer the consequences. Although we did not know what the signs were, because he wouldn't explain. He always just took off and left us behind to face our mother alone, which didn't alleviate her mood. It was hard enough dealing with three rowdy boys on those weeks she didn't have to deal with that as well. I have a completely different respect for her now and wish I'd better understood when I was younger.

I'm still not sure I comprehend what it is like to have to deal with all that, though. However, I have a better understanding now that I've gotten to witness it firsthand. If this is normal, what all women experience when that time comes around, then I don't know how they manage to survive.

I don't believe it is, though. Normal, I mean. I recall Winnie discussing this subject with Dr. Wilson when we first arrived and heard the good doctor notifying her it wasn't. Not that it matters, or makes me any less sympathetic to all the other women out there. I still can't imagine having to deal with it, or everything that goes along with it. Women, in my mind, are superior and should be considered the dominant sex.

My wife will forever get my respect after having witnessed her suffering, but not complaining. I'll make certain to take extra care of her during these vicious spells. Do my best to pamper her even more than I planned to do regularly. Make sure I am around to handle some of the extra burdens she might experience while going through it. I'll make sure she has those items required that will make her feel better. If for some reason we don't have something, I'll gladly go out to get it for her.

It was why I'd called her doctor in the first place. I knew she hadn't taken Dr. Wilson's suggestion seriously about coming and seeing her when it began. So, I'd taken it upon myself to make the appointment. If the doctor could somehow make this easier on her, relieve some of the discomfort, and hopefully reduce the amount of blood she was losing— because in my non-professional opinion, it seemed like more than it should be—it was worth suffering the wrath of my wife. Whatever the doctor could do, however she could help, was why we were here.

The door to the office opens and both women step inside, so, of course, I stand. I wait for Winnie to get closer before I reach for her and wrap her in my arms. Extra hugs are always good, right? I once read women need hugs more than men do.

"Please have a seat." Dr. Wilson instructs us.

"Everything okay?" I ask as I release Winifred and notice she seems a little upset. "What's wrong? Have you been crying?"

"Prince Esteban," the doctor says my name to grab my full attention. "Everything is fine, or it will be. Your wife has a very common diagnosis I am confident we can take care of with a few different treatments. I believe she is a little overwhelmed at the moment. Her concerns have always been ignored until now, but we will no longer allow her to suffer unnecessarily."

I squeeze Winnie's hand as I bring it to my lips. "No, we will not. Whatever needs to be done will be done."

Winifred hiccups next to me as she tries to catch her breath and settle down.

"For now, I've placed Princess Winifred on oral contraceptives to help control her symptoms and protect her from getting pregnant. I want her to start them immediately. You'll need to refrain from penetrating sex for five days after she's started the first pill to make certain an accidental pregnancy does not occur. Or you'll need to use condoms as a precaution. In three months, I'd like to reevaluate her condition."

She looks directly at me. "It is my recommendation we perform a D & C, to lightly scrape her uterus and remove a thin layer of it before you two attempt a pregnancy. Your wife's condition often results in miscarriages, and I strongly believe we can prevent that from occurring if we do this right. If all looks well in three months, if I'm satisfied the pills are doing their job, then I'd like to schedule the procedure at that time. That will hopefully relieve her symptoms even more. Afterward, we will give her body time to heal, so when you two decide you'd like to perhaps try to get pregnant, it has all been taken care of."

"That sounds serious." I am trying to process everything the doctor has just told me. I wasn't prepared for this overload of information or this particular subject. Naïvely I'd come here in full man-denial mood, assumed this was only a female issue, forgetting how essential this is if we ever hope to have children together. Now I'm glad we came because it sounds like this isn't exactly normal and requires some action.

"It isn't as serious as it may sound. The good news is that we caught it early, before you two decided it was time to try to produce some offspring. I'm not confident Princess Winifred would have been able to carry a child to term if her condition had gone undiagnosed. Diagnosed and treated, her chances increase. It also provides me with the information I will need later to understand what to watch for, how to make certain we are successful when that time arrives."

For the first time, Winifred speaks since walking in. "But that doesn't mean there won't be complications. It's still very possible I'll... I'll not be... not be able to carry a child or even get pregnant."

"That is a possibility, yes," Dr. Wilson confirms. "The D & C could cause scar tissue or not work as well as we hope. We could have to try something else. Worst-case scenario, should your condition not improve with our efforts, at that point, it might be best to do a hysterectomy. We are not to that point yet, Winifred, so there is no need to believe that will be the end result.

"I've had a lot of success with the treatments we've discussed. Your bleeding is heavy, heavier than I am comfortable with, but not so heavy I feel we need to worry ourselves that it can't be controlled. If it gets worse, and it could, then we will deal with it."

Tapping her finger on the desk while she talks, "I need your family history if you could get that for me. Talk to your sisters, other female relatives on both sides of the family; establish if anyone else has ever had issues. It might clarify how we proceed. It might not. You need to be proactive, but you don't need to be concerned about not being able to get pregnant. Or if a pregnancy should occur, then worry about carrying that pregnancy to term. Like I told you in the exam room, your first successful pregnancy might be our hardest to achieve. Once a patient has successfully had her first child, this condition often corrects itself. You let me worry about all that. It's my job, and I'm very good at it."

"Wait." I shift in my chair, so I am now facing my wife. "Are you worried about that?"

She shrugs as she stares down at her left hand. "If I c-can't g-give you an h-heir..."

I lift her chin to force her to look at me. "Do you think I'm concerned about that, Winnie? That I care one way or the other about your fertility?"

"Your family cares." Winifred sniffles. "They will expect—"

"Nothing. They will expect nothing." I cut her off from saying something that is not at all true. "So what if they do? It's not up to me or you or even them when it comes to this. If God's design is for us to have biological children, then we will have them. If his plan is for us not to have them, then we'll figure another way to get our children.

"Who am I to say how that comes to be. Maybe God knows there is a child out there who needs us, and if he were to bless us with one of our own, we'd never get to meet him or her. My family would accept any child we brought into our family unit, biological or not. So, stop with this nonsense and let the doctor and God guide us."

Tears are spilling down her sweet face, as relief seems to wash over her. How could she think any of that mattered more to me than her well-being? It is more important she is healthy. Healthy enough for me to continue to love her for many more years.

"You're not just saying that?" Winnie sniffs, still the ever-unsure woman who never wishes to disappoint those in her life. "It's not too late—"

"Don't. I didn't marry you, Winnie, because I had this vision of the children you'd one day give me." I can see the doubt in her eyes. "I married you because I loved you. I wanted to share my life with you, be a part of your life as well. There were no stipulations put in place, no premarital agreements discussed. Do you know why?"

A slight tinge of a smile begins in one corner of her beautiful mouth. I've come to recognize this as her tell, so I should have been prepared. I, however, was not, and I don't believe Dr. Wilson was, either, if her reaction expressed her shock and enthusiasm.

Winnie huffs out, "Because you're not a very smart man, obviously. A smart man would have had a list of stipulations. Forced me to sign one very tight prenup, so I didn't rob you blind one day. Now you are stuck with an emotionally damaged, penniless, and now likely a barren woman, who can only offer you one thing."

If we were anywhere else, I'd not let her get away with talking about herself like that. Since we are not, I decide to take the bait and find out what that one thing is she believes she has to offer me. I can name way more than one, but I'll list those later, after we've had time to deal with this first.

"And what is that, *princesa*? What one thing do you believe you can offer me?"

"My love." Her words are soft but potent. "All I can offer you, Your Highness, is my unwavering love."

If the sigh that escapes the good doctor wasn't enough for Winnie to understand, then perhaps my reaction to her words will be. I haul her into my arms and kiss her with everything I have inside of me. Once I've done a thorough job, I draw back and wait for her to open her eyes. "I need nothing else. Your love is more than adequate. It is all I will ever need; all I have ever hoped for."

"And here I thought our king and queen had something unique." Dr. Wilson taps her desk with her pen. "What a privilege for me to have witnessed that. We are going to get through this, and I am going to do everything I can to offer you the best care out there. I believe we are on the right course."

I hate to ask, but I need to make sure we take the proper precautions. "Would it be best if we used condoms until this has all been taken care of?"

"Stan, no," Winnie protests.

I'm not going to lie; I hate the idea as well. It's not something I desire to mess with. Not exactly an item I ever really thought I'd use. However, if it is best, then I'll suck it up and do what is necessary to keep her safe.

"Love, please. I'm just making sure." I kiss her cheek. "Would that be best? I don't want to put her body through more than necessary. You mentioned a pregnancy would not be ideal right now. Oral contraceptives are not absolute."

"You are correct. Nothing besides a hysterectomy or vasectomy can prevent a pregnancy from occurring when a couple is sexually active. That being said, I don't see the need to go to such extremes. You could, I suppose, but then again, condoms are not foolproof, either. If a pregnancy should occur while the princess is on contraceptives, I'd go so far as to suggest maybe it was because it was meant to be. The dosage she is on should be strong enough that unless she misses a pill, the risk is extremely low."

"I won't be missing any," Winifred verbalizes confidently.

"Then it should be enough. Make sure you also take the iron pills I prescribed, along with the recommended PMS medications I wrote down. I believe those will aid in offering you some relief. Do you have any more questions or concerns?"

When we both shake our heads no, the doctor stands. "Take a deep breath. This is not going to get better if you stress about it, Winifred. Relax and enjoy being married to an incredible man. Let him take care of you like I imagine he has been doing all along. If you have any questions that pop up later, call me, and I'll do my best to answer them."

I stand and extend my hand. "Thank you."

"It is my pleasure, Prince Esteban. You have an incredible wife. She is one very lucky woman." The doctor informs me as she shakes my hand. "I wish all my patients had husbands or significant others like you. I'll see you in about three months. We will decide then how to move forward. Until then, enjoy being newlyweds."

We are escorted out the back way to where our car is waiting for us. This appointment was tougher than I anticipated.

We are both in some need of good news, and I'm hoping the next part of our day goes better. I've been doing some research and took it upon myself to get the ball rolling. It's time to get my wife what she has been dreaming of and to see how high she will soar.

Winifred

The Royals

A s soon as we are inside the car, I am engulfed in the only arms I've come to find comfort in. That appointment was loaded with overwhelming amounts of information I'd not been ready to deal with.

My concerns about my heavy monthly visitor had never been taken seriously. Mother always excused it as a weight issue or diet problem. I'd been told many times, if I'd just take better care of my body, then those issues would resolve themselves. Eventually, I accepted that I was going to have to learn how to deal with them, so I did. I sucked it up and learned to function, recognizing how to read my body so I didn't get caught off guard. Knew what items worked best and understood when the heaviest times would occur. Always having those items on hand when I needed them.

Five hours is how long it took my husband to decide my symptoms weren't normal. I hadn't complained about the horrible cramping. Even though I'd not had the proper items I always had with me in the past, I'd made do with what was available. Even caught off guard, it wasn't as awful as it could have been. Perhaps I've just gotten used to the severity of it. A little embarrassed he'd made such a big deal about it, I'd almost written off his concerns, because he was a man and didn't have a clue how a woman's body reacted once a month.

Dr. Wilson took one look at me and began firing off questions. Was this my normal? How long did the heaviness last? How many days total did I bleed? What other symptoms did I have? Was sex painful?

I'd ask her to describe *painful*. Did she mean the first time? Or was she asking me if it still sometimes hurt? Since I was new to sex, I wasn't completely sure if the discomfort I sometimes experienced when he first entered me had to do with my body still adjusting to him or something else.

After a ton more questions, she'd smiled and deemed it was the newness since the pain subsided after things got going. That had been a relief, well, sort of, I guess. I wasn't exactly thrilled about discussing our sex life with her. She'd asked some fairly detailed questions I'd not been prepared to answer.

Finally, she wanted to know why I'd not sought medical assistance until now. So, I'd told her the truth and watched her irritation grow. Once I was done, she'd explained it all to me. I'd sat there and listened carefully. When she was finished, I broke down on her for so many reasons, I couldn't even begin to explain. After I was finished, she'd asked me to trust her, not understanding that she was asking the impossible.

In that office, I suddenly realized how silly I was being. The man I married, the man I was in love with, was unlike any other out there. Proving once and for all that, we were really in this together. I wasn't going to have to deal with this very personal issue on my own. He in no way blamed me for my condition and was way more concerned about it than anyone else had ever been. It was nice, more than nice, to have a person looking out for me like only he could.

"Better?" he whispers against my hair.

I nod and soak it all in.

"Feeling good enough to check something out with me?"

"What are we going to check out?" I ask, still tucked securely against him.

"Some property I own." Stan runs his fingers through my hair.

I tilt my head back suspiciously. "What kind of property?"

"Well, right now, that's debatable. At present, it's not much, honestly. Rundown and in some dire need of renovations. I've recently acquired it and am trying to figure out exactly what I should do with it." He's not fooling me. It's clear he is up to something.

I lean back so I can determine where we are. I take all of five seconds to recognize the neighborhood. "What have you done?"

"What have I done? I just told you." His smug face only pisses me off.

"You bought a piece of property you'd like to renovate," I repeat flatly. "I didn't realize you did that sort of thing."

"Don't be coy. It doesn't suit you, love," my husband informs me just as flatly.

"Fine. Let's discuss this property you've purchased, then. Do you have a plan for it?" I ask, crossing my arms defiantly. "Know what business you might want—"

Damn the man for knowing how to shut me up. His lips crash against mine, so I have to discontinue speaking for the moment. He doesn't stop until he knows I've lost some of the fire that was building inside of me, and my brain has gone all mushy.

"Are you finished?" Stan dares to ask against my lips.

"No." I sound in no way certain about that, so I try again. "No. No, I'm not. You had no right to purchase a building for me without first consulting me. I can't afford that, Stan."

His mocking chuckle makes me want to punch him. "I'm sorry, did you say you can't afford it?"

Shoving him back the best I can, I scowl at him while I do my very best to make him understand. "Yes. The money I was planning on using to start my business is gone. I'll never see it again. Which means I have no money to start a business unless I acquire a loan. No bank is going to give me a loan once they realize I'm penniless and can't pay them back. What?"

He is laughing. Laughing, without making any noise. Those dang eyes of his are bouncing around in amusement, and his smile is so huge it takes over his face. "You are adorable."

"Too bad I can't use my adorability in my favor, then, isn't it?

Adorability doesn't pay the bills." I pout because I am still extremely peeved about the fact my parents screwed me.

"In this case, I believe it just might."

"Ha, ha, Stan." I turn away from him and stare out the window.

"Tell me who you are, Winnie." He instructs me.

"What?"

"Say your name for me, love. Tell me who you are. Remind me for my sake." The smugness only irritates me, but I do as he requests.

I roll my eyes. "Winifred Reyes."

"Close enough. Now tell me how much money you have in your bank accounts."

I shake my head and rattle off the number I recall was on my most recent statement. It's not a sad number, but it won't buy me a third of the material I need to run the type of business I am interested in.

"No, that is how much money Winifred Batista had when she was a single woman." Stan corrects me. "Try again."

"I have no idea, I guess, then." I throw my hands up in the air, frustrated. "However, that isn't business money, money set aside to invest. It is our personal capital that is there for financial freedom and used to run the households we both keep. I cannot allow you to use that money on something so risky. It just isn't what should be done, and I won't put our family in financial trouble."

The stupid, arrogant man smiles at me again. I'm clearly entertaining him. And that only makes this entire situation more embarrassing to me.

"Don't laugh at me, Stan. This isn't funny. None of this is funny to me. I went to business school, remember? I know how it all works. And I'm not an idiot when it comes to finance. I know all the arguments between smart investments and risky ones. I understand why it isn't wise to invest personal funds into a new business that hasn't even proven itself yet." Listen to me go on makes the smile on his face grow.

"Which is why I had a plan, a solid one. I had a step-by-step plan of attack, where I would grow at a smart pace, with minimal risk. Rent a space in a heavy foot traffic area, where I could have a small storefront with a nice kitchen in the back. Establish a solid customer base and get my name out there. In the store, I'd sell pastries, cookies, and cupcakes—items that had a few days of shelf life. Then I'd offer others that could be ordered and ready within a day or a few days; items like cakes for birthdays or cookies for a small party. Items that are easy to keep up with, ones I could also turnover quickly. Slow and steady wins the race. It would allow me time to learn how the business differs here compared to over there. Eventually, if it all worked out, then I'd think of buying or even renting a bigger space, because that's smart business. What you've done isn't, and I'm afraid you'll be disappointed when I turn you down."

"Are you finished?" He is still freaking smiling.

I nod once.

"You're right, none of this is funny. However, I believe a good business plan allows for investors. Investing personal funds is never a wise idea. I agree with that, which is why the money I'm offering you is money I set aside about two years ago."

The words fly out before I can stop them. "You set money aside two years ago?"

Esteban lifts his hand and brushes my hair behind my shoulder and caresses my cheek. "Yes. I threw out this crazy business proposition on a tarmac, to a beautiful woman with a dream. I'm not going to lie; I did it purely for selfish reasons. I thought if I had enough startup money set aside to invest when she was ready, it would give me the in I needed to be a part of her life. She'd feel obligated to entertain me when I stopped by regularly to check in on my investment. Which is when I'd charm her enough to convince her I was also a good investment she'd be smart to take a chance on.

"So, as you can see, I, too, had a plan in action. Luckily for you, my money is still there and waiting. Of course, I realize that I'd forgotten one very important detail. In order for this incredible woman to get a chance at that dream, she needed a physical location. So, I did some research, and when I saw this place, I knew it was perfect, or at least I hope it is, so I bought it for her. What do you think?"

I hadn't even realized the vehicle had come to a stop. Just outside my window, on the corner, is an older brick building. It's actually one of the places I had planned to look into but never got the chance. This area has been renovated, and several small boutiques have popped up. It's busy with foot traffic and patrons prowling the shops.

The door opens, so I climb out and stand there, visualizing the possibilities. The large windows are inviting and would be a perfect spot to display some yummy treats to lure customers inside.

A large hand presses against my back, guiding me to the front door. "Let's have a peek inside."

I allow Stan to direct me through the door once he has it open. Listen to the bell above the door announced our arrival. This space is small, just big enough for a counter and display case, maybe a few small round tables but not much else. The old bricks add character, and the lighting is excellent.

"The flooring will need to be replaced," Stan points out as we walk around. "The windows as well, I imagine. Maybe even a few bricks, but for the most part it's in good shape."

I nod, knowing if I speak, my emotions will take over.

He once again places his hand on my back and guides me through a large doorway that leads to the back. The space is empty and in need of some tender loving care.

The ceiling has been ripped out partially, leaving exposed pipes and air vents. I honestly like that look better than I do the dingy ceiling that covers the rest. If done correctly, it would give it a friendly atmosphere, while making it easier to get to them if any problems arise.

The walls aren't much better. Many have been destroyed, with vast holes all over them. They'll need to be replaced, but that was inevitable anyway. I'm positive the wiring will need to be updated to accommodate the commercial size ovens and other equipment required. I can start small, and when I need to add more, then I can. There is enough room back here to expand as my business grows.

I am no longer able hold back the tears. As my mind envisions this space, they fall freely.

"So?" Stan steps up behind me and wraps his arms around me, resting his head on mine. "What do you think, Winnie? Are you going to allow me to assist you?"

"I shouldn't," I whimper. "I should tell you no."

"But you're a smart businesswoman, and you know a good thing when you see it," he whispers in my ear as he lowers his head. "There is only one problem. I'm not sure I'm sold on the name we once discussed."

I laugh. "You don't like the name Stan's Dreamland, why?"

Spinning around slowly, so I am facing him, Stan holds me tight as he explains. "It doesn't sound like an establishment that sells delicious goodies, at least not the type of treats you will be selling."

Now I outright laugh. "What does it sound like I'm selling?"

"Very naughty items, that in no way are suitable for the crown princess to be selling. It needs a more refined name, one that is simple but sounds prestigious." He leans forward until he is but a breath away from my lips. "I was at first thinking 'Winnie's' sounded perfect. But call me selfish, I don't want others calling you by the name I have been calling you while courting you. So, then I thought it might be fun experimenting with what you will serve and who you now are. *Iguarias de Royal*, in my mind, has a very nice ring to it."

Iguarias is Portuguese, and it means delicacies. It is one of the three languages commonly spoken in Hermosa Islas. I have to admit I like the name. It sounds like a specialty shop, one that serves only the best of the best.

"Well, *princesa*, what do you think?" He squeezes me. "You will be offering delicacies correct? Ones that are good enough for a royal to enjoy and approve of?"

"Which royal?" I tease him.

"Well now, that is a wonderful question. I'm quite positive the Royal Crown Prince, will insist on tasting every treat you decide to sell in this shop. You could have a signature slogan that states, *Crown Prince tasted and approved*. It would not be a lie, and it would surely draw attention to your little bakery," he grins. "My pudgy midriff will be proof enough that I spend way too much time being your official taster."

I pinch his very firm abs. "You are not allowed to get pudgy. That would be poor form on my part, feeding you too many sweets. You'll ruin me before I get started. Plus, I'm quite fond of this body you work so hard at maintaining. I'll have to ban you from my kitchen if you aren't careful."

Then I kiss him. Get up onto my tiptoes and kiss him.

"What was the for?" He asks when I finally release those soft lips.

"This." I motion one hand at the space we are standing in. "Earlier. For knowing how to make my day turn around."

"I see." He captures my lips again. "So now that you have your space and a solid investor, it's time to speak to the expert about renovations, and I believe I know just the person we should talk to about that."

"You're not suggesting we bother the queen with something so mundane as this?" I shove back so I can look at him. "No, Stan, that's crazy."

"This is a historical district, my love. Plus, the queen caught wind of my investment and requested I allow her to get first dibs at it. She said something about wanting to assist her partner in crime so she'd feed her well when a craving hit her."

"But she is busy getting her family home..." I try to figure out the words I need to blow her off, but then I hear a female voice echo behind me.

"Oh, wow. So many possibilities." Larkin is standing in the doorway between the kitchen and the storefront. "I hope I'm not interrupting, but I wanted to stop by before I had to head back to Homero. I need to take measurements and maybe a few photos, so I can sketch out a few proposals before I return next weekend. Since you are here, Winifred, I'd like to hear your ideas on the space."

"Your Majesty." I step away from Stan. "You really do not need to do this."

Larkin waves her hand at me. I notice she is dressed down in clothing that looks like she is ready to get her hands dirty. Then I watch as she drags an old ladder across the floor and begins climbing it, so she can check out the ceiling.

"It will be a fun little side project for me. Get my mind off the chaos taking place in Homero. Now, why don't you tell me what you envision while I poke around."

"Should you be climbing ladders like this Larkin?" Esteban rushes over and holds it for her. "I'm not sure how sturdy this one is."

"Please." She ascends with ease. "I've been scaling old stone walls in the citadel. Crawling around in spaces just big enough for me to squeeze through. This, dear prince, is a piece of cake." Then she laughs at her little innuendo. "I'm well-trained, and promise not to break my neck on your watch."

"Oh, geez," Esteban grumbles. "Please do not do that. Your husband would never forgive me."

After that, we follow her around and discuss my vision. She continues her inspection of the space. Giving us a few more scares as she peeks behind walls, climbs the old rusty ladder that leads to the roof, so she can establish its integrity. I'm not sure either of us breathes again until her feet are firmly back on the ground. The smile she offers her security team enlightens me she has heard their complaints and voiced many times over how she knows what she is doing.

We walk back out to the vehicles parked out front and don't miss the crowd that seems to have gathered. It's not every day they get to watch their queen investigate a roof for the princess and prince. I'm sure they are wondering why we are here.

"Madam, we need to get moving." one of her guards informs her as she tries to chat it up with us on the sidewalk.

"Yes, fine." She leans over and gives me a genuine hug. "I'll come by your place when I make it back next weekend. We'll look at what I've drawn up and decide which one you are most interested in. I'll have a crew out here that next week to clear things out, and then we will get started. I'm very excited about this, Winifred."

"As am I, Larkin." I feel weird using her given name, but she has insisted on it, so I vow to do as she has requested. "If it becomes too much, please don't feel obligated, just tell us, and we will manage."

"You and I are going to get along perfectly." She kisses my cheek. "I better go before the revolution begins."

Larkin grumbles at her team when they start to speak again, as she climbs into the car that is waiting for her. Shortly after I watch them drive away, we are climbing inside our own vehicle and departing the area.

So, it seems I have something to think hard about now. I'll need to make some phone calls this week and seriously start the process of acquiring the right equipment I'll need.

Wow, this is truly going to happen.

CHAPTER 31
Winifred

The Royals

Winter has hit hard. The snow is piling up and keeping everyone tucked inside. Thankfully, we made it to my favorite private residence before the storm was upon us. My husband and I are snowed in at our home in Cabrera with our good friends Darius and Ingrid. They came for a holiday, wanting to ring in the New Year together now that everything has worked out the way it should have.

We haven't spent a great deal of time together in the last couple of years. Not since my best friend married the duke and moved to his home in Switzerland. While Darius has remained employed as the lead investigator of the royal family, he has executed his job from afar. His obligations changed once his time became more centered on his wife's needs rather than his own. Now that Ingrid is finished getting her alternative degree in business, he is free to travel again, with her close by his side.

She is his new assistant, a job my friend first thought ridiculous. That was until she realized how badly he needed one. Someone he could count on being discreet, while fielding his phone calls, working out his schedule, helping organize all the men who work for him, and making sure everyone was where they needed to be when required to be there.

How the man ever ran a successful business without an assistant to do all that for him, while he did both full-time jobs, was beyond Ingrid's understanding.

Ingrid and I are currently camped out in my kitchen as I whip up some pastries. That's what I do most days while I wait for my shop to be renovated. Larkin has an excellent team working hard at getting everything completed. In a few more months, the place will be ready for business. It will be time for me to decide what recipes I want to start with. For that reason, I bake at home right now, while I experiment with them, perfect them. Send test treats with Stan regularly to the palace, where his staff samples those treats and provides feedback. Of course, I also deliver treats to our security. They have even accused me of forcing them to train harder to work off all the extra calories. Although, it is done in a playful manner as they devour them almost immediately.

"How have you not put on any extra pounds?" Ingrid mumbles as she licks off the spatula before washing it.

A male voice answers her. "She runs like a madwoman."

True. I tend to put in at least five miles daily, sometimes more. A habit I picked up when I was trying my hardest to keep my mind off the man who has taken over my life. When I am really lucky, he joins me on my runs. I get inspired to not let him get too far ahead of me, so I can maintain the perfect view.

"We both do. If I didn't, I'd be soft in the center and my very fit wife might get bored with me," he informs our guests as he steps in behind me and dips his finger into my filling.

I slap his hand away, but not before he gets a good finger full of the fruit filling. "You can't do that when I am making these for others. The health department won't appreciate that."

"Good thing these aren't going up for sale then, isn't it?" Stan leans down and kisses my floured cheek. "Delicious as always, my love."

"Are you taking notes?" Darius takes a seat at the counter across from his wife.

Ingrid points the spatula at him. "No. Do you remember the last time I attempted to bake?"

A wicked smirk crosses Darius' face, and then he chuckles. "Shall I explain?"

Ingrid shrugs and begins snickering to herself. "I warned you before I began it was a dreadful idea."

"What happened?" I ask as I pull out the finished pastries and place another pan in the oven.

Darius looks hungrily at the unfinished product and starts to rise.

"I wouldn't do that, man. Fingers have been lost touching her goodies before she is finished. You take your own life in your hands if you ruin them before she is ready to present," Stan warns, and Darius seems to debate if the warning is real.

"Patience, Falcon. If you touch them now, they will fall. Plus, I need to fill them still. I promise you, as soon as they are ready, you will be the first to sample them." I glare at the hand hovering over the hot, flaky shells.

Deciding to heed the warning, he sits back down and finishes his story. "I believe we had been married for almost a year. My love, as you all know, is very good at scrambling up a meal. I mean, it took her some time to learn, but over time I have no complaints."

We have all heard those stories. Ingrid even called me several times during those first months for some advice. It had been her idea to cook for her husband; he was more than okay with letting his staff continue to do so for him. However, my friend learned the basics so she could cook for him on the weekends. Now they didn't need to rely on the chef. It had taken her a while to get the hang of it, but once she had learned how to read a recipe, it all came together.

"So, I mentioned I wanted her to make me my favorite cake." He smiles widely as he recalls the memory. "My beloved did her very best to persuade me it was a terrible idea asking her to attempt such a task."

"What type of cake?" I probe.

"Carrot," Ingrid announces with a vivid eye roll. "With dates. His mother made it with dates, so how difficult could it be, he said."

Darius shrugs and then pats his leg, inviting her to sit. "How was I to know she lied all those years about baking it herself? I believed her, although now that I think about it, I should have known better."

Ingrid moves over to settle between her husband's legs. "I was clueless about how one even begins, but I didn't want to disappoint, so I did my best." She snickers and shakes her head. "I opened a box of premixed white cake, cut up a few dates, shredded a few carrots, threw in a handful of nuts…"

"Oh no." I can only imagine the disaster they are about to reveal.

"It had a pleasing aroma." Darius squeezes his wife. "My darling wife drizzled it with icing, and we let it cool."

Leaning her head against her husband's shoulder, Ingrid chuckles. "We returned to a collapsed cake that, when he cut into it, oozed out of the uncooked center. I haven't attempted to bake for him since. His mother then enlightened him that she purchased the cake he so loved from the bakery."

"It wasn't so awful." Darius kisses his wife's lips. "Not the way I ate it at least."

Ingrid blushes. "Please, no."

"I'm certain Este has partaken of his own delicious dessert, where his wife was the salver. If he has not, then I highly recommend he gives it his best shot," he announces as he nibbles on Ingrid's neck. "Waste not is my philosophy, so I figured out the best way to devour my love's best attempt at providing dessert. I do believe the dessert I devoured was way better."

"Oh, geez," Ingrid and I both mutter at the same time.

"I'll keep that in mind." Stan dips his finger in the filling again. "When my lady is feeling better, it might be fun."

A little over a month ago, I had the procedure Dr. Wilson suggested. It's been touch and go for a while now. In the beginning, I had a lot of cramping. Not any worse than before, but enough to make me moody. It's been sort of a dry spell for us while my body recovers. During that stage, I wasn't at all interested in sex, but now that I am feeling better, I've started missing it. My dear husband, however, has refused to even suggest it, determined to give my body as much time as it needs. It was recommended we wait at least four weeks—it's been five—but that it might take as long as six. Dr. Wilson told me it was my decision after four, and when I felt ready, then it would mean I was ready. I felt ready five days ago, except Stan isn't getting the hint.

Ingrid and I discussed this earlier in detail. She made a few suggestions on how I could entice my husband, but I've yet to make the first move since we've been married. It's always been difficult for me to put myself out there like that. A part of me still remembers how rejected I felt for so many years, and therefore I lack the confidence to follow through.

"I thought you said you were feeling better?" My friend blurts out.

I nod and try to decide how I want to respond with Darius in the room. "Yes. Like my old self."

"Did you hear that, Este? Like her old self?" Darius smirks. "Honey cakes, I believe that is excellent news. I hear you had a rough go for a while."

I blink a few times while I dig deep. "Did he tell you that?"

"Do you talk with my wife about matters?" Darius motions between Ingrid and me. "Are you to believe that us menfolk don't speak of these issues when they are close to the heart? I understand that you women assume the only topics men discuss have to deal with business and sports, possibly politics. I'd like to enlighten you on your confusion, while I let you in on a little secret. We have a few trusted mates, where any topic is up for grabs. Now understand, we don't always dive into the details like you ladies do, we skate around the issues at best, but we do speak of such subjects when necessary."

"Like what sort of topics?" Ingrid seems just as intrigued about this as I am.

"All right, I'll go there, if you promise not to get upset," Darius challenges her. "Both of you."

"Now I have to know." I plate up a pastry and place it in front of him. "This sounds serious."

Stan pulls out the other pan and turns off the oven. "Sometimes it is. When I was courting you, Darius was the only person with the knowledge of what was happening. I needed to vent, so to speak. I needed someone who could offer me sound advice, while we did our best to grow during our time apart. Those were some tough times, Winnie. If it hadn't been for him, I'm not sure I'd have survived those years without breaking, and making demands you'd not agree to."

"And what about you, my brilliant man? What did you need to discuss?" Ingrid lays a hand on his arm.

"Oh, you know the usual." He smiles down at her. "We had some mechanical issues, in the beginning, to deal with, I do believe."

"You... you shared that stuff with him... things about... Oh. My. God." Ingrid ducks her head and sighs. "Seriously."

"I didn't explain the situation entirely. I only shared that we were experiencing a few minor setbacks. That we were both getting a little frustrated while doing our best to make the most of a situation beyond our control. He advised me to be patient, and give us both some time, and not push. Suggested I speak with a women's doctor to establish if maybe she had some answers for us. I'd considered that, but was afraid you'd think I was overstepping into your territory. He pointed out that as a couple, any issue one of us was having affected both of us, so it was my duty as the husband to do what needed to be done."

When I glance over at my husband, he simply shrugs.

"You are so getting lucky tonight," I inform him and hear the other couple snicker. "That advice you gave him was what finally fixed the issue?"

"I guess." Stan clears his throat. "I only suggested what I would have done if in a similar situation with you."

"Yes, I know." I finish with the pastries and hand him the dishes. "A proven point when you as much as dragged me to my doctor. You two, I am certain, are a rarity. My best friend and I are so very lucky, so very lucky."

Darius shoves the last of the pastry I gave him in his mouth and moans. "So delicious, honey cakes. You have the touch, and it's a good thing we only visit a few times a year. Otherwise, my waistband would expand, and I'd be forced to join you both on those crazy runs."

He kisses his wife's cheek and rests his head on her shoulder. "So, is it close enough to midnight for me to share, or do I have to wait for the clock to actually strike?"

Ingrid glances at the clock on the wall and nods. "Close enough, I suppose. You don't think it is too soon?"

"No. If we were sharing with a crowd of nosy buzzards, then I'd hold off. But these two are our confidants. I believe we've proven that already. It's not like I will be able to keep this secret much longer." He nuzzles into her neck. "I'm bursting."

"I knew it." Stan reaches for the champagne flutes behind him. "A sip will not hurt in the celebration."

Apparently, I'm the only one still in the dark. "What are we celebrating? Did you solve that dreadful case you've been on for months now?"

"Please do not bring that up tonight. I'm literally about to wring a few necks if I don't get to the bottom of that." Darius grabs the champagne and pops the cork, licking up the spillage as it bubbles over. "You do the honors, love."

Ingrid runs her hands through her hair and waits for us all to have a glass before she announces. "We are going to have a baby."

Darius is all smiles.

While I notice Ingrid is smiling, it doesn't quite meet her eyes. She is doing her best to pretend; except I know her well enough to notice the truth.

I take a savor of my flute before I respond. "How wonderful."

My friend's husband reaches over and pulls her against his side. "It is, isn't it? I mean, I know this was unplanned and took us a little by surprise."

Ingrid huffs and then takes a sip of her drink. "You can say that again."

"Sweetheart?" Darius grabs her face and turns it, so she is looking him in the eye. "This is good."

"We... we just started working together. We said in a few years we'd be ready for something like this. I'm twenty-two." She glances down, looking guilty about not being as ecstatic as her husband is.

"I get it, Ingrid," I notify her. "I mean that. I really do. I can't imagine finding out Stan and I were going to be parents right now."

"Thank you." She glances up but doesn't look any better about it.

"I'd probably be uncertain about my feelings as well. I mean, because all those thought-out plans of mine would have to once again be revisited." I point my glass at her.

"I'm just getting settled in my work, you know. I love my job. I like working with Mr. Falcon, keeping him in line, and knowing all he does. I just... I don't want... I don't want to go back to living separate lives." The truth comes out like I knew it would.

"I hate to break this to you, Mrs. Falcon." Darius shoves her playfully. "Your boss isn't so keen on that as well. He's thinking it's time to change how he runs the business. Stan and I discussed that earlier. I thought it might be nice to set up a home base closer to those we are closest to. And since the Heir Crown Prince cannot just pick up and leave his home, because of his responsibilities, not to mention the Reyes family is my biggest and most valuable client. I thought it might be best to move it here."

"That's how you figured it out so easily." I lean against my husband. "I wondered how you picked up on that."

"I read between the lines. It was always in the long-term plan for them to move back once they started a family. Keeping his family safe from the influences he grew up in, making sure his children aren't exposed to all of that." Stan informs me as we watch our friends easily speak to each other.

I'm not exactly sure what that means. Ingrid hasn't elaborated on the semantics of Darius's strange family. All I know is he isn't close to them and that they look down on him for marrying outside the realm. For that reason alone, I don't like them, because, in my opinion, Ingrid is just as good as anyone else; better, actually, than most.

"Okay?" Darius whispers against Ingrid's lips.

Through tears, she nods and finally smiles for real. "Yeah. I think I like that idea. So, wow. Wow. Oh, wow. Darius, we are going to have a baby!" She squeals like she is just realizing what that means.

"I know, sweetheart. God help us." He turns to look at us, and this time appears a little worried.

Stan and I both glance at each other and then laugh.

How quickly the tables have turned. I imagine there will be a common flip of worry that takes place between them over the next several months. Both flipping out at different times while making sure the other person stays as sane as possible.

CHAPTER 32
Esteban

The Royals

The four of us went our separate ways slightly after one. Both ladies were yawning, so Darius and I thought it best before being forced to carry them to bed after they fall asleep. It wouldn't be the first time we'd done that. These two liked to drag it out for as long as possible and end up crashing while catching up.

According to my lovely wife, it was a common occurrence. They were roommates in boarding school and often talked until one lost the fight, the other followed close behind. They woke up more than once in her New York apartment, still seated on the couch or relaxing on the piles of pillows on the floor. That was how it was with them, and I suppose how it will always be.

I drag her tired body behind me as I lead her to our suite. Listening to her babble about how I did this same thing for the first time a few years ago, when she made a secret trip home.

"Do you remember that, Stan?" she asks me as I guide her into our bedroom and sit her down on the bed.

"Yes." I lean down and kiss her forehead. "Of course I do."

"I was so naïve back then." She kicks off her shoes and flops onto the bed. "I had no idea what I had gotten myself into. So innocent."

I listen as I unbutton my shirt and toss it in the bin. When I turn to face my wife, I am blown away.

Somehow, she has slipped out of all her clothes and is now lying on her back, staring up at me. I swear I practically combust.

"What are you doing?" I ask as I stand there and admire her. "You are so beautiful."

"As are you." She licks her lips and rolls over onto her stomach, propping her head into her folded hands. She crosses her feet with bent knees, and that is when I notice the heels she has slipped on.

"Are you trying to seduce me, Winnie?" I kick off my shoes and unbuckle my belt so I can remove my pants.

"If you have to ask..." She drops her head onto her folded arms and sighs.

I point at my tall and proud member, standing up to greet her. "It's just that you've never..."

She rolls over onto her back and lets her head hang slightly off the edge. "Come here."

My feet move all on their own until I am in front of her. It is clear to me that she's had a little too much to drink, causing her to loosen up a bit. I do believe she drank Ingrid's share of the champagne, since her friend had to decline, for obvious reasons.

"I'm here," I inform her as I stare down at her. "Now what?"

"Don't judge me," she whispers, and I can feel her fiery breath heating my thighs.

I watch as her lips land on my skin. Pressing soft precious kisses along my thighs, that have my knees getting weak. As I watch, her earlier words make sense, and I feel the need to make it clear this is unnecessary.

"How have I never thought about giving you this pleasure until now?" Those words, however, steal the ones I was about to speak.

Flipping back to her front, she settles on her knees and encourages me to move closer. Her arms wrap around my backside, and before I can stop her, she drops a kiss to the tip of my erection, and I swear.

Those green eyes turn up to find mine, so she can watch my reaction as she lets the head slip between her soft lips. A smile breaks across her gorgeous face when she catches me gasping for air. I never thought watching her suck me off would be so mesmerizing. Watching my shy and timid wife take control while doing her very best to give me some pleasure is as good as it gets.

"Winnie." I speak her name as she takes me deeper. "Winnie, stop."

Pulling her mouth off like I suggested, she looks up, concerned. "Did I do something wrong?"

I shake my head as I gather her in my arms and fall on the bed next to her. "Not at all. That was perfect."

She kisses me with a smile pasted on her face. "Then why did you stop me?"

"Because if you kept going like you were, I was going to lose it, and I didn't want to shock you." I watch her blush as she understands my meaning.

"Oh." Her gaze travels down my body again. "Would that be something—"

I don't let her finish. I kiss the words right off her lips, kiss her so hard, I swear I am bruising both of our lips. It has been weeks since we've been intimate and I've missed being this close to her.

"Stan," she pants, when I finally break the kiss.

I brush my fingers along her collarbone as I admire her. My eyes find hers again, and I watch her as I allow them to travel down to her breasts. "What do you want, Winnie?"

Her eyes roll back into her head when I pinch her nipple lightly. She withers with each manipulation and arches her chest closer. "Please, Stan."

I lower my other hand, so I can make sure she is ready to take what I have to offer her. The last thing I ever want to do is hurt her. Once I've played with her long enough, I kiss her lips again before I drag her on top of me.

We've had sex like this a few times. I don't last long in this position, because the sight of her does me in. But it also gives her control. And since tonight she is the one to have decided she is ready for us to resume our sex life, I find it only fitting she gets us started.

"Take what you want from me, Winnie," I instruct as I run my hands down her back and squeeze her bottom.

She does just that. Slowly, she takes me inside of her and rides me. I have to do everything I can to not flip her onto her back and take over.

There will be time to do that later. Right now, I need to give my wife the chance to show me what she needs, so that the next time she is feeling needy, she takes it as well. I want us to be equal in all things, and this is a huge step for a woman like my Winnie.

Her body quivers and it sends me into my downfall. I explode, and when I come back down, I discover she has collapsed on top of me.

How long has she been out? How long was I out after one hell of an orgasm that rocked my world?

I caress her back as I turn us onto our sides. When I start to pull out, I hear her mumbled protest. "Stay."

"You sure?" I kiss her nose.

Titling her head so she can look up at me, she nods and yawns. "Weirdly enough, I am. I've missed you. Missed how our bodies rock in slow motion together while we sleep. Stay."

Staring my wife in the eyes, I express my thoughts. "I never dreamed we'd have this connection that was so much more than a physical need. It's so much more than that. It only goes to prove that when a person finds the right one and loves them unconditionally, waits for her until the time for both is right, when that happens, the bond between them is unimaginable. I love you, Winnie."

"I love you too," she whispers against my lips.

Now it is my turn to casually bring both our bodies to heights unknown. I roll her over onto her back and begin rolling my hips in that way we both like. Hitting that spot deep inside of her, while working that sensitive nerve between her folds, just enough to make her moan softly.

I don't rush the process, even when I start to experience the burning heat travel down my spine. When my mind tries to coerce me to pick up the pace so it can get there faster, I push those thoughts aside and keep moving slowly. I do so because I know from practice that when I reach the ultimate high, it will be better and send us both into a deep sleep.

"Stan." She whimpers beneath me. "Oh wow. Yes."

I feel her body tremble and tighten around me. Each and every time that happens, I fall behind her, and this time is no different. My body tightens from the top of my head all the way down to my toes, and all the pressure is released deep inside her. It is the most pleasant sensation, and knowing my love has given it to me warms me all over again.

As soon as we have both relaxed again, I roll back onto my side, bringing her with me. This time I don't attempt to free myself, instead I draw her close and hold her while we both fall into a deep sleep.

Past experience alerts me that our bodies will leisurely do this off and on all night while we sleep soundly. When we wake, we will be exactly as we are now, still riding the high that only comes from being with the one person who is your entire world.

CHAPTER 33
Winifred

The Royals

W e've been open for nearly a month now. I must admit,
Larkin is very talented. Her vision matched mine, and
somehow, she even managed to get this done while still
working hard on her own home. I felt guilty pulling her away from that
project when I know how badly King Antonio wants to get out of
Aragon. However, Larkin assured me I was in no way interfering and
that she had two very capable teams working hard on both projects.
That it was common for her to be working on more than one project,
dividing her time between them, showing up to work on those sections
she felt required her more experienced hands. I couldn't be more pleased
with the final results.

I have three employees working for me. I hired another baker a few
months before we ever opened our doors, knowing it would take two of
us to do this right. She reminds me of myself at nineteen, with a dream
to one day open her own business. The day I met her, I realized then she
was the one I wanted, and I haven't regretted that decision yet.
Together, we have made this place a success, with only a few minor
hiccups.

I hired two employees to work at the front counter. An older
woman, who gladly comes in early during the week to get us through

the rush. The other is a teenage boy who arrives after school and works weekends. So far, they are both working out just as I need them to. And if business continues to flourish, I might need to hire at least one more to help them out.

As you might imagine, keeping my husband far away from my kitchen is nearly impossible. I leave the house around four every morning to make sure I have fresh goodies for my early commuters during the week. I am even gone by six on Saturdays, so he starts his days early, too. I learned he was always an early riser, got his mileage in first thing most mornings before heading to the office.

I am kneading out the dough for our newest creation when I hear Florence greet someone as they step inside. The backdoor opens around that same time, and it is no surprise to find my husband making his way inside. His guards, of course, are flanking him, taking up their spots just inside, like always, when he stops by before heading to the palace.

They don't need to give the place a once over, I'm sure you've figured out I have two of my own guards stationed somewhere in the vicinity. Something I've gotten accustomed to, and have come to realize there is no point in fighting since I am now a princess.

"Hello, Ellie." Esteban greets my kitchen mate. "What are you working on this morning?"

Ellie blinks slowly as she tries her best to remain calm. It has taken her a while to get familiar with the prince stopping by regularly unannounced, making normal conversation with her.

I, however, love the fact that he treats my staff no differently than he does his own. It's refreshing to watch since I understand how unusual it is for someone so prestigious to interact with those below him.

"Birthday cake for a young girl, Your Highness," she answers, acting as normal as she can.

Rolling his eyes, he approaches the young woman and then leans over to inspect her project. "Esteban. One of these days, Ellie, I am going to get you to address me less formally."

"No, you are not." She giggles as she does her best not to let his closeness bother her. "My mother would be very displeased with me if I were so rude."

Flashing her his genuine smile, one that I swear melts hearts and turns minds to mush where all females are concerned, he then places a simple kiss on her forehead. "It will happen. You will in due time see me as Winnie's significant other, and not some well-to-do prince who can't be bothered with the commoners."

The poor girl nearly swoons and has to put down her icing bag so she doesn't mess up the beautiful cake she is diligently working on. I can't fault her for reacting like that; all the Reyes men have that effect on women. They enter a room and then begin flattering them with their manners and charm without even trying.

He leaves her and begins strolling my way. "Hello, beautiful."

I blush like I always do when he gives me such an undeserving compliment. When I work in the bakery, I can assure you I look anything but. I don't bother with makeup and pull my hair up into a bun to keep it out of the way. Most of the time, I am covered in flour and sugar. I wear loose clothing that allows me to move more freely, with an apron wrapped around me to keep my clothes as clean as possible.

"You are going to ruin that amazing suit of yours if you get too close," I warn him as I check out his dark charcoal trousers; he obviously left his jacket in the car.

"Don't care," Esteban informs me as he steps behind me, so he can place a meaningful kiss on my cheek. "What delicious treats are you elbow deep in?"

I bump into him with my backside so I can continue working. "Cinnamon pretzels. A few of our clientele have mentioned how they would like some bread alternatives. I will also bake some loaves later for the evening crowd."

"What kind of bread?" I hear his voice take on that tone that always makes my skin tingle.

"Rye, sweet loaves, and French loaves for now. If they sell, I might add them to our daily items." I cut long strips before making them into pretzels.

"You are bringing home samples, correct?" He steps to my left, then peeks into my large fridge, knowing I keep my ideas inside. "That looks like a lot of bread."

"That is because it is." I open the oven and shove a full tray of pretzels inside. "I'm playing around with a few more ideas, but I am not ready to let my customers try them just yet. Hand me the red bowl, please."

Esteban reaches inside and grabs it, doing his best to inspect the contents. "I have time to get my hands dirty if you need help."

I glance at his clothing again and laugh. "I'm good. You will be covered in flour and then be required to return home if you attempt to assist me. I need to get these in the oven if I plan on getting them ready for later. You should go."

"Is that your subtle way of enlightening me I am bothering you?" My husband carefully rotates my face so we are looking at each other. "Tomorrow, then. Tomorrow, I'm getting up with you and coming here to lend you my very talented hands."

Ellie sighs, and I can see her agitating her head, as if shaking off a visual. The man has talented hands, all right, and it is clear my assistant is thinking the same thing I am.

It's not unusual for him to join me on Saturday when his schedule permits. I have no problem putting him to work, giving him tasks that need to be done. I leave the big stuff to Ellie and me—like baking and decorating—but he washes dishes well and can even scoop batter into cupcake pans like a pro. Sometimes I even allow him to cut the sugar cookies into fun shapes, since it isn't all that difficult to do. On a few occasions, he has manned the counter with Moses, and I must say, seeing my customers not know how to react is quite entertaining.

"I could use a little assistance out here." Florence sticks her head through the door. "We have a late crowd."

"Be there in a second," Ellie informs her as she finishes the flower she's currently working on.

"I got this." Esteban doesn't even hesitate. "You two are busy, and I'm just standing around watching. Don't worry, Florence and I will get them in and out in no time flat."

I don't bother arguing with him. "You do that, then."

Twenty minutes later, I have the loaves rising in the pans and decide I need to establish what is taking my husband so long. I've watched Stew check his watch twice now, which means time is of the essence. However, they have been warned to not remind him, unless it is absolutely warranted. Meaning, if the world isn't going to come to a halt, because he takes a few extra minutes to arrive for some boring meeting, then so be it.

I take the time to remove my very messy apron and wash my hands before I glance up at the clock. No wonder his men seem to get a little antsy. It is approaching nine.

"I'll see what's keeping him." I aim my thumb toward the front. "If anything, I'll take over and send him back ASAP. Sorry."

Stew nods with a gentle smile on his face. "No apology necessary, Your Highness. He does as he pleases when it involves you. We have learned to just let a few matters go and deal with the rush later."

Ellie snickers as she spins the cake, checking all sides are even. "I often forget who it is you are. It is so weird, but at the same time extremely cool."

I wish I could convince our security to use my given name when addressing me, but they refuse to do so. Years of training on the magnitude of respect, and the importance to set an example for others, means I just need to get used to my permanent title.

Larkin and I have discussed this a few times. She feels much like I do. We both are having a difficult time remembering our place in society, accepting we aren't common women, hoping to make a name for ourselves any longer. Everyone knows us the moment they lay eyes on us. Well, everyone in this country, at least.

As soon as I step through the doorway, the atmosphere changes. I notice the tension immediately, and it takes me all of five seconds to understand why.

Standing just inside the main entrance is my sister Dalia with her husband, Hector. A very unimpressed man is blocking them from coming inside. No words have been exchanged, although it is clear he is silently ordering them to leave.

Thankfully, the lobby only has a handful of patrons, who haven't yet noticed the conflict. Florence is handling it all very well, filling orders quickly to get them out of here before all hell breaks loose.

It is no secret to anyone who reads or watches the news, that there is bad blood surrounding our two families. The Colóns have made it clear they believe the Reyeses' reign needs to come to an abrupt end and a new regime rise in its place. They are campaigning to do away with having a sovereign born into power, saying it is barbaric, and long past time to move into a more modern government spectrum.

I do what I can to assist her. Smile the best I can, while I help her ring my customers up, thanking them for visiting us this morning. I even add a few extra pastries, hoping once they witness the turmoil at the door, they'll just move along and leave it be.

"We just love this little gem you've got here," my last customer tells me as she hands me her money. "I have to say, I was a little concerned at first when I heard our new princess was opening a bakery. But then I thought if the queen can work, why shouldn't you be able to as well? Then, of course, after I've tasted your delicacies, it would be such a shame to push your talents aside, all because of who you are. Not to mention, how lovely it is seeing our handsome prince serve the people with a smile. He is rather unique, is he not? He and our king, seem to know how to make the women they love very happy, and making their women happy seems to make them happy as well."

I glance toward the door and nod. "Yes, I agree. Men like them are difficult to find. Thank you for your support. I wasn't sure how it would all work, but so far so good."

She kisses the air and then makes her way to the exit; thankfully there is a separate exit. Larkin designed it that way to keep traffic moving, and since there is no handle on the outside, and it is right next to the register, it works perfectly.

Altercation avoided, and now I only need to see if I can defuse the tension before more customers walk in.

"I believe you are going to be late if you don't get moving." I place my hand on my husband's back. "Hello, Dalia, Hector. What brings you to this part of town? I do believe it's a little under you."

"Looks like I'll be late, then. Lord Colón will be as well it seems, since he is expected to be at this meeting I've been told is important," Prince Esteban announces, not backing down. I use his official title because there is no doubt that he is the man I am dealing with right now.

"Then you should depart together, Your Highness. If my memory serves me correctly, that particular meeting is one the king and you were discussing in detail the other night. Would be a shame to put in all that work, to only prove Lord Hector and Governor Colón's point. Do you not agree with me, my prince?"

I don't miss the smirk that appears momentarily on my husband's face. He is doing his best not to give away how very pleased he is with my knowledge on all matters occurring in his world.

Dalia is equally aware that it would not look good if her husband showed up late. "My sister is correct, my lord. You know how important this is, and I am more than capable of handling myself. Make me proud and let them all distinguish where your loyalty lies."

Lord Hector adjusts his suit as he spins and makes a speedy exit. We watch as he approaches a dark vehicle and climbs inside. I guess he agrees with his wife, even though he didn't say so, or even tell her goodbye.

My husband, however, isn't going to just walk away without properly addressing me. "I should go. Are you going to be all right?"

"I always am, Stan." I spin to face him. "Hillary and Vincent, as you know, are close by. As I am sure are a few others who cannot be as easily detected. My customers had better actually be customers, and not on the payroll of the prince."

"I can promise you they are, in fact, not on my payroll. You feed them all well enough with your treats you leave for them in the guardhouse. They don't need to pose as customers, nor do I need to encourage foot traffic. You, my *princesa*, do that without interference from me." He wraps one arm around my waist and leans close. "I love you."

"I love you too," I tell him before his lips drop to mine.

Any kiss from this man gets to me. It always takes me a few seconds to regain some ground and speak in complete sentences.

"Well, that was certainly some show," Dalia proclaims with venom surrounding her words. "It is not proper, my dear Fred, to so publicly display affection with a man like the prince. You are only making a fool of yourself, and no one is buying into this lovesick story you two are trying to sell."

I return to my place behind the counter, while I do my best to not let her get to me. "Did you come here to tell me that, or would you like to purchase something?"

"Like I'd buy anything you made." She glares at all the items on display. "I see you are fattening up the people to win them over, that's low, even for you."

Right then, a little girl and her mother walk into my store. The little one makes a beeline for the front counter and stares with delight at all the yummy goodness inside.

Her mother places an order with Florence and then asks the little one what she wants. It is clear she is having a tough time deciding what looks best.

Dalia scowls down at the little girl, who is about five. She still carries some of her baby fat; she's got a round little face but is in no way overweight. "You should probably pass my darling child. Sweets aren't going to help you win the battle you are noticeably fighting."

The woman gasps as she steps closer to her daughter. "Hurry up, love."

"I'm just being honest. You very likely should reconsider your choices as well." She looks the woman over judgmentally, and I know how that feels. I've suffered those judging eyes more than once growing up, and they were always accompanied by harsh, hateful words as well.

"Dalia!" I scold her.

The woman shakes her head and studies my sister just as shrewdly. "Perhaps I should buy you something. Seems you could use a little sweetening up with that sour face and attitude. Starving yourself has obviously made you a very bitter woman."

I am unable to hold back my laughter. I've finally met someone who isn't at all deterred by my bitter sister and her spiteful words. "Pick two, little one. They are on me today."

Once the little girl decides what she wants, Florence bags them up with a smile. She hands her mother both bags and sends them on their way.

Dalia is still taken back a bit by the woman who dared speak to her like that. "Well, one should only expect that kind of rudeness in this neighborhood."

"Are you going to say what it is you came here to say, or do you plan on insulting all my customers while they shop?" I lean my forearms on the counter and wait.

"I only came to determine what the fuss was all about." She looks at her polished nails and sighs. "Karina and Paschal have been raving nonstop about your little adventure."

"Would you like a tour of the place?" I offer.

"I suppose." She glances around as if not at all impressed. "You certainly have gone all out."

I smile as I admire the décor. It looks nice. Esteban insisted we spruce the store up to appear worthy of the queen and king. Said it would give the right impression, even draw in more prestigious clients.

"Do you cater?" My sister motions with her hand. "I only ask, because I am sponsoring this charity event, and more than one of my chairpersons has suggested we use you."

Oh, how hard that must have been for her to say.

"We are capable of taking large orders, as long as given enough time to fill them. I'd need the details, of course, and a date. If we have the time, I'm sure we could accommodate your needs. If you have time now, I'd be more than happy to sit down with you in my office to discuss it." I motion for her to follow me to the back.

"I have a few minutes." She lifts her chin. "If you're sure it won't be an issue, with all that is going on between the families."

I lead her to my large office and take my seat behind my desk. "I hold no grudges against you, Dalia. How are you?"

My sister takes a seat in a chair and sets her purse on my desk. "Okay, I suppose. How are you?"

"Wonderful," I tell her as I open up the calendar on my computer. "Life is good. Marriage is better than I expected. Of course, that all has to do with the man I married, and his determination to keep me on my toes and happy."

I peek up to find my sister uneasily staring down at her lap. This is so not like her, and I am worried, really worried. "You okay, Dalia?"

"Yes, of course. Why wouldn't I be?" She boosts her head, and I swear I see my mother's sad face reflecting in hers.

Seeing her like this only makes me appreciate my life that much more. She isn't at all happy with her life. It is clear in the way she carries herself. It makes me sad to think, had I not been so heavily pursued by my husband, I, too, might have ended up like that.

"If you ever need to talk, I'm here," I find myself offering.

A sadistic laugh comes out of her. "Talk. What could we possibly discuss, Fred? We have nothing in common. We indubitably live two completely different lives. No, I don't believe I will be calling upon you to *talk*."

"Don't say I didn't offer," I tell her as extend my hand for the paper she is now holding. "Let me see if we can fit you on the schedule. I'll give you a brochure with our fees and all the items we have to offer. That way you can take it back to your committee before making a final decision."

We only discuss business for the next ten minutes. It is clear to me Dalia has no interest in acknowledging the elephant in the room. I can easily play this game as well as she can.

I escort her back out through the front and say my goodbyes.

Florence is sitting on her stool, taking it all in. "She is one of your sisters?"

"My oldest." I watch Dalia climb into the car, still waiting. "She and I never saw eye to eye on anything."

"She's a jealous woman, that one," the older woman states. "I imagine she was always jealous of you."

"I'm not sure what she ever had to be jealous of. I was the black sheep of my family growing up. The one that could never do right in the eyes of my mother or my sisters. Father had his moments, but I even had a challenging time getting his approval."

"And yet, you are the one living the most authentic life. Married to a man who loves you to the moon and back. Running your own business, one that makes you happy. Seems to me, she has always known you'd eventually get what she always wanted." Florence points out before she answers the phone.

I suppose that is true, although in my mind Dalia had her chance to have what I have. She could have walked a different path if she wanted to. Instead, she decided on the life she now lives, and no one forced her to choose that life. She freely did it all on her own.

CHAPTER 34
Esteban

The Royals

I couldn't care less I was running about thirty minutes behind. If I am going to be completely honest, lately my drive to do this mundane work has vanished. The problem is that I feel like I genuinely don't have a purpose, a reason to wake up every day and show up.

Let's be real here. I'm not the one who will one day inherit the crown. I guess there is a chance, should a tragic event befall my brother the king. But in all likelihood, it will be his firstborn child who will accept that job one day.

Which means what for me, exactly?

My entire life, I was informed I'd take over the family business. It was to be my contribution to our family. Then my father died long before expected, so all that changed. I got stuck in a role that has no worth to it. All those once well-thought-out plans I had on how I would manage the family business went down the toilet. I became the Heir Apparent and now am forced to learn a job that doesn't have any future or room for advancement. Which makes going to work day in and day out seem rather pointless, even though deep down I know it's not.

I step into the king's outer office and am immediately greeted by his newest secretary, Violet. She is in my mind a little shy and mousy, although she is doing a very fine job not letting anyone get past her.

"Your Highness, King Antonio is ready when you are."

I rest my hip on her desk, doing my best to stall while I try to get to know her better. "Did you enjoy the treat I dropped off for you yesterday?" My lovely wife sent a tray of turnovers for the office to enjoy. She was trying something new, of course, and our staff benefits from it.

"Very much, sir. It melted in my mouth. It was very nice of her to think of us." She blinks rapidly, giving me the impression she is still getting used to the fact she speaks daily to highly regarded people. "Please tell her I said thank you. Perhaps one of these days I'll make it to her bakery."

"When you do that, make sure to mention you're our secretary, and she'll give you the good stuff. Probably throw in a few extras from the back. She is always working out new recipes she wants opinions on. I stopped by this morning and she was making cinnamon pretzels, even getting some loaves of bread ready."

Snapping my fingers, I point at her. "Tomorrow. You should stop by sometime tomorrow for sure. I will be in the kitchen, assisting her then. Come by, and be sure to announce yourself, so I can give you the tour. The queen designed and saw to all the renovations, you know. Her vision, I swear, is quite impressive. It just goes to show how talented the woman is. Promise me you'll come by." I wait for her answer.

"Oh. I umm... I guess that would be okay." Violet weakly replies.

"Stop harassing my secretary and join me in here before they summon us." Antonio stands at his now open office door.

Violet rises to her feet swiftly. "I told him you were ready for him, Your Majesty, when he arrived."

He nods and motions for her to sit back down. "I know you did, Miss Blanc. Just like I realize my brother is doing his best to delay the inevitable to get on with his day. When Lorenzo arrives, make sure he joins us ASAP. We've wasted enough of this day away. Before I have to spend it with a group who aren't exactly going to like what I have to share, I'd like to hear his thoughts on his latest project."

"I have to head down to personnel in a few. I didn't realize Prince Lorenzo was stopping by." Violet seems unsure what to do now. "I'll call

UNEXPECTED PRINCESS

down and let them know it could be longer before I am able to get there."

"Go. Lorenzo is more than capable of letting himself into my office. He has no problem letting himself in my home unannounced, even when he knows I haven't seen my wife in over a week." Antonio seems to recall a specific event.

"Please do not mention that again," Lorenzo's voice echoes from the door. "I told you I was stopping by hours before I did. How was I to know you gave everyone the night off so you could get busy the moment you stepped inside the front door?"

A devilish grin takes over Antonio's face. "One day, little brother, you will understand. Your day will come and when it does, I hope your wife greets you like mine often does."

Lorenzo glances over at Violet, who, of course, is blushing something fierce. "Do you have to put up with his arrogant arse all day long? You just let me know when you're sick of him, love, and I'll find a place in my office for you."

"Do not recruit from my personal office staff, little brother. It is poor form, and I'll not stand for it." Antonio motions for us to follow him.

I do, of course, but my little brother seems to lag behind now. His voice has softened quite a bit. Meaning, I am not sure what he is saying to the woman who is uncertain how to deal with the three of us and our banter.

"He'll be a few minutes." Antonio takes his seat as if expecting this.

"What?" I flop down on the couch and do my best to get comfortable.

"I believe our little brother has a thing for Miss Blanc. He spends more time harassing her than you do. While she speaks to you when you take the time to converse with her, she all but ignores him." Antonio grabs a pen and holds it out in front of him. "It drives him completely insane. Watch."

Lorenzo comes stomping in a few moments later with a confused expression on his face. "I don't get that woman."

"Why is that?" Antonio tilts back in his seat and smiles widely. "She blow you off again?"

"Blow him off? Violet is just shy." I do my best to defend the poor woman.

"Shy?" Lorenzo drops into one of the larger chairs. "That woman is not at all shy, Esteban."

I glance over at Antonio and see him shrug. "Why do you say that?"

"Because shy women don't just not talk to you or ignore you when spoken to. They don't make eye contact with you and make you wonder what you did to piss them off in a past life. Nor do they point out how they are not at all impressed with your chivalry, or tell you to save it for someone who cares." Lorenzo shakes his head.

My eyes once again find Antonio's, and I can see his dancing around in delight. It is clear he has witnessed those two go at it and finds it very amusing. I've never seen my little brother so affected by a woman before, and it has me wondering why he cares so much.

I don't get to ask more about it, though, because Antonio is ready to move on. He wasn't kidding about wanting to hear what Lorenzo has been up to and how things are going over at Reyes Capital. Hearing him give his report only makes me miss what I never had a chance to do with that company. I'm happy to discover Lorenzo is making a name for himself, and that he is getting more and more comfortable running things. Since February, I've all but taken a solid step back and let him make the big decisions. Sounds like he was more than ready to do just that, and soon he won't need either of us looking over his shoulder to make sure he is coloring within the lines.

"So, what are you two working on?" Lorenzo asks, as he gathers up his reports. "Anything exciting?"

"I'm officially letting them know I will move the king's office as soon as Isabel's school year ends. Larkin promised me my new office will be ready soon, and we are both more than ready to make the official move," Antonio announces.

Meaning, I'll be left behind to deal with everyone while he works out of his nice, quiet home in the country. "Must be nice to have that option."

My eldest brother must hear the bitterness in my voice. "You have options as well, Esteban. You only need to speak of them, so I can help you decide how we move forward. Don't think I haven't noticed your less than enthusiastic desire to be here."

We stare at each other for a long moment, while I do my best to figure out what I want to say. "It's fine. I'm fine. What can I do about it, anyway? Nothing. Therefore, there is no point in discussing a topic none of us can change, or even wish to. So, let us just move on and forget about it."

"You seem to forget that I've done your job before. I understand more about it than you think I do. The only difference is when I was doing your job, I was doing so with the knowledge that one day everything I learned would benefit me once I took over this very seat." He taps his desk. "You, however, don't have that same knowledge about taking your place here. It could happen, I suppose, should I resign or God forbid die before my heir is old enough to do this job."

"Do you have news?" Lorenzo's eyes bug out.

"No. Not yet. As far as I know, anyway. But it is a possibility. We've been doing our best, as you are aware." Antonio seems rather proud to be rubbing that in, and I guess I don't blame him. Serves Lorenzo right if he witnessed something he shouldn't have, since he seems to believe our homes are still open doors for him to freely walk through.

"Why do you have to keep bringing that up? I promise, you have my word, I will not walk into your home until invited inside ever again. Meaning that until someone opens the door, wearing clothing, preferably, I will remain outside of it. I have no desire to witness what I witnessed last night in your foyer. Your entryway, may I remind you, where all your guests must walk through to enter. I do so hope you sanitized every surface, so as not to offend the unsuspecting souls who have no idea how you two have perfected wall sex." At that, he stands and runs his hand over his face several times. "You do realize I am ruined now?"

"I doubt that." Antonio also stands. "Violet is counting on you not being."

"That is never happening. She has made that perfectly clear. Not that I... never mind." He ignores both of us laughing and makes his way through the office.

"So, you are predicting those two have the hots for each other?" I stand as well, knowing it is time for us to make our appearance. "I thought she was shy."

"She is a little timid. But when it comes to Lorenzo..." He stops at his door, and we watch them stare each other down.

"It was just a simple invitation, Miss Blanc. You were invited, were you not?" Lorenzo is standing with his arms crossed in front of him.

"Yes. I have other plans that night, though." Violet must have noticed us because she forces a smile on her face.

"I don't believe you," Lorenzo challenges her.

Tilting her head toward the ceiling, she takes a deep breath. "Like I bloody care if you believe me or not, Your Highness. I said no, and like always, you refuse to accept that I am not interested in your advances. Do women never tell you no?"

Antonio nudges me as he snickers. "See."

I step forward. "What is he bothering you about now?"

Her eyes fall to her desk before she answers. "Nothing, Your Highness. He's not bothering me. I just don't believe he gets rejected all that much. Women, desperate women, fall to his every demand and trip over themselves to please him. I, however, am not one of those women; therefore, he seems determined to figure out why. It's simple, really. I am frankly not interested, that is all."

"Out." Antonio grabs Lorenzo's shoulder and shoves him toward the door. "You heard her. She is not interested. Now, go, before I embarrass you and tell her what I believe is going on here."

Violet squints her eyes and glares at Lorenzo. "Nothing is going on, sir."

"I know that," Antonio addresses her calmly. "Nothing, however, seems to be getting you a little riled up, and I can't have that. You are a critical employee I require to help me make my transfer to Homero run smoothly. Which is why I am determined to make sure nothing gets in the way."

Violet nods as she falls back into her seat.

There is definitely something transpiring between these two, and I believe it might be fun to watch. Little shy and mousy Violet obviously has some fight deep inside of her that Lorenzo triggers. Why is that exactly?

The three of us walk out, leaving Violet to calm down and get back to work. Lorenzo doesn't even bother to speak to either of us. He continues moving when we pause outside the conference room, where Alejandro, the king's personal secretary, is waiting.

"I was just about to come and get you two," he informs us as we step closer, handing us the agenda that explains the topics this meeting will cover. "Number five should be addressed immediately."

Antonio reads it and then glances my way. "So, it begins."

"So, it does. Shall we?" I motion for him to enter first. "It will be fun watching those two slither away with their tails between their legs."

"Yes, it will." Antonio gestures for Alejandro to open the door.

CHAPTER 35
Winifred

The Royals

T he last time I celebrated my birthday was when I turned
nineteen.

My twentieth birthday was unquestionably the biggest
letdown. It occurred only a few months after the man I'd been falling in
love with stepped out of my life. I didn't feel like celebrating a day he'd
made special for me twice before. It only reminded me of what I had
lost. So, I went back to not celebrating it while doing my best to forget.

Last year, my birthday came only days after my mother's sudden and
unexpected death. So, celebrating it was the very last thing I wanted to
do. I had so many other obligations to take care of. It had come and
gone before I realized it.

This year I will turn twenty-three. My life is going better than I ever
imagined it would, but that doesn't mean I have sincerely thought much
about celebrating. I guess so many years of not having celebrated the day
of my birth, I became accustomed to those around me not
acknowledging the day at all. There were only a handful of people in my
life who ever cared to mention it, my closest friends in boarding school,
and my now-husband.

So, when Stan made a request, I did what he asked me to do and
took the day off. I even closed up shop, uncertain that was the best idea

since we had only been open a little over a month. He took it upon himself, however, to post a note on the front door, informing my customers that we would be closed and why. It stated the prince demanded his wife take the day so he could pamper her properly. As you might imagine, that sparked many conversations and had them all questioning me how exactly a prince pampered, several giving me that knowing eye. Oh, if only I could explain it, although I honestly hadn't a clue to the extremes my prince had planned to take his pampering.

This morning I was awakened in the best possible way. If the man who so clearly loves you hasn't ever woken you up gently, then you have no idea what I'm talking about. I'll do my very finest to paint a vivid picture, so hopefully, you will understand.

It started off with the scent of bacon—I see you were going in an entirely different direction. Fear, not my good friend we will get there. My nose picked up the scent seeping through the door to our bedroom, the one that leads to the inner patio. Forcing the rest of my senses to awaken and causing my eyes to flutter open slowly.

Since my mornings were typically quite early, I often crash as soon as the sun sets. My adoring husband puts me to bed at least three to four times a week. The other nights he still tucks me in, even lays down next to me until I drift off.

Last night, I put in a few extra hours, because we were going to be closed for the next couple of days, and I had orders that needed to be filled. So, I'd crashed in front of the television quickly after dinner and somehow ended up in bed. My guess is that my man carried me there once he was ready to call it a night.

So, I'm not at all surprised to discover I am in one of his university t-shirts and my more comfortable knickers. Reminding me of the first night I ever slept in this particular bed a little over a year ago. Things that night got out of hand, and we both allowed our emotions to lead us, not at all considering how risky that was. It most certainly was a turning point for us.

Imagine sharing a shower with someone you care about. The one person who you know makes you lose your mind in the best of ways. It changes everything. There was no turning back for us at that point; we couldn't go back to being friends or acquaintances. It was either move forward together or separately; thankfully we had chosen the together option.

I climb out of bed and dig through my drawers for a pair of yoga pants to slip on. We are never truly alone here in this residence. Unlike our home in Cabrera, which is way bigger than this one, so you'd think it would have staff lingering about, but it does not. There are usually at least five staff members on the grounds somewhere here, however.

I exit through the patio door and make my way to the kitchen, which is just across from our suite. Esteban is clearly in there since I can hear the clanking of pans and his voice as he talks to someone.

When I reach the doorway, I have to grab onto the frame, to keep myself from fainting at the sight of him dancing around in there. He is doing the best he can to multitask and doing a fine job at it. His back is facing me, and my eyes are fixated on the globes of his naked arse, which are hanging out of the apron he has wrapped around him.

I take a few seconds to recover from the most perfect scene. "A woman could get used to waking up to such a sight."

Not missing a beat, he shakes that fine arse of his and peeks over his shoulder. "Pants aren't required today. Today we wear the suit you wore on the day you entered this world."

I can't help but giggle at that thought. "I hope you gave everyone the day off if you plan on walking around in your birthday suit all day."

"I did. House staff left last night around eight, and will not be returning until later this afternoon. I have ordered security to stay in the guardhouse or walk the perimeter. They are not to step foot inside the house without my verbal permission. How can I properly pamper my adoring wife on her birthday, if I am not allowed the freedom to do as I please?" He has been plating up our breakfast while talking and then placing them on the tray next to him.

"I see." I push off the frame and step toward him. "French toast, bacon, and scrambled eggs. Impressive."

"Back to the bedroom, *princesa*. This is a full-service breakfast, and I was planning on serving it to you while in bed." He nods at the door I just stepped through. "Move it, birthday girl."

I do as I am told with a smile on my face, wondering what a full-service breakfast consists of. When I walk through the patio door, I head straight for the bed and crawl back in with my back against the headboard. Because I had done as told, I hadn't realized my husband discarded the apron until I was settled in the bed and looked up at him.

"Do I get to choose what I want first?"

Stan rolls his eyes as he places the tray between us and then sits down. "No. Eat first while it is still hot. I worked hard in there, I almost burned—"

"Is that why you had the apron on? It's probably not a good idea to cook naked, Stan," I inform him as I take my plate and pick up a piece of bacon.

It all looks delicious and I can't decide what I want to try next. This isn't the first time my husband, the prince, has cooked for me. While he can only cook a few items since he has always had staff who did that for him, what he cooks he does well.

"I put the apron on because I didn't think body hair in your breakfast was ideal." He cuts a piece of French toast, forks it up, and offers it to me. "The first few pieces I made were questionable. Do you know how hard it is to cook for someone who is very well-established in the kitchen? There is a ton of pressure to get it right."

I fork up a bite of mine and offer it to him. "It is very good. No pressure at all."

We finish our breakfast with small talk and a few laughs. As soon as I shove the last of it in my mouth, my dear husband confiscates my plate as he gives me orders. "Strip."

"I thought we had all day," I tease as I remove my clothes, surprised he allowed me to remain dressed this long.

"Susie set the massage table up in the solarium." I cannot help but grin at that statement.

Susie is our masseuse. She has magical hands that work out those kinks I now get from being on my feet all day, bent over a table. Baking is hard, meticulous work. My hands, neck, back, and even my legs and feet take a beating weekly. My incredible man hired her to knead those out once a week, usually on Saturday evenings, when I will have the following day off.

"Susie is here?" I ask as I stare at him dressed in the same suit as earlier.

He also does a once over of himself and raises his eyebrows. "No. I don't make it a habit of running amuck like this when there are others around to witness. Nor would I suggest you, my dear, expose yourself."

"Stan." I wait for him to nod, notifying me I have his full attention. "Susie sees me like this regularly."

"I am aware of that, my love. But I would not suggest you follow me in that beautiful state without slipping a robe over you first. I believe she covers you with a sheet, to ensure you are comfortable." He reaches for my hand and then guides me through the patio door again, to where Susie has it all set up. The sun is shining down on the table like a spotlight, warming the leather from the cool morning air.

"So, she isn't here?"

Patting the table in front of him, he encourages me to climb up and even helps me get situated. "Comfortable? I have a sheet I can cover you with if you are cold."

Lifting my head, I look at him. "Who's giving me my massage?"

Reaching for the bottle of oil, he applies some to his hands as he answers. "That, my *princesa,* would be me."

Seizing my right hand, he begins much like Susie would, using the perfect amount of pressure. I sink back down but keep my head turned, so I can watch him work the magic. My words fail me while he works both my arms for a good fifteen minutes.

"Head down," he orders as he steps in front of me. "You are going to get a kink in your neck, and then I will have to work even harder to get it loose."

Those magical fingers begin to massage my scalp, forcing a satisfying moan from my lips. "When did you learn to do this?"

"Susie has been giving me pointers for a few weeks now." He digs into the spot behind my ears, and I moan. "Do you regularly make those sounds?"

"What sounds?" I mumble as he does his best to drive me insane.

"Sex noises, Winnie. Do you make those distracting sounds regularly?" he asks as his lips land on the top of my head.

I begin to raise my head, except it is pushed back down quickly. "No. Stay still."

I moan again when he digs his fingers deep into the tender tissue at the base of my neck, relieving all the tension. "I don't. Or at least I don't believe so. Perhaps I do and just don't realize it. Susie has never mentioned it before."

He drops something and bends down to pick it up. My eyes instantly find his arousal, and I giggle. "I don't believe it is proper protocol to get turned on while working on a client."

Stan's gaze finds mine, and he flashes me one hell of a grin. "I'd be rubbish at this job, then. Those sexy noises are doing that to me, and I suppose if you were an actual client of mine, this might be grounds for dismissal."

I tilt my head again, so I can keep my eyes on him. "I don't know. I believe my sisters have gone to special massage parlors, where that wasn't taboo. I recall them discussing it after an overseas trip where they visited a very private and exclusive one. Discussed how all massages should end with the masseuse bringing them to orgasm. I was twelve at the time, and clueless about what that meant, exactly."

"Your sisters have lived an adventurous life." He forces my head to rest correctly again as he works the tension out of my back and shoulders. "I believe that is called a happy ending massage. A few of my university comrades visited establishments like that as well. They thought it would be funny to buy me one of those special massages for my birthday when I turned twenty-one. I was likewise as clueless until—"

My head jerks around in haste. "You had some prostitute masseuse—"

"No." Stan shakes his head, disgusted. "No. Thankfully, I realized rather quickly what she was about to do when she removed the tiny cloth covering me, so I stopped her. Ruined all my chaps' fun. I then told them under no circumstance would I dare trust them ever again."

Not very many words are spoken for the next hour. My very talented man does his best to relax me, and I have no complaints.

He even turns me over, so he can work those muscles as well. That is when things take a turn in a completely different direction. It's much more difficult to ignore how intimate this is when our eyes lock and the heat behind them is clear as day.

"This is by far the best massage I've ever received," I inform him as he manipulates my breasts.

He leans down and kisses my lips softly. "I'm doing it some justice, then."

I nod as I watch him move until he is standing by my feet. With a devious smile on his face, he lifts one leg and gently places soft kisses along the inside, making my breath hitch.

"Okay?" he questions as his hands squeeze my thighs and make me shiver.

"Stan." I say his name, hoping to send him a message.

I then watch as he straddles the table and rests my thighs on top of his. Those hands travel up and work over my most intimate area, with all kinds of promises. They land on my hips and press wonderfully in the right spots, which makes my belly tingle and has me wiggling.

"What do you want, Winnie?" He tugs me closer so that his hard member is now sliding through my wet folds, bumping and rubbing that sensitive spot perfectly.

"Stan, please." I whimper as a mild orgasm is set free.

Grinning as only a man can when he knows what he is doing, I realize this is going to be a long, slow process. I'm not sure how many times I go off mildly, but each time, it is only enough to just relieve the pressure, but not enough to satisfy. It only makes me want more, while I do my best to trust him to know what he is doing.

When he has me quivering in the best of ways, he slides his hands behind my back and hauls me up, until I am sitting up facing him. "I want to try something a little different."

I nod, not at all fearful.

"Relax against my hands and wrap your arms around my neck. Leave your legs where they are, but lift slightly, so I can work my way inside, love." He grabs his shaft and places it at my entrance, then guides me down on him. "Good?"

Once again, I nod.

"Don't move," he instructs me as he brings my head close to his. However, he doesn't allow our lips to touch. We are as so close that we are breathing in each other's breath. Our eyes shift from our lips back to our eyes as we watch.

My husband's hands squeeze my hips ever so gently that I can feel all the pressure building inside of me again. It is so slow and intimate I don't even realize our bodies are slowly moving until his lips contact mine, and we kiss.

Nothing is rushed or frantic. It is all a gradual process that seems to take on a power all its own. I have never felt closer to him than I do at this moment, as we melt into each other, letting our bodies just do what seems natural.

My orgasm is long and drawn-out, powerful, and it sends Stan into one just as impressive. His body trembles and breaks out into goose pimples as I watch the pupils of his eyes expand and then get small again. It is so intimate; I don't even realize I am crying until I feel the warm, wet tears fall onto my legs.

"Happy birthday," he whispers.

"I'll never top this when your birthday comes around," I inform him as I wipe my face off.

"It's not a competition, my love. I only want you to feel cherished while understanding how lucky I feel to be a part of your life. This day is important because it was the day God allowed you to enter the world, making it possible for me to one day find you in it." He somehow moves us, so he is now standing with me still attached to him.

"We also celebrate it, because I believe it is also the very date we came together as a couple when you were only nineteen. How we have both changed since then. I am so very glad we found each other again, Winnie. That you forgave me for not knowing how to handle matters back then when I feared for your safety. This, my love, is how it will be from now on, and I promise to never not celebrate another birthday with you for as long as I live."

I believe this day may become my second favorite day of the year, my first, of course, being the day we married. Every day with this man, I often wonder how I got so very lucky to be the one he chose to be his.

CHAPTER 36
Esteban

The Royals

I surprise my wife with a party after a day of lazing around the house and making love unhurriedly off and on all morning. When the day ends, I inform her it is time to get dressed for the evening.

We shower together for the second time when I lead her to her closet and point to the garment bag hanging there. "Put that on." I slip into my own clothes and listen for her reaction.

"Stan. I cannot possibly wear this."

"What is wrong with it?" I holler back at her.

The dress is a deep purple, tight-fitting cocktail dress that stops just above her knees. There is a sheer overlay that falls down the sides and back, stopping right before it reaches her ankles. I have no doubt she will look stunning in it and be the talk of her party.

"It is too small for one," she protests. "Two sizes smaller than—"

I peek my head around the corner and shake it. "You are crazy. I bought the smaller size, because you, my love, have lost weight again. If I had bought you the size you typically buy, it would not have fit correctly. Try it on."

I step back into my closet and begin putting on my dinner suit. We are going to a nicer restaurant, I told her, so I am going to dress the part. I, of course, have rented the establishment out for the evening, invited those who are important to us. Not just family and friends, but also staff members who see to our daily needs, people my lovely wife interacts with and treats with respect. This is a private event, a party to celebrate her birthday. I didn't want a bunch of stuffy people there, those who would make her feel uncomfortable. She has to attend enough of those types of events as it is.

"You are crazy, Stan," she grumbles back. "This dress will…"

I wait for her to finish, but she doesn't. "Will what?"

There is no response, so I button up my shirt and step back into her side of the closet and pause. Winnie is standing there in front of the mirror, gaping at her reflection. The dress fits like a glove, exactly like I knew it would.

"Shoes are in the box under the bag. Finish getting ready. I'll meet you downstairs, in about thirty." I smile, knowing how perfect she looks.

Forty minutes later, Winnie steps into the foyer where I am waiting, looking gorgeous. I say nothing; instead, I walk up to her and then wrap my arm around her as I draw her in for a nice, passionate kiss.

"Aren't you tired of me yet?" she whispers breathlessly against my lips when I draw back.

"Not possible. I will never tire of you, my love." I kiss her again. "Tonight, when we get home, there will be none of that slow, easily loving we've done all day. After having appreciated you in this stunning dress, I'm going to be more than ready to rip it off."

Her hands land on my chest as she pushes me back. "There will be no ripping off of this dress."

"Spoilsport." I laugh as I take her hand and escort her to the car waiting for us.

It takes about thirty minutes to get to the restaurant. At first glance, the place appears to be filled with patrons enjoying their dinner. It isn't until the hostess leads us through the dining hall to our table, does she seem to catch on.

"Stan." Winnie pauses and peruses the room. "Why do I know every single person here?"

Right then, Ingrid stands and everyone sings *Happy Birthday* with her. My wife's hands cover her mouth as she spins and realizes I pulled one over on her. "You are throwing me a surprise birthday party?"

I nod.

"You invited all these people?" She scans the room. "People I truly like. People who are important to us."

I nod again.

Her eyes find mine, and I notice the tears filling them. Then, to my surprise, she throws herself against me and kisses me hard, causing the crowd to cheer and whistle.

"Thank you," she mumbles against my lips. "Thank you so much."

Little did my wife understand what kind of night she was in for inviting those closest to us. We not only have a wonderful, delicious dinner, filled with laughter and stories. So many of them shared, even more, when they took the microphone to wish her a happy birthday.

The crowd was small, only about fifty guests. Her sisters Karina and Paschal were there with their father. I had invited Dalia and her husband, although I wasn't surprised to not find her in the crowd.

As you might imagine, my wife insisted on making the rounds to thank every person there for coming and sharing this evening with her. We are there for almost two hours when things turn more interesting. Two events transpire before our eyes.

First, is when my younger brother approaches us, seeming unhappy about something.

"Something wrong, Lenny?" Winnie asks him.

"What? No." He glances around the room. "Have you seen Miss Blanc? I seem to have misplaced her shortly after dinner ended."

"Miss Blanc? Violet? I spoke to her an hour ago. She informed me she needed to leave. Said something came up that needed her attention," Winnie tells him.

"Are you serious?" He sounds pissed. "She just left without a word?"

"I got the impression it was important, Lenny. Why do you ask?" She reaches out and takes his arm, forcing him to look at her. "Are you and Violet..."

He scowls at her. "No. That woman is impossible to read. It doesn't matter. I'm over it now. Message received. I'm not sure why she has a beef with me, but I'm done playing nice."

Lorenzo leans down and kisses Winnie's cheek. "Happy birthday, Freddie. You look divine. Happiness looks good on you. I'm going to head out. I have a meeting in the morning and I need my beauty sleep, so I can impress the heck out of this new investor."

I shake his hand and wish him luck, knowing this will be a big deal for him and our family's company.

"Him and Violet?" Winnie asks me, confused as she watches him walk away.

"Antonio says it's been going on for a while now. I must admit it is quite an interesting thing to watch. I always considered Violet a shy woman, a woman who was doing her best to figure out how to deal with the job she was now performing." I wrap my arm around her shoulder.

"You all are very intimidating men, Your Highness. Miss Blanc didn't grow up in a home like the one we both did. She is as simple as it gets. Her father is a seaman who is gone for months at a time. I believe he works on a shipping vessel. Her mother died when she was twelve, leaving her to take care of herself when he was off working." Winnie gives me a brief history of the woman I once thought was a bit mousy.

"How do you know all that?"

Rolling her eyes, Winnie explains. "Women talk, Stan. I think it came out when she was giving me her condolences about my own mother's death. She told me as a way to explain how she understood the pain and confusion I was experiencing. Did you know she has younger siblings? Quite a bit younger, around the same age as Isabel."

I was going to ask more about that but don't get the chance. Something across the room catches my wife's attention, and she darts that direction as fast as her feet will carry her. Not only do her feet seem to move, but so do the feet of every single security personnel in the room. They swarm the princess and try to stop her. But she is too quick and determined to get to whatever it is she sees before they can prohibit her from her destination.

I cannot see what she sees but I know I hear her correctly, which is what gets my feet moving almost as quickly. "Dalia? Dalia! Oh my,

Dalia! Dalia, are you okay? Help! Someone, help. Dalia! Oh, God, please, Dalia."

When I break through the crowd, I catch sight of what Winnie saw that got her moving. Standing in a complete daze is Dalia Colón wearing a peach-colored dress. The color is barely recognizable since most of the dress is stained in bright red blood. Her face and hands are covered in it as well. The tips of her hair are dripping with it. The question, of course, is whose blood is it? Is it hers or someone else's?

Braden, Isaac—one of Antonio's guards—Vincent, and Dane—Larkin's personal guard—step in between the two women. Braden and Vincent do their best to keep Winnie back, which as you might expect isn't a simple task. The other two men slowly step toward Dalia, while the remaining security puts themselves up as a wall between everyone else and her.

"Lady Dalia," Amanda, another one of Larkin's guards, addresses her in a calm voice. "Are you hurt?"

"Let me through!" I hear Ivan Batista demand. "She's my daughter. Let me through!"

Antonio appears to my left. "Dalia."

The disturbed eyes of a distraught woman fall on him. "Your Majesty."

Lifting a hand, not at all interested in what his guards have to say, Antonio slowly begins walking. "Are you okay, Dalia? Are you hurt? You're bleeding, I do believe."

"Bleeding?" Dalia blinks sluggishly and looks down at her hands. "I'm bleeding?"

I am now directly behind my wife and place my hands on her back. "What happened, Dalia?"

"Your Highness." She blinks a few times. "I don't know. I was fighting with Hector as usual. He forbade me to come here and socialize with the likes of you all. I told him I was tired of all this stupid animosity between us; that I was coming with or without him."

Hillary steps in now wearing black latex gloves. "May I look you over, Lady Dalia? Make sure you are okay?"

"Sure, I suppose that would be okay." Her eyes are so blank it is scary.

"I started to leave." She reaches up and touches the back of her head. "He grabbed my hair and yanked me back, I might have fallen. Hector started kicking me, then, while telling me I wasn't leaving. Over his dead body was I leaving."

"Did he hit you with something ma'am?" Hillary asks.

Dalia just looks at her blankly.

"You have a gash back here on your head." Hillary informs her, motioning to those now approaching. "Why don't we get her a seat and something to press against this until the paramedics arrive."

Both appear quickly.

"She has no weapons," Hillary announces, having taken the time to pat her down while assessing for more injuries.

Winnie shoves her way forward again now, even though it is clear the guards are still leery about it. "Dalia, how did you get away from Hector?"

Dalia's eyes find her sister's. "When he paused to catch his breath, I crawled into the kitchen. I opened the cutlery drawer and pulled out the sharpest knife I could get my hands on. When he grabbed my hair again, I caught him by surprise. He fell backward, stumbled, and collapsed behind the counter. I had to be certain he wouldn't follow me. I had to make sure he wasn't able to come after me."

"Stop! Stop!" Karina orders as she breaks through the crowd. "Dalia, do not say another word. Keep quiet."

Dalia nods and blinks heavily, very dazed, clearly not aware. "I had to stop him, Karina."

Karina kneels next to her older sister. "I know, honey. You've said too much already."

"Dalia." Winnie stares at her sister. "Oh, Dalia."

"I'm sorry I ruined your party, Fred." Dalia is still not all there. "I only wanted to come because I am tired of all this fighting. I don't want to fight anymore. I'm sorry."

"Don't worry about it, Dalia. I'm glad you came," Winnie tries to reassure her. "We will figure this out and... and Karina will make sure... Oh, Dalia."

CHAPTER 37
Winifred

The Royals

D alia ended up shutting down completely once admitted into
the hospital. She was in a state that had my family and me
deeply worried about her.

I can honestly say I have never seen my oldest sister in such a state.
Dalia is the one who always has something to say. Even at her worst, she
voiced her thoughts and ordered everyone around. However, the Dalia
I've spent the last couple of days with is a shell of that person. I'd do
about anything to see a sign of her, just so I'd know she was still in there.

Her eyes are as hollow as I imagine they can get. There is no life
inside of them; no fight or light shining behind them. The last thing she
said when the paramedics took her away was how very sorry she was as
she stared into my tearful eyes. The doctors haven't been able to get her
to respond in any way. It is as if she has given up and lost all hope.

It took an hour to learn Hector Colón was still alive, just barely.
He'd taken a nasty slice to the neck, nicking his main artery. The reason
everyone believed Dalia was covered in so much blood. He had
somehow slowed down the loss of blood with a towel hanging in the
kitchen, but unable to move much more than that.

The police reported the home had been in dire shape, evidence that a struggle had occurred. Bloody handprints were left along the pristine walls and front door. They questioned Hector the best they could, but his muffled words were inaudible and random. They were waiting to get the green light from his doctors before doing so again.

Dalia's first accounts were the clearest explanation so far, although the police believe there is more to the story and would like to hear what that is. The problem is, she hasn't been able to elaborate since. Her defensive bruises suggest she is telling everyone the truth, but until they can confirm, there isn't much else they can do.

My father has stepped into the protective role as expected. He has taken it upon himself to keep the Colóns far away from his daughter, who is undeniably traumatized by whatever happened in her home. Karina and he have joined forces. They are doing the best they can to keep Dalia out of jail. The plan is to have her placed in a facility that will hopefully get her the treatment she needs.

We are sitting in her room at the moment. They are talking about her like she isn't even there, much like they have done to me my entire life. It bothers me. For that reason, I asked them to leave and not return until they are finished with their business.

The silence is better than listening to them bicker about where they believe she should go. I hate thinking of my sister locked in some institute, instead of out in the world living a full life. I guess it is better than jail, and until she starts talking, the possibility of her going to jail is exceptionally high.

Governor Colón is doing his best to pull as many strings as he can. Painting my sister as a disturbed woman, one who finally snapped and attacked his innocent son. Hector is far from innocent.

If necessary, I will testify on Dalia's behalf. Reveal how the Colóns were, at one time, ready to kidnap me, and force me to marry into their family. That in itself, I imagine, would paint a lovely picture, and give my sister a chance to heal her mind so she can explain what happened.

"Why are you still here?" Dalia's cold voice echoes in the silent room.

I do my best not to smile when I hear her. "Where else do you think I should be?"

"How should I know?" She stares out the window, looking at nothing. "Do you not have a business that requires your attention?"

"I do. I went in early and made certain all was well. Made sure there were more than enough items available and then left." I can't help but get a little tickled about her concern for my business. "Not true, I guess. They kicked me out. Stan took over for me, with Ellie supervising. He brought reinforcement as well."

I will never forget the look on Ellie's face when she stared open-mouthed at Lorenzo, who was ready to do whatever she told him to do. I laughed, knowing her day was going to be one she'll never forget.

"Dalia." I reach over and take her hand in mine. "Dalia, talk to me."

She shakes her head.

"Dalia, please." I squeeze her hand.

"Why do you care so much, Winifred?" She pulls hers out of mine.

The last time my sister used my actual name was so long ago, I don't remember.

"How long has he been hitting you, kicking you?" The bruises all over her body suggested it wasn't the first time she suffered from such an attack.

I'm shocked when her head spins around and I find tears in her eyes, tears that are about to spill over and run down her cheek. "How long have we been married?"

"How did that happen, anyway? I mean seriously, Dalia." No matter how angry my sister was about her life, I never understood why she let someone like Hector Colón convince her marrying him was a good idea.

She winces as she shifts in her bed and shrugs. "How come you found someone who cares so deeply for you? Why did it seem so easy for you?"

The laugh that escapes me surprises us both. "Easy? Are you serious? Nothing about it was easy, Dalia. We had a rough go at it for a very long time. In the beginning, I... I had a really tough time understanding what Stan saw in me. I had no idea how to act, honestly. I was a nervous wreck and knew I was screwing it all up just by talking. We sort of struck up an odd friendship during that first year I was away.

"He showed up out of the blue in New York on my nineteenth birthday, and at the time, I was contemplating dating someone else. I thought he had come to realize over that year how we weren't compatible and moved on. That night I made a complete fool of myself, dancing with two guys to prove to him I, too, had moved on. It of course backfired on us, and later, after we left the bar, I had a major panic attack on him and ended up sprawled out on the sidewalk."

Dalia stares at me strangely for a few moments. "You danced with two guys?"

"I did." I snicker, remembering that night as if it happened yesterday. "Like dirty danced with them."

"You played him, Winifred. You let him witness that naughty side of you, and it worked." She shakes her head.

"Not really. Maybe just a little. I hated it, though. I hated that I was allowing myself to go there, just to make him jealous." I remember it clearly. "The only thing I guess it did was force us to address the issue between us. His reaction was sort of aggressive, and it felt like I had coerced that response out of him. Made him act in a manner that wasn't him. You know what I mean."

Dalia nods. "You are a good person, Winifred."

"Thanks." I know I blush at the compliment. My sister doesn't give them often, if ever.

"Yeah, so we dated for almost nine months. He regularly made visits as often as his schedule allowed. Flew me home to his place in Cabrera around New Year's. He didn't like the fact I was alone during the holiday, and since it would have been too obvious for him to fly to where I was..."

I hate remembering what happened after we had such a wonderful time together. We lost two full years, all because someone thought I was involved with a man I was not. Falcon came close to dying, and my best friend almost lost the love of her life.

Dalia seems shocked to hear all the trials my husband and I have gone through just to be together. That we somehow found our way back to each other, after all these forces tried their darnedest to keep us apart. Our determination to not let others interfere with the choices we were free to make on our own has somehow affected my sister.

I can see it in her eyes, and I wonder what she is thinking. Before I can ask, she spills. I soon realize how mother played a huge role in the way each one of us girls interacted with each other and those around us.

"You have no idea how hard it was being the oldest, Winifred. Just like I have no idea how difficult it was for you to grow up with three sisters who constantly put you down." Dalia blinks emptily as her eyes drop to the floor.

"I'm so ashamed, Winifred. All those years I was taking out my fears and uncertainties on you, making you suffer more than I did. Treating you like I believed mother wanted me to. If I brought you down, made you feel unhappy about who you were, then at least I knew I wasn't the only one who felt like she just wasn't good enough."

I can hear the pain in her voice when she talks about what was expected of her. "The pressure mother put on me to attract the right man, a certain type of man who held a particular place in society, always weighed heavily on my shoulders. After I messed things up with Antonio, took her greatest chance of being the mother-in-law of the future king away from her, it got even worse. Looks like she was focused on the wrong daughter to get what she wanted."

"That is why Esteban was so determined to keep it between just us. He didn't want me to undergo the pressure from others, those who were only concerned with what he could give me because of the family he came from. Those who were less concerned I marry him because of love."

I know that is a sensitive subject for her, since she lost Antonio to a woman he fell in love with. Taking all her chances of ever convincing him to reconsider, while making our mother even more unbearable to live with.

"I knew agreeing to a quick marriage with Hector was a bad idea. Not only because I'd heard the rumors about him, but because I witnessed how angry he got when you disappeared at the wedding. He came looking for you, practically broke into my apartment. Made me go to father's to check and see if you'd returned there."

Dalia flinches as if she is recalling something specific. "When I returned to inform him you weren't, he went crazy. Said if you'd done something stupid—like run off with the prince—then I was going to pay for it.”

“All you had to do was come to me, Dalia. I would have helped figure it out with you,” I tell her. “No matter what animosity there was between us, I never wanted you to be stuck in a marriage like the one you are now in.”

Her eyes become hollow again as she gazes off into the distance. “He knew things about me, things no one should have been able to find out. Things that if they got out, would ruin my chances of ever making—”

“We’ve all done things, Dalia.” I can’t imagine what he could have had on her that would have ruined her in a way that wasn’t forgivable.

“I slept with the king while I was dating his son. I became pregnant. My plan had been to get Antonio to sleep with me after we were officially engaged, so he’d assume it was his. I was only a few weeks along, so I figured I could play it off. But when he ended it, I had no other choice. King Ramon was not about to father another child, especially not one with his son’s ex-girlfriend. It became such a mess that I knew if it should ever come out, I’d never win Antonio back. He’d forever hate me and I’d be the laughingstock of society. Forever the mother of the king’s bastard child. Worse than one of his whores he snuck into the palace regularly, because I was supposed to be his son’s woman. So, I did what I had to do to keep my sanity, and somehow Hector knew all about it. He had the medical records, claimed he planned on making them public if I refused to go along with his plot to ruin the Reyes family.”

To say I am speechless is an understatement. I have no words. That would certainly ruin her, most likely make her the laughingstock of the kingdom if it ever got out. Those who didn’t hate her before would afterward. She’d never be able to escape such a past, possibly even have to move to another country under a pseudo name where she’d be forced to live an uneventful life. And Dalia would never survive a life where she was not in the spotlight, where everyone looked to her for approval. She was truly the woman our mother had raised her to be. My sister didn’t know how to do things differently.

“Oh no, Dalia.” I finally whisper.

"I did what I had to do." She shivers as if the thought of what she has done sickens her. "Now the truth will come out."

"Or not." A deep, familiar voice echoes from the doorway.

Dalia's eyes bug out and she pales. "What did you... what did you hear?"

The stutter in her voice declares she is alarmed he might have heard her confession. King Antonio is standing there with Esteban and Darius by his side. She appears mortified and unquestionably distressed about anyone ever knowing her deepest, darkest secret.

"Nothing we didn't already know." Darius enters the room first and takes a seat in the chair. "We've known for a few years now. It came out when I started my investigation into your family. We tracked everything, went back years to determine if there was any reason your mother seemed so obsessed with getting her hands-on Reyes money. It became obvious to us that she did not know about the child, because if she had, then she wouldn't have allowed you to abort it without retribution."

"I'm sorry, Your Majesty." Dalia recoils slightly. "I never meant to... but he was the king... he came to me... one does not deny a man like him. He said he would... it doesn't matter what he said. I knew even then when it was happening, we would be over if you ever caught wind of it."

King Antonio remains emotionless as he stares at her. It is clear he only recently learned of this news as well and is still processing the truth about how Dalia planned to set a trap for him.

"It all worked out as it should. I am with the woman I was always meant to be with. What is in the past, is the past, and nothing or no one can change that." He finally tells her with recognizable bitterness in his voice.

"I think we have what we need on Lord Hector now, and can use it against him. Tell me, Lady Dalia, did you and your husband have sexual relations?" Darius seems to know something and wants my sister to confirm it.

"I'm sorry." Dalia stiffens, visibly not comfortable with this conversation. "What kind of question is that?"

"A legitimate one." Darius hands my sister a folder, and when she opens it, I notice she seems shocked.

Esteban takes my hand and tugs me to my feet. "We need to leave so Darius can speak with your sister in private."

"Dalia?" I wonder what is going on now.

"She can stay." Dalia shakes her head in disgust. "No. Hector and I were not intimate like most married couples are. He only visited me during the nights he knew I was ovulating, and he only stayed long enough to get the job done."

"Were you alone?" Darius asks. "I'm sorry I have to ask, but in order to help you out of this mess, I need to know."

"No." Dalia makes a disgusted face. "He always invited a young male to join us. He liked to watch his invitee masturbate. Had the young man touch him until he was primed and almost there, then he'd do what was necessary. Afterward they'd leave without saying a word to me."

"Is this the young man?" Darius hands her a picture, and she nods. "Thank you, Lady Dalia. That gives us exactly what we need. I can assure you, unless Hector and his father, the governor, want this getting out—which I can promise they do not—they will keep their traps shut. I don't care what a man does, or who he has consensual relations with. That is between him and God. A man who isn't true to himself, open about who he is, must not want others to know about this for reasons I don't understand living in today's world. I thought we were past all this, but this information allows us some leverage to get him to listen to reason. I guess I will hold on to this, keep it in my back pocket if we need it."

His eyes turn sympathetic. "Plus, I do believe spousal abuse is a criminal act, one that holds strict punishments if we can prove it in the courts. It is also undisputed grounds for divorce, and one most judges will grant immediately. I believe your sister Karina is already writing up the papers to turn into the courts first thing in the morning. Are you ready to give your account to the officers who have been patiently waiting?"

Dalia nods her head. "It was self-defense."

"That is what the doctor's report suggests. They only want to clarify, and once you do so, we will make an arrest." Darius stands and reaches for the folder on her bed. "Tell them the truth, the entire truth, and you will have nothing to worry about."

Karina steps inside with two officers flanking her. "I don't want her talking to you without me present. Dalia, are you feeling up to talking to these men?"

Dalia nods as she looks at everyone in the room. "I am. I'd like it if Winifred stayed as well, if that is okay. The rest of you may leave."

CHAPTER 38
Esteban

The Royals

A few months have passed since the drama that frequently surrounds my wife's family came to a head once again. The Batista family has been through more than enough over the past few years, so hopefully, things will finally settle for them.

I honestly have no idea how my love survived that family and turned out so normal. I've only been dealing with them for a short amount of time, and the stress of it all is a bit overwhelming.

The three older Batista sisters may finally be getting along better with their youngest sister, but that doesn't mean all is perfect and well. Some habits are hard to break, although it is nice to see them at least trying. Even though I want to strangle them before shipping them off to some secluded island where they can't cause trouble.

Dalia is no longer married to Lord Hector Colón. They dissolved the marriage only weeks after the incident that made headlines. The support the Colón family had recently gained suddenly went away after the story broke and shone a light on what they had been up to. No one wanted to support a family who seemed unstable and willing to do about anything to make the royal family look bad.

Hector would not be Governor Colón's successor, like they had once hoped. New blood would get the chance to take over. That could be good or bad, depending on which person running for that office could convince the people he or she was best suited for the job.

Just last month, Dalia moved to Italy. She wanted a fresh start, knowing the best way to do so was to get away from the drama that surrounded her here. She calls Winnie at least once a week to check in, and from what my wife says, her sister is happier than she has been in a long time. Dalia is working for a real estate agent and doing very well at it, evidently. That is all Winnie has ever wanted for her sister, for her to thrive and be happy. One day, maybe, she will meet someone; although Dalia insists, she is not sure it will ever happen. She wants to focus on her life and forget about men for now.

Karina stops by the bakery a few times a week on her way to and from work. When she does, she always makes certain to poke her head in the kitchen and briefly chat with her sister. They don't have the best relationship, but they are working on it. Winnie is way more tolerable of her jabs than I am, because if I hear her belittle my woman, I put an immediate stop to it. I have noticed a slight change, but I guess it takes time, and this one is as stubborn as they come. I also don't miss how she never misses the chance to speak to Stew when he is around. I believe she might have some kind of crush on my poor guard, and he has no idea how to take her.

Paschal is the sister who has changed the most. She is still seeing the married man; the same one she had been involved with for quite a while now. I've tried to figure out the best way to handle that situation. I don't like him for so many reasons. Winnie tells me it is pointless to put my nose in her business. Because until Paschal is ready to see him for who he truly is, I'm only feeding that side of her that enjoys the shock value it displays. I'd call my wife crazy, but the more I get to know this sister, the more I believe my wife is right. She likes to push the envelope more than the other two do. Surprisingly, it doesn't bother her that people know she is having an affair with a married man.

I also see her the most, since she has no problem stopping by unannounced. Paschal reminds me of Lorenzo. She is the most social of her siblings, and not always understanding that not everyone enjoys her company.

One thing I don't believe I considered when I married Winifred was how much her family would become a part of our lives. I don't know why I thought we could remain in our little bubble and keep everyone else out. I should have understood how impossible that was going to be since I, too, was raised in a large family. It was as if I understood Winifred would gain my family, two extra brothers and two more sisters, along with an adoring mother. That they would look out for her, accept her, welcome her just as they did Larkin when Antonio made it clear she was there to stay. I somehow overlooked that I, too, was gaining three more sisters who I'd come to care about, even though I didn't always agree with them. I even gained a father-in-law who had very strong opinions. And because he was one of the justices, he was unashamed to voice all those opinions to me as often as he pleased.

This is my brother's last full week here in his office at the palace. Maximiliano Chateau has been deemed suitable for occupancy, even though it is not completely finished. As soon as my brother got word of that from his wife, he finalized the move and instructed his staff to pack.

Not much will leave the office he uses here; most of it will stay because he will need it when he returns for his weekly visits. The plan is to spend at least one full workday in Aragon, so he can meet with those who need face-to-face time with him, but conduct the majority of his business from afar. Should someone need to speak personally to the king while he is away, they can make the trip up to him to do so, or speak with him via satellite. Or if it can wait, they can have the secretary at this office put it on his schedule for when he is to be in Aragon.

I am currently in my office, which is directly across the hall from the king's. Since I will now represent Antonio, be his voice and face, so to speak, when he is not around, it works out well. His secretary can send those wishing to talk to the king to me easily. Should she have an issue that needs to be handled with care, I will never be far and can intervene.

"Is he in?" I hear Darius ask as he keeps moving, heading straight for my office.

"Yes, but you can't just..." My secretary tries to stop my best friend, but Darius never listens and does as he pleases.

"Have the king join us," he hollers back as he steps through my open door.

"Falcon, I didn't expect to see you today." I study him closely to determine if I can get a read on him.

He is standing there in a firm stance, wearing a serious expression on his face that concerns me. "Nor did I expect to be seeing you today, my friend, but it seems other forces thought it would be a good idea."

Antonio brushes past him. "Make this quick. I have a full schedule. I assume we have news."

"News about what?" Seems my brother is more informed about this than I, not that I should be surprised.

"You had me look extensively into the law dealing with who could be a governor and then—" Darius starts, but I interrupt.

"Why would you do that? Who are you thinking of supporting to take over for Colón?" I turn to my brother for answers.

Antonio holds up his hand, a sign I need to be patient, so he can hear what Darius has to say.

"Like I was saying," Darius continues. "The support the Reyes family has received from your people has risen extensively."

"Why are you looking into this stuff? Do you not have enough other investigations that would be more useful ways to spend your time?" I again interrupt.

"Are you sure he is best suited for this new endeavor? He can't even sit still and keep his mouth shut long enough for me to get through a simple report." Darius seems frustrated.

Antonio smirks. "Continue."

"While it has never actually been done before, there is nothing that states a member of the royal family cannot hold an elected position."

"Which member is thinking of running for an elected position?" I know my continuous interruptions are irritating, but I can't help it. I am completely lost here.

"You are so irritating. Would you shut up and let me finish?" Darius grumbles.

"By all means, Duke of Falcon, you have the floor. I'm sorry I interrupted you. Although, I believe this is my office. You showed up unannounced, and for some reason are discussing top-secret plots, so I'm just trying to figure out how I fit into all this." I cross my arms and lean back in my seat. "Go on, I'll keep my mouth shut."

"Justice Batista has been an excellent resource and ally. He thought it was an interesting proposal and wondered why no one else had thought of this until now. A person only needs to hold a residence in that region once elected, and since Cabrera is part of the Southern Region, we have that covered. Not to mention the area in which *Iguarias de Royal* is located, is also in the district. I would suggest obtaining a home in the region if the plan is to remain in Aragon, Este. That allows those who are represented to see this as a legitimate representation, and not just the king trying to pull the wool over their eyes."

I start to say something but stop myself. The number of questions running through my head right now is extensive. I'll learn more if I keep my mouth shut.

"And it isn't too late to get him added to the ballot?" Antonio asks.

"No. Right now, the only candidates are Lord Valor, who, as you know, has Colón's support, and Lady Garza, his opponent. Neither candidate is very popular in the region, and Garza holds the lead at the moment, but only because she isn't associated with the Colóns." He scratches his chin.

"As you are aware, Aaron lost a great deal of support after that incident with his son. People don't trust him like they once did. They are waiting for their king to announce his supported candidate. In that region, you've become quite popular. The sooner you announce who you support, the better. That way, we can get out there and do a little campaigning."

Darius smirks. "The downside of it all means he'd have to step away from this while in office. It doesn't mean he can't take over should something tragic happen to you. It only means he would need to focus on the South and the needs of those people in that region. Find his own office space outside of the palace and represent the family less than he does right now. It might put extra work on you, or you could hire a liaison who you trust to do the job he is currently doing."

"Thank you, Darius. That gives us plenty to think about. I appreciate you working so quickly on this, and I promise to let you get back to more important matters that require your attention." Antonio shakes his hand and then dismisses him.

I am still straining to decipher what that was all about. Why do are these two plotting my next career move? Why didn't anyone ask me what I wanted? Maybe I have an opinion on the matter, and it would have been nice to be allowed to give it. Although it might be fun winning a governor seat just to prove a point.

"Confused yet?" Antonio takes a seat on one of my couches. "I know you aren't necessarily pleased with this role you've been forced into."

"What choice do I have? It's not a terrible role, just—"

"One that has no real meaning for you, not like it did for me. I get it, Esteban. I'd be equally bored if I were stuck in the role forced on you to accept. Which is why I've been trying to figure out how best to make you feel you are contributing, while also being useful to all this, and not feeling like you are not a critical part of it all."

I stare at him blankly.

He then explains, and I can hardly believe my ears. It never crossed my mind to run for office. Why would it?

"I don't know, Antonio, that sounds risky. What if I don't get elected? Then it only goes to prove that our family may not have the support we thought we had. It could give those who want to take us down serious firepower."

"I've thought about that as well. But it is a risk I'm willing to take. You're more valuable to me in this seat than you are as my second. Your loyalty to protect the realm and its integrity from a different post could give us what we need to continue governing the same way we have been doing for nearly one hundred and twenty years. I'd like it to go on for one hundred more. Allow my heir to get the chance to take over when I'm ready to step down." Antonio smiles widely and I suddenly believe I understand where all this is coming from.

"Do you have news you'd like to share?" I ask, wondering how I hadn't figured this out yet.

"We didn't want to make the official announcement until we were well into our second trimester. After suffering through a miscarriage once already, we were trying to keep it between us for as long as possible. But the queen is starting to show, and it won't be long before everyone speculates. So, after the move, we plan on making our announcement, letting everyone know our little bundle should arrive sometime in November." The expression on my brother's face is priceless.

He is beaming, and suddenly, I wish Winnie and I were ready to take that step. Right now, however, I know she is busy getting her business underway. In a few years, once she has it exactly how she wants it, we will discuss adding a little one.

"Congratulations. How very exciting! Do we know if we will be expecting a prince or princess?" I think it would be great if he shakes things up a bit, gives this country their first true reigning queen since the ever-popular Queen Victoria. I do not doubt that whatever heir he and Larkin produce will be a great leader with a heart of gold.

"We are going to let it be a surprise." He smiles widely. "Break all the rules and wait it out until our child decides to make his or her debut. It will be the suspense this country needs.

"So now that you most likely are no longer obligated to take my place and crown, tell me how you feel about being a governor. Of course, you will still maintain the title of prince, no matter if you win the election or not, they cannot take that away from you, ever. I won't allow them to refer to you with a lesser title, should you win, even. They can refer to you as Prince Esteban, Governor of the South."

I laugh at the long, obnoxious title. "That is a mouthful."

"Well, I'm just stating I won't allow them to degrade who you are, no matter what. They like their titles, so we will give them one that works. You'd be an excellent governor, Esteban. You would do right by the people in the southern region and only let me influence you marginally."

Again, I laugh. "Marginally, of course. Not that you ever really listen to me, anyway. You've always done as you pleased, even when you knew I was right. I need to discuss this with Winnie before I make any decision, but I think it might be more up my alley than this cushy job. Who do you have in mind to take over this position for me should I decide to go play the political game?"

"Gabriela is still a little young to step into the role, although I believe when she gets older it would suit her well."

My poor sister is worse off than I am when it comes to where she fits in the family dynamic. Clearly, if she wanted, she'd have a place in the family company, could even be Lorenzo's right hand. The kid is a whiz, smart as a tack, knows the ins and outs of the business, and often shares her ideas with all of us. She also hates how women in her particular position are looked at as objects or trophies and would like nothing more than to see that all change.

"Agreed," I respond.

"So, until Gabriela is older, and I can convince her how much influence she will have in that particular role, I thought I'd go with another female who is older and wiser. I need someone who can relate to the generation above mine, those who are not always agreeable with change. Not only does this person have a great deal of experience dealing with this crowd, she also wants to see me do the very best job I can do. She won't be afraid to call me out when she feels the need to do so."

"Mother." I nod once as I wrap my head around her stepping in and taking control. "There will be those who think she should have no part in what goes on in the king's office. They will say she gave that right up when she divorced her husband, the former king."

"Yes, they will. But since she is also the mother of the current king, I can think of no one else I'd like taking over for you, brother. When and if Gabriela ever wants to take over the office, then I have no doubt Mother would train her properly, before passing it off to her to run with. We both know Her Royal Highness Angela, is an excellent ally to have standing next to us. I am only moving her into an office where others recognize her role. It's no secret she has often counseled me when I needed advice. She will only step out of the shadows and into the light."

"Sounds like you've genuinely thought this through. Now I guess I need to do some thinking. When do you need an answer?" I'm pretty sure the sooner the better.

Antonio folds his hands under his chin. "As soon as you can give it to me. The sooner the better."

My best guess is he'd like to make all three announcements at the same time. Shock everyone by announcing I will be running for Governor of the Southern Region. Then let them know if I am elected, my mother will step in as his advisor, taking over my current office. Then he will make everyone happy again by announcing that the next heir to the throne is cooking. This will allow everyone to grasp the bigger picture. That my job as the Heir Prince is ticking hastily to an end.

CHAPTER 39
Winifred

The Royals

I t's been almost a year since I decided to let the man I love sweep me off my feet and whisk me away to marry him. I haven't regretted that decision, not once, in this last year.

There have been several complications that have arisen since that day, but we've joined forces and got through unscathed. My family hasn't made it easy, but Stan has been there by my side, taking it all in stride.

He's sacrificed some of our time together because of my dream to open the bakery. Or maybe I should say he's given up some of his free time, and spent it with me at the bakery, just so we could spend time together. I don't know many princes out there who would roll up their sleeves and wash dishes, take orders, or learn how to bake a few goodies, just so they could spend those extra minutes with their wives. I don't know very many men who would do that, which means I realize how very blessed I am.

He's added a few of his own complications, of course. I had to learn how to survive without him when he was forced to travel. His travel time slowed down once Lorenzo fully took over Reyes Capital, but he still traveled with Antonio to help with the political relationships they have with other world leaders.

Then, of course, a few months back, he dropped the biggest bomb yet when he gave me his thoughts on running for office. I looked at him like he was crazy. Why would anyone want to run for office when he was already a prince? But after his long explanation, I understood that my dear husband was only looking for his place in the country he so loved. Accordingly, I gave him the *okay, I guess that would be fine*, answer.

And wouldn't you know it, by the end of the summer my prince became Prince Esteban, Governor of the Southern Region? He won by a landslide in a very controversial election. One that had several swearing they needed to construct a law that stated a member of the royal family could not hold a government office outside of the king's/queen's. My guess is once they realize how awesome my husband is going to be in his new role, they will change their tune. But then again, there will always be those who want to protest, no matter what.

So, in one year I've graduated from university, become the wife of the Heir Prince, am a business owner of a thriving bakery, and also the new First Lady of the Southern Region. It's been a very busy and challenging year, and I wouldn't change a thing about it.

I was, however, hopeful that this next year would be a little less chaotic. I figured we'd learn all about how holding an office as a governor would change the dynamics of our family unit. We'd adjust to his and my schedules, and make the necessary changes to make this all work for the best. He was going to spend less time in my bakery piddling around, and I was hoping to figure out how to do it all without him underfoot. Probably end up hiring a few more staff to make up for his absence.

What I hadn't accounted for was that during all this bustle, something else would sneak up on us. I believe there is a saying about expecting the unexpected, because it's bound to happen when you least expect it. Well, I was not at all expecting this, nor do I imagine Stan was, either.

"If you knead that bread anymore, it's going to lose its elasticity," Ellie informs me as she takes a cake out of the oven to cool.

"Yes, of course. I'm just distracted and lost in my thoughts," I tell her as I separate the dough and place it in the loaf pans.

"You've been distracted all afternoon. Added the raspberry filling to the dinner rolls, instead of the pastry I sat out." She gathers my pans and takes them to the sink. "What's going on?"

The backdoor opens as my smiling husband strolls inside. "Hello, everyone. Are we having a good day?"

"Hello, Governor." Ellie giggles. "I've always wanted to say that. Yes, it's been very productive for the most part. Why are you here bothering us before the day's end? Don't you have important government business that requires your attention?"

"Probably." Stan and Ellie have formed a teasing relationship. She is not nearly as intimidated by him anymore and freely harasses him when he shows up unannounced. "But someone has to make sure you aren't slacking and taking advantage of your boss."

"I never slack." She points a knife at him. "Today, I've been doing double the work, however, because she is distracted about something. Are you not letting her sleep? We've talked about this, and just because you have magic hands that unmistakably work on her, you promised to only use them on her days off."

"You are getting too comfortable, Ellie. Now you sound like Paschal, lecturing me on when it is proper to pamper my wife," he declares with a laugh. "I'll tell you the same thing I told her. Booger off."

Ellie laughs hard as she washes the dishes.

I remember the night he told my sister to booger off. It was about a month ago, right after a long night of campaigning. We were taking a holiday at Esteban Palace. We thought we were alone in the garden area, where there is a pool. As far as we knew, the others had called it a night and headed to their designated suites for the evening.

It was a hot summer evening and one thing led to another. Having never gone skinny-dipping, I took my husband up on his offer. Thankfully, I got distracted as I watched him strip out of his clothing before removing my own. That gave me just enough time to notice Paschal seated in one of the lounging chairs sipping on a drink. She hadn't noticed us until Stan did a cannonball into the water and splashed her. She scolded my husband for getting her all wet, scolded us for not remembering there were others around. Then gave us the fifth degree on how she would never be able to forget how naughty we truly were. An act she never expected from me, she left us rather quickly. Stan hollered after her to booger off and then climbed out of the pool to get me out of my clothing. We had a lot of fun in that pool, next to the pool, in the garden on the way back from the pool.

"I think I finally found us a place we are both going to like." I hear him say as I clean up my area. "Do you think we can go see it now?"

"How big is it?" I ask, knowing we had discussed my ideas on getting a place that was small, two maybe three bedrooms.

"Four bedrooms." He answers as he raises a hand. "I know, bigger than we discussed, but I don't want to live in an apartment or a condo. I want a home, where we have a private entrance and a yard."

"Ellie, can you close?" I ask as I remove my apron. "If not, I'll be back to do so."

"I can close." She grabs a few cupcakes that need icing. "See you in the morning."

I go to my office and grab my purse, and then we climb into the car waiting outside for us. The drive is short, only about ten minutes away. Which means it is just as far for Stan since his new office is right down the block from the bakery. He hired Larkin's firm to renovate it. In a few months, it should be done, and we can commute together if we want.

We pull up to a metal gate that opens almost immediately. There are several trees in the yard to offer that secluded feeling, even though we are still in the city. I am pleased to find the home isn't exceedingly large. I know that may sound silly, but why do we need another twenty-bedroom home? We don't. So, I requested we keep it small, if possible. Even though I knew that with our family's security needs, that might not be feasible, I wanted to at least try.

"What do you think?" My husband asks as we pull into the circle drive and stop in front of the porch. "There is a guard station close to the gate. Not as big as the one we have at the other homes, but big enough for them to work from. Braden suggested taking over the room in the external garage for the command center, between those two areas, they should be comfortable."

I glance around and notice the small garage he is talking about. It is two stories, and I guess if he thinks that will work, then it will. What do I know about that kind of stuff? So, I nod and wait for him to climb out.

The home is brick and looks to be fairly new, although, I am not good at identifying all that stuff. For all I know, they could have renovated recently it. There is a large black door with frosted windows on both sides of the entrance, iron rails leading up to it, with a few large potted plants.

When we walk inside, I pause to take it all in. The floors are wooden. A staircase leads to the second floor. Immediately to the left is a dining room that looks as if it opens to the kitchen. To the right is a library that has a fireplace and large windows that open up to a view of the side yard. It's a beautiful view.

The entry connects to a large living room with an even greater view of the backyard. I notice a pool area, and what looks like a side yard where there is a play set ready and waiting for a child to play on it.

"Come look at the kitchen. You are going to love it." Stan grabs my hand and starts directing me that way.

He was right. I love it. There is more than enough counter space to create. It has a large island where I can picture myself standing around, surrounded by those I love. Us, all there, preparing a meal, and me shooing Stan away when he distracts me. I can barely keep it together. There is even a smaller area where we could place a table; that would be a great place to serve breakfast.

"Well?" I can hear the anticipation in his voice.

"So far, I like it. It's nice and simple. An average home much like those you represent." I glimpse around again. "Is it new? Everything looks so new."

"It's a renovation. Larkin brought it to my attention. One of the architects in her firm bought it and fixed it up. They are selling it now, moving to a home in Prieto. The children will attend the boarding school there while they work on de la Peña Citadel. Larkin and he will take the project on together, but because of her situation, they felt it best to have someone else live near and take the lead." Once again, he takes my hand and guides me up the back set of stairs that take us to the second floor.

The first thing I notice is the large sitting area, one that could easily be made into a playroom or a family area. Across from it are two bedrooms that share a bathroom, they are both large with window seats and built-in bookshelves. The third room is a little larger with its own bathroom, Stan informs me it was the master bedroom at one time.

"Where is the master now?" I ask, knowing I don't believe there is enough room on this level for it.

His entire face lights up as he takes my hand and opens a door I thought was a closet when I first saw it. It has a set of stairs that extends to a third floor.

"They turned the entire attic into an extensive suite." He guides me up the stairs. "There is even a small room off to the side that they used as a nursery, according to Larkin."

I step onto the landing and am blown away. This space is big enough for a large bed and all the accessories. There is a fireplace with an area spacious enough to construct a sitting area, one enormous bathroom, and two huge closets. Then I notice the small nook, the one that is suitable for a crib, a dresser, and even a rocker. It even has a cute little duck border that enhances the space.

I can no longer keep it together. I walk over to the window, which also has a seat, and sit down. As I glance around the space, the tears I have felt building begin to fall.

Stan drops to his knees in front of me. "What's wrong?"

"Nothing." I hiccup. "I-it's p-per-perfect. T-this sp-space. T-the area o-on th-the second fl-floor."

"Why are you crying then, sweetheart?" He reaches up and wipes my tears away.

"I-I need to t-tell you s-something." I blink a few times as I gather up the courage to just say it.

"What?"

I know he is going to be surprised. This was not at all part of our five-year plan, but it is what it is.

"I'm pregnant," I whisper, but I know he heard me because I watch the realization sink in.

Stan stares at me for several seconds, then glances down at my stomach, then back up at my face. Slowly the most amazing smile takes over his face and I cry harder.

It becomes clear to me, then, that pregnancy hormones are going to suck. Larkin was right; it is as if you just can't control the tears once they start. She and I talked about it a few weeks ago when we were suffering through a state dinner. It was after she had a meltdown when they ran out of the chocolate truffles she had been devouring all night. I made her some the next day and had them shipped overnight to her. She called me crying because she couldn't believe I'd done something so nice, over something so silly.

"Are you sure?" He takes his hand and places it on my stomach. "When did you find out?"

"I couldn't figure out why I was so sluggish. Thought I was coming down with the flu, so I called Dr. Wilson. She took one look at me and demanded I pee in a cup for her." I remember handing her the cup, wondering how she was going to tell I had the flu from my urine sample.

I know, right, but it hadn't even occurred to me I might be pregnant. I ritually took my pill daily, at the same time every day, like directed. Well, until I was trying to run a bakery and keep up with my husband's campaigning. During that time, I might have forgotten to take them and then took them later. Or I might have skipped a few and then taken the missed doses as soon as I realized it. I figured one or two missed doses wouldn't be a big deal. Surely my body wouldn't drop an egg that soon or make a nice cushiony place for one to hang around and wait for it to be fertilized. Seems I was so very wrong about that, and now we have a stowaway, that will be escaping in the next eight months, maybe sooner, I guess.

"Why didn't you call me?" He sounds disappointed.

"I don't know, Stan. Maybe because I was in shock." I lift my hands in protest. "I thought I had the flu or something like that. I was fatigued. I thought maybe my thyroid was acting up, even, and that she needed to adjust my medication. I never once suspected I was growing a child inside of me."

"Calm down." He grabs my face and stares into my eyes. "A baby, Winnie."

I blink several times and, dammit, I start crying again.

"Wow, sweetheart. I don't even know what to say." Although his face expresses it all to me; he is thrilled. "How do you feel about this?"

"I'm freaking out a little. It's not that I don't want this baby, I do. I just... we are... this is so not part of the plan."

"Does one ever really have a plan? We have what... nine months?"

"Eight months, maybe less. Dr. Wilson suspects I'm about eight weeks, maybe ten. She will know more when we go back in four weeks to confirm, and I get my first ultrasound. If I should have any spotting or cramping, I am to call so they can see me immediately, but so far all I've been is tired and a little forgetful. All normal pregnancy signs according to her."

Once again, he smiles. "Is this the home you want to raise our baby in, Winnie?"

"Yes," I whisper cry. "Here and Cabrera. This place is our everyday home, the other will be our holiday place. How are we going to manage, Stan? We are both so very busy. Me with the bakery, you with your new job as a governor, it seems so impossible. I don't want someone else raising our child, not full time, at least. I want to do both, work and parent, but how are we going to do that?"

"We do what every other working parent does, we find a person we trust to watch them while we work. Hire more people to help out around here, at the bakery, and I find me an assistant who will run my office like clockwork.

"I want to be an equal part of our child's life, Winnie. I don't wish to be an absent father who is only around to discipline or educate. I want to be there for them all the time. I want to change diapers, give baths, read them nighttime stories, wipe their tears away when they are hurt or sad, make them giggle, and sit with them while they share all about their days. I want them to see me loving on their mother like it is normal. And have them make those noises of disgust because we are embarrassing them. I want our children to have the life we both wished we had growing up. I never want them wondering if they are loved or if their parents even love each other, I want there to be no doubt about it or us."

"You make it sound so easy." I hiccup.

"That's because it will be," he reassures me. "With you by my side, Winnie, I know we can do anything we set our minds to. I love you."

"I love you too," I tell him before I kiss him.

Epilogue

The Royals

Esteban
Fourteen Years Later

B eing the father of four keeps me rather busy these days.
Two years ago, my third term as Governor for the South
ended. I served them faithfully for twelve years. It was a good
run. I enjoyed my time in office, even though I had to often defend my
actions to those who didn't support a member of the royal family in an
elected position. Every time I was up for reelection, my opponents
desperately tried to convince the people that our family was
monopolizing the government by having two of us in office. Aiming to
guilt the community, by suggesting they were providing the king with
power to do as he pleased with me in that seat. Thankfully, the people
saw through the lies. They knew the truth, knew I had opposed my
brother on several occasions. They also understood that by electing
someone else, it was giving the other side of that debate power, a power
they lost each time I won.

Now that my days as a governor are finished, I have moved on to an educator, so to speak. My dear brother has asked me to do my best in assisting him in getting his children ready for the roles that will be theirs one day. I happily took it on, even included my two oldest in the education as well.

Princess Nicolette—Antonio's oldest, also known as Nicky—and our oldest, Duke Danilo—Dan—are only four months apart. They are quite close, getting in all kinds of trouble together. I swear what one does not think of the other one does. They are both thirteen, close to being fourteen, and showing us all why so many parents go gray before the age of fifty.

Prince Lucas—Antonio's second oldest—and my Duchess Liliana —Lili—share a birthday. They are both ten and much better behaved than their older siblings. Lili is her mother reincarnated, I swear. Lucas is undeniably as uptight as his father was growing up. So, they also get along well, do their very best to keep the rest of the gang out of trouble.

Winnie and I have two more. Duchess Noelia—El—is going to be seven in a few days. She is quiet for the most part, but she without a doubt has a feisty side. Duke Simon—Sy—surprised us a few years ago. He is two. We assumed we were done having children, but I guess he thought differently. That child, I get the feeling is going to be difficult when he gets older. He has that gleam in his eye that states he is always thinking and taking in his surroundings. He's taking notes on his siblings, I swear, learning from them about all the ways to manipulate us. By the time he gets old enough to give us trouble, we will be too worn out to care.

Antonio and Larkin have two more as well. Princess Juliette is six. She takes after her older sister, and I almost have to laugh. How my brother got two girls who are mouthy and very active, to me, is certainly funny. A few years ago, when their family made a trip to Belize, they visited an orphanage and met their youngest son, Tomas. He was two at the time but was so malnourished that he looked to be barely even one. Larkin heard his story, about how he was abandoned in the streets where drugs and prostitution were the primary sources of income. She looked at her husband and that was all it took for him to understand what she was thinking. She stayed behind an extra month until the paperwork came through, and could bring him home. Having lived a similar life of abandonment and then being taken in later by a very loving family, her heart broke for the little boy. She always said she felt they were meant to have one more, and when she saw Tomas, she realized he was the one God intended to be theirs. He is now four and thriving.

I'm returning home now with my three oldest in tow.

My primary job now is parenting. I get the children up and ready in the mornings and then take the oldest three to school. Sy and I hang out together until his mother returns home around two every afternoon. After I make sure my wife is fed and our littlest one is changed and ready for his nap, it is time for me to leave and retrieve the other three.

Five days a week we do that, we dismissed hiring a nanny again right before Sy was born. Since I was now available to take on those responsibilities, Winnie and I agreed we didn't need the extra help this time around. May I just say how much I love my new job? It has rewards and challenges daily. Just when you think you have it down, something materializes, and you are racking your brain to figure out how to best solve the situation before all hell breaks loose.

Saturdays are a little different. Winnie no longer works them, because the kids' extracurricular activities always take place on that day. After Lili was born, we offered Ellie a partnership in the business. We knew we needed someone to take on more responsibility. Someone who would work just as hard as Winnie, even take as much pride in the store. We could think of no one better than Ellie. She has become more like a little sister to my wife, family to me, and bringing her into the business was the smartest move for that area of our lives.

As soon as I pull up to the house, the troops scramble out. I barely get the car stopped before they are running inside. Like always when I enter after they've trampled in, I can hear everyone in the kitchen. They are all talking at once to their mother, who has a pre-dinner snack waiting on them.

"Jordan told me that Blaine told her that Henry Sullivan—you remember Henry right? He is the new kid who just moved here—she said that he likes me," Lili announces in a high-pitched voice.

"Oh, I don't think so," Dan announces. "You are too young for a boyfriend."

I can't help but grin as I walk into the kitchen and hear my son's disapproval.

My wife catches my eye and shakes her head. "That's sweet, Lili."

"Mom, seriously. Don't encourage her." Dan sounds appalled.

"He's not my boyfriend, Danilo. I was just telling mom what Jordan said." Lili states. "So, tell us why you were stalking Petra on the way to the car. Do you want her to be your girlfriend?"

"No!" my son replies way too quickly. "Gross, Lil. Girls are gross."

Dan isn't fooling anyone. He so likes this Petra girl. I've watched him this last week waiting for her to arrive, and even caught him walking her to her car after school. I'm not ready to deal with that yet, but I know it is coming. Antonio has been dealing with it for a few years now with Nicky, girls unquestionably start noticing the boys earlier—or maybe it's that they admit it sooner.

El adds her two cents to the conversation. "If you don't like her, then why did I hear you tell her you'd call her later?"

"Because we have a project we are working on." Dan finishes up his snack and grabs his backpack. "I am going to call her about school work."

"Then why did she kiss you on the cheek, then say she can't wait?" El is so stirring up trouble and she knows it.

"Okay, enough." My wife snickers, also realizing what our youngest daughter is doing. "Chores need to get done before Simon wakes. Then if you all hurry, you can help me with dinner."

They all scurry off, still bickering amongst themselves.

I step up behind Winnie and nuzzle her neck. "How do you do that? Make them disappear almost instantly, ready to return in another hour to help with dinner."

She shrugs and shivers at the feel of my lips against her skin. "I don't know. So, tell me about this little hussy who is after my son."

I chuckle and bite her neck. "I don't think she is a hussy, first of all. She's cute in her own way. Not one of the popular girls. It is clear those girls don't like her or the attention Dan is not giving them."

"A chip off the old block, then." She glances over her shoulder at me.

"If you are referring to me and you, suggesting this is similar, then I have my doubts. He is just beginning to figure it all out." I kiss her neck again.

"And you already had it figured out when you met me?" my wife questions and then moans when I nip her ear.

"I was sixteen, Winnie. I had a better understanding of it, yes. But since you were only eleven, there was nothing I could do about it, except wait it out. Which is what I did. I waited it out until you were old enough for me to make a move." I reach down and spin her around, so she is now facing me. "In the garden that night, when you were only eighteen, I had dreamed of kissing you so many times." I lean forward and let my lips linger just above hers. "I knew if I kissed you then, I'd want to keep you. I was right."

I lean forward and kiss her softly at first. But like always, it is impossible to just kiss her without getting carried away. Even all these years later, she affects me like no other woman before her ever did.

"Stop, please," I hear Lili order as she enters the kitchen. "Parents should not be kissing like that."

I draw back, but don't let my wife move. "You better be glad we do or you'd not exist."

"Stan!" Winnie scolds me.

"Ugh. I don't want to think of that ever," Lili grumbles as she grabs what she needs, then hurries off. "Stay out of the kitchen. Mum and Papa are at it again."

The other two children groan loudly and then make those grossed out noises kids make. I do love hearing how they find us totally rude, and not at all impressed that we are so affectionate to each other.

"How long is Sy expected to be out?" I ask as I push a small section of her hair behind her ear.

"He went down later than usual, so possibly another hour," she informs me and then squeals as I bend down and toss her over my shoulder. "What are you doing?"

"Grossing our children out even more," I inform her as I carry her through the doorway that leads into the living area, where I find them all hard at work. "Your mother and I are heading to the third floor. We need to clean up before dinner."

They all make grossed out faces, knowing very well what that means.

As I carry my wife up the stairs, she enlightens me of something. "I cleaned up already, Stan. I took a shower after I put Simon down."

"Then it looks like I need to make a mess of you again before I clean you up," I tell her as we take the final stairs to our little haven, our hideout that is far away from nosey ears. Once we are there, I toss her on the bed and fall next to her.

"Tired after carrying my fat arse up two flights of stairs." She shakes her head to get the hair away from her eyes.

Winnie is far from fat. Sure, she has added a few extra pounds after having four children. I adore every part of her shapelier body and have no complaints.

She still runs a couple of miles a day when she can, sometimes more. We even ran a 5k as a family a few months after Simon was born. I pushed him in the jogger, while the rest of us ran as a unit, encouraging each other every step of the way.

Two weeks ago, we drove up to Seville, so Winnie could run a half-marathon. The kids and I moved along the racing trail and cheered her on in several spots. We were all at the finish line to catch her as soon as she was done and even walk with her while she recovered.

In another month, the two of us are leaving for France, so we can run in the marathon there. The kids are going to stay with her sister Karina, her husband, and their three children. Yes, I know what you are thinking, but surprisingly it works and everyone gets along perfectly. It will be the first time we have been alone since Simon was born.

Who is Karina's husband you ask? My man Stew figured out that Karina was not so easy to get rid of after she set her eyes on him. It took them a few years to work it all out. Stew wasn't about to put up with her attitude or conniving ways. Funny how the right person can make a person change and become the best version of themselves. I'm not saying Karina is a pussycat. She most certainly is not. But she has calmed down considerably and is more like Winnie now and less like the spiteful woman she was when I first met her.

"Careful love or I'll hold on to that arse while I make you ride me," I warn her.

"Is that a threat, Your Highness?" She knows what calling me by my proper title does to me.

I roll over on top of her and grind my hips into hers. "You are asking for it, *princesa*."

She wiggles underneath me and that is the end of the game. I quickly remove all of our clothing and roll over again with her straddling me. My hands firmly on her lovely arse, I guide her onto me while I watch her body take mine.

"Your sister called earlier," she says as she bounces up and down, driving me insane.

"Please, do not mention my sister while I am inside of you." I grip her hips hard and thrust upwards. "Which one?"

"Isabel. She... oh shit... met someone. Harder."

I flip us over and slam into her. "Tell me later about it. Why do you always bring those things up when we are in the thralls of it?"

Winnie moans and digs her nails into my back. "Probably because as my mind starts to empty, I begin to recall important stuff. So I don't forget it, I tell you. It's your fault."

I slam in again, and she cries out. "Yes. Again. Your mother called too."

This time I stop what I am doing. "If you want this to continue..."

"Sorry. I just... if I don't tell you... my mind, remember it needs to shut down soon, and... never mind." She whimpers as I move, slowing everything down now.

Fifteen years of marriage has told me that this is the best way to get my wife to just let it all go and enjoy. Slow lovemaking always stops her mind from overthinking, and it is something we both love to do when we get the chance.

After we have collapsed onto the bed, I rub her shoulders, caressing her back to the here and now. "You were saying?"

"Hell, if I know, Stan." She turns her head and smiles. "I love you."

"I love you too. Now let's shower before the kids decide to wreck the place." I take her hand and help her to her feet.

I love my life, my family, and my adoring wife. We've had some tough times, but we've survived them because we let no one else dictate how we live this life.

Winifred Josephine Reyes was the unexpected princess I always wanted by my side, and if I had to do it all over again, exactly how we did it, that is what I would do. There is no one better suited out there for me than her.

If you enjoyed the story of Prince Esteban and Winifred, I ask you to consider leaving me a review on Amazon, Goodreads, and BookBub.

Here is the link to My Noble Fight, book 3 in The Royals, the story of Lorenzo and Violet.

I have several books available for you to read, they are listed in the back of this book.

Thank you and Happy Reading!!!!

The Duke

FALCON GLOBAL NOVELLA

One kiss was all it took...

All I want is my freedom. All my father wants is to chain me to the highest bidder. I have one last opportunity to live on my terms before my choice is taken from me.

Darius Falcon, also known as The Duke, enters my world. He's an arrogant prick who won't take no for an answer. Refusing to change course once he sets his sights on me. Too bad he won't get to keep me for more than a week.

Then one day he materializes from the shadows to save me from a monster. It's then I wonder if now is my chance to take control of over my future. Maybe when you wish upon a hunk, dreams really do come true.

Only Available to Newsletter Subscribers.
https://dl.bookfunnel.com/xn53pw0g4o

Acknowledgments

I'd like to first of all thank my readers. You are who I write for, the people who keep me writing. Thank you, thank you, thank you.

To my beta readers, Sarah, Terry, and Stacey. You guys had some great suggestions and stepped up to help me out in ways you will never know. This book would not be what it is without you.

Last, I'd like to thank my family. I couldn't do this without their support. While they don't always know what I'm writing about, they never complain when I put them off whenever I'm deep in my writing. Recently my daughter has even become a fan, an edited for her age fan, but still. It has been so much fun sharing my writing with her while she asks all the right questions, feeding my crazy obsession. I love you all beyond words.

*updated 4/20/24

Also by C. R. Riley

Crystal Lake Series

Facing the Storm

Uncharted Waters

Light in the Shadows

When the Fog Lifts

Life Series

The Good Life

A Transformed Life

Love of the Game

Sneaky Quarterback

Tight End Comeback

Scoring the Birdie

Fielder's Choice

Catcher's Interference

Kohl Family Series

Untouchable

Unbreakable

Unforgettable

Unavoidable

Undeniable

The Royals

Suddenly Enthroned

Unexpected Princess

My Noble Fight

Her Royal Highness

Fearless Warrior

About the Author

Contemporary romance author C. R. Riley is celebrated for creating worlds and characters that don't always follow the rules, including those she futilely tries to set herself. But the best characters always find a way around them, often surprising her with their willingness to make each and every journey unique, if not emotionally satisfying.

Her Kohl Family series has been called the perfect epitome of contemporary romance with a twist of the unexpected. The characters tackle tough topics while making you fall in love with them, and despising those baddies who deserve it. Each story is a unique standalone. That cares over in her Modern-Day Royals series, which features characters who are unlike any royal put to the page before. And of course, combining her love of football and baseball she adds a steamy sports romance, Love of the Game which follows a family of athletes on their separate journeys to find true love.

You can find all her romantic and out-of-the-ordinary series on Amazon and free in Kindle Unlimited. Never miss a new project update or book release by signing up for her newsletter or follow her on social media, accounts listed below.

I'd love to hear from you and do my best to personally answer emails.
crriley@crrileyauthor.com